D0594851

BLACK ANGEL

BLACK ANGEL

Graham Masterton

First published in the UK in 1991 by Mandarin
This paperback edition first published in 2021 by Head of Zeus Ltd

Copyright © Graham Masterton, 1991

The moral right of Graham Masterton to be identified as the author
of this work has been asserted in accordance with the Copyright,
Designs and Patents Act of 1988.

All rights reserved. No part of this publication may be
reproduced, stored in a retrieval system, or transmitted, in any form or
by any means, electronic, mechanical, photocopying, recording,
or otherwise, without the prior permission of both the copyright
owner and the above publisher of this book.

This is a work of fiction. All characters, organizations,
and events portrayed in this novel are either products of
the author's imagination or are used fictitiously.

9 7 5 3 1 2 4 6 8

A CIP catalogue record for this book is available from the
British Library.

ISBN (PB): 9781801101189
ISBN (E): 9781786695567

Typeset by Siliconchips Services Ltd UK

Printed and bound in Great Britain by
CPI Group (UK) Ltd, Croydon cro 4yy

Head of Zeus Ltd
First Floor East
5–8 Hardwick Street
London EC1R 4RG

www.headofzeus.com

"I found in Punta Arenas an American sailor, almost 100 years old, who claimed that he was the sole survivor of the sailing vessel Charlotte, which had sunk in a terrible storm off the False Cape Horn, in 1837. He spoke of a strange cargo, the nature of which the ship's master had been sworn to secrecy. He spoke of terrible screaming in the night, which had frightened some of the crew so direly that three of them had jumped overboard, believing the ship to be possessed. He would say very little more, except that Chilean fisherman had refused to take any of the Charlotte's crew out of the freezing water, and that he himself had escaped only by a miracle. He said that the beach on which the wreck still lay was spoken of by Chileans as a place of unspeakable evil, and that they called it 'the Place of Lies'."

Randolph Miller, "*Travels in South America*",
Chapter XII

I

Joe Berry fastidiously wiped up the last circles of spaghetti sauce with a torn-off piece of sourdough and then pushed his plate away, and that was the end of the last meal he would ever eat.

"Food of the goddamned gods," he remarked, and took a pack of Merit Menthols out of the pocket of his plaid shirt.

On the other side of the kitchen, Nina Berry was carefully crimping the pastry around the edge of an apple-and-cinnamon pie, a pie that she would never bake. "Do you want a cup of coffee?" she asked him.

He lit his cigarette, and shook his head. "I need my sleep. I'm starting that flat in Cow Hollow tomorrow."

"I bought some fresh decaff."

"Decaff isn't coffee. Same way lite beer isn't beer."

Along the corridor of the Berry's two-bedroom Fulton Street condominium, seven-year-old Caroline Berry and five-year-old Joe Berry Junior were both fast asleep in their bunk beds.

Caroline's rag-doll Martha lay sprawled on the Navajo rug. Caroline would never again pick Martha up. Joe's favorite stuffed rabbit Joe Berry Junior-Junior sat propped in the red-painted basketwork chair. Joe Berry Junior-Junior would never be called Joe Berry Junior-Junior again. The next name that Joe Berry Junior-Junior would be called would be "People's Exhibit H."

It was 9:03 on the night of Thursday, August 11, 1988.

Joe stood up with his cigarette dangling between his lips and carried his plate to the dishwasher.

"I wish you'd quit," Nina chided him, taking out the cigarette and kissing him.

"Two a day, is that smoking?" he appealed.

"Two too many. I want you to live for ever."

There were marginally fewer than eight minutes left to go. Joe said, "I'll try to cut down to one, okay? But you'll have to give me time to decide which one. I need the morning one to get me going and the evening one to calm me down."

"Oh, decisions, decisions," Nina teased him.

Joe took back his cigarette and walked through to the living-room, where the huge Zenith television set was flickering with the sound turned down. Former 49er Dwight Clark was being interviewed about his new restaurant, Clark's by the Bay. Without turning up the sound, Joe heaved himself down on the couch and propped his thick green socks on the coffee-table.

He picked up the *Examiner*. "Did you read here that they're thinking of scrapping the Mounted Patrol?" he called. "They've worked it out that they're costing the city a million-and-a-half bucks a year, just for a bunch of fancy cops on fancy horses."

"I *like* the Patrol," Nina replied. "They give the city character."

"Oh, sure. And for every thousand dollars spent on character, that's a thousand dollars less for the poor beleaguered bastards in the combat zone."

Nina came through to the living-room, carrying a mug of coffee. "Combat zone! You make it sound as if we're in a war, or something."

"Are you kidding me? Four cops have been killed this year already. If that's not a war, what is?"

Six-and-a-half minutes left. Not even enough time for Joe to finish the afternoon paper, or for Nina's coffee to grow cool enough for her to drink.

Once, nine years ago, when they were staying the night with friends in Mill Valley, Joe had asked Nina, "If you had a choice, what would be the last thing you would ever do, before you died?"

She had kissed his ear. The sunlight had dropped through the slatted wooden blinds like freshly culled honey. "Make love, of course," she had giggled.

He had kissed her ear.

Five minutes. Not even enough time for making love.

Joe was thirty-three years old, lean and wiry, with thinning black hair but a surprisingly boyish face, which his drooping grandad mustache did little to mature. After leaving college, he had trained as a cop, because his father had been a cop; but after eight years of active service on the streets of San Francisco he had suddenly decided not to go to work any more. He had lain in bed, unable to rise. The doctor had diagnosed nervous exhaustion, but Joe had recognized it for what it was. A total drainage of the spirit—an emptiness caused not by shock, not by trauma, not even by seeing his friends shot or old ladies beaten to a purple pulp or swollen bodies bobbing in the Bay, but simply by giving away a little piece of his soul day by day, night by night, to those who needed it.

He knew why priests drank. He knew why doctors took drugs. He knew why policemen couldn't get out of bed in the morning. There was such an emotional famine in the world. such a hunger for human spirit, that sooner or later there came a point when you had nothing more to give.

These days Joe was a skilled joiner, working for Fastiff Interiors in Ross Valley—constructing limed-oak closets and mahogany floors and redwood decks. He loved the peace of joinery, the measured pace, the smell of different woods. He loved the way that carefully cut joints dovetailed into each other. But he still woke up occasionally in the small hours of the night and saw the silent needy faces of all of those people who had stolen his soul, pale as death, pale as a shoal of poisoned fish, floating on the tide.

Joe didn't care much for crowds any more. It had been three seasons since he had gone to Candlestick Park. There were just too many faces, mouths open, eyes wide, all of them hungry for a piece of his soul.

Nina didn't exactly understand what had happened to Joe, although she knew several other police wives whose husbands had suffered what was fashionably called "burn-out". Some of the more hard-bitten officers called it "cop-out".

Nina had remained her gentle, supportive, and slightly bewildered self – skinny and pretty in a dated flower-child kind of way. She had been born in 1962 to the owner of The Red Flag book store on Haight Street, the irrepressible Thad Buford, and a vague college girl named Vanessa Grade (who in 1967 had legally changed her name to Star Lover.)

Nina had met Joe in 1981, at an Independence Day jazz concert at the Frost Amphitheater at Stanford University. They had just started talking to each other, sitting under a tree, as if they had known each other for years. She hadn't found out that he was a cop until it was much too late, and she was in love with him.

It had been almost impossible at first for Nina to persuade her spaced-out friends that Joe wasn't going to run them in every time they lit up a roach; and at almost every party and weekend get-together, Joe had suffered insults both implied and direct. One of Nina's friends always called him Himmler. Another called him Berry-My-Heart-At-Wounded-Knee. As time went by, Joe and Nina had lost contact with all of those chatty nutty people who felt uncomfortable in the presence of a pig, no matter how much of a regular guy he could prove himself to be, and their social circle had been reduced (as the social circles of all policemen and their families are inevitably reduced) to other policemen and their families.

Nina remained friends with at least a dozen policemen's wives, but didn't regret that she wasn't still one of them. Whenever she met them, they were all fudge cake recipes and high-pressure cheerfulness. They all had the same bright brittle way of talking, as if at any second they were going to shatter into a thousand pieces. It was bad enough living on the fault line without living on the edge, too.

She sipped her coffee. "Did I tell you that Caroline won a Snickers bar for painting today?"

Four minutes to go. Joe looked up. "They give away candy at school, as prizes? I thought candy was a punishment, not a reward."

"Oh, Joe, one small Snickers bar isn't going to hurt."

"Well, I don't know. It kind of usurps parental discretion, don't you think? You try to bring up your kids right, take care of their teeth, take care of their weight. It sure doesn't help when their teacher starts handing out candy."

"She did a beautiful painting of the family. She called it 'We're The Berrys'."

"Did she paint herself with her teeth falling out?"

"Joe, for goodness' sake, it was only one candy bar and she brought it home and asked me before she ate it."

"And you, of course, said yes?"

Nina shook her head. "You're impossible sometimes. You smoke, you eat pasta like there's some kind of award for it, you drink beer until you're so full of gas that you practically float away. And then you nag me about one measly Snickers bar that your daughter won because she was so good at painting."

Three minutes. Scarcely enough time to play one last record. Certainly not their favorite, Barbra Streisand singing *Evergreen* (3:23).

"Okay, okay," Joe grinned at her. "I surrender. But don't blame me if she grows up fat and toothless."

"Go look at the painting, why don't you?" Nina suggested. "She's pinned it up on her bulletin-board. And you can kiss them both goodnight, while you're at it."

Joe sighed, dropped the newspaper back on to the couch, crushed out his cigarette, and stood up, and stretched.

"I think I'm getting old," he told Nina. He leaned forward and kissed her forehead. That was the last time he would ever kiss her. "I laid sixteen square yards of oak parquet today, and I feel like Quasimodo."

He walked along the corridor to the children's bedroom, lightly drumming his knuckles on the wallpaper. As usual, the children's door was about an inch-and-a-half ajar. A flowery ceramic plaque announced that this was Caroline's and Joe Junior's Room. Joe eased the door open, and stepped inside, breathing the warmth and mustiness of sleeping children.

It was too dark for him to see Caroline's painting clearly. As far as he could make out, she had represented the Berry family as four bright blue packing-cases with startled pigs' faces and yard-brooms for arms. Why did kids always draw people with about a hundred fingers on each hand? He smiled, and went across to the bunk-bed, and stood watching Caroline sleeping.

She was blonde and skinny and pretty, just like Nina. He had seen so many families in which the daughter had grown up to look like Dad and the son had grown up to look like Mom. His old sergeant George Swope had produced three daughters who had all looked exactly like him. Thick eyebrows, jutting jaws, and bulbous noses. The guys in the bunko squad had called them "The Sergeant Swope Sisters".

But here was Caroline's thin blue-veined wrist lying on her My Little Pony pillow, and her shining blonde hair spread everywhere, like the gold that Rumpelstiltskin had spun. Her lips were slightly parted, and she was breathing with a slight catch in her throat.

Down below, almost totally buried in his comforter, so that Joe could see only the back of his dark-brown sticking-up hair, Joe Junior was dreaming of something unguessable. Space, or school, or Kraft cheese-and-boysenberry jelly sandwiches. Joe leaned into the recess of the bunk bed and kissed Joe Junior's hot little ear. He, too, sounded slightly clogged. Maybe a quick squirt of Dristan room-spray might help them both to breathe more easily.

One minute, fifty-five seconds. Not even enough time to go find the room-spray. Not even time to think about all of those moments when the Berry family had been truly happy.

Joe went to the window to tug the drapes straight. He looked down on Fulton Street, almost deserted except for parked cars and two men in hats walking slowly uphill, gesticulating and weaving from one side of the sidewalk to the other, as if they were drunk, and arguing.

The house itself was unusually quiet. No television from Mrs. Caccamo upstairs, because she had fallen and fractured her ankle, and was spending a week in the hospital. No opera from the Linebargers below.

The silence made the foggy night seem even more spectral. Joe had always promised himself that one day he would move out of the Bay area, maybe to Napa or Sacramento, where the weather was drier, and the kids wouldn't keep getting snuffles.

But he had been born here, and his mother had been born here, and his grandfather had been property-boy at the Chutes, one of the few theaters to survive the great earthquake and fire in 1906, and where else in the world could he possibly live?

One minute to go. Then less than a minute. Then fifteen seconds. Then ten. Not enough time to say the Lord's Prayer, even if he had known that he ought to.

He tugged the drapes. Instantly, he heard a noise like a bomb going off. Garrunchh! – a deep, wrenching, grinding explosion. He cried out, "Jesus!"—because for one ridiculous splinter of a second he thought that he had caused the explosion himself, by tugging the drapes.

He listened. There was silence.

"Nina?" he called.

Silence. Or maybe a faint cry? He couldn't be sure.

His life began to fall apart all around him, moment by moment, as if God wasn't going to be satisfied until he and his family had suffered all the punishments of hell.

"Nina!" he screamed. (Or did he? Maybe he was incapable of saying anything, he wasn't sure. As a cop, he had listened to tape-recordings of men under severe stress—hostages, suicides, men trapped in gradually flooding sewerpipes. These men had all believed that they were speaking calmly and rationally – but all that anyone could hear was an almost alien gibberish, and the huge gasping of hyperventilation.)

He thought: earthquake? But it hadn't felt like an earthquake. No queasy sensation beneath his feet. Gas explosion? Maybe the Linebargers had left their gas on when they had gone to see their daughter in Eureka.

He stepped out into the corridor. *Nina?* "Nina? Are you okay?"

The blood in his ears rushed *Nina Nina Nina Nina Nina*.

The first thing he saw was that their front door had gone. Not just the door, but the frame, and great lumps of the surrounding brickwork, too.

Lying in the rubble was a full-sized jack, the kind used by firefighters to break down security-locked doors in burning buildings.

Nina!

He didn't know how he managed to reach the living-room so quickly. It was as if he had simply blinked and thought "living-room", and he was instantaneously there. It was then that he saw at once what had happened, and it was worse than anything he could have imagined.

Something inside of his mind said: *This is madness. This is too terrible to be true. This is the nightmare that haunts every hardworking taxpaying middle-class man and woman, and it simply doesn't happen outside of dreams, or movies.*

A huge towering man in a strange and terrifying black horned mask was standing in the middle of the living-room, one booted foot resting on the kicked-over coffee-table. He was gripping Nina tightly by the roots of her hair, and up against her thin bare neck he was pressing the blade of an enormous triangular-bladed butcher knife. Nina was white-lipped, and her eyes were bulging. Her arms dangled limply by her sides, as if she were a life-size marionette of Nina whose strings had been cut. The man was holding the knife-edge so tightly against her larynx that the skin had been broken just enough to make her bleed, and even if she had done nothing more than swallow, her throat would have been sliced open.

Joe cautiously raised both hands, breathing heavily. His police training told him: *hostage situation – don't go crazy, don't panic. She may be your wife, but that's all the more reason to stay in control. Act calm. Act conciliatory.*

The man's grotesque mask made it impossible for Joe to judge what he looked like, or what age was, or what state of mind he was in. The mask was jet black, glossy, plastic or papier-mâché, like the head of a huge beetle, with antlers rather than horns. The eye-sockets were dead-black, and foxily slanted, and they were as dead as velvet and they gave away nothing at all.

The man was stripped naked to the waist, although his chest was streaked in glistening rust-and-crimson-colored oil, or maybe oil mixed with paint, or blood. He had the knotted muscular chest of a dedicated weight-trainer, although Joe thought: *weird, this guy's extra-weird*, because his nipples were both pierced with shining gold rings, from which hung ragged collections of beads and feathers.

He wore a heavy black-leather belt with a silver buckle in the shape of a grinning skull, and tight black jeans, and boots. Slung from his waist was a heavy canvas sack. He was enormous—six-three, easily, and well over 200 pounds. And what made him so frightening was that Joe had never seen anything like him, ever before.

He didn't look like a Hell's Angel; or one of those overdressed homosexual fetishists who came clanking into San Francisco General to visit their dying friends; or any one of those archetypal crack-maddened freaks whom you could encounter unexpectedly around any street corner, and without whom the San Francisco Police Department would have been almost a normal place to work.

This man was different. This man was decked out like an emissary directly from Satan himself.

What was more, he had smashed down their front door with a firefighter's jack, and unless he had known for sure that the other two apartments in the building were empty this weekend, he obviously hadn't cared how much noise he made. To Joe, that meant that he didn't particularly care whether he lived or died, and if he didn't care whether he lived or died, that meant that he wasn't afraid to kill.

A long time ago, on Green Street, one of Joe's partners had made the mistake of trying to cajole the shotgun away from a man who didn't care whether he lived or died. His face had splashed Joe's shirt like a tipped-up plateful of minestrone soup.

Nina's eyes pleaded, but she couldn't speak, and if the man hadn't been gripping her by the hair, she would probably have collapsed.

Joe spread his arms, to make it clear that he wasn't carrying a weapon; to show that he wanted to talk.

"What is it?" he asked, his throat clogged with tension and phlegm. "What do you want?"

The great masked head turned slowly as Joe circled around the coffee-table.

"What do you want?" Joe repeated. "Is it money? Is it drugs? Just tell me what it is, come on, anything, and we'll talk about arranging it. Come on, you've got my wife there, friend, you don't think I'm going to fool around, do you?"

"Joe—!" gasped Nina, in desperation.

"It's okay, sweetheart, it's okay," Joe told her, knowing all the time that, *Jesus, this guy could go crazy at an instant, and cut her throat, and kill me too, he's totally irrational. Who the hell busts into somebody's condo with a jack? Who takes out their whole door, when there's nothing to steal but silver-plated baseball trophies and a four-year-old video recorder?*

Who the hell wears an insect mask and smothers themselves in blood?

"Come on, friend, what is it?" he repeated.

The man hesitated for a long, long time. Minutes of dark-sliding silence, like oil pouring over a weir. Then he said, in a deep muffled voice, "I'm not your friend, friend. I'm your worst nightmare."

Joe nodded, and tried to clear his throat. "Okay, I'm sorry. I apologize. No offense meant, huh? I'm just interested to know what you want."

Another long silence. Then, "You know what I want." Joe couldn't stop his heart from scrambling; couldn't stop his lungs from constricting. *Calm, Joe, calm for Christ's sake. But don't let him know how frightened you are.* "I don't know, no, how could I know?"

The great shiny black head nodded and dipped. "What does *everybody* want? Power, money, revenge, sex."

Joe was beginning to panic. "You won't get any of those things here."

"Oh, no?" the man replied. He drew the knife backwards and forwards across Nina's throat, so that it tugged at her skin. "What would you call this, revenge or sex? Maybe you'd call it power."

"Listen, listen, you want money, I'll give you money," Joe promised him. "I have at least two and a half thousand dollars in my savings account, you can have it all."

The man let out a deep, harsh cry of mockery. "What are

you going to do, write me a check? You don't have the first idea, do you?"

"Then what?" Joe demanded. "Just tell me what it is, and I'll do my best to give it to you!"

Again the man was silent for what seemed like hours. Joe strained his ears to pick up the warble of a distant siren – anything that would tell him that help was on the way. Hadn't the *neighbors* heard his door being broken down. for Christ's sake? Were they stone deaf, or stupid, or what?

He could hear the fog-lagged noises of San Francisco at night, but that was all. Traffic, aircraft, and the long animal cry of a ship's foghorn. No sirens. He and Nina and Caroline and Joe Junior were trapped with their nightmare, in a city that seemed to have turned over and gone to sleep.

Nina choked, "Please. Please don't hurt us."

The man turned to Joe. "You want to live?"

"What kind of a question is that?"

"Under the circumstances, pretty reasonable, wouldn't you say?"

Joe smeared the sweat from his forehead with his sleeve. "Of course we want to live. We have kids to take care of."

"Sure you do," the man nodded. "So what I want you to do is, to kneel down on the floor, and to place both of your hands flat on the floorboards."

Joe hesitated. "That's all? That's all you want me to do?"

"Just kneel down on the floor, like I said, and place both of your hands flat on the floorboards."

Joe did as he was told. The man looked at him for a while, and then said, "Okay, that's good."

He released his grip on Nina's hair, but when Nina started to sag, he nudged at her neck with the butcher knife, keeping her upright. With his left hand, he rummaged in the canvas sack that was tied to his belt.

Joe said, "Can't we talk? There must be something you want. I can arrange to have some cash brought around. My brother-in-law—"

"Screw your brother-in-law," the man growled. With some difficulty, he tugged out of his sack a small heavy-headed hammer, and then probed inside with two fingers, and brought out a long steel rail dog – a flat-sided nail used for pinning rails down to railroad ties.

"Here," he said, shuffling forward a few paces, bringing Nina with him, and shoving them aggressively under Joe's nose.

"What?" asked Joe, bewildered. He felt a sharp wetness down the side of one leg, and suddenly realized that he must have squirted pee into his pants. Fear beat against his forehead like an endless monotonous drumbeat. *Please go away. Please don't be here. Please let me open my eyes and find you gone.*

"Here," the man repeated. "Take the goddamned hammer, will you?"

Mutely, Joe took it, and tried to take the nail, too.

"Unh-hunh. Not the nail. Your lovely wife's going to hold the nail."

The man reached down and tried to press the nail into Nina's hand. But Nina's fingers were trembling uncontrollably, and she dropped the nail on to the floor, and it bounced and rang.

"Pick it up," the man told Joe. "Give it back to her."

Joe picked it up, and placed it gently back in Nina's hand, and closed her fingers around it.

"What do you want us to do?" Joe asked. His voice didn't even sound like his own.

The man grasped Nina's hair again, and slowly levered her head back. Her bare throat was stretched. White skin, visible veins, highlighted by the white triangular reflection of the knifeblade. The knife's reflection didn't waver once. *This man isn't even human*, thought Joe. *Not only isn't he scared; he isn't excited, either. He's calm, he's relaxed. He's not even threatening us because it turns him on.*

"You spread your left hand on the floor," the man instructed Joe. "That's right. nice and flat. Now your lovely wife's going to kneel down beside you nice and slow, and she's going to hold that nail for you right in the middle of your hand, she's going to hold it real steady. Then you're going to knock it right in."

Joe stared at those dead black eyes in horror. "You want me to nail my own hand to the floor? Are you crazy?"

"You can do as you're told or you can watch your wife die, up to you."

"You're out of your mind!" Joe gasped at him.

The man grunted, dipped his masked head. "It doesn't matter squat to you whether I'm sane or I'm crazy. All that matters to you is staying alive. And the only way you're going to have any chance of staying alive is if you do what I tell you."

Very slowly, still tightly gripping her hair, the man forced Nina to kneel down next to Joe.

"The nail," he told her.

"I can't," she choked. A thin runnel of blood had slid straight down the center of her larynx and pooled in the hollow of her neck.

"Tell her, Joe," the man coaxed him. "Tell her what's going to happen if she doesn't behave."

"Nina," said Joe. "You're going to have to be brave."

"But I can't do it! I can't!" She was close to becoming hysterical; and Joe knew how dangerous it could be, if a hostage became hysterical. That was when you had to go in with guns blazing, because anything could happen, and usually did, and all you could hope to do was keep the casualties down to the minimum.

"The nail," the man insisted.

Shaking wildly, Nina held the nail between finger and thumb, about two or three inches above the back of Joe's hand. Joe took hold of the point and placed it between his finger-joints, well clear of his veins.

"I can't do it," Nina panted. "I can't do it. Please don't ask me to do it."

"Listen," said Joe, "it won't even hurt. You remember Bill Gates? He caught a .45 slug in the middle of his hand, just like he was playing baseball. He didn't even feel it, and he's fine now. Absolutely fine."

In spite of his soft words of reassurance, Joe was sweating iced-water, and he could feel his spaghetti knotting and churning in his stomach like a jarful of tomato-flavored worms. If he had to do it, if he *had* to nail his own hand to the floor, he wanted to get it over as quickly as he could.

"Just hold the nail there," he begged her. "Hold it there and close your eyes. You won't be doing me any favors if you don't keep it real steady."

Nina stared into his eyes, and swallowed. "I love you," she said. "Don't ever forget that I love you."

"I love you too, sweetheart," Joe told her.

"Get on with it, for Christ's sake!" the man snarled. "You want to see her die?"

Joe could feel the point of the nail trembling against his skin. He had to hit it hard and accurate—think about it as joinery. He didn't want to hit his fingers with a 5lb hammer, he could smash his knuckles and never be able to work again. And he didn't want to hit Nina's fingers either.

A drop of Nina's blood fell on to the back of his hand and that decided him. If she could shed her blood to save him, then he could certainly shed his blood to save her.

He swung the hammer back, shouted "*Ahh!*" and banged the nail right through the flesh between his index and middle fingers, right through muscle and cartilage, and into the hard oak flooring.

He hadn't imagined that it would hurt so much. After all, Bill Gates had told him that he hadn't felt a thing. But the nail sent a hideous spasm of pain all the way up his arm to the elbow, and his fingers contracted as if he had been electrocuted.

"Oh, Jesus, Jesus, Jesus!" he babbled. It was partly a release of tension, partly surprise, mostly agony.

But the man in the mask wasn't going to let up. "Again," he ordered, his voice harsh. "Right in, as far as it can go."

His eyes filled with tears, Joe lifted the hammer again. The man had forced Nina to stand up now, well away from him. She hadn't been able to close her eyes, but she had turned her face away, and she was gray with shock.

Joe looked down at his hand. The L-shaped head of the nail protruded about an inch-and-a-half above the skin, but apart from a narrow red line that ran between his fingers, there was surprisingly little blood.

"Again." the man commanded him.

Numbly, Joe lifted the hammer, hesitated, and then banged at the nailhead again, and then again, until his hand was pinned flat to the floor. He felt as if he were suffering from severe frostbite. He was overwhelmed by a relentless aching that seemed to penetrate every bone in his body. He dropped the hammer and knelt shaking and silent, not even thinking what might happen next.

"Now," said the man. "Mrs. Berry's turn."

Joe lifted his head. "What?" he asked, fearfully.

"The lovely Nina's turn," the man replied. No emotion. No gloating. As matter-of-fact as an airline steward, announcing that it was time for them to board their flight.

"What do you mean, what are you going to do?" Joe demanded.

"Will you just cut out all the fucking questions?" the man told him, his voice still muffled but rising.

"But you're not going to—"

"I said shut the fuck up!" the man screamed, and this time Joe was seriously frightened. The man might sound calm most of the time, but it was clear that he was right on the brink. One wrong move, one smart answer too many, and he could kill them both. Joe closed his eyes tight, in excruciating misery, and thought of Caroline and Joe Junior; and tried to think of something hopeful, too, some way out of this terrifying insanity.

But the masked man had crowded the whole apartment with such a suffocating aura of illogical dread that Joe couldn't think of anything constructive or optimistic at all; except that he wanted this over. No matter how it ended, he wanted it over.

He opened his eyes and found that Nina was kneeling on the floor facing him, her hands flat on the floor. Their fingertips were almost touching. The man was hunkered down beside her, his belly rolled over the belt of his jeans, and now he was holding the point of the knife close to her jugular vein.

Joe could smell him. He smelled of sweat and automobile grease and something else indefinable: a smell like stale hay, or dry leather, or poor-quality marijuana.

"We're going to do the same thing again now," the man said. "Nina's going to hold the nail and Joe's going to hammer it in."

He produced another railroad dog from his sack, and laid it carefully on the floor close to Nina's left hand.

"They're going to gas you for this," Joe told him, his voice fragmented, like all the bits and pieces inside a child's kaleidoscope.

"Shut up, please," the man said, much more softly this time. "They're not going to gas me for nothing."

Joe, wincing with pain, said, "You can't expect me to— Jesus, she's my *wife!*"

"Sure I can expect you to. I can expect you to do anything. It's up to you, do it or die. What could be simpler?"

Nina breathed, "Joe, do it. For God's sake let's get this over with."

She picked up the nail with her right hand and carefully positioned the point over the back of her left.

"Do it, Joe. Come on, we've shared everything before."

"Yes, come on, Joe," the man urged him, digging the point of his knife into Nina's neck. "Double your pleasure, double your fun."

"God, you maniac," Joe cursed him.

He lowered his head. There was a moment when he didn't know whether he would be able to do it or not. After all, what guarantee did he have, after he had nailed Nina's hand to the floor, that the man wouldn't kill them anyway? But his police training kept telling him: *compromise, take the line of least resistance*. He had seen too many times what had happened to people who had tried to be heroes.

Nina said, "Go on, Joe. Be brave."

Joe shivered. Why did he feel so cold?

"Go on, Joe," he heard Nina repeating.

He tried not to think about anything at all. He lifted the hammer and beat at the nail in Nina's hand with all his strength, hoping to save her the pain of a second or a third stroke. She let out a strange cry like nothing he had ever heard before; except for a seagull with a broken wing, which he had once seen crushed by the wheel of a slowly-reversing truck, on the Embarcadero.

He dropped the hammer heavily on to the floor. But the man in the mask said, "Again! Come on, Joe! Again! It's only half of the way in!"

He picked up the hammer. He tried to look at nothing but the head of the nail. He beat it again, and still it wouldn't go in. He beat it again, and again; and at last Nina's hand was pinned flat to the floor, like his own.

The man peered closely at Joe, and then at Nina, and they were both weeping.

"You did good!" he exclaimed. "You did really, really good! I'm proud of you!"

Joe said nothing. He couldn't speak out of pain; and humiliation; and complete disgust. Nina kept on sobbing and sobbing; but Joe knew that she was sobbing more out of pity for him than she was for her own pain.

The man took his knife away from Nina's throat, and eased himself back so that he was sitting on the floor. "Well, well," he said. "That's good. That's just the way I wanted to see you. Kneeling, you know? Obedient. And sick at heart."

He dug the point of the knife into the floorboards, and it vibrated backwards and forwards, like a tuning-fork.

"Joe's had his turn and Nina's had her turn. Now it's *my* turn."

"Aren't you satisfied yet?" Joe asked him, wretchedly.

"Satisfied?" The glossy black mask turned toward him in apparent curiosity. "Don't you know that his Satanic Majesty is *never* satisfied?"

"For God's sake," Joe pleaded.

"Oh, no," the man replied, and his voice was rich with lewdness. "For Satan's sake."

He grasped Joe's right hand, and forced it flat on to the floorboards.

"No," said Joe, dully, although there was nothing he could do.

The man kept Joe's hand flat against the floor with his knuckles. Then, with a jingle, he sorted another nail out of his sack, and dug it directly into the back of Joe's hand.

"No," said Joe. But with three or four hard, insistent bangs, his right hand was nailed to the floor, too.

Joe cried, "Ah! Ah! Oh God, ah! Oh God, that hurts!"

But the man said coarsely, "Shut up, please, will you? This is all going good. We don't want to spoil it, do we?"

"Jesus," wept Joe.

He kept his head bowed and his brain closed while the man nailed Nina's right hand to the floor. But the sound of the hammer struck through every bone and nerve in his body.

The man stood up, and paced around them. "Good, Joe, you're looking good. That's the way I like to see you, don't you know? Kneeling down, showing the proper respect."

Eventually, he hunkered down behind Joe, and said. "This is going to hurt. But I want you to think about something that takes your mind off things that hurt. I don't know, think about your mother. Your dear sweet little old mother."

Joe's hands, cold at first, now felt as if they were blazing. He hung his head in pain and exhaustion.

"You don't want to think about your dear sweet little old mother?" the man chided him. "You bastard! What kind of an American are you? Next thing you'll be telling me you don't like Pee Wee Herman!"

He spent some time rummaging in his sack. Then he produced a nine-inch rail dog and held it too close to Joe's face, so that all Joe could see was blurry black-and-blue. "Look at that! Is that a nail or is that a nail? That's hand-forged. No expense spared on *you*, Joe."

He pressed the point of the rail dog into the soft hollow just in back of Joe's knee. Joe thought: *holy shit, he's going to nail my legs to the floor, too*. He hesitated for a moment, while the man picked up the hammer. Then he lashed out with both legs, like a donkey. His right foot caught the man on the elbow, and the man rolled over, unbalanced. But the next thing Joe knew, the butcher knife came slicing right up between Joe's legs, cutting through his pants, opening up his scrotum, and digging halfway into his penis. Missing his urtery by an eighth-of-an-inch.

Joe stayed motionless, crouched, hunched, with blood soaking his pants. *Oh God. One more inch and he could have turned me into a woman.*

"That's good, Joe," the man told him. "You just stay still like that; don't move; and everything's going to be fine and dandy."

Another kind of crucifixion followed. The pain was so terrible that Joe openly cried. The man drove nails right through his bended knee-joints into the floorboards, so that he was fixed into place, on all fours. Then he did the same to Nina.

When he had finished, he tossed the hammer aside, and it bounced and bounded across the floor.

"There, Joe! There, Nina! Crouching like servants! Crouching like slaves! I like you like that, Joe! That's the way you were born, crouching. That's the way you lived your life! It suits you to crouch! Servile, yes? That's it, servile!"

He walked around and around them, so that Joe lost touch of where he was. But at last he stopped, right behind Nina, and hesitated, one booted foot drumming quickly on the floor. *Oh dear God. the pain*, thought Joe. But he was past weeping; at least for now.

"Servants, yes!" the man decided. "That's what you are, servants!"

He slowly knelt down, flexing his chest-muscles as he did so, jangling the beads that dangled from his nipples. He lifted Nina's flowery green-and-yellow dress, all the way up to her waist, until her bottom was exposed. She wore shiny tan-colored pantyhose, with white lace-trimmed panties. The man trailed his fingertips around the cheeks of her bottom, gently, musingly, but confidently too, because he knew that whatever he wanted to do, neither Nina nor Joe would be able to stop him.

"I'm going to fall," whispered Nina. "I can't stand it any longer. I'm going to fall."

"You couldn't fall if you wanted to," the man cooed. "You're nailed in place, Mrs. Berry. Fixed in slavery. Fixed, you housetrained bitch!"

"Leave her alone!" Joe bellowed. "You touch her, so help me, I'll see you in hell!"

The man raised his black masked face. The lamplight shone on every glossy curve. Only the eyes remained dead. "That, Joe, has been on the cards since you were."

With finger and thumb, the man fastidiously rolled down Nina's panythose, down to her bloodied knees. He couldn't pull them down any further because she was firmly nailed to the floor. Then he tugged down her panties, a little at a time.

Jesus so help me if we ever get out of this I'm going to strangle this man with my bare hands and happily die for it.

Joe closed his eyes. He heard the man's belt buckle unlatching. He heard Nina whimper. *Please Jesus spare me this. Please don't let this be happening. Please may I now wake up.*

He caught a blurred glimpse of the man with his leather

pants pulled down to his thighs. Black shaggy hair, white shaggy thighs, and a rearing red totem. Then all he could do was concentrate on Nina's face, in agonizing close-up, as the man reared up behind her, and dragged the cheeks of her bottom apart, and forced himself into her.

She winced in agony, although by now she was almost beyond agony. Her green-flecked irises contracted. Her mouth opened, as if she couldn't breathe.

"I love you," Joe told her. There was nothing else that he could do. He wished now with an agony that made the pain in his hands and his knees seem like kisses by comparison that he had struggled and fought for her. Even if the man had stabbed him to death, he could at least have died like a man—died like his partners had died, when he was a cop—out on the streets, fighting injustice, fighting for something they believed in.

But Joe—no, Joe was nailed to the floor, while a brutal sadist raped and tortured his wife, right in front of him. The great tough husband and protector Joe Berry was nailed to the goddamned floor!

Perspiration quivered on Nina's forehead like a crown of pearls. The man thrust harder and harder, and she was starting to pant.

"She's a good hump, Joe!" the man grunted. "She might have given you two kids, Joe—but no problem, she's still as tight as a nut!"

Joe saw Nina's face with her eyes tight shut and her teeth gritted. Then all of a sudden the man shouted, "Oh! That's it! That's fucking it!" and Nina cried out, and the worm-spaghetti wouldn't stay down in Joe's stomach. It filled up his mouth with a huge hot rush which he couldn't contain, and splattered over his hands.

The man stopped his jerking and thrusting.

"Oh, come on, Joe. That's not nice. We're just trying to have a little fun here. That's not nice."

"*You're killing me!*" Nina screamed. "*It hurts so much! I can't stand it any longer!*"

The man hesitated, then sat back on his haunches and tugged up his pants, and buckled himself up. "I see," he said, and although his voice was soft, it was filled with a terrible cold resentment which made Joe feel even more frightened than before. "I see, so that's the way you feel about it."

Joe heaved again. A string of scarlet saliva swung from his chin.

"Can't you leave us?" Nina begged. "Can't you see that we've had enough?"

"Enough?" the man repeated, as if he couldn't believe what he was hearing. "What do you mean, enough? This is the sixth ritual of the seven rituals. Don't you understand?"

The sixth ritual, thought Joe, lowering his head. Now, at last, he understood who their attacker was, and it filled him with such fear that he could have screamed, and gone on screaming. Every month this year, a family had been butchered somewhere in the Bay Area... Forest Hill, Crocker Amazon, Pacific Heights, Bernal Heights, College Park. The murders had been deliberate and ritualistic, and in most cases the victims had been killed so horribly and in such bizarre ways that the TV and newspapers had withheld most of the details.

How do you report that a man was forced to push his own hand down a sink-disposal unit, in order to save his wife from being set on fire?

The murderer had left scarcely any circumstantial evidence; but he had called KGO Radio after every killing and claimed responsibility. Joe had heard his tape-recorded voice on television, blurting, *"Every one of these sacrifices has brought the great day closer. Soon my master will rise again, as it was written in the scrolls."*

Joe couldn't remember if the voice was anything like the voice of this maniac who had nailed them to the floor. He hurt too much to think with any kind of clarity.

KGO had dubbed the killer the Fog City Satan. His killings had followed no particular pattern; except that they had all been ritualistic, and that nobody had survived to tell the police what had happened; not even a child. When the Fog City Satan visited your home, that was the end of you and all of your kind.

There had been no discernible logic behind the Fog City Satan's choice of victims. One had been white-collar, two had been blue. One family were Mexicans, another were Chinese. Two had been Catholic, three had been connected with the hotel or catering business. None had been gay. None had served in the armed forces. Two had owned Pontiacs. One had owned a Volkswagen.

Either the Fog City Satan chose his victims at random; or else he was following some obscure personal vendetta which nobody else could explain. Once, Joe had arrested a man who had been shooting anybody whose name began with a G and ended with an D—"in case they got uppity ideas and tried to claim that they were God."

The brutality of what happened on the streets had eventually led Joe to hand in his shield. It was almost too much for him to accept that he and his family had fallen victim to the madness that he should have stayed on to fight.

"Do you know what I'm going to do now?" the man whispered. "I'm going to bring in your children, that's what I'm going to do. I'm going to rouse them up from their beddy-byes, and I'm going to bring them in here to see you; and they're going to say goodnight. In fact, they're going to say more than goodnight, they're going to say goodbye."

Joe roared, "If you so much as touch one hair on their heads—!"

The mask dipped closer; black and shiny; its eyes dead. "You'll what, Joe? What will you do? Rip half the muscle out of your leg, and crawl after me? Or maybe you'll curse me, Joe—maybe that's what you'll do! Well—curse away, that's all I can say! Because there's no curse worse than me."

Joe swallowed, and spat out fragments of ground beef. Then he said, "Listen, if you need a sacrifice, I'll be your sacrifice. But don't touch the children, please. Just let them sleep."

He coughed, and then he said, "You can kill me now. Go on. You can kill me now. But please don't touch those children, please."

The man listened thoughtfully. He turned away. It seemed as if time had come to a premature end; as if logic had melted like one of Salvador Dali's buttery pocket-watches, draped over a branch.

"You know something?" the man said at last. "You just don't get it, do you? Fate, destiny, call it what you like.

You just don't see where it's going. You don't see what's happening, all around you. The old order's coming back. Not those fusty old farts from pioneer times. The *real* old order. Pure evil, Joe. Pure and cold! They've waited and they've waited; but now's the time! The time that was told of. And there's nothing you can do to hold it back."

Joe said, "Don't touch our children, okay?"

The man waited, tapping the tip of his knifeblade against his teeth. Then he said, "Give me a minute, will you?" and walked quickly out through the living-room door.

"*Don't touch our children!*" Joe roared.

There was a lengthy silence. Nina began to cry.

"It's okay," Joe told her. His throat was sore with vomity-tasting phlegm. "Everything's going to work out fine. He's a headcase, that's all. He just wants to make us feel scared."

"I'm so scared! I'm so scared! What more does he want?" blurted Nina.

"Just hold on, please," Joe begged her. He felt as treacherous as a lizard; as stupid as a clown. Worst of all, he had allowed the most vicious and irrational killer that the Bay Area had ever known to break into his house and terrorize his family. And he had allowed himself to be rendered totally helpless, so that if the killer wanted to torture and sacrifice his children, there was nothing he could do to stop him.

"Joe," Nina panted. "Joe."

Joe rocked his hands, just a fraction, from side to side. Each movement was critically painful, and fresh blood bulged out around the nailheads, and slid warmly down between his fingers, so that his hands were soon paddling in it.

Left, right. Left, right. Jesus, I never knew anything could hurt so much.

"I'm working myself free," he told her. "Don't you worry, Nina. It hasn't gone through bone. I'm working myself free."

Inside, he wept. Inside, he felt as tiny as a child.

Nina whispered, "Joe, listen, don't. You'll hurt yourself. Joe, listen, if this family has to die then we'll all die together. Joe, don't try to fight him."

"*He raped you!*" Joe screamed. "*He raped you!*"

And he used that anger to shout out, "hah!" and to tear his right hand free from the floorboards, with a hideous crackling sound, leaving a string of scarlet muscle clinging to the nail, and his hand spraying blood in every direction. He sucked in his breath in a sharp "*theeeeeee!*" of agony, and pressed his hand close to his chest. The pain was worse than anything he had ever experienced. And it was even worse because he knew that would never have the courage to pull his other hand free from the floor, because it hurt too much, because he didn't have the balls. And there wasn't a chance in the world that he could possibly tear out the nails that were buried in his knees. He would rather stay crouched on the floor than try to pull those out.

This is the point when pain overcomes bravery—when you have to admit that you simply cannot take any more.

"Joe," Nina whispered. "Joe?"

He raised his head. "What is it?"

"I just want you to know that whatever happens, I still love you, and you're not to blame."

He wiped his torn hand against his face, and streaked his cheek with blood. He started to sob. Deep, braying sobs, like an animal in pain. He sobbed and sobbed, and he thought that he would never be able to stop.

Not until the man appeared in the living-room doorway, leading Caroline with one hand, and Joe Junior by the other. Both children were pasty-faced and swollen-eyed and staring with terror. Joe immediately damped his hand back to the floor, as if it were still nailed down.

"Mommy?" whispered Caroline. "Daddy?"

The man squeezed her wrist. "Come on now, kids. You promised you'd be quiet, now didn't you? So just stay quiet."

Joe said hoarsely, "It's all right, kids. It'll soon be over. Just do what he tells you, and everything's going to work out fine."

The man let out a muffled laugh. "You're some kind of optimist, Joe, I'll say that for you!"

"Just don't hurt them, all right?" Joe insisted.

"The great one requires pain," the man replied. "Pain and humiliation, and a prayer of forgiveness."

"If you so much as scratch those children, you're going to burn in hell, I promise you. You think the police department wouldn't hunt you down and make absolutely sure that you die the most painful death they can think of?"

The man laughed again. "Even Satan's entitled to a trial."

"You'll burn in hell for this!" Joe yelled at him. "You'll burn in hell!"

Joe Junior started a high-pitched terrified crying, almost like a whistle, and tried to twist himself away from the man's grip. But the man swung him around and growled, "Shut up, you little bug!"

He dragged both children across to the couch. Joe turned his head away. He didn't think that he could bear to watch. But Nina, trembling, couldn't take her eyes off them; and all the time she muttered under her breath "*Don't hurt my children, dear God don't hurt my children, dear God don't hurt my children.*"

The man dragged a length of thin nylon yachting cord out of his sack, and deftly lashed Caroline's left wrist to Joe Junior's right wrist. Neither of the children was crying now, but they whimpered and shivered so pitifully that Joe decided that however much it was going to hurt him, he was going to try to tear himself free from the floor.

Up, Joe! he told himself. *You have to get up.*

He clenched his teeth, and reached behind him, gripping his ankle with his bloodslippery hand, so that he could lever his leg upwards, and drag the nail out of his right knee. *One—two—three—*

He screamed, but he didn't hear himself scream. The pain put him into convulsive muscular spasm, and he ground his teeth so forcefully that he crushed one of his ceramic crowns. He still couldn't get up. He couldn't do it, he couldn't do it. The nail had been driven too deeply into the floorboards, and he didn't have the strength or the will to have another try at tugging it out.

"Are you all right?" the man asked him, with creepy solicitousness.

A strange quietness came over the Berry family, all four of them. The quietness of complete terror. The quietness of looking death, real death, straight in its dark and velvet eye.

The man ushered the children against the wall. Then he

took hold of Caroline's right arm, and lifted it high above her head Joe saw the hammer and the nails coming out, and screamed, "*No!*"

Why didn't the children cry? It must have hurt them just as much as it had hurt Nina and him. Yet they were uncannily silent, and their silence was far more agonizing to Joe than their screaming would have been. It was as if they prepared to endure anything, because they trusted their father to save them. Daddy wouldn't let us die.

The knocking sounds echoed in Joe's ears like somebody knocking on the doors of a mortuary. The children said. "Ow, ow, ow, ow," in a terrible soft unending appeal to a world that could hurt them so much. But they didn't scream, and they didn't cry, and with every knock of the hammer. Joe withered away inside of himself, until it was all finished and his spirit was as frail as a dried-up leaf.

The man had nailed the children to the wall like two paper dolls, their arms outspread, their feet scarcely touching the floor. Neither Joe nor Nina could look at them, or the expression on their faces.

"Mommy it hurts," whispered Caroline. "Mommy it hurts so much." And all Nina could do was kneel and weep.

The man paced around the room, his shadow swiveling from one wall to the other, admiring his handiwork, and slapping the head of the hammer in the palm of his hand.

"Now we're going to say a prayer, yes? Now we're going to ask the great one to forgive us. Now we're going to pledge our lives to the old order, the way it was always supposed to be."

"Please," Joe begged him. "You can kill me if you like, but let the children go."

The man shook his head. "This is it, Joe. This is where you make your peace with the god that you and all your kind turned your backs on. The real god."

He rummaged around in his sack yet again, and this time he produced a red plastic bottle of barbecue starter fluid.

"Oh, God, not that," Joe breathed.

"What?" asked Nina. "What?"

But Joe wouldn't answer; and if there was anything merciful about being nailed to the floor, it was that Nina couldn't see what he was about to do.

"Joe?" she pleaded. "Joe?"

The man walked backward and forward in front of the children, jetting them with fluid. All over their hair, all over their pajamas, all over their hands and feet. Joe Junior coughed and gagged at the smell of it, but although their eyes ran with tears, still neither child cried out.

"How about praying for forgiveness?" the man demanded, his glossy black mask dipping and swaying like the head of a huge black insect performing a ritual dance. "How about saying with me, 'o great Beli Ya'al, whose day has now come, forgive me, forgive me, forgive me.'"

"Are you crazy?" Joe screamed at him, in a sudden surge of panic and temper. Jesus Christ, who cared what the man did to him. Things couldn't get worse.

"Come on, now, that's not going to help any," the man told him. "Just say after me, 'o great Beli Ya'al, whose day has now come…'"

Joe remained mute; but Nina said, "O great Beli Ya'al… whose day has now come… forgive me."

It seemed to Joe that the lights in the living-room flickered and darkened.

"Come on, Joe," the man urged him. "'O great Beli Ya'al, whose return was written in pages of dust, whose name lived on when every other name was taken by the wind…'"

Joe shook his head, and began to recite his own prayer.

"Our Father, which art in Heaven… hallowed be Thy name… Thy Kingdom come, Thy will be done… on earth, as it is in Heaven…"

But he stopped; because he knew that he would have to ask God to forgive him his sins—as he was supposed to forgive those who had sinned against him. And he would never be able to forgive this man in his black antlered mask, not even in heaven, not even in hell.

"Come on, now, Joe, we're depending on you," the man coaxed him. "'O great Beli Ya'al, whose return was written in pages of dust…'"

As he spoke, the man approached the children, where they hung on the wall. Caroline appeared to have gone into some kind of fit, because her eyes were rolled back in her head, and she was quivering and bubbling at the mouth. Joe Junior had his eyes tightly closed.

The man said, more softly now, "…whose name lived on, when every other name was taken by the wind…"

Then he bent down in front of the children, and struck a match, and played it backward and forward beneath their cringing feet.

2

Larry was eating linguine pescatora and talking with his mouth full when Deputy Chief Burroughs came in through the swing doors of Salvatore's restaurant and stood with his fists on his hips, shortsightedly peering from left to right.

At first, Deputy Chief Burroughs couldn't see Larry through the curved glass screen which separated the doorway from the dining area. But then Larry saw him catch hold of Vito, the waiter, and mouth *Lieutenant Foggia* above the noise and clatter of the restaurant. Vito beckoned him around the screen, and along to Larry's table under the mirror.

"God damn it to hell," cursed Larry, trying to shield his face with his hand. "The first free evening in two months."

"What is it?" asked Linda, turning around, and frowning.

"Dan Burroughs, wearing his Saint Joan face."

"Oh, not here!" Linda protested.

"A visitor for you, Larry," said Vito. "Hey, I'm sorry. I tried to tell him you were at "Prego", but he wouldn't believe me."

"Who eats at "Prego"?" Larry replied.

Dan Burroughs pulled out a chair without being invited

and sat down. He was dry, gray man, with sunken cheeks and pursed lips and eyes that looked as expressionless as ocean-washed pebbles. His voice was harsh from years of smoking and years of San Francisco fog.

"Hi, Dan, be my guest," said Larry, sarcastically. "How about something to eat? The gnocchi's good tonight."

Dan said, "Spare me, Larry, will you? I wouldn't of interrupted your dinner without good cause. Hallo, Linda, sorry about this."

Larry poured Linda some more orvieto, and filled his own glass, too. He guessed that this was probably the last glass of wine he was going to be able to drink this evening. Dan was marble-hard and totally unforgiving, but he wasn't the kind of man who canceled anybody's R-and-R just because he was feeling out of sorts.

"There's been another killing," he told Larry. "Linda, I apologize for this, but you may want to excuse us for a moment. I don't have what you might call the delicate touch when it comes to stuff like this. It's going to upset you: so maybe you'd better hear it from your husband, rather than me."

Linda slowly put down her fork. "I don't mind, Dan. I'd just as soon hear it from you."

Dan shrugged. "Please yourself. But I'm afraid it's real bad news. Our ritual killer's been out on the town again."

"You mean this Fog City Satan?" asked Linda.

Dan gave her a sour, scarcely perceptible nod. He hated the hyped-up glamorized names that newspapers gave to killers and rapists and drug-runners. As far as he was concerned, they were nothing more than human detritus, on the same level as all those hundreds of pounds of dead skin and discarded hair that had to be swept every day out of San Francisco's transit system.

"Four dead," he said. "A father, mother, two children. Very, very ugly. You don't want to know how ugly. But there's something else, too. This time, the people he wasted were ours."

Larry swallowed wine. "He killed a cop?"

"Good as. An ex-cop, you know him. Joe Berry. The whole Berry family."

Linda raised her hand over her mouth in horror. "Joe Berry? And Nina? And the kids, oh God! I can't believe it!"

Larry felt as if Dan had suddenly smacked him across the face. Numb, stunned; and suddenly much more vulnerable to sudden death. He crossed himself.

"What happened?" he asked, soft-voiced. "God almighty, we saw Joe just last Friday. He brought round a coffee-table he'd made for us. God almighty, I can't believe it."

Linda said, "They're really dead? Nina, and the children?"

Dan nodded. "I'm sorry. All four of them. I told you it was pretty upsetting news."

Linda started to weep. Larry reached across the table and grasped her hand.

"Hold on," he told her. "Hold on." Damn it, he could have cried, too.

Dan took out a pack of Marlboro, and lit one. "It happened just over an hour ago. A neighbor heard shots, and raised the alarm."

"Is Arne up there?"

"Arne's up there, yes. Well, let's put it this way. He's up there at this particular moment in time."

Larry caught the intonation. He could guess what Dan had in mind without even having to ask. But all the same, he asked.

"Am I totally misguided, or do I get the impression that you're thinking of taking him off it?"

Dan blew out smoke. "He's off it as soon as you can get to the scene."

"Me?"

"That's correct. I'm passing this one over to you, Larry. From now on, the Fog City Satan is all yours. I've already detailed Sergeant Brough to help you, as well as Jones and Glass. And anybody else you want, except for Gates and Migdoll."

Larry glanced anxiously at Linda and then turned back to Dan. He didn't like this one bit. He was good on neighborhood killings, family vendettas and domestic quarrels. He was comfortable with Italian brothers who had shot sailors for insulting their sisters; or Chinese restaurateurs who had hacked up rival restaurateurs for stealing their recipe for frog-shaped chicken. But he certainly didn't relish the idea of working on the grisliest series of ritual massacres that the Bay Area had ever known. What was more, Arne Knudsen would be sure to hit the ceiling if his precious Satan case were taken away from him. Arne liked to think of himself as a kind of one-man nemesis, a Swedish Shadow, inexorably pursuing murderers through jungles of deception and shoals of red herring, until at last he arrived at their door with a warrant and a grim grin.

Larry said, "Dan... with all respect... I'm not so sure that this is my kind of assignment."

"Your kind of assignment is the kind of assignment which I assign you to."

"But Arne's on top of it, isn't he? I know he's a grouch, but he's a terrific detective. Look at that work he did on the Petrie killings."

"For sure," Dan nodded. "But the Petrie killings were systematic. The Petrie killings had a mathematical pattern. Knudsen's unbeatable when it comes to systems and patterns. He's more logical than Mr. Spock. But this Fog City Satan guy doesn't kill by systems or patterns—no system or pattern that *we* can work out, anyhow. He just tortures and kills and each time he chooses a different location and a different family and a totally different m.o."

Salvatore came up to their table, frowning anxiously. "The linguine's no good?" he asked Larry.

"If God's tears taste of anything, this linguine is it," Larry told him. "But I'm afraid we've just received some terrible personal news. Another time, okay?"

Salvatore saw that Linda had been crying. "I'm real sorry. You want something? Maybe a coffee? Maybe a brandy?"

"That's all right, Salvatore. Maybe you could call us a cab, so that Linda can get home."

Linda said, "You're not going to start on this tonight?"

"I'm going to have to," said Larry.

"He's going to have to," Dan repeated. "Believe me, I feel like shit for breaking up your evening. I feel like shit for bring you such bad news."

"But why does Larry have to take it on?" asked Linda, defiantly. "He's buried in work already!"

Dan puffed out more smoke, and coughed. A large

black-haired woman at the next table gave him a look of disgust that threatened to wither the pink carnations on their table.

"Linda, we're *all* buried in work. Knudsen's buried in work. Pasquale's buried in work. Rossetti hasn't seen his wife in so long he passed her in the street last week and didn't recognize her. Larry has to take it on because Mayor Agnos is urgently demanding some fancy high-profile police work, and there is nobody on the roster who is fancier or high-profiler than your husband."

Larry said, "Two Armani suits doesn't make me fancy and high-profile."

"Don't shit me, Larry," Dan told him. "You're media-friendly and you look like you're doing something useful even when you're not."

"Has it occurred to you that this assignment might be a little beyond my abilities?" Larry asked him. "Besides, Joe was a personal friend. I don't want to make this into some kind of vendetta."

"Vendetta? Don't make me laugh. You're Italian. Your uncle was Vincent Caccamo. Your whole life is one long vendetta."

Dan coughed – a hacking, hoarse, rib-wracking cough that led the woman at the next table to drop down her fork in disgust. Her nervous-looking partner called, "Pardon me, sir, we're trying to eat here."

Dan heaved himself around in his chair and stared at the young man stonily. "Any luck yet?" he asked him.

Linda said, "Dan... tell me. Did the Berrys suffer much?"

Dan flicked a quick glance at her. But before he answered,

he crushed out his cigarette and turned back to the young man at the next table and said, "Sorry. I apologize. It's been a terrible day, is all."

"Don't mention it," the young man replied. But the woman hissed at him, "Don't *mention* it, for God's sake?"

Dan said to Linda, "As far as we know, they suffered very badly. This guy is a maniac, it's like he sits at home thinking up terrible ways to hurt people. Believe me, you don't want to know the details, except that when they died it was a merciful release."

"Is there anything I can do?" asked Linda. "Any relations you want me to call?"

Dan said, "Tomorrow morning I have to go break the news to Joe's mother. She's in a convalescent home in Berkeley. Maybe you'd like to come along. I could use the moral support."

Linda nodded. "Whatever you need, Dan, just ask."

Vito came up to tell them that the taxi was waiting outside. Larry guided Linda to the door, and Dan followed behind.

"What do I owe you for the meal?" Larry asked Salvatore, but Salvatore shook his head.

"Don't worry about it, Larry. Come and enjoy next time. And all our sympathy, yes?"

They stood outside on Polk Street. It was one of those ghostly nights when San Francisco seems like a huge sailing-ship, becalmed in the fog. Dan Burroughs coughed into his hand. For the first time in a very long time, Larry felt unsure of what he was doing; uncertain about the future. He didn't like the feeling at all. It reminded him of his first few weeks in homicide, when he had broken out into laughter – terrible high-pitched unstoppable laughter—every time he had been called out to look at another body. What had set him off was the almost-daily revelation that no matter how vain and pompous human beings could be, they were made up of nothing but meat and string and mess. He had once said to Linda that he was close to hating God, working in homicide. Unlike everybody else, except for doctors, you knew how disgusting humans were inside; even the most brightest; even the best. He used to watch Miss America and see nothing but muscles and skulls and heaped-up intestines—a parade of potential corpses in bathing-costumes.

Larry didn't look like the bitter type; or the hysterical type. He didn't particularly look like a detective. People at cocktail parties who tried to guess what he did for a living usually thought that he was a moderately successful musician, or something to do with commodities. He had that air of slight superiority; coupled with a very quiet way of talking; and a line in sardonic humor.

He was a shade too thin to be classically handsome. His face was long, with deeply-lined cheeks, almost gaunt. His hair was black, and stuck straight up like a brush, as if he were trying to grow out a crewcut. His best features were his eyes, which were always darkly circled, but green-emerald-green, and bright, and always sharp. And Linda loved his slow-developing smile.

All through her teenage years and early twenties, Linda had always been too small for most of the men she liked best. Her high-school hero and first serious crush, Glenn Basden II, had called her "the mighty midget". She was abundantly brunette, curvy, brown-eyed, irreverent (and she liked to sing); but she had a face like Bernini's Saint

Teresa, white as ivory, with heavy-lidded eyes and a perfect nose. Just the kind of looks to stir the blood of a professional Italian like Larry. And Larry hadn't minded at all that she was only 5ft 2¼ins. She made him feel supremely protective.

Feeling protective was an important part of what made Larry tick. At least he liked to think so. If it wasn't, then he didn't know why he subjected himself year after year to all of the sleaze and all of the brutality and all of the reminders that the Life of Man is solitary, poor, nasty, brutish and short.

He felt that he had a mission, kind of. If not a mission, then a duty for sure. Linda thought that he was vaguely peculiar, but she never brought him down. Without his mission, she didn't know what kind of man he would be, and she wasn't at all sure that she wanted to find out.

Larry took hold of her shoulders and kissed her forehead and then her lips. "Tell the kids goodnight if they're still awake."

"Okay," said Linda. "When do you think I might see you?"

Dan coughed again. "You know better than to ask that, Mrs. Foggia. Just tell him what you want for Christmas, and give him a goodnight kiss."

Linda gave Larry a quick, light kiss on the cheek. "I hope it's not—well, I hope it doesn't give you any nightmares."

Without another word, she climbed into the taxi and Larry leaned over to the driver and said, "Russian Hill, the quick way."

"*In un amen*," the driver replied.

Larry watched the taxi drive off, its brakelights briefly

GRAHAM MASTERTON

glaring at the intersection with Union Street. "Do you know what the trouble with this town is?" he told Dan. "Too many goddamned Italians."

They climbed into Dan's bronze Caprice, and drove toward Fulton Street.

As he drove, Dan carefully placed another cigarette between his lips and pushed in the lighter. "I didn't give you the full picture because I wanted to spare Linda the grisly details," he said. "But I think you'd better be prepared before we get there."

Larry said nothing, but watched him as he lit his cigarette. The Caprice bucked over Van Ness.

Dan said, "The guy gained access to the building by forcing a window in the first-floor apartment, which was unoccupied at the time because the owners were away. The guy then broke down the front door of the Berrys' apartment using the same kind of jack that the engine companies use. It took out the whole Goddamned door, frame and lintel and everything.

"It's impossible to say exactly what happened next, but judging by the cuts on Nina Berry's throat, the guy probably persuaded Joe to co-operate with him by threatening Nina with a knife. That's Arne's theory, anyway."

Dan looked at him sideways, his cigarette dangling between his lips. Then he said, "Are you ready for this? The guy got Joe to crouch down on his hands and knees, and then he nailed him to the floor."

"He did *what?*"

"He nailed him to the floor. Then he nailed Nina to the floor, facing him. One nail through each hand, one nail through each knee. Damn great railroad nails."

"Mother of God," said Larry. He knew better than to ask how the killer had persuaded Joe to stay still while he nailed him down. He had once been caught in a deserted building close to the Embarcadero by a wild and homicidal young Neapolitan, who had threatened to blow out his stomach with a pump-gun. Larry had heard himself saying nothing but "yes, sure, whatever you want."

Dan impatiently blew his horn at a taxi that was dawdling in front of him. "There's worse. The guy raped Nina, right in front of Joe, by the looks of it. Also—we don't know when—we don't like to think when—he got the kids out of bed, and nailed them to the wall. That's right, you heard me. He nailed them to the wall."

His voice was rough and dry and expressionless, like somebody dragging a mail sack across a concrete yard. He repeated the words as if he had memorized them, and didn't want to think what they actually meant.

"They may have seen their mother raped, they may not. But whatever happened, he doused them with some kind of inflammable fluid, and set them alight."

Larry stared at him. "He burned them? And they were still alive?"

"That's right. But he didn't stop there. He set fire to them, but he didn't let them die. After a short while, he smothered the flames with a blanket. Then he walked right out, leaving two seriously burned children hanging from the wall, and their parents nailed to the floor—presumably to witness their children's agony."

Larry swallowed. but couldn't speak. Dan spun the Chevrolet's wheel with the flat of his hand, and turned into Fulton.

"We've seen some bad ones, right?" he remarked. "But how the hell can you begin to understand something like this? How can you begin to understand one human being wanting to hurt other human beings so much?" It was the first time that he had shown any real rage.

Larry said, "If the guy walked out. leaving the kids to suffer and Joe and Nina nailed to the floor to listen to them—how did they die?"

There were red and blue lights flashing through the fog, and almost a solid block of Fulton was crowded with police cars and fire-trucks and ambulances and TV vans. Dan pulled in behind the medical examiner's car, crimped his tires against the curb, and pushed down the parking-brake.

"It must have been more than Joe could stand, listening to his children suffer. He dragged himself up off the floor. God knows how he did it. He pulled huge lumps of flesh out of his hands and his knees. Then he crawled into the bedroom and got his gun. He shot his children, and then Nina, and then he shot himself."

Larry took a deep breath. He didn't know whether he wanted to get out of the car or not. What he really felt like was going home.

"What does Arne think?" he asked. "Is he sure that there was just one assailant?"

"No question. Male, and physically powerful. And despite the fact that he didn't kill them himself—the way he killed everybody else—Arne's sure that it's him. Satan, no less."

"No eye-witness descriptions?"

Dan shook his head. "Not yet—although it's quite

possible that somebody saw him enter or leave and doesn't have the nerve to say so. You remember what happened after the last two killings? Those warnings that were sent to the *Chron?* 'Anybody who points the finger will lose it.' 'Anybody who saw anything will lose their eyes.' Great way to encourage public-spiritedness, don't you think?"

"What about the press?" asked Larry, rubbing his eye. "How much do you want them to know? Have you told them yet that it was Joe who wasted the family, and not the assailant?"

"Unh-hunh. All we've released so far is that the Berry family were attacked and tortured and that they're all dead. I don't want to say any more until we have a clearer idea of what really happened."

A reporter from the *Examiner* had caught sight of Dan and Larry sitting together in the car, and was hurrying up the street toward them, followed by nearly a dozen more reporters, and the jiggling light of a TV camera.

"'Grief for a while is blind, and so was mine,'" Larry quoted. He had always liked Shelley. Shelley was kind of strange, and good on death. "'I wish no living thing to suffer pain.'"

Dan smashed out his cigarette, and gave him a counterquote. "'Gentlemen, it's time to grab the bull by the tail and look the facts squarely in the face.' James McSheehy."

Already one of the reporters was rapping her knuckles against the car window. Larry recognized her as Fay Kuhn, who had been writing sensational features about the Fog City Satan ever since the ritual killings had begun. Fay Kuhn, ex-*Oakland Tribune*, was pretty and educated and always well tailored. Her most controversial story so far had been to link the killings with comparable murders that had taken place in San Francisco in 1906, when five families had been ritually slaughtered, as well as nine prostitutes in a bawdy house on O'Farrell.

Dan Burroughs' answer to *that* story had been: "You're trying to suggest it was the same guy? What should we do? Hit the sunset homes?"

Larry climbed out of the car. Fay Kuhn was on him at once.

"Lieutenant Foggia, can you tell me what you feel about taking over the Fog City Satan case?"

Larry gave her a small, carefully packaged smile. "I haven't yet been officially informed that I *am* taking over the case. And, besides that, we don't really like to call the perpetrator the Fog City Satan or anything else. He's not the devil, he's not superhuman. No matter how sick or sadistic his behavior might have been, he's a human being with a father and a mother and friends and family and a name of his own. All I'm going to say tonight is that we're going to find out what that name is."

Fay Kuhn tossed back her shining brunette bob. She always reminded Larry of Jackie Onassis, when she had been Jaqueline Bouvier – very groomed, and very young. Platinum Card Cunt, as Detective Linebarger would have put it – the kind of woman that any man with an income less than $350,000 a year shouldn't even attempt to ask out for lunch. She said, sharply, "Do you seriously think that *you're* going to be able to find out what that name is, where Lieutenant Knudsen has failed?"

Dan slammed his car door shut and called, "That's enough, Fay. We have work to do."

But Larry said, "Lieutenant Knudsen hasn't failed in any respect. For instance, you wouldn't say that a space-shuttle shot has failed, just because it hasn't landed yet. Lieutenant Knudsen is a supremely good detective, and if I *was* to be allocated this assignment, I know that I would find his preparatory work to be impeccable."

"It's 'were', actually," Fay Kuhn corrected him. "Not 'was' to be allocated—'*were*.'"

He looked at her narrowly, trying to work out if she were serious or not. "That's your department," he said, at last. "You look after the wasses and the weres, I'll find your Fog City Satan."

Rick Tibbies, from the *Chron*, piped up, "Larry! The rumor is that these are all revenge killings… somebody settling some old scores. Is there any basis in fact for that?"

But Fay Kuhn grinned at Larry, and said, "So you admit you're taking over the case?"

"No, ma'am," Larry replied. "But I have one small favor to ask."

"I'm booked for dinner all this week," Fay Kuhn retorted. There was no doubt about it, she was quick, quick, quick.

"It's not that, Ms Kuhn. I just want the *Ex* to cut out those cute headlines. You know the ones. 'Foggia in a Fog.' 'Befogged Foggia Hunts Fog City Sicko.'"

Rick Tibbles repeated, "What do you think, Larry? Are these revenge killings or what?"

Larry shook his head, but he didn't take his eyes off

Fay Kuhn. "Who knows? If they are, we still don't see the connection."

"Foggia in a Fog, hunh?" asked Fay Kuhn, with a wicked smile.

Dan came around the car and took hold of Larry's arm. "Come on, folks. Lieutenant Foggia has work to do."

They walked shoulder to shoulder down the sloping incline of Fulton Street, jostled on both sides by reporters and cameramen. Larry turned around once to see where Fay Kuhn had gone to; and glimpsed her powder-blue suit on the opposite side of the street. For some reason, she obviously felt that she had everything she needed, for now; and Larry wondered what he might have given away.

Dan led the way through the police lines and up the front steps of the condominium. The stairs were marble, with black-painted cast-iron banistairs. The walls were papered with yellow-and-black flowers. Somebody had attempted to make the building look very turn-of-the-century. On the first landing, there was a framed reproduction of *The Stomach Dance* by Aubrey Beardsley, a devilish creature grinning and dancing.

As they climbed, police officers and photographers and paramedics came clattering down the stairs in a constant stream, their faces pale, like extras in a Fellini movie, and the whole building echoed with voices and flickered with reflected camera-flash.

At last they reached the Berrys' apartment. Larry stood on the landing looking at the demolished doorframe for three or four minutes, while Dan waited patiently beside him. The firefighter's jack lay where the Berrys' attacker had dropped it, on the plaster and rubble and broken brick.

The front door hung sideways at a crazy angle, security chains dangling uselessly. A brass nameplate on the door announced *Berry*.

"How many apartments in this building, Dan?" Larry asked thoughtfully.

"Three. The occupants of both the other two apartments were away."

"Do you think this guy would have known that? Or cared?"

"I don't know. He didn't seem to be too worried about how much noise he kicked up."

"Next door, that way?"

"Empty. They use it for storing carpets. On the other side, they're Armenian. They don't hear nothing, they don't say nothing. They don't even speak Armenian."

"Who reported the shots?"

Dan brushed plaster from the sleeve of his suit. "Somebody who said they were a neighbor. No name, surprise, surprise."

Larry said, "Did you ever see anything like this, Dan? The whole Goddamned door taken out, just for the sake of a killing? I mean, robbery, for sure. They'll dig their way with coffee-spoons from one side of Nob Hill to the other, for a few thousand bucks. But this is strange. This doesn't fit with anything at all."

They stepped into the apartment. The living-room was unnaturally lit with halogen lamps, so that it looked as bright as a TV-set. Larry could already see Arne Knudsen standing in the center of the room, wearing the vivid grass-green raincoat which had earned him the nickname Jolly; and Phil Biglieri the medical examiner, salt-and-pepper bearded, baggy-eyed, tired, in brown corduroy slacks and a brown tweed sport coat; and Houston Brough, Arne's partner, leather-jacketed, stocky and gingery and cropped, with his lower lip permanently set at "belligerent".

Dan laid a hand on his shoulder. "Take a deep breath, okay? This is something like you never saw before."

Larry hesitated. "Can I trust you, Dan?"

"What's that supposed to mean?"

"It means I want reassurance."

"Reassurance? What are you asking me for, a security blanket?"

"I just want to hear it from your own lips that you haven't dropped this truckload of blood and guts straight in my lap because you know for sure that it's going to bury me. I just want to hear it from your own lips that you've assigned me to this case because you really believe in what I can do.

He paused, and then he said, "I just want to hear it from your own lips that you're not bailing out Arne Knudsen and using me for your fall guy."

Dan sucked in his cheeks; and then coughed. "You know something, Larry?" he said. "You're too damned paranoiac for your own good. You can invent punishments for yourself that never even crossed my mind."

"We'll see," Larry told him. He knew how devious Dan Burroughs could be. He had seen too many promising detectives diverted to cases that looked glorious; but which had eventually taken all the steam out of their careers. In particular, he remembered Bill Hyatt, a brilliant and enthusiastic officer—the kind of guy who looked right, spoke well, and could handle almost anything that came his way. Dan had given him the Murisaki homicide—one of the most complicated ethnic killings that the San Francisco police had ever had to handle—and after three months Bill Hyatt had turned in his badge. "Either I kill myself, or turn into a Japanese, or quit. Given the alternatives, I quit."

Larry said, "Never mind. You want me to crack this assignment, I'll crack it."

"Larry—" Dan began; and for a moment Larry saw something on that gray crumpled valise of a face that he had never seen before, which was caution, and possibly concern. Caution, for sure – and that reassured him more than any words that Dan could possibly have spoken.

"You know something, Dan?" he told him, squeezing his elbow as he passed through to the living-room door. "You're a fuck. A total fuck."

Dan grunted in amusement. "Gone are the days, Larry."

Arne Knudsen glanced up as Larry came into the living-room, but said nothing. He must have guessed already what was going down. Houston Brough looked shifty, and mumbled something that could have been "How're you doing?" Larry was about to say, "Hi, Jolly," or "How're things, Jolly?" but he found himself face to face with the most stark and hideous tableau that he had ever encountered in twelve years on homicide, and his mouth simply refused to work. He just stood and stared, and his whole body seemed to dissolve, like a plate-glass window slid into clear running water.

He saw Nina Berry first. She had fallen forwards, so that her white cheek was pressed against the floor; but she was still half-crouched in the position in which she had been nailed. A dark crimson map of congealed blood spread from her head, a slowly-creeping continent of wasted life. The blood had already begun to soak into the oak: and it occurred to Larry, oddly, that they would have to tear up the whole floor before they could sell this condo again.

About two feet from Nina Berry's parted hair, there were two large nails sticking out of the floor. Each of these nails was decorated like a matador's lance with fragments of bloody flesh. The other two nails still protruded from Joe's kneecaps. Joe was now lying on his back on the far side of the living-room, with a .38 revolver still clenched in both hands, the muzzle stuck in his mouth. His brains had been blasted up the wall in a tall triangular spray, and then halfway across the ceiling.

Joe's knees were torn and bloody and his hands were torn and bloody. Larry could even see the tendons and ligaments, like Rembrandt's anatomy lesson. There were bloody tracks all around the room, showing where Joe had been crawling.

There was no way of imagining what Joe had suffered, as he had shuffled from one side of the room to the other, first to kill his family, and then to kill himself.

The children were the worst, and when Larry looked at them he knew that he would never be able to forget them, and that this spectacle would haunt him asleep and awake for the rest of his life. They were pinned to the wall, side by side, and they were both charred black and scarlet, although they were still recognizable, and part of their nightclothes was still intact. Their arms had broken free from the nailheads, and were clenched up in front of them as if they were two dancing monkeys, and their feet were clenched.

Joe had shot both of them in the face. From the angle at which they had been hit, he had probably been kneeling. Caroline was unrecognizable. No face, nothing, just a hole crammed with minute steak. Joe Junior, although his face was lamp-black, like an 18th century blackamoor statue, and the top of his head was missing, could have been peacefully asleep.

Larry took a long, long look at them, and then turned away.

Arne said, in his distinctive Swedish lilt, "It's not so pretty, is it?"

Larry's mouth was filled with garlic-tainted bile. All he could do was shrug, and swallow.

Arne turned around on his heel, his raincoat rustling. "He broke down the door, and he tortured them... but unlike all the other incidents, he left them alive, and walked out."

Arne had tight wavy hair, like Shredded Wheat, and expressionless agate eyes. Sue-Anne in Records had said that he was the best lover she had ever had. Maybe that was why Larry disliked Arne so much. For his reputation, for his analytical coldness, and for his bright green raincoat. He didn't think much of his bulbous conk, either.

"Why do you think he walked out?" Larry asked. "There was no way that he could have been sure that Joe was going to go for his gun and kill them all. There was no way that he could be sure that Joe was even going to be able to *move*. Supposing one of them had survived? Even one of the kids?"

Arne slowly shook his head. When he spoke, he spoke with almost fastidious certainty. "I think that he walked out because he was quite sure that they wouldn't *want* to stay alive," Arne replied. "I think that he was quite sure that he had taken away their whole reason for living."

"That's the way you read it, is it?" asked Larry.

"What else?" Arne wanted to know.

Larry had to admit that Arne was probably right. But it was odd that a killer who had tortured and slaughtered five families without any compunction should suddenly decide that he was going to leave the sixth family to kill *themselves*. There was no pattern to it, no logic. None of that identifiable rhythm that lets you know almost immediately that one sickeningly familiar fruitcake is out on the rampage again.

"I don't know…"said Larry. "It seems pretty damn risky, leaving the victims alive."

"Maybe the mother *wants* to get caught," Houston Brough remarked, his mouth crammed with Hubba-Bubba.

"No, no," Arne replied. "When they *want* to be caught, they usually adhere even more closely to their predictable pattern. It seems to me that this fellow doesn't particularly care whether we catch him or not. He's marching to quite a different drummer."

Phil Biglieri came up to them, closing his case as he did so. He always reminded Larry of one of those henpecked husbands in Thurber cartoons. The kind of round-shouldered man who arrives home to find that even his house has acquired the thunderous face of his domineering wife.

"We'll be taking away the bodies now," he announced. He set down his bag. "It's a pretty bad one, for sure."

Larry said, "Gunshot wounds?"

Phil Biglieri made a face. "No doubt about it. You can

have an interim report by late tomorrow. Well, maybe after lunch."

Larry and Arne and Houston Brough stepped back while the medical examiner and two medics almost religiously took Caroline and Joe Berry Junior down from the wall. There were burned outlines on the wallpaper, where their bodies had been. As soon as the children were lifted gently into body-bags and carried away, the medics took Nina and Joe.

Arne took out a stick of green chlorophyll chewing-gum and folded it into his mouth. "I suppose that you're very happy, about winning this assignment?"

"I didn't choose it, Jolly, I was asked," Larry replied.

"Bullshit, you've been *told*," Arne retorted. "The same way that I've been told to fold my tents and move on to Pacific Heights. Three elderly widows found poisoned in three months. Potassium cyanide, no apparent motive. Very Sherlock Holmes, yes?"

Larry glanced back at Dan Burroughs, who was standing in the hallway with his hands in the pockets of his slack gray suit, smoking furiously and staring at nothing.

"Jolly, for Christ's sake, you're not going to give me a hard time for this, are you? I don't want to take on this goddamned Fog City Satan any more than you want to give it up."

"I never gave up on anything," said Arne. "I never gave up on Stan Williams; I never gave up on Jack Couderc. Three years it took me to find Jack Couderc. But okay, fuck it, if I have to give it up, I give it up with good grace. You're welcome to it. So what, it's nothing but grief! Torture, mumbo-jumbo. Go on, take it. I'm happy for you."

Larry didn't know what to say. He didn't like Arne, but he liked even less the way that Dan Burroughs had re-assigned the Fog City Satan case because of political pressure rather than proper police procedure. The case was Arne's; and Arne had solved more than sixty-two percent of the cases to which he had been assigned, and Arne was proud of his reputation. Arne spent untold hours working on the police computers. He built up files that looked like telephone directories. He analyzed his assignments like a chemist, searching for traces of this and traces of that. Motive? Antecedents? Aliases? Addresses? Automobile ownership? Blood type? He had the closest relationship with the coroner's department of any detective, ever.

Compared to Arne, Larry always felt as if his only talents were intuition, a passion for opera, a terrific set of teeth, and a blood-relationship to almost every Italian in San Francisco. Arne made him feel like something between Peter Falk, Sylvester Stallone and Frank Langella. Too romantic for a cop. Too inspirational.

But maybe Dan Burroughs knew what he was doing. Maybe logic just wasn't enough. Maybe the only possible way to catch the Fog City Satan was by flying blind. By hunch, and guesswork, and sniffing the wind.

Larry said, "Tell me—have you built up any kind of picture of this guy in your head? Some kind of psychopath, maybe? One of the Press boys mentioned revenge."

"Could be revenge," Houston Brough ventured. "Joe was a cop, after all. And let's face it, some ex-cons hold a grudge for ever."

Arne shook his head. "I don't believe that this was done for revenge. What could Joe Berry have ever done to anybody, even to an ex-con, to deserve something like this? This isn't revenge. This is like some kind of madness. This is like some kind of disease! The perpetrator set fire to Joe's children! He nailed his wife to the floor! This was done because the perpetrator likes to see people suffer."

"You think the motive is cruelty, and that s all?"

"What else? What makes that so hard to believe? The guy likes hurting people. He's a hundred-percent sadist. The only thing that makes him different is that he's a very inventive sadist. He can think up ways of hurting people that you wouldn't believe. He's like a nightmare; only you can keep on pinching yourself, and he's still there. He's worse than a nightmare, he's real."

Dan stepped reluctantly into the room. "How're you two boys rubbing along?"

"With this investigation, or with each other?" Arne asked him.

Dan ignored him. "Goddamned pitiful," he remarked, looking around, as if he were considering buying the place. "Poor Joe Berry. Who'd have thought he'd've wound up like this? God damn it, I remember shaking his hand, the day he quit the force."

Arne said, "We can find him. I don't have any doubts about that. But it's going to take time."

Dan went to the window, and stared out at the fog and his own gray reflection, and sighed. "Trouble is, Arne, time is exactly what we don't got."

"But, be reasonable, chief," Arne protested. "This isn't the kind of case you can solve with a snap of the fingers. With a killer like this, you have to scrutinize every single movement, every single footmark, every single fiber. You can't just go kicking around down doors and pulling in faces you don't like and beating confessions out of them. I'm sorry, chief. I know that the mayor and the media have been riding you hard. But this one can't be hurried. We only have to make one wrong move, and we could easily frighten him off for ever, or frighten him into doing something ten times worse than he's done already."

"Arne," said Dan, growing impatient. "I've made up my mind. Larry is going to take over this investigation as of now."

Arne took a deep breath. "And I suppose you want me to give him my fullest co-operation?"

Dan turned away from the window and gave him a lopsided smile. "Of course you will, Arne. We want this bastard caught."

"I know, I know," Arne replied. "Not only caught, but *seen* to be caught. You want the investigative equivalent of grand opera."

"Arne—I want this maniac on death row," Dan told him. "And I want him on death row soon."

"Yes, sir," said Arne. "I think we all want that. But I can't pretend to be happy. I'm not saying anything about the way Larry works. He's a good detective, everybody knows that. But this investigation... well, it needs science, you know? It needs finesse."

Dan said, "Finesse, for Christ's sake? We're not dancing the fucking cha-cha."

"But it's the detail—"

"Arne," said Dan. "Maybe, for a change, this investigation needs somebody who can see a wood, instead of nothing but a whole bunch of fucking trees."

Arne didn't answer. Whatever he said, it wouldn't do him any good. When Dan made up his mind about something, it couldn't be changed except by weeks of intense and closely argued lobbying. The trouble was, Dan had worked on the force for nearly thirty years—and even if you could prove that you were technically correct, he was almost always right when it came down to practical, street-level detection.

Larry cleared his throat and said, "Maybe I can—uh—take a look around."

"Well, of course," Arne told him. "It's your pigeon now. But we didn't discover anything unusual."

"Four people were nailed down, and you don't call that unusual?"

"Of course it's unusual. But what I'm trying to say is, we didn't discover anything that added to what we already know about this Fog City Satan, which is pitifully little. No good old-fashioned clues. No stray buttons from a cable-car driver's pants; no free pens from the Hair Replacement Center. No Chinese fortunes found crumpled under the couch. No pizza flour sprinkled around the room. Well, not until *you* walked in, anyway."

"Do you want to die quick or slow?" Larry retorted.

"Quick. I don't know, slow. I want to see the look on your face as I stay alive from one week to the next. I want to see the slow, slow realization on your face that I'm not really going to die, after all."

"One more crack about pizza and you'll die, believe me."

Arne led the way out of the living-room and along the corridor. He laid his hand on Larry's shoulder and his demeanor suddenly changed.

"Actually, Larry, there is one thing. But I didn't want to discuss it in front of so the chief. It's the only clue that connects this killing with all of the other killings. The one and only thing. If I told the chief, he'd be round to Mayor Amo in five minutes flat, telling him something ridiculous, like we'd all but arrested the guy, and of course we'd have blown the whole thing.

"This is important. It *must* be important. But the trouble is, I don't know *why* it's important. I want to see what you think of it."

"Why should you care what I think of it?"

"Because everybody can contribute something positive to a complex case like this, even a Neapolitan kamikaze pilot like you."

"I hope you realize that I didn't actively volunteer for this assignment," Larry told him.

"No, for sure, of course you didn't," Arne replied. "On the other hand, did you actively turn it down, when it was offered to you? Did you say, 'No, Dan, thanks very much, this is Arne's baby'? You know how I feel about this assignment, Larry. This assignment is the bee in my bonnet. This is the birdhouse in my soul."

"Why don't you tell me about this Fog City Satan," said Larry. He had read all the Press reports and listened to all the television bulletins. Ritual Slayings In Forest Hill. Family Massacred in College Park. Satan Slays Four On Farragut. But he wanted to know where Arne's thinking was at. He wanted to pick up for himself that same scarcely perceptible scent that Arne was following. That faint but certain aroma that all killers leave on the wind.

"Sure," said Arne. "But come take a look at this first."

Larry followed Arne along the corridor to the children's bedroom. "I nearly missed these, you know," said Arne. He ushered Larry right into the room, and then half-closed the door. "There," he said. "What do you make of this?"

"Jesus," said Larry, and crossed himself.

A rag-doll and a toy rabbit were nailed side by side to the back of the paneling. They were grubby with years of loving—years of being sucked and cuddled and dragged around the streets. In their heads were embedded the same kind of railroad dogs that had fastened Caroline and Joe Berry Junior to the living-room wall.

The sight of them pinned to the bedroom door gave Larry a chill that was almost worse than seeing two dead children. It was like a final, terrible assault on everything that normal people held dear.

"I don't know what to say," Larry breathed...

"I thought that would set you back," said Arne.

"Do you have any idea what it *means?*" asked Larry.

"Not the faintest," Arne replied. "Not even a clue. But we came across something similar in four out of the five previous killings. In Bernal Heights, we found live goldfish nailed to the kitchen counter. Well—mashed, more than nailed. In College Park we found a cat nailed by its ears to one of the garden fences. In Crocker Amazon, there was a dog nailed to the garage door by its tongue."

"I didn't hear about any of that," said Larry.

"There's a whole lot you didn't hear, my friend," Arne told him. "I've been trying to keep this case really low-key, play down the panic, play down the fear. This beast has an appetite for other people's fear. To him, other people's fear is like food. Tonight, right here in this condo, he brought these people such terror and despair that he was able to make them kill themselves! Imagine what a feast he had tonight!"

Arne was angry, and wildly distressed. Larry had never seen him so emotional before. By the way he was staring up at the rag-doll and the rabbit nailed to the door, it was clear to Larry that he would have done anything to force this so-called Fog City Satan over his knee and broken his back. Arne was quite capable of forcing anybody over his knee and breaking their back.

Arne said. much more quietly, "Who knows? Some of what's been happening, I've been keeping quiet for the sake of my investigation. Other things—I don't know. I guess I just didn't want to give this scumbag the satisfaction of picking up the *Chronicle* and reading about every single stomach-churning little thing that he's done. Some of it was too sick to be published, especially what he did to the women. Truly sick stuff, you wouldn't even want to know. Well, I guess you'll *have* to know, now that Dan's turned the case over to you. But—hah! You never came across anybody like this before.

"Apart from that, of course, I was worried about copycats. If I released that stuff about the goldfish to the Press, the next thing that would happen is that dogs and cats and canaries would be nailed to every fence and every telegraph pole between here and Pillar Point.

"And most important, I guess—I wanted very much to keep this one particular thing secret, in case the killer tried to contact us, and we needed some way to verify that it was really him. Nailing pets and toys to the wall has been the only consistent connection between all of the killings that we've managed to keep out of the media."

"Do you have any idea what it *means?*" asked Larry. He couldn't take his eyes off the rag-doll and the rabbit. He thought of Frankie and Mikey back home, asleep— Frankie cuddling his matted blue Cookie Monster and Mikey sucking that gray-looking thing called Thing.

"Do *you* have any idea what it means?" Arne retorted.

Larry shook his head. "Crucifixion, maybe? Who knows? Maybe the guy just likes nailing things together. Maybe his parents refused to give him a woodwork set, when he was little."

"Do you think this is *funny?*" Arne demanded.

Larry said, "I think it's time we pulled the plug on this guy, that's what I think. He's done enough. I respect your technique, Arne. Believe me, I'm not bullshitting you. I think you're one of the best detectives we've ever had. But personally I think it's time for a little gonzo detection."

"You'd better not screw this up for me, Larry," Arne warned him, his eyes pale. "I've put my heart and soul into this assignment. More than my heart. My career, too."

Larry took a last look around the children's bedroom. It was almost too painful to think that less than three hours ago, Caroline and Joe Junior had both been sleeping snugly in their bunk beds, dreaming children's dreams.

"Is there anything else that I'm missing?" Larry asked Arne. "I mean, anything ritualistic, anything really weird, like these toys?"

"No, that's it," Arne told him. "From now on, it's all spadework."

"Thanks, Jolly," said Larry.

"Oho, shit, Larry, don't thank me! This isn't my idea. You're just about the last guy in the world I would've assigned to this investigation. You may respect my technique, my friend, but I sure as hell don't have any respect for yours."

"Come on, Jolly," said Larry, slapping his shoulder. "We'll get this guy *di riffe o di raffe*. And, by the way, I may respect your detection, but I still hate that fucking raincoat. No wonder you never get wet. No self-respecting drop of rain would even want to fall on you."

"You can make jokes?" Arne asked him, his eyes hard.

Larry said, "Yes, Jolly, I can make jokes. You know why? Because Joe and Nina were dear, dear friends of mine, and I loved Caroline and Joe Junior like they were my own. I can make jokes because there isn't any other way I know of dealing with something as Goddamned fucking terrible as this short of catching the guy who did it and tearing out his throat. And don't try to kid me, Jolly, because you feel just the same as me, except you're Swedish and Swedes don't understand that when human beings feel so bad about something that they can't even breathe, they have to laugh."

Arne took out a clean handkerchief, unfolded it, and patted the front of his raincoat. "You know what your trouble is, Larry? When you talk, you spit."

"Jesus," said Larry; and walked out of the bedroom feeling like fire, feeling like Vesuvius, feeling sad and furious and explosive, all at the same time.

He came home at seven o'clock in the morning with armfuls of files and a warm brown paper bag containing four *focaccia*, the thin, flat, crusty bread which he bought from the Danilo Bakery on Green Street. He had to find a space for his Toyota in the street because Linda had parked the Buick wagon in their small angled driveway. The city was still masked in fog, but up here on Russian Hill the fog was faintly gilded by the sunlight above it, and in the garden the birds were throatily singing.

Larry laid his files and his bread down on the white-painted porch while he searched for his door-key. A quail perched on the fence nearby, watching him inquisitively.

"What do you want, pal, breakfast?" he asked it. "You and me both."

He stepped into the small hallway, with its pale wooden floor and its antique sea-chest and its oil-paintings of old San Francisco. He leaned against the door to close it. The cottage was silent: it sounded like the whole family was still asleep. He propped the files on the chair just inside the living-room door, and eased off his shoes.

His first stop was the master bedroom. The white-painted door was two or three inches ajar, and through the gap he could see Linda, lying on her back on the pale yellow ruffled bed, her eyes closed, her hair spread out across the frilly pillow. Above her head was a framed Currier & Ives' print depicting two self-satisfied cherubs spooning cream from a sundae-dish.

He didn't open the door, didn't attempt to wake her. Somehow he felt that if he entered the bedroom, he would drag into her dreams all the blackness and brutality of the previous night. Fire and blood, nails and flesh.

He watched Linda for a while. He felt sad for her. He felt sadder still for Joe and Nina Berry. Dan Burroughs had once said to him, after half-a-bottle of Jack Daniel's: "When you work for homicide, my friend, you're in permanent mourning."

Larry didn't know whether "mourning" was quite the right word for it. It was closer to rage than grief—at least for him. He left the bedroom and tiptoed across to the kitchen.

He opened the icebox, and inspected the contents. While he made up his mind what he was going to have for breakfast, he gulped orange juice straight out of the carton. He was just about to place the carton back in the icebox door when a firm young voice behind him said, "How come you can do that and we're not allowed? You said it was unhygienic."

He turned around. Frankie and Cookie Monster were standing in the doorway watching him, one solemn, one bug-eyed. Frankie was wearing one of Larry's old shirts instead of pajamas because that was what Frankie liked to wear. Cookie monster was naked if blue fur constitutes naked. Frankie was dark eyed and curly haired and so thin that Linda's mother had accused her of starving him. "Look at this child, like a bird! It's all that pasta! Pasta has no nutritional value whatsoever! You might just as well eat the box as eat the stuff that's in it!"

Linda had explained often enough that Larry insisted on fresh pasta whenever they ate pasta, and as a matter of fact they didn't eat pasta particularly often. But Linda's mother had set her heart on her beloved only daughter marrying into serious San Francisco money; gold and hotels and limousines, not to mention Anglo-Saxon *Protestant* money. The wedding picture of Larry and Linda outside

Grace Cathedral was framed in black, as if they were both already dead. Linda's father, however, couldn't have cared less: his brains had been gently frittered by years of golf at Burlingame. The biggest excitement of his life was the annual swimsuit edition of *Sports Illustrated* and he still hadn't come to terms with the fact that Ronald Reagan was no longer President.

Larry opened the oven and switched on the grill. "Hey, Frankie, you want a *focaccia coi ciccioli?*"

Frankie climbed on to one of the woven-topped kitchen stools, and sat Cookie Monster on the tiled counter. "I sure would."

"In that case, keep your mouth shut. Parents have a special indulgence from the Holy Father to drink from the carton, just like they can put their elbows on the table and make rude noises whenever they feel like it. We have it in writing, direct from Rome. Okay?"

"Yes, sir," said Frankie. "Can I have plenty of bacon?"

Larry laid strips of bacon on the grill. He wasn't exactly a purist when it came to making *focaccia coi ciccioli*: strictly, you were supposed to do nothing more than roll crispy bacon scratchings in with the dough. But just like the heresy of pizza heaped with sausage and peppers and sweetcorn and tuna and God knows what else, his *focaccia* had been changed by American affluence for ever. Larry's father used to take a *focaccia* to school in his satchel, topped with nothing but sea-salt, or a little fresh sage. For a treat, maybe, a few slices of onion.

"Mommy says you had to work all night," said Frankie.

"I sure did. Is Mikey awake?"

"Mikey's in the yard."

"What the hell is Mikey doing in the yard?"

"Mikey had to do twos."

Larry stared at Frankie intently. "Am I hearing this right? Mikey went into the yard to do twos? What's wrong with the bathroom?"

"We saw Tarzan and Mikey wants to be Tarzan."

"And that's his idea of being Tarzan? Doing twos in the bougainvilleas?"

Frankie shrugged. "Tarzan doesn't have a bathroom."

Larry opened and closed his mouth. "Tarzan-doesn't-have-a-bathroom," he repeated. "Tarzan doesn't have a car, for God's sake! But that doesn't mean that Mikey has to go to school by swinging from tree to tree."

The door to the laundry-room opened and Mikey appeared, frowning. He was completely naked except for his Fred and Barney slippers and his pajama-top knotted around his waist. His belly-button was sticking out and his forearms were all goose-bumpy.

Larry eyed him with a wry, pretend-angry expression, and Mikey stared back at him with six-year-old defiance.

"Well?" asked Larry. "How was it?"

Mikey made a half-hearted attempt to pummel his chest. "Me Tarzan."

"Sure, I know that," said Larry, turning over the bacon. "What I asked was, how was it? You know, two-ing *al fresco*?"

Mikey hesitated for a long moment, his eyes searching the kitchen as if some kind of magical answer to life's problems was hidden in one corner.

"Does Tarzan use leaves?" he asked, eventually.

A pause while everybody thought about it.

Then, "Sure, I guess," said Larry.

Mikey nodded, quite seriously, hesitated, and then plodded off toward his bedroom.

Larry called after him, "Didn't you realize? That's why Tarzan keeps yelling out 'Owwoowwwooooow-wwoooooh!'"

"Not funny!" Mikey snapped back, and slammed his door.

"Will you shut up!" Linda called, unexpectedly, from the bedroom.

They ate *focaccia* and crispy bacon in blissful masculine silence in the dimness of the kitchen, Larry and Frankie and Mikey. Three guys, big and little and littlest, bonded by humor and love. Cookie Monster tried to snatch some of Mikey's *focaccia* but Thing retaliated by swallowing one of Cookie Monster's eyeballs.

Larry tried not to think about Caroline and Joe Berry Junior but he couldn't help it, and his grief and his anger was almost too much. He scraped more than half of his *focaccia* into the sink and stood looking out into the gilded fog and wondering if there really was a Blessed Virgin, who would take those two poor children into her arms.

When he was a boy, he had always imagined that the Blessed Virgin's arms would be cool and pale, cool like ivory; and that when She kissed him, She would leave tears on his cheek—crystal tears, like dew. Mothers cry for their dear dead children, after all. But only the Blessed Virgin could cry for all of us.

Frankie said, "Did somebody murder some kids?"

Larry turned and stared at him. "Yes, they did," he said, quietly. "How did you know?"

"I always know when somebody murdered some kids because you always cook us nice breakfasts and you never say 'Don't talk with your mouth full!'"

Larry thought about that, and then nodded, and scruffled his boys' hair. "I guess I do. I guess it always makes me appreciate you guys extra much, when somebody else's kids get killed."

Mikey said, "Tarzan could sic 'em."

"Oh, yeah? The first thing that Tarzan has to do is show Daddy where he fertilized the yard."

Later, when Frankie and Mikey were watching television, he carried a tray of espresso and orange juice into the bedroom, and sat on the edge of the bed while Linda continued to sleep.

She looked like Snow White, poisoned by her husband's occupation, waiting for the kiss that would finally release her from lonely nights, guns in the bedroom closet, and the endless anxiety that one of those rabid crack-brained psychos would one day decide that he was going to take one of those pigs down to hell along with him, no matter what the cost.

She looked like a woman who had attended too many funerals, and who was sleeping so that she wouldn't have to go to any more.

"Linda?" he said, at last, and immediately she opened her eyes. "I brought you some coffee."

She rubbed her eyes. "What time is it?"

"Eight."

"As late as that? I promised myself I was going to be awake for you, when you got back."

"Doesn't matter. The boys were up. I made them breakfast."

"Oh, I'm sorry," said Linda, taking hold of his hand. Italian hand, short-fingered, neatly formed, with streaks of black hair. An engraver's hand; or an architect's hand; or the hand of glassmaker.

"What are you sorry for? I needed some time, you know? A little time to breathe."

She drank half of her orange juice, then she lay back on the pillow. It never ceased to please and amaze him, how beautiful she was. Every time he looked at her, he knew exactly why he had fallen in love with her.

"Snow White," he said.

Linda smiled. "Snow White was wakened by a kiss, not a cup of espresso."

He kissed her forehead, oddly warm from sleeping; and then he kissed her orange-tasting lips. "You get both."

"Was it bad?" she asked him.

He nodded. He knew that he was very tired, and that if he tried to explain to Linda how bad it had really been, he would probably upset them both, and the boys, too.

"Was Arne mad?"

"Oh, sure. Arne was mad. He tried not to be, but he couldn't help himself."

"Do you know *why* Dan gave you this assignment?"

Larry sat up straight. "Not at first. But I guess I do now."

"He's not doing a Kevin Defendorf on you, is he?" Kevin Defendorf was another of those up-and-coming young detectives whose careers had been suddenly sidetracked, and who had found themselves, in the words of Lawrence Ferlinghetti, "out on the rusty spur which ends up in the dead grass where the rusty tincans and bedsprings and old razor blades and moldy mattresses... lie."

Larry shrugged, sniffed, said, "Maybe. But it doesn't really matter."

"Of course it matters!" Linda protested. "This is your career!"

"Unh-hunh," Larry disagreed. "You didn't see what I saw. If you'd seen what I saw, then you'd know that it doesn't really matter. Somebody has to find this guy, no matter what it takes."

"Larry...?"

He tried to smile. He almost succeeded. "Linda, this job isn't worth turning up for, unless once in a while it becomes a crusade."

"But you have your whole life to think of! What about Frankie and Mikey? What about me?"

Larry took hold of her hand and twisted her wedding-band around and around. "And what do you think will happen if I refuse to accept this assignment? What do you think Dan will do to me then? What do you think everybody else on the squad will do to me then? Arne and Brough and Migdoll? They'll treat me like I'm chickenshit, which is exactly what I will be, if I try to tell Dan that I'm not taking it on.

"Anyway, it's nothing to do with Dan. I *want* to take it on. For myself; for Joe. For Nina. Somebody has to do it. Somebody has to find who killed their kids."

Linda watched him twisting her ring. Then she said, "You know what Nina always used to say to me? She said there was something inside of Joe that made him a cop, and she could never understand what it was. He didn't even *like* being a cop. But he was born with it. The day he couldn't get up and go to work, she went to the church and she lit a candle, and she thanked God for sending her a miracle."

Larry said, "Is that how you feel?"

Linda shook her head. "I hope I understand you better."

There was a strange and lengthy silence between them. Outside the bedroom window, the day remained adamantly foggy. They wouldn't see the sun today. They wouldn't see the sun for days. Larry had a feeling about it.

"You want some breakfast?" he asked Linda.

She shook her head. "I want to do my yoga first. Besides, I'm meeting Marjorie for coffee."

"Oh, the painting society," said Larry. "Well... if you don't mind, I'll seize some zees. But you can interrupt me if you want to. No Foggia ever complained about being raped. You can check it on police records." After Linda had taken Frankie and Mikey to their summer sport class, Larry showered in the green-tiled shower. Afterward he stood in front of the bathroom mirror and stared at himself. Lean, muscular, but not in outstanding shape. Dark slanted nipples like almonds, black hairy chest. A heavy penis, and balls like ripened fruit. Curved thighs like Italian furniture.

He dressed in sand-colored slacks and a mauvish Hugo Boss polo-shirt. Then he sat in the kitchen on his own and drank two poisonously strong cups of espresso and read the *Chron*. It was the fiftieth anniversary of Herb Caen's column. Larry knew Herb Caen well, and liked him: as much as an over-romantic thirty-eight-year-old Italian detective could ever know and like a perverse and puckish seventy-two-year-old newspaper columnist. But they had breakfasted at Sam's together a few times; and Herb had written a piece about policework in San Francisco, saying that it was like composing an opera, all highs and lows.

The fog clung, the cable cars clanged, but those were the symptoms of San Francisco, rather than its mystical essence. It was the Gold Rush that had made San Francisco what it was; and even today, in 1988, it was still a Gold Rush city, haunted by bravado, haunted by greed; a city of hills and superstition; a city of ghosts and get-rich-quick and Lady Luck.

It was a city on the brink of the world; and Larry lived on the brink of the world, too; and maybe there was something about living on the brink of the world that nurtured the bloody irrationality of the Fog City Satan.

For seven hours, until the fog began to darken, layer on layer, like grimy net curtains, Larry read all of Arne's files. He was interrupted again and again—first by Houston Brough, who was painstakingly doorstepping everybody who lived within a half-mile of the Berrys' condominium, then by Dan Burroughs, then by Phil Biglieri the medical examiner, with preliminary reports on how the Berrys had died. After five o'clock, he took no more calls, although he heard his answering-machine clicking and recording again and again. He read notes, diagrams, laboratory reports, forensic analyses, interviews. He couldn't have wished for better groundwork. Arne had covered every aspect of every murder that Larry could think of; and a few more, besides. He had reconstructed cleaver-wounds with computer graphics, and identified the type of cleaver that the killer had used, and even the brand of cleaver, and then located the hardware store in Berkeley where it had been bought.

He had commented on the extreme force which the Fog City Satan had used to gain entry to all of the premises that he had violated. In each case, he had burst in like a bombshell, taking out whole windows, wrenching out doors. But Arne could think of no logical reason why. In almost all of the six cases, a crowbar would have been sufficient; and in the College Park murders, where a whole living-room window had been ripped out the back door of the house had actually been left unlocked.

Larry leaned back in his Western-style armchair and stared for a long time at all the papers on his desk. They were comprehensive; they were brilliantly cross-correlated; but somehow they were incomplete. Arne talked about motives, for sure. He had interviewed social workers and criminal psychologists; he had attempted to find parallels with other ritual-type murders from all over the United States, and some from Europe, too. He had even looked into Fay Kuhn's far-fetched report that the killer was repeating the ritual murders of 1905. He had gone so far as to show some similarities between two of the ritual killings with similar murders in Port-au-Prince, in Haiti.

But what was missing was *purpose*. What was missing was *why?* What was missing was any kind of convincing reason – logical or illogical – why anybody should want to inflict such elaborate torture on so many innocent families.

What was missing was that inspirational leap into homicidal madness that was needed to put the detective behind a killer's eyes. The same leap that Larry always tried to take when he was dealing with an enraged Neapolitan father who had beaten his daughter's lover to death; or a cold-blooded Korean shooter who had killed a crack-dealer in a Haight Street doorway; or a spaced-out relic from the City Lights days, who (from no other motive but mercy) had suffocated his dying middle-aged mistress with a Victorian tapestry cushion.

He folded back a large legal pad and wrote himself a list of all the ritual murders to date, with the basic details of each killing, along with Arne's suppositions.

Forest Hill, 3/9/88: the Tessler family home on Magellan was broken into shortly after 2 a.m. when the garden door was sledgehammered. Mr. Alan Tessler, 47, and Mrs. Irene Tessler, 42, were forced to strip naked. They were bound tightly together face to face, and gagged. Their daughter Jeanette, 24, and their maid Maria, 26, were also stripped and bound together. Both young women were raped in sight and hearing of Mr. and Mrs. Tessler, and both were then sexually violated with glass rolling-pins from Mrs. Tessler's antique collection. The killer sawed off Mr. and Mrs. Tessler's legs with a chainsaw, halfway through the thigh. Mr. Tessler died of traumatic shock; Mrs. Tessler died of massive loss of blood. Jeanette and Maria were both killed by blows to the back of the skull from the same sledgehammer which had been used to break down the back door. Mr. Tessler's thirty-eight cage birds had all had their legs broken.

Crocker Amazon, 4/20/88: the Wurster family home on Farragut was broken into sometime around 11 p.m. when the side door was pickaxed. Mrs. Pamela Wurster, 40, was tied to a kitchen chair and doused in inflammable fluid. Her husband Douglas Wurster, 39, was apparently ordered to thrust his right hand down the sink-disposal unit, under threat of his wife being set alight(?). His fingers were severed and his hand was badly mangled. With his hand wrapped in a towel, he was then tied to a chair next to his wife. Their three children—Lance, 17; Andrea, 12; and Peter, 9—were brought from their bedrooms and tied to chairs facing their parents. Mr. and Mrs. Wurster then had their tongues cut out with their own kitchen knife, in front of their children. Afterward the children were strangled one by one with nylon cord. Then Mr. Wurster, who remained alive, was killed by a single pickax blow to the back of the head. The Wurster's Labrador dog was found with its tongue nailed to the garage door.

Pacific Heights, 5/8/88: the Yee family home on Vallejo was broken into approximately 3 a.m. when a sledgehammer was used to break down the front door. Mr. Kim Yee, 51, and his wife Mrs. Sheila Yee, 46, were stripped, gagged, and then bound face-down to their kitchen counter. Their two sons Kingman, 20, and Hsu, 17, were tied back to back in the jacuzzi, and then their wrists were cut and they were left to bleed to death. Mr. and Mrs. Yee had their forearms chopped off at the elbow with a heavyweight cleaver, and after approximately twenty minutes both were killed by having six-inch nails hammered into the backs of their heads. Nine goldfish were nailed to the kitchen counter, too.

Glen Park, 6/19/88: the secluded McGuire family home in College Terrace between Mission and Bosworth was broken into shortly after 9:30 p.m. by the removal of the entire living-room window by a steel hawser attached to the rear bumper of a 4x4 vehicle. Mr. Grant McGuire,

35, and his sister Mrs. Blare Furst, 29, were stripped and tied together. Apparently threatened with the death of Mrs. Furst's 6-year-old daughter Gardenia, Mrs. Furst cut off her brother's ears, (an act substantiated by the blood on her hands) and Mr. McGuire then cut off Mrs. Furst's ears. After this, Gardenia Furst was drowned in a plastic washbasin of water in front of Mr. McGuire and Mrs. Furst; and then Mr. McGuire and Mrs. Furst were both killed by a shot in the left ear with a nail-gun usually used by construction workers for erecting plywood paneling. The family cat had been nailed by its ears to the garden fence.

Bernal Heights, 7/6/88: the Ramirez family home on Moultrie was broken into at 5 a.m. when a huge French window was smashed in with slabs of concrete. Mr. Hector Ramirez, 45, and his wife Isabella Ramirez, 33, were stripped, gagged, and partially bound, lying on their backs on the living-room floor. Their two children Juan, 11, and Nadia, 9, were tied back-to-back close by. Concentrated sulphuric acid was then dripped on to the top of the children's heads until (presumably) Mrs. Ramirez agreed to blind her husband by dropping concentrated sulphuric acid into his eyes. Afterwards the entire family was killed by having their throats cut. No known pets.

When he had finished writing. Larry dropped his felt-tip pen and stood up. It was dark outside now. Linda would be home in five or ten minutes, bringing the boys. He knew that he should have walked around the house, switching on lights, making the place more welcoming. But somehow the horror of Arne's reports on the Fog City Satan had numbed him. He kept on asking himself what he would have done, if he had been asked to drop sulphuric acid into Linda's eyes?

He tried to imagine what it must have been like, to have to do it. To be so terrified, to be so desperate, that you didn't feel you had any choice.

He pressed his forehead to the cold window. It was so dark and foggy now that all he could see was his own reflection; the ghost of Larry Foggia. He tried to imagine what kind of man could have asked those people to mutilate themselves. He tried to think what it must have been like, standing beside them, watching them sacrifice themselves. But for the first time in years and years, he couldn't even begin to think what kind of man this could have been.

He had witnessed torture and cruelty before. Most times, however, the purpose had been obvious. Men and women had been tortured for information; for sex; or out of sheer bloody-minded revenge. He had never seen people tortured in such a variety of terrible ways, just for the sake of torturing them.

The Fog City Satan seemed to have no purpose. Some of the killings had involved sexual assault, but not all of them. Some of the killings had involved theft, but not all of them.

In some cases, the family's pets had been tortured in ways that reflected what had happened to their owners, but Arne had been unable to decide what the significance of these particular acts of cruelty might have been.

In every case, people had been tied (or in the Berrys' case, nailed down) and then mutilated—but never in the same way twice. Larry had thought fleetingly of Jack the Ripper, and the way that he had dabbled and played with his victim's organs after slashing them open. But Jack the Ripper – although he had been sickening – had been consistent.

There was no hint of obsessive behavior in what the Fog City Satan was doing—apart from the way in which he seemed to pick on contented families, and subject them to fear and pain beyond any kind of sanity. There was no geographical pattern. The excessive force used to gain entry to the victims' houses was noteworthy—but not especially helpful. All it confirmed was what they knew already—that the same man had perpetrated each of the killings.

There was a wealth of forensic evidence. There were closely comparable bruise-marks on the necks and arms of those victims who had been strangled or manhandled. There were closely comparable footprints on tiled kitchen floors and shagpile rugs. There were smears of reddish grease which the FBI laboratory had identified as a home-made mixture of STP gasoline additive and Revlon lipstick.

There were no fingerprints, but there was semen, and stray pubic hair. These had been the most useful evidence of all. They had enabled Arne to establish that the Fog City Satan was Caucasian, blood-type AB, with a darkish complexion. From his shoe-size, the span of his hands and his obvious physical strength, Arne had been able to build up a picture of a man in his mid-forties, approximately 6ft tall, weighing 180–185lbs.

If they ever caught him, they would be able to use genetic fingerprinting to identify him beyond any shadow of a doubt.

After each killing, a man purporting to be the killer had called the radio station KGO, and issued warnings that anybody who identified him would be punished. Arne had given Larry copies of his recorded voice (as well as voiceprints), and although it was muffled and obviously disguised, it certainly sounded like a Caucasian male of about forty-five or forty-six.

Arne had guessed that the Fog City Satan was a native of San Francisco, or that he had lived in the city long enough to know where and when he could attack his victims openly, and quite noisily, but with very little chance of discovery.

Unless, of course, he didn't care about being discovered.

Larry heard the key in the front door. That was Linda coming home. He was still standing in the dark when she came into the study and switched on his Anglepoise lamp.

"Larry?" she said. "You gave me such a fright. I didn't think there was anybody in."

He turned away from the window. "I'm sorry. I was miles away."

"I called you just after five. How come you didn't answer?"

"I didn't answer after five. I had too much reading."

"You look terrible. Did you eat anything?"

He shook his head. "I guess I forgot."

"I was going to make *messicani di vitello*. I bought some beautiful *scallopine* at Parma's."

"Sounds good to me," he told her.

She approached his desk, and looked at the medical reports and the computer printouts and the maps. She picked up a photograph of six-year-old Gardenia Furst, drowned in a blue plastic washbasin in front of her mother.

Larry said, in a thick voice, "You don't want to look at that stuff."

Linda lowered the picture with a trembling hand. "Is it really bad?"

"It's worse than you want to know. We haven't been telling the Press even half of it."

"Why does it have to be you?" Linda wanted to know.

Larry shrugged. "If it isn't me, it has to be somebody else."

"You know better than that."

Larry could hear the boys fighting in the hallway, and suddenly he didn't want to think about the Fog City Satan any longer. He put his arm around Linda's shoulder, and led her out into the living-room, and closed the study door tightly behind him.

"I guess Dan wants me to do it because he thinks I can understand what this lunatic is all about. Like, it takes a lunatic to know one, if you follow what I mean."

"Larry..."said Linda, and her eyes were dark with worry.

"It's okay," he reassured her, squeezing her close and kissing her forehead. She smelled of Chanel No. 19 and fog. "When it comes down to it, he's just a man. Men can be found out. Men can be caught."

Frankie and Mikey came running up to him, and caught hold of his hands. "Daddy! Benny's dad says he's going to take us to the Marina for frisbee and football tomorrow!"

"Benny's dad said that? He actually volunteered?"

"Oh, daddy, can we go, daddy? Please can we go?"

Larry lifted up Mikey in his arms and gave him a pretend punch under the jaw. He saw Linda looking at him and he knew what she was thinking. How come you never take

your kids to the Marina for frisbee and football? How
come it's always somebody else's dad?

He set Mikey back on the floor. "Okay," he said. "You can
go with Benny's dad if Benny's dad genuinely volunteered.
But Sunday we're going to Muir Woods. The four of us.
Muir Woods, and then lunch at Basta Pasta."

"Muir Woods? What a drag!" said Frankie, pulling a
face.

"Muir Woods is awesome and natural and beautiful,"
Larry retorted.

"Who cares?" Frankie retorted.

"I *hate* Basta Pasta," put in Mikey.

Larry said to Linda, "I need a drink. How about you?"

"I brought back some Verdicchio."

They went through to the kitchen. Larry opened the wine
while Linda unpacked her marketing, and rinsed the veal
scallops.

"You can talk to me if you like," she told him.

"I'm not sure there's very much that I can say," he replied,
pouring out the wine.

"You can ask me what kind of a *day* you had, darling?
How was your class? What did you have for lunch?
Did Mr. Chabner make any more passes at you? Did
Mr. Kotch's toupee fall off again? And *I* don't want to go to
Muir Woods, either."

"All right, for Christ's sake," said Larry. "We won't go to
Muir Woods. God, I only wanted to give this family some
environmental uplift."

Linda came up to him and kissed him. "I'm sorry. I
know this has hit you real hard. I could kill Dan for giving
you this assignment."

87

"You and me and Arne—all three of us."

There was a long pause between them; a long moment of relaxation. One of those moments in a good marriage when you don't have to talk because talk isn't necessary to say what you mean.

But the moment was interrupted by the phone ringing. Larry lifted the receiver out of its wall-bracket and said, "Foggia."

"Larry, it's Houston. KGO just called us. They've had a call from our boy."

"Another warning?" Larry asked him.

"I don't know. Kind of. But not like the others. This time, he said—hold on here, I can't read my notes—'*He's coming from the other side. He's coming.*'"

"Who's coming? Did he say who?"

"No names," said Houston. "But apparently he sounded really pleased with himself. Almost like he was celebrating."

"Was that all he said?" asked Larry. He kept thinking of Caroline and Joe Junior, their flesh burned to a dark maroon, twisted and gnarled like incinerated wood, nailed to the wall.

Houston cleared his throat. "No. There was quite a lot more. He said something about '*bringing him back.*' Then he said, '*They gave their lives willingly. Just like a sacrifice. Just the way it was always meant. And now's the time. The steps are almost complete.*' Something, something—the next bit was indistinct. Then, '*He's coming from the other side. All he needs is feeding. You won't know when he's coming. You won't know where. Be warned if you must. Be dust if you don't.*'"

Larry had scribbled everything that Houston had told

him down the left-hand margin of Linda's *Sunset* magazine. "That was it?" he wanted to know.

"That was it. Apart from a few background noises. We never had background noises before."

"What kind of background noises?"

"Hard to say. I've sent them down to Norm Dandia, for analysis. Sounds like rustling, and some sort of music."

"Okay, Houston. You did good. I'll get down to headquarters in maybe an hour."

He hung up. He said, "Shit."

"Larry sweetheart?" asked Linda.

"I don't know," said Larry. There was something about these killings that upset and irritated him beyond all reason. *Be warned if you must. Be dust if you don't.* What the hell was that supposed to mean? It was senseless, illogical. Yet it was frightening, too. And in a strange lateral off-the-wall way he understood its meaning, like one of those double-Dutch songs they used to sing at school.

"*See the little babies cry.*
Eat the meat and hope to die."

Linda watched him as he read and re-read what the killer had said to KGO *The other side, He's coming from the other side.*

The other side of what?

Linda came up to him and laid her head on his shoulder. "The other side?" she asked him.

He had doodled the words in capital letters, and circled around and around them. THE OTHER SIDE.

"Nothing," he told her. "It was just something that Houston said."

"You don't want to tell me?"

"It's nothing, okay? It's just—nothing."

"Oh, come on, Larry. Don't act weird. Tell me what it means."

"Jesus, Linda. I don't *know* what it means."

"See the little babies burn,

See the way they twist and turn."

Linda shrugged. "Okay, if that's the way you feel. *Messicani di vitello* coming up."

She began to mash bread into a bowl of milk, while Larry stood beside her, silent, with his glass of wine.

"You're upset," she said, after a while.

"I'm fine. I'm not upset."

"Larry, I know when you're upset. And right now, you're upset."

"Of course I'm upset!" Larry burst back at her. "I've been spending the whole goddamned day looking at pictures of dead families! Jesus, *you'd* be upset! Any one of them could have been us!"

Linda set the bowl aside and began to chop ham and pork for the filling. Although she was Anglo-Saxon (Danish, from way back) she had acquired that calmness that characterized Neapolitan women, no matter how volatile their menfolk were. When the ceiling's coming in, don't panic—cook.

"So what's this 'other side'?" she asked him.

"I don't know. I don't have any idea. It's something the killer said to the radio station."

"Your momma's always saying that, isn't she? Least, she used to."

Larry frowned at her. "My momma was always saying what?"

"'The other side.' Like, 'when your poppa went to the other side.'"

"What do you mean?" he demanded.

"It's what she says instead of 'died'. Haven't you ever noticed? She never says, 'when your poppa died'. Not once. She always says, 'when your poppa went to the other side.'"

Larry thought for a while, and then his eyes slowly narrowed.

"You're right," he told her. "It was something to do with that spiritualist stuff she used to be into."

"You mean that spiritualist stuff she's *still* into," put in Linda, quickly, as if she had accidentally-on-purpose let it slip out.

"She still does it?" asked Larry, surprised. "How do you know?"

"Well… I shouldn't really tell you—"

"Tell me," he insisted. He didn't have to insist very hard.

He listened while she told him what his mother had said. Then he finished his glass of wine, and poured himself another one.

Linda said, quietly, "What are you going to do?"

Larry swallowed wine. "What does any good Italian boy do? He talks to his momma."

3

His mother still lived in the same Edwardian house in Ashbury Heights where Larry had been brought up, 144 Belvedere. When Larry's father was alive, the Foggia family had occupied the whole five-bedroomed house; but now Eleonora Foggia lived in the ground-floor apartment, and rented off the rest of the house to two earnest young executive couples, one violently avant-garde painter and a former dancer from the Joffrey Ballet with a bad ankle and a Valium habit.

The fog refused to lift. It was beginning to give Larry a headache. Everywhere he drove, he could see transparent tadpole shapes swimming in front of his eyes. His mother's cream-painted house looked like a half-developed photograph – three stories of pale brick and carved lintels and complicated balconies – fashioned from what his father used to call "overwrought iron".

He climbed the steps and rang his mother's doorbell, and she answered so quickly that he knew that Linda must have called her in advance. She was sixty-nine now, two months away from seventy, and she was going through a phase of quite remarkable handsomeness, when her age really suited her. Her hair was very white, cut in a simple bob. But her face was sharp and elegant and sculptured; her eyes were big and gray and bright; and although she was always dressed in black, she looked both cultured and vivacious...

"*Ciao, momma*," he told her, and hugged her close. He was always amazed how thin and birdlike she felt.

"Hallo, stranger," she greeted him. He hadn't called by for over a week and a half. "The coffee's ready."

He followed her along the lilac-wallpapered hallway to the front parlor which was now her principal living-room. It was huge and gloomy, with an impossibly high ceiling and heavy brown drapes. When he was a boy, it had seemed like church, with a darkly polished hardwood floor and massive pieces of austere and hideous furniture. But now that his mother had been reduced to living in an "owner's unit", the room was crammed with all of her favorite pictures and ornaments and rugs. A tatty parrot scratched and muttered to itself in a domed cage; and everywhere he looked there were mirrors, so that the parlor seemed like one of a hundred gloomy overfilled rooms, occupied by one of a hundred black-dressed Eleonora Foggias and one of a hundred tatty parrots.

"Hallo, Mussolini," he said to the parrot. The parrot viciously clawed and bit at him, and then ruffled up its gangrenous feathers and croaked, "*Che violino! Che violino!*"

"It's time you gave that bird's body to the Audubon Society," Larry remarked.

His mother was pouring *capuccino*, with chocolate flakes. Larry never drank *capuccino* anyplace else, too sweet and creamy for his taste, but his mother liked to make it for him, and how could he refuse? Especially when a huge oil-painting of his father hung over the fireplace, dark and lean and censorious.

"You'd like some cake," his mother asked him, although it wasn't really a question. "*Torta casereccia di polenta*."

"Sure, sure thing," Larry reassured her. "But not too much. Detectives have to keep in shape."

They sat down in big velvet-upholstered spoonback chairs – almost knee-to-knee, as if they were about to play chess, or hypnotize each other.

"Well, then, what is it." his mother wanted to know, noisily stirring her coffee. "Linda said you were worried."

"Linda called you?"

"Sure Linda called me. You don't expect a daughter-in-law to call her mother-in-law when her husband's acting strange?"

"I haven't been acting strange. Linda didn't say that I was acting strange. Or did she?"

"Linda said that you'd been given those terrible murders."

"That's right. The Fog City Satan."

"She said you were acting abnormal."

"Abnormal? Not me."

"That's what she said: abnormal. Over-excited. Anxious."

Larry took a mouthful of polenta, filled with raisins and figs and pine-nuts. "The *case* is abnormal," he told her, in a muffled voice. "And maybe the only way to crack it is to *think* abnormal. But I wasn't conscious of *behaving* abnormal."

"Linda said you were abnormal. Have some more cake."

Larry lifted his hand. "No thanks. That's plenty."

"I made it all for you," his mother protested.

"Give it to Mussolini, maybe he'll do us all a favor and choke."

"*Tieni duro! Tieni duro!*" croaked Mussolini. "Stick to your guns! Stick to your guns!"

"It's about time they did Kentucky Fried Parrot," Larry observed.

Eleonora Foggia leaned forward and laid her dry, long-fingered hand on her son's knee, with all of those huge white diamond rings. "You wouldn't have come to talk to your *momma* if you weren't worried."

"Well, you're partly right," Larry agreed. "The point is, you were always into that spiritual stuff, weren't you? All that hocus-pocus you used to do with grandma, ouija boards and crystal balls."

His mother's eyes slitted; exactly the same way that *his* did, when he was suspicious. "How come all of a sudden you're interested in that?"

"Because of this case, that's why. We've had six mass killings so far—six mass killings in six months."

"I've been reading about them," his mother nodded. "Terrible, all of them. Terrible."

Larry said, "The weird thing about all of these killings is that they're all different, but in some way they're all the same. I just can't work out what that sameness is. There's a connection, right? But I can't understand what it is."

"And you think *I* will?"

"I don't know. Maybe you will, maybe you won't. The point is that, up until now, the guy has always called up KGO radio and given out some kind of warning. Like, 'If you tell what you saw, I'll cut out your tongue and feed it to the fish.' But this time, he said something different. This time he said—here, hold on a moment, I have it written here—this time, he said, '*He's coming from the other side... he's coming. They gave their lives willingly, the same way that Jesus gave* His *life... and now's the time. The steps are complete, and he's coming from the other side. Be warned if you must, he dust if you don't.'*"

Eleonora Foggia was silent for an uncomfortably long time. Then she looked up at Larry and Larry realized for the first time that she was not only momma, not only handsome, but old. Her skin was finely crumpled, like white tissue-paper out of a hat-box...

"I still don't understand why you came to me," she replied; although she must have done, by now. She just wanted him to spell it out loud and clear, the way she had always insisted he did when he had asked her for anything. Don't mutter, don't mumble. Speak up, and tell me what you want. And don't forget to say "please, *momma*."

Larry said, "Come on, *momma*. You used to talk about 'the other side' all the time, especially when you used to hold those what's-their-names—seances with grandma. I just figured that you might have some kind of inkling of what this maniac's trying to tell us."

Eleonora Foggia turned and stared up at the oil-painting of her late husband, Larry's father. Then she said, "You look so much like him, do you know that? You look so much like him, I used to think when you were growing up that maybe you *were* him, reborn. Your grandma used to think the same. She lost a son. I lost a husband. But we always had you. Your grandma used to call you 'Mario's Little Ghost'."

"Just tell me about the other side," Larry asked her.

"The other side is where you live when you're dead but you're not ready to be dead."

"And what happened when you held these seances with grandma? Did you ever get in touch with anybody on the other side?"

His mother looked a little sad. "We thought we did. But maybe it was just our longing that was talking to us. We used to hear whispering. We used to feel people touching us. But, who knows? It was probably nothing. I gave it up years ago; long before you grew up."

"You went to a spiritualist session on Nob Hill on June 17 this year. The address was 1591 Jackson, if you want to be picky about it. The host was a man called Wilbert Fraser."

She slowly withdrew her hand. "Have you been having me *followed?*" she demanded, in motherly horror.

"Of course not. Are you crazy? I'm a detective, that's all, and detectives detect. Besides, you told Linda all about it, and you didn't think that Linda wasn't going to tell me?"

"Women don't keep secrets any more," his mother complained.

"Of course they keep secrets. But Linda's my wife and you're my mother. Why should we have secrets?"

Eleonora Foggia squeezed her son's fingers, and smiled. "*Cuore di Mama,*" she told him.

"Sure thing," said Larry, and leaned forward to kiss her. "But tell me something about the other side."

"For years I wasn't sure," his mother told him. She scraped back her chair and stood up: silhouetted thin and attenuated like a Giacometti sculpture against the fog-whitened net curtains. "Sometimes I used to believe it. sometimes not. Sometimes, I used to lie on my pillow at night and I could hear your father's voice whispering. I could hear him breathing, slow and regular, the way he always used to! Sometimes we held a seance and I could *feel* him standing in the room—standing real close, just next to my shoulder—I could feel him and I could smell him, too. His tobacco, his cologne. But then my friend Anna told me to go to Wilbert Fraser."

"And what happened at Wilbert Fraser's?" asked Larry; a little sadly.

His mother turned and smiled at him. "I saw him. I spoke to him. That's what happened."

"You've *seen* him? You've *seen* poppa? Are you kidding me?"

"Of course not."

"You've seen him and talked to him? Why didn't you tell me before?"

Eleonora shrugged. "You wouldn't have believed me, would you? You would have thought I had Alzheimer's or something, and stopped me from going to see Wilbert any more."

"You're right. I *don't* believe you. Jesus, momma! I can understand you feeling that he's still around, but *talking* to him—!"

"It's true, Larry," his mother said, with great simplicity. "The other side really and truly exists."

Larry put down his coffee. "You're telling me that you've been to Wilbert Fraser's and you've actually seen poppa and talked to poppa and everything?"

"That's right."

"So, what did he say? Did he tell you what it's like, being dead?"

"Don't mock me, Larry. I'm your momma, and it's true. As a matter of fact your poppa asked after you. I said you were doing well."

Larry stood up; circled around the furniture with his hands in his pockets, and then sat down again. "I don't know what to say."

His mother seemed completely calm. "You asked me about the other side and I told you. What *can* you say?"

"All right, then," said Larry, "let's suppose for a moment that it *does* exist. Do you think that it's possible for people on the other side to—how can I put it?—to come back to this side?"

His mother raised one eyebrow. "You're asking me if people can come back from the dead."

"I suppose I am, yes."

"Well... I don't think so. Once you're gone, you're gone. That's what I believe, anyway."

"Was there ever anybody at Wilbert's who thought different?"

Eleonora Foggia thought hard. "There was one... a girl. She believed that she could bring back her dead son. She really believed it. But nobody else took her seriously. I certainly didn't. Oh... and a young man once. He argued with Wilbert about something, I don't know what."

Larry said nothing for a long time. Quite frankly, he didn't know whether to follow up this line of investigation or not. He had always been superstitious (salt tossed over his left shoulder; never walking under ladders). But he didn't seriously believe that it was possible to talk to the dead; or even to smell the dead's tobacco. However, all of the Fog City Satan's killings had displayed a ritual quality; almost a religious quality; and his final boast that somebody was coming through from the other side was enough to convince Larry that the killer believed in some kind of spiritualism, even if *he* didn't.

The question was: what religion, with what ceremonies? What did the Fog City Satan worship? A cruel god, a bloody god, for sure. But why were all of these sacrifices necessary? What were they meant to achieve? They were all savage, they were all indescribably cruel. In fact they were so cruel that Larry refused to believe that they hadn't been done for a purpose; and that he could still work out some kind of pattern behind them, if he tried.

A pattern would mean predictability; and predictability would allow him to be standing in the next would-be victim's home, ready to put the cuffs on the Fog City Satan just as soon as he smashed his way in through the door.

"Are you going again?" he asked his mother.

"Going? Going where?"

"To Wilbert Fraser's, for another seance?"

"I wasn't planning on it."

"Supposing I asked you to go? And supposing I asked you to take me along?"

"Why should you want to do that?"

"I just want to understand what this 'other side' stuff is all about, that's all. It may have nothing to do with the Fog City Satan, but it's something I have to check out."

Larry's mother said, "Well... I wasn't *planning* on going

again. But if that's what you want. They meet Tuesday evenings. There's only one thing, though: I'd have to make some conditions. You must promise me that you won't tell everybody there that you're a police detective; and you must also promise not to embarrass me."

"*Momma*," Larry told her. "Would I embarrass you?"

"Yes," said his mother, sharply. "You've been embarrassing me all my life. Children always embarrass their parents, just the same way that parents always embarrass their children. I haven't stopped. Why should you?"

"*Momma!*" Larry protested.

She leaned over and kissed his forehead. "You can have as much help from me as you wish. But don't ever take me for granted."

She went to the other side of the room, and he watched her face in the gloomy mirror as she opened the polished lid of her record-player, and put on *Si, mi chiamano Mimi* from *La Boheme*.

"You should have remarried," he told her. "You're a beautiful woman. Years ago, you should have found yourself somebody else."

Her reflection looked at him and smiled. "There was nobody like your poppa. Nobody that I ever wanted."

"Hard to please, hunh?" Larry asked her, finishing his *capuccino*. "And I always thought you were such a soft touch."

"*L'abito non fa il monaco*," she replied. "And there's one thing more you to remember, if you come with me to Wilbert's."

"What's that?"

"You may see poppa. You may even talk to him, if the vibrations are good. But you must promise me not to be frightened."

"I'm not too sure that I *want* to see poppa. You know, dead is dead."

"No, Larry. Dead is just like living in another place. Close by, very close by, but very different."

Mussolini screeched out, "*Pesci in fascia! Pesci in fascia!* Fish in your face!"

"Do you believe in euthanasia for old parrots?" Larry asked his mother.

That evening, Houston drove him back to Fulton to talk to a woman who lived across the street from the Berry condominium. She claimed to have seen a man "pacing up and down" outside the house shortly before nine o'clock on the evening that the Berrys had been killed.

She lived in a second-floor studio apartment that smelled of cat-litter and sour milk. She kept herself wrapped in a large multi-colored blanket while they talked to her, creaking from side to side in a basketwork chair. Larry stayed by the window, looking down into the foggy street. Everything was covered in cat-hairs, he didn't feel like sitting down.

Houston asked her, for Larry's benefit, "You told me he was tall."

"Tall, that's right," she agreed.

"How tall would you estimate? Six? Six-one? Taller?"

"Tall, that's all. And big, too."

"And how was he dressed?" Houston asked her.

"I told you before. Jeans, and a kind of a loose shirt. And he had some kind of a pouch or a bag hanging around his waist."

"What color was his hair? Dark, do you think, or fair?"

"I told you before," the woman replied. "He was bald, or what looked like bald. It was foggy, just like tonight. Hard to see anything too well."

"So he was pacing up and down, that's all? You didn't see him enter the building?"

The woman shook her head. A marmalade cat jumped possessively onto her lap and started to rub the top of its head against her arm. "Now, Basil," she admonished it. "Don't be so jealous."

"Did you see the man do anything else?" Houston demanded, as loudly as a prompter in a bad amateur play.

"Of course I did. I told you before," the woman snapped back.

"Would you please tell me again, just for Lieutenant Foggia's benefit?"

The woman creaked around in her seat and stared at Larry with penetrating eyes. One of her cats let out a doleful miaow, and then they all joined in.

"My cats don't like you," the woman told him.

"They can smell parrot on me," Larry replied.

"Would you just tell the lieutenant what you saw?" Houston asked her, desperately.

"Well… I saw him put a bag on his head."

"A bag?" asked Larry, "What kind of a bag? Or was it a hood? Or maybe a scarf?"

"It was a bag, stupid I know a bag when I see one. Like

a big black sport bag. Or a bowling bag. He bent down and he put it on his head."

Larry peered across the street. It was difficult to make out anything at all in this fog. "You looked out of the window and you saw a tall bald man put a black sport bag on his head?"

"That's correct."

"All right, then What did he do next?"

"He just stood there for a while."

"I see. With this bag on his head?"

The woman drew her blanket more tightly around her. Her nose was hooked, and she reminded Houston of a tattered eagle sitting in a tattered nest. "Are you trying to tell me that I was mistooken?"

Larry shook his head. "Of course not. How's your eyesight?"

"Better than your manners, boy."

Larry said, "I'm sorry. I didn't mean to offend you. But we get so many people calling us up with false information— well, we have to be certain, that's all."

"And you don't believe that I saw a man standing outside that house with a sport bag on his head?" the woman retorted, defiantly.

Larry hunkered down in front of her, trying to smile, trying to be warm and reassuring. Close up, the woman stank strongly of dried urine. "I believe you saw something that *looked* like a man with a sport bag on his head. But, let's face it, how often do you see people wearing sport bags on their head? It's not the kind of thing you see very often, is it?"

"That's why I told the officer about it," the woman

retaliated. "I said those exact words, almost. It's not the kind of thing you see too often, is it?"

"Well, you're right; and thank you for your help." Larry told her.

Halfway down the darkened staircase, Houston said, "I'm sorry. She sounded more rational, the first time I talked to her."

"That's all right, don't apologize," Larry told him. "I want to see everything. Every interview. Every report. There's something hidden in all of this. Something that's staring us right in the face, but which we can't understand. Do you know what I mean?"

"What about this bald guy with a bowling bag on his head?"

Larry opened the street door, and shrugged. "Who knows? Maybe he thought that if his head looked like a bowling ball, he might as well carry it around in a bowling bag."

"I can taste cat litter," Houston complained. "I can actually *taste* it."

Norm Dianda took off his earphones and blinked at Larry like a disturbed bush-baby. "Okay... we have several different auditory events going on here. I've separated each of them as far as I possibly can, but it's hard to be specific about some of the sounds in the distance."

"Let's just hear what you've got," Larry told him. He was sitting on the edge of Norm's workbench, drinking espresso. Norm Dianda was the police department's resident sound expert. He wore terrible peaky-shouldered sweaters that his mother had knitted him, and diseased-looking turquoise Kickers, but he could set up the most complicated wiretaps that Larry had ever known, and his work with directional microphones was legendary. Here, in his basement laboratory, amid stacks of speakers and amplifiers and tape-recorders, he had devised one of the most sophisticated systems of sound analysis in the country—better than anything that the CIA or the FBI could boast. Or, at least, that was Norm's claim.

He had spent almost the entire weekend working on the tape-recording that KGO had made of the Fog City Satan's last telephone call. For starters, he played the traffic noises in the far background. To Larry, they sounded just like traffic noises in the far background.

"What does that tell us?" he asked. "The guy was calling from someplace close to the street."

"Oh, not just any street," Norm told him. "You listen up some more."

Larry listened intently. He could hear cars, trucks; an occasional motor horn. He looked at Houston but all Houston could do was shrug.

"You're hearing it but you're not listening," said Norm. "This traffic noise has two distinct characteristics. One is, that the traffic keeps starting and stopping, and changing direction. You can hear the change in direction from the change in echo and Doppler effect. This indicates that our boy was making his call close to an intersection where there were traffic signals. First of all the traffic goes one way, then it goes the other."

"Norm, do you know how many intersections there are in San Francisco?" Larry protested.

"Sure... but there's another sound, too. Listen. Every time the traffic goes in one specific direction, there's a kind of a clonk-rumble-clonk."

"A clonk-rumble-clonk?" asked Houston, in amusement.

"For sure. Listen. There it goes. Clonk-rumble-clonk. Clonk-rumble-clonk. When a truck passes, it sounds louder, and different. There you are. Clonk-clonk-rumble-clonk-clonk-clonk. Two sets of wheels at the front, three sets of wheels at the rear."

"Do you have any idea what it is?" Larry asked him; knowing that Norm was just itching to tell them.

"Well..." said Norm, a little archly. "My guess is that it's a sheet of heavy-gauge steel covering an excavation in the road surface. It's close to the traffic-signals, and it's only on one side of the intersection."

Larry was impressed. "That sure narrows it."

"There's more," said Norm. He played the tape again, this time emphasizing the music and the conversation in the middle-distance. The voice of the Fog City Satan boomed indistinctly in the foreground, like blurred summertime thunder over the Berkeley Hills.

The conversation was unintelligible. There was laughter, and a knocking noise. An occasional *shug, shug*. The music sounded like the lambada.

"The phone call was probably made in a bar," said Norm. "There are six or seven different voices in the background, and although it's impossible to distinguish what they're saying, their intonation sounds Spanish. You can hear glasses knocking on a wooden counter, and that *shug, shug* sound is probably the sound of the bartender shoveling glasses into a sinkful of crushed ice. You can hear two distinct tunes, and from the smooth way in which they segue together, I'd say they were probably on tape, rather than any kind of juke-box. The first tune is the *Hot Lambada* by Juan Ochoa and the Antics. The second tune is *Love in Guadalajara* by the Border People."

"Listen to this guy," put in Houston. "He sounds like a deejay on one of those Latino FM stations."

"A Mexican-style bar located at an intersection with a steel plate in the roadway," said Larry. "I guess that shouldn't be too difficult to find."

"You'll know for sure when you've found the right place," put in Norm. "There are no commercially issued tapes in which the *Hot Lambada* by Juan Ochoa and the Antics is immediately followed by *Love in Guadalajara* by the Border People. In other words, the tape was probably recorded by the owners of the bar, and is the only one in existence with those two songs in that particular sequence."

"You're some kind of genius, you know that?" Larry told him.

Norm said, "It's analysis, that's all. Of course, this is the first time that we've picked up any distinct background noise on a call from our boy, so presumably he made all the previous calls from his home, or someplace quiet like that."

"It's the same guy, though?"

"Oh, sure, it's the same guy. Just listen." He played the tape again, this time emphasizing the voice of the Fog City Satan.

Larry had heard the tape on Saturday afternoon, and had played it six or seven times. The coldness of the man's voice had chilled him then. But Norm's remixed and amplified version was horrifying. He could hear the man breathing. He could hear his tongue clicking in the wetness of his mouth. It was like having the Fog City Satan whispering directly into his ear.

"*We're bringing him back. They gave their lives willingly. Just like a sacrifice. Just the way it was always meant. And now's the time. The steps are almost complete. All we have to do is to call him. All we have to do is to feed him. Then you'll pay. Then you'll suffer. He's coming from the other side. All he needs is feeding. You won't know when he's coming. You won't know where. Be warned if you must. Be dust if you don't.*"

Larry shook his head; and Houston said, "Jesus. What a creep."

Norm said, "As far as I can tell he's male, Caucasian, around mid-forties. He's a little hoarse; so he's possibly a cigarette-smoker. His accent sounds local, although there's a slightly Latin lisp in the way he pronounces his 'esses'."

"I never heard that middle-section before," Larry remarked. "All that stuff about '*Then you'll pay. Then you'll suffer.*'"

"That was very indistinct on the original," Norm agreed. "But I managed to enhance it with the computer."

"You've done an incredible job," Larry told him, slapping him on the back. "In fact, when we catch this guy, the credit's going to be yours, not mine."

"Please," said Norm. "Credit I can live without. But a pay hike would be good." He took a sip of Larry's espresso and grimaced. "How do you drink this stuff?"

"It's good for the chest-hair," Larry told him. "Did you ever see any self-respecting Italian without chest-hair?"

"Sure," said Norm, flicking off rows of switches. "Sophia Loren, for one."

The fog was as impenetrable as gray flannel by the time Houston called to say that they had "probably" located the Mexican bar from which the Fog City Satan had made his call. Larry took his Toyota out of the police garage and met Houston twenty minutes later at the intersection of Front and Green. Houston was sitting in his battered beige Saratoga with his mouth open and his eyes closed. Larry knocked on the window.

"What's this, bedtime?"

Houston climbed out of the car and stretched. "I haven't been sleeping too good."

"None of us has been sleeping too good. The time for sleeping is when we nail our boy."

Houston said, "Okay—this is the only intersection in the city that has a metal plate covering a hole in the street *and* a Mexican bar."

The night was still foggy. This particular corner of Front Street looked like a set for a made-for-TV detective movie; all fog and unfocused neon and dew-glossed sidewalks. A few cars bounced past, their marker-lights dipping as they crossed the intersection, then *clang-bonk-clang* as they bounced over the metal plate.

"Alphonson's Cantina" stood on the south-west corner of the intersection, between Rainwater Fine Arts and Anselmo Imports, Inc. It was a rundown sausage-and-tequila-and-fajita joint with windows obscured with scratched red paint and a fitfully buzzing neon sign advertising Sol

Cerveza. Obviously its owner had missed out on the surge of popularity that had turned the "Border Cantina" and "Alejandro's Sociedad Gastronomica" into the hot places to eat.

"Have you checked inside?" asked Larry, as they crossed the street.

"Not yet. Front Street used to be my beat, back when I was a grunt. I didn't want to risk being recognized."

Larry pushed his way in through Alphonson's double doors. Inside it was gloomy, smoky and almost empty, although mariachi music was playing from the stereo system at deafening volume. There was a long battered bar, a collection of tables with checkered red cloths and empty wine bottles with candles stuck in them, and a huge mural of bullfighting in Tijuana, with an anatomically impossible bull being slaughtered by what looked like a transexual matador, painted blood everywhere.

A man with a fleshy pockmarked nose and greased-back hair was polishing glasses and talking to a big-hipped black-haired woman in a purple dress. The woman was drinking margaritas and smoking a small cigar. Larry came up to the bar and stood beside her and said, "How are you doing?"

The woman looked him up and down. She had a big white-powdered face that had obviously been battling for years against the effects of gravity. Her wrinkled cleavage was thick with powder, too; and around her neck she wore six or seven gold chains with crosses and pendants and a rabbit's foot.

"Do I know you, my darling?" she asked, in a rasping voice.

"You do now. Larry Foggia. Can I buy you a drink?"

"Don't mind if you do. I suppose you want something in return."

"Such as?"

"It depends what you're into. I gave up blowjobs years ago, but I can read your palm."

Larry said to the man behind the bar. "Are you the owner?"

The man shook his head. "The owner's in Vegas. I just work here."

"What's your name?"

"Herve, why?"

"Were you working here last Friday evening, Herve?"

"Sure. I work here every evening. What are you, a cop or something?"

Larry produced his badge. The woman in the purple dress raised one overplucked eyebrow and noisily blew out smoke. "Good thing I only offered the palm-reading, hunh?"

Larry ordered her a margarita, and two beers for himself and Houston. "I'm looking for a guy who made a telephone call from here round about seven o'clock on Friday. A hefty guy, dark-haired, mid-forties."

The barman lifted a glass to the light, then polished it some more. "I don't know. I'm usually pretty busy around that time."

Larry looked around. The telephone was on the wall beside the double doors. It was covered by a yellow-painted pegboard hood to keep out the noise, but anybody making a call could have easily been seen from the bar, and if the Fog City Satan looked as distinctive as the forensic and circumstantial evidence suggested he did. it would have been almost impossible for the barman to have missed him.

Larry took out a $20 bill, folded it, and offered it to the barman between two uplifted fingers. "Tall... could have had his head shaved. Muscular. too; like he worked out a lot."

The barman ignored the money and shook his head. "I didn't see nobody."

"Come on, Herve, be serious," Larry persisted. "There's no way that you could have missed him."

"You're wasting your time," interrupted the woman in the purple dress. "About three years ago, Herve had his fingers broken because he told some guy's wife that he was drinking in here with another woman. Since then he's suffered from complete customer blindness. But don't you worry about it, my darling. I think I saw the character you're talking about."

"Really?" asked Larry. He wasn't sure whether the woman was putting him on or not. But there was something he liked about her. She was upfront and earthy, and he liked people who were upfront and earthy. Maybe it was a reaction against the unreality of his upbringing, walking through the rooms of 144 Belvedere, haunted by his father's ghost.

The woman held out her hand. "You don't think I'm going to tell you for free when you were going to give this bozo a double sawbuck?"

Larry handed over the bill, and the woman tucked it carefully into her cleavage.

"What's your name?" he asked her.

"Edna-Mae. Edna-Mae Lickerman. *Mrs*. Edna-Mae Lickerman."

"You live around here, Mrs. Edna-Mae Lickerman?"

"I run the Hand-Made Pottery on Vallejo. I pot by day and I drink by night." She let out a bright, harsh laugh.

"All right, then," said Larry. "Tell me about this guy you saw."

"He came in Friday evening at a quarter after six," said Edna-Mae, assertively.

"How come you're so sure of the time?" asked Houston.

"I was on my third margarita, my darling, and I time my margaritas. I have the first margarita at a quarter after five, I have the second margarita at a quarter of six, and I have the third margarita at a quarter after six. It's called pacing your drinking, haven't you ever heard about that?"

"Okay," said Larry. "So what did he look like?"

"I've seen him before. He doesn't come in all that often, maybe once every four or five weeks. But you can't mistake him. He's built like a bulldozer. He wears this kind of scarf knotted around his head, but I never saw his face too clearly."

"What do you mean by that?" asked Larry.

The woman blew out cigar-smoke. "I don't know. He has these perfect looks, you know? Blue eyes, good strong chin. A little bit like Yul Brynner, only taller than Yul Brynner. But he's weird, like there's something missing in the thinking department."

"Have you ever talked to him?" asked Larry.

"Nossir, no way. He always sits and drinks alone. He doesn't look like the type who's going to be interested in small-talk."

"Have you any idea where he lives?"

"Nossir."

"Have you ever heard anybody call him by name?"

"Nossir."

"What was he wearing last Friday?" asked Houston, making notes.

"Jeans, and a sweatshirt, and a black leather motorcycle jacket, or maybe it was dark brown."

"Is that the way he's usually dressed when he comes in here?"

"Pretty much, yes."

"What color was the sweatshirt?" Houston wanted to know. "Anything printed on it?"

"I think it was red, my darling. It had some kind of writing on it but I don't know what it said. I don't go around reading strange men's sweatshirts."

Larry checked his watch. "Do you have some time to spare?" he asked the woman. "I'd like you to come down to headquarters with me and take a look through some pictures. Maybe you can pick this guy out for us."

"Well..." said the woman. "I was planning on getting drunk."

"You can send out for a bottle of tequila. Believe me, this is very important. You could help us to catch a killer."

Edna-Mae widened her mascara-blobbed eyes. "You mean he's a killer? That young guy?"

"We're not sure yet," said Larry. "But there's a possibility, yes."

"Well... a killer! I never met a killer before. Apart from my former husband, of course, Mr. Lickerman, and all he ever killed was love and devotion."

"Do you want to finish your drink?" asked Larry. "Then we can go."

"All right, then," Edna-Mae agreed. "But let me read your palm first. I did promise, after all. Unless you'd rather have the blowjob?"

Larry grinned. "I think I can live without either."

"But I insist, my darling! I never take a free drink! I'm not a kept woman, you know!"

"All right, then," said Larry, holding out his hand. "I'll settle for the palm-reading."

Edna-Mae bent back his fingers and examined the lines on his hand. Her fingernails were very long and painted lilac. On her left hand, instead of a wedding-band, she wore a silver ring with a bright blue human eye enameled on it. The eye was startlingly realistic, and Larry had the odd feeling that it was watching him.

"Now these are what I call interesting lines," said Edna-Mae. "I mean, these are not your normal marriage-mortgage-kids-and-a-station-wagon lines. These are very artistic, very individual. You draw, right? And you cook? And you like music? Don't tell me, you like opera!"

Houston rolled his eyes up in exasperation. "His name's Larry Foggia! Larry Foggia, one of the Bay Street Foggias! And don't tell me you didn't know that all along! And now you're asking if he likes opera? Does Pavarotti like opera? Hey—what about pasta? Does he like pasta?"

Edna-Mae bared her discolored teeth. "Yes, my darling, he likes pasta. See that line there, just around the thumb? That's his linguine line."

"Come on, then," Larry laughed. "Let's see what interesting un-normal future I've got in store."

Edna-Mae traced Larry's line of fortune, right up the middle of his palm. "You'll never make any money, believe me. You'll be poor but honest for the rest of your life."

Houston shook his head in amusement. "He's a cop; and she says he's going to be poor but honest."

"Here's your heart-line," Edna-Mae persisted. "You're extremely passionate, but you're loyal, too. You're the type of man who gives all of his love to one woman, for all of his life. But here—look—your heart-line's broken. You're going to have trouble with your marriage. I'm not sure what it is, but it looks like it's going to be soon."

"I know, Linda's going to ask her mother to stay," put in Houston.

But Edna-Mae was frowning; and she raised her hand to keep Houston quiet. "No, no. It's not that. You're not going to fall out of love. You're not going to argue. But for some reason, there's going to be some terrific disruption in your marriage. I mean something really volcanic."

Larry gave her a tight smile. "Is that all? Can we go down to headquarters now?"

"Wait, wait, let me check out your head-line," said Edna-Mae. "You see here? Your first finger belong to Jupiter, your second to Saturn, your third to the Sun, and your fourth finger to Mercury. Your head-line runs from Jupiter, right across your palm, to here, the mound of Mars."

"And what does that tell you?" asked Larry, trying to be patient. Herve the barman glanced at him, and breathed on a glass, *hah!* and the look on his face said that there's one born every minute.

"You're going to argue with some people who are important to you," said Edna-Mae.

"Arne Knudsen, for starters," put in Houston. "And probably Dan Burroughs, too."

"You're going to meet somebody who will change your life, but let me warn you, my darling. You will wish more than anything else in the world that you had never met this person."

"Is this a man or a woman?" asked Larry. To begin with, he had felt completely skeptical about Edna-Mae's palmistry, but she spoke with such hoarse conviction in her voice that he almost found himself believing her.

"Who?" she said, staring at him.

"This somebody… this person who's going to change my life. Is this a man or a woman?"

"It's a—it's—"

Her eyes clouded. She stared down at Larry's palm as if she couldn't understand why she was holding it or where she was.

"It's—" she stuttered. "It's—"

"Looks like the margaritas got the better of her," said Houston, out of the side of his mouth.

But Edna-Mae suddenly dropped Larry's hand—almost threw it away. Her eyes were staring and her face was rigid. Larry could see the muscles convulsing and shuddering in her cheeks. "Hey… are you okay?" he asked her.

She nodded, dumbly, trying to swallow, trying to speak.

"Edna-Mae, what's wrong?"

Houston said, worriedly, "Hey, Larry. She looks like she's having a fit."

Larry said, "Hold on, hold on."

Edna-Mae sat up stiffly on her bar-stool and began to quiver. If Larry hadn't known that it was impossible, he would have guessed that she was suffering an electric shock. Her face—which had already been powdered white—began to turn purplish-gray, as if she couldn't breathe.

"Hey, Herve, give me a glass of water, will you?" Larry asked him.

Herve reluctantly filled up a glass in the sink and handed it over. Larry held it to Edna-Mae's lips and said, "Come on, Edna-Mae Lickerman. Have a drink."

She stared at him. "Your hand," she breathed. Her cigar dropped on to the floor, and Houston leaned over to pick it up.

"My hand? What about it?"

"Your *hand!*"

Larry lifted his left hand, palm upwards, and stared at it. "Can't you see it?" gasped Edna-Mae.

She took hold of his fingers again, and stretched them back. As she did so, Larry began to feel an extraordinary crawling sensation in his palm, as if a large centipede were walking across it. He looked down, and with a prickly feeling of alarm, he saw dark shadows and patterns moving across his skin.

His first reaction was to look up toward the ceiling, to see if a light was playing on his hand. But then he realized that the shadows were actually flickering and dancing on his skin. They were mottled, gray and purplish, like birthmarks.

"Houston!" he said. "Houston, look at this!"

Houston leaned over and stared at his palm. "That's weird," he remarked. "That's truly weird." He touched the patterns with his fingertip, but they were no more substantial than shadows. "I never saw anything like that before. Never. And they're *moving*."

Edna-Mae said thickly, "It's your future, don't you see! What will happen to you tomorrow! The man who will cause you such grief! He's coming!"

"Come on, now," said Larry, trying to tug his hand away from her. "This is just some kind of a stunt, right? Let's get serious here."

But Edna-Mae shook her head violently, and uttered a cackling, choking noise. "He's coming! He needs to feed!"

Larry tried again to prise his fingers away from her, but she clung on tight. "Come on now, Edna-Mae, let's call it a day."

She began to toss her head wildly from side to side. "Future! Future!" she blurted.

Suddenly, Larry felt a deep pain in the palm of his hand, as if somebody had dug a nail into it. He looked down and saw that the shadows had formed themselves into the indistinct shape of a man's face—eyes, nose, and mouth.

"Look at that," he breathed to Houston. "What the hell is that?"

The barman Herve crossed himself twice, and gabbled in a high-pitched voice.

"*Uade retro Satana,*
Sunt mala quae libas
Nunquam suade mihi uano
Ipse uenena bibas."

It was one of those little rhymes that children learned in Jesuit schools to ward off the devil.

The face on Larry's hand grew darker and more distinct. The smudged eyes appeared to open, and Larry saw the image staring at him. Shadows still crossed the palm of his hand, like the shadows of smoke or passing clouds; and as they passed the man's expression appeared to alter and shift. He seemed to smile. He seemed to turn his face. He seemed to be trapped inside the palm of Larry's hand, like a holographic face on a credit card, yet he looked self-satisfied and calm.

It's an illusion, Larry quaked. He couldn't stop himself from quaking. *It has to be! An optical illusion. Or some kind of rash. Maybe I'm overtired. Maybe there's some kind of drug in the air here... maybe Edna-Mae was smoking something.*

But he could actually feel the face crawling and flexing on his hand; he could feel the eyes opening and closing, he could feel the coldness and wetness of the mouth.

And all the time, the middle of his hand ached as if it had been nailed to the bar.

The eyes turned. Then the mouth breathed, "*It's feeding time, my friend.*" And Larry heard it. He actually heard it speak.

Edna-Mae screamed. Larry yelled too, and wrenched his hand away from her, and squeezed it tightly into a fist. He thought he felt the face against his skin. He thought he felt hair and teeth and lips. But then his fist was filled with a searing pain, and dazzling white light burst out between his fingers. He opened his hand again, and for a fleeting, blinding second, a bright light flared and danced on his palm, and then vanished.

Edna-Mae tilted sideways on her barstool, and then dropped onto the floor on her hands and knees. Larry, shaking, sweating cold sweat, stood staring at his hand.

His skin was reddened, as if he had burned it with scalding water, but the face and the shadows had gone.

"He's coming, he's coming, oh God he's coming," coughed Edna-Mae. She began to crawl on all fours across the floor. "He's coming and there's nothing you can do. He wants to feed! He wants to feed! On us! He wants to eat us! Eat our lungs, eat our livers! He wants to eat us!"

Houston snapped at the barman, "Dial!" and then cautiously approached Edna-Mae, as if he were trying to corner a rabid dog.

"*Si, senor,*" Herve gabbled, and came around the bar. "*Crux sacra sit mihi lux.*"

"Larry? Are you okay?" Houston asked him. "Come on, let me take a look at your hand."

Larry stared at him. His features seemed to be disconnected—eyes, nose, mouth, mustache. For a moment Larry couldn't work out who he was.

"Did you see it?" he said. "Did you see it?"

Houston cautiously explored the palm of Larry's left hand with his fingertips. "There's nothing there, lieutenant. Nothing at all."

"But you saw it, too?"

"Sure I saw it. Like a face."

"And you heard it speak?"

Houston looked at him guardedly. "I didn't hear it speak."

"It spoke, believe me. My own hand spoke to me. Can you believe that?"

"I didn't hear it, lieutenant. I saw it, but I didn't hear it. Maybe—"

"Maybe what? Maybe I've lost my marbles?"

"I didn't mean that, lieutenant, but—well, you know. Maybe you heard something else and thought it was saying something. Easy mistake to make, you know, in the heat of the moment."

Larry kept wiping his hand against his sleeve. "I need a drink," he said. He felt as if he had just walked away from an auto accident; as if time had stopped and then restarted. "I don't know what the hell kind of trick that Edna-Mae was playing on me, but it felt like—Jesus, I could *feel* it, like a real face." He wiped his hand again. "Jesus. That practically scared the nuts off me. What do you think, Houston, hypnosis? Or maybe she's got some kind of hallucinatory drug on her fingers."

Edna-Mae was still crawling on her hands and knees across the floor. Herve kept trying to help her up, but she was far too heavy for him, and she kept pushing him away. "Leave me alone... leave me alone, you little runt! It's feeding time! Did you hear that? It's feeding time!"

"Houston," said Larry, "for Christ's sake give the poor bastard a hand."

Houston and the barman tried together to lift Edna-Mae off the floor, but she went completely limp, and they had to drag her across to one of the tables. She sat there staring at nothing at all, quivering and scratching herself, and muttering "Feeding time! Do you hear me? Feeding time! Oh, yes, that's the future! Did you see it in your hand, Mr. Clever-clogs? Nyum, nyum, nyum, feeding time!"

Herve went to the phone and prodded out the number for the paramedics. "'Alphonson's Cantina'. Jes. A woman gone crazy. Jes. How should I know? No, no, juss went crazy." He hung up, and then he came and stood next to Larry and stared at Edna-Mae. "This is the devil's business, jes?"

"Just give me a drink, will you?" Larry asked him. "Large whiskey, straight up."

Herve poured them both a Johnnie Walker, and then took a swig himself, directly from the neck of the bottle. "Devil's business," he repeated. "You be marking my words."

"You don't say anything about this to anybody," Larry instructed him, and passed him a $20. This time, Herve pocketed the money without a complaint.

"Nothing to nobody. I swear."

Houston came over, tapping his ballpen thoughtfully against his thumbnail. "Maybe we should stake this place out. See if our boy comes in again."

Larry was still staring at the palm of his hand. "It was there, wasn't it? A face."

"I don't know," said Houston. "I guess it was. But you know what they say. Things aren't always what they seem to be."

Larry smeared the palm of his hand against the edge of the bar. Somehow he felt as if his hand was dirty, as if it had been soiled. And he couldn't rid himself of a deep, persistent itch. "It must be some kind of hypnosis," he repeated. "Like mass-suggestion. They do shows like that, don't they? Making people see things that just aren't there."

"Sure they do," nodded Houston, trying to be reassuring. "My uncle used to see this black spotted dog all the time, two or three times a month. He saw it all his life, no matter where he went. He even saw it in Italy, during the war."

"No kidding," said Larry.

"No kidding, it was true. He used to mention it all the time. Like, 'I saw the black dog today, over in Mill Valley.' Then about three years ago he was driving north on business and a black dog stepped out in the road. He swerved to miss it, and hit a tree by the side of the road."

"Are you kidding me?"

Houston shook his head. "He didn't die, but he broke his back. He's in Sausalito now, in a home. Can't walk, can't speak. He might as well be dead. And he still sees that damned black spotted dog."

They heard the distant warbling of the paramedics' siren. Uphill, downhill, temporarily muffled, then uphill again—louder, and closer. Edna-Mae raised her head and listened.

"We called for an ambulance," said Larry, loudly.

She frowned at him. "You!" she said. "You're the one with the hand!"

Larry put down his drink and circled around the tables toward her. Immediately she stood up, noisily knocking over her bentwood chair, and backed away. "You mustn't touch me!" she said. "Whatever you do, you mustn't touch me!"

"Listen," Larry appealed. "You had a—I don't know—you had kind of a seizure. Something like a fit. Just let the paramedics test your heartrate and your blood-pressure. We don't want you collapsing on us, do we?"

"*Collapsing?*" she shouted at him, harshly, as if he had suggested some sort of obscenity. "*Collapsing?*"

Larry stepped nearer to her. He raised his hand, trying to appear comforting and reassuring, but that made her shrink even further away. "It's you!" she kept hissing. "It's you!"

Larry heard the ambulance cross the intersection,

clonk-rumble-clonk, and pull up outside the front of the bar. Houston said, "Hold on, I'll tell them we're here," and stepped outside into the street.

Larry turned to say, "Don't forget the—" but as he did so, Edna-Mae Lickerman backed into the cheaply varnished door marked *Senoras* and slammed it behind her. Larry heard her lock it.

"Oh, shit," he complained, and immediately went up to the door and rapped on it with his knuckles. "Edna-Mae? Edna-Mae? Come on, Edna-Mae, you don't have anything to worry about! That was just an illusion, that's all! You want to see my hand now? That was just an illusion!"

"Stay away!" Edna-Mae shouted back. "You're the one with the hand! You stay away!"

"For God's sake, Edna-Mae, you've had a bad turn, that's all. Come on out and we can help you!"

"I don't want your help! You go away!"

There was a long silence. Larry rapped again, but Edna-Mae didn't reply. He didn't know what the hell was going on, or how he had managed to get himself involved in rescuing an hysterical woman from the toilet of a rundown Mexican cantina, but he suddenly felt angry and frustrated, as he always did when his life got temporarily out of control, and he bashed against the door with his fist. His mother always said that it was his Neapolitan blood; the fire of his dead father.

Houston came across the cantina with a Chinese paramedic in tow. The paramedic's name-tag announced that he was Bryan Ong.

"What's the problem here, lieutenant?" the paramedic asked him.

"I'm not too sure," Larry told him. "We've got ourselves a panicking middle-aged woman locked in a washroom. From the way she behaved, she may have had some kind of fit. Maybe it's nothing more serious than menopausal freak-out. Or, it could be DTs. She practically lives on margaritas."

Bryan Ong nodded without expression. "Your sergeant here said something about your hand, too."

Larry lifted his hand as if he were pledging allegiance to the flag. "Nothing. My hand's okay. Little sore, maybe, but that's all."

"What happened to it?"

"Kind of a flash-burn, I guess. Static electricity, I don't know."

The paramedic stared at the washroom door and cleared his throat. "Well... I guess we have to get her out of there."

"Herve, you got a spare key?" Larry asked him.

The barman shook his head. "Only one key, *senor*."

Larry leaned against the washroom door and rattled the handle. "Edna-Mae, are you going to come out quietly, or what?"

Again, there was no reply. But Larry was sure that he could hear a suppressed mewling sound, like somebody weeping into a bunched-up handkerchief.

"Edna-Mae, are you all right?"

"Let's get the door down," said the paramedic, setting his bag on one of the tables. "It sounds like she could be convulsing."

"Okay, then, whatever you say," Larry agreed. He gripped the doorframe in each hand, leaned back as far as he could, and kicked at the lock. He didn't manage to break it completely the first time, but then he kicked again, and the door juddered open.

He was greeted, alarmingly, by a freezing-cold draft, and a dazzling light that flickered erratically on and off. The draft sucked at his ankles and ruffled his hair.

Houston held his arm. "Go easy, lieutenant. Looks like the fuses have shorted out."

"Edna-Mae?" Larry shouted out. "Edna-Mae, can you hear me?"

He pushed his way into the washroom. There were only two cubicles, with red-painted doors covered in graffiti.

"Maybe she went out the back," Houston suggested.

"No," said Larry. "The door's padlocked, look; and there's a mesh over the window."

"What the hell's that *light?*" Houston protested, shielding his eyes with his hand.

Bryan Ong stayed back, by the broken door. "Are you sure she's in there?"

"Of course she's in here," said Larry. "Edna-Mae?"

He kicked open the first stall. It was empty, with a broken toilet-seat and a floor heaped with unrolled paper. He kicked open the second stall. He could hear her mewling, he was sure.

Houston, right behind him, said, "Jesus, Larry, what the hell's happening in here?"

He didn't see her at first. She was so small. God almighty, *she was so small*! She was crouched down in the corner behind the toilet-bowl, her hands covering her balding, tufted head. Her eyes were as wide and as dark as a Rhesus monkey's. Her wrists were wizened and thin as sticks.

"What's *that?*" asked Houston, his voice brittle with fear.

"It's her," said Larry. "I don't know how, but it's her."

"How can it be her? It's no bigger'n a dog!"

But there was no mistaking the purple dress. There was no mistaking the gold chains and the rabbit's-foot which were dangling around her scrawny neck.

Larry's mouth was dry as glasspaper. He held back the cubicle door, and slowly approached her. The little creature that had been Edna-Mae stared up at him with both malevolence and fright.

"Edna-Mae?" Larry whispered. "Edna-Mae, is that you?"

The little creature whined and cringed, and lifted its arm to protect its face. Its skin was papery and flaky, the color of wasp's-nests.

Houston said, "What happened to her? What could have done that?"

"Will you stop asking damfool questions and give me a hand here?" Larry snapped at him.

"What do you want me to do?" Houston asked. "Christ, lieutenant, this is unreal!"

"Yes, it's unreal," Larry agreed, testily. He leaned back and called, "Medic! Let's have a stretcher in here, please!" Then he turned to the creature that was Edna-Mae, and said, "Come on, Edna-Mae. We're not going to hurt you. Just come out of there, okay? Everything's going to be fine."

The paramedic pushed a gurney with squeaking wheels into the washroom. "You need some assistance in there?" he wanted to know. His offer sounded distinctly unenthusiastic.

"Come on, Edna-Mae," Larry coaxed the little shriveled creature in the corner. "Nobody's going to hurt you, I promise."

He knelt down on the wet tiled floor and reached around behind the toilet-bowl. Edna-Mae suddenly scratched him and scuttled and twisted away, and Larry shouted out, "*Ah!*" more in surprise than pain. But he managed to snatch the sleeve of her dress, and then the chicken-bone arm inside it, and her skull was too big for her to squeeze past the pipe at the back of the toilet. She struggled and scratched and fought and squealed, but eventually Larry managed to drag her out, and lift her kicking into the air. She weighed almost nothing. She was only the size of a five-year-old child, and her dress was tangled around her in purple bunches. He felt as if he could crush her ribcage like a bird's-nest.

All the time she kicked and scratched and spat, and hissed at him between clenched teeth. He could scarcely recognize the bawdy, hoarse-voiced woman who had first accosted him at the bar.

Between them, Larry and Houston and the paramedic managed to strap her on to the gurney. Her eyes darted furiously from side to side, and her thin wrists quivered in their restraints. Her slimy blue tongue writhed between her lips like a fat slug half-crushed under the wheel of a car.

"Cover her up," Larry ordered. "Cover her right up. I don't want anybody to see her."

The paramedic unfolded a blanket. As he tried to drape it over her, however, she raised her scrawny head and snapped at his hand. He shouted, and twisted his hand away, but not before she had ripped a large piece of skin and muscle away from the bone. Bright red blood suddenly stained the blanket, and spattered across the washroom floor.

"Oh God," said Larry. He yanked the roller-towel off the wall, bundled it up, and pressed it against the paramedic's hand. The paramedic had gone gray. He leaned back against the wall, panting and swearing in Cantonese. Almost immediately his colleague appeared, a big crewcut man with forearms like Popeye.

"What the hell's going on here?" he asked. He squinted in bewilderment at the flickering light.

"Don't ask," Larry replied. "Just get us to the hospital. This woman, your friend here, and me. My sergeant will follow behind."

"Ong, you okay?" the crewcut paramedic wanted to know.

"He got bit, that's all," Houston explained. "This woman bit him."

The paramedic leaned suspiciously over the gurney. Then he lifted the blanket and stared at Edna-Mae with an expression that was hewn out of solid corned-beef.

"Be careful," Larry warned him. "She could be dangerous."

The crewcut paramedic paused for a moment, then let the blanket drop back. "This is a woman?" he asked.

Larry nervously rubbed the palm of his hand. "This is kind of a woman, yes."

"*Kind* of a woman. Shit."

"Just get her out of here," Larry told him. "And don't say a word to anybody. You understand? Otherwise I'll have your guts."

"Yes, lieutenant, sure thing, lieutenant, whatever you say, lieutenant," the crewcut paramedic replied. He laid an arm around his partner's shoulders and said, "Come on, Ong, let's go."

That night Larry said hardly anything at all over dinner. Linda had sent Frankie and Mikey to bed early because tomorrow they were going on a Cub Scout outing to Kirby Cove. They had already laid out their T-shirts and their sneakers and their lunchpails, and Mikey had bought a magnifying-glass with his pocket-money in case they got lost and needed to start a fire to attract attention.

They finished the wine, and Linda started collecting up the dishes. "What's wrong?" she asked him. "You look like you're out of it."

"I don't know. Something happened today; something weird."

"Dan Burroughs said something nice to you?"

He didn't even smile. "No, no. Weirder than that."

"Weirder than Dan Burroughs saying something nice to you? I can't imagine *anything* weirder than that."

He raised his left hand, palm outwards. "Do you believe that—" He hesitated. "Do you believe that—"

Linda stood still, with dirty dishes in each hand. "Do I believe that *what*, Larry?"

"I don't know. Do you believe that somebody could have pictures on their skin?"

She frowned. "I'm not following you. What pictures? You mean, like a tattoo?"

"Well, kind of like a tattoo. But moving."

"Moving?"

"That's right. Like, moving pictures. Pictures of somebody's face."

She looked at him for a long time. Then she gave him the smallest shake of her head. "I really don't understand you. Whose face? Where?"

He tilted his chair back. "We went down to a Mexican bar today, on Front and Green. We think our boy made his last telephone call from there. Anyway, there was a woman in the bar, and she said that she'd seen him, or somebody who looked like him."

Linda put down the dishes, pulled out a chair, and sat down, listening, her chin in her hand. It was obvious that she could sense how disturbed he felt.

He lifted his hand. "She offered to read my palm. It sounded like a joke, that's all. But while she was reading it, these marks appeared, right on the skin, and they were moving."

"You're sure it wasn't a rash, anything like that?"

He shook his head. "They were more like shadows. To begin with, I thought they *were* shadows. But then they all gathered together and formed into this face."

"Was it a face you knew?" Linda asked him.

"I don't know. No, I don't think so. It was very indistinct. It could have been anybody."

Linda said, "It sounds like some sort of hallucination."

"That's what I thought. But then the woman had a fit, like an epileptic fit. She kept screaming about my hand, and telling me to keep away from her. She locked herself in the can and wouldn't come out. In the end I had to break down the door."

He hesitated. He could still see that shrunken tufted head. He could still feel those chicken-bone arms. He could still hear that rasping, high, malevolent voice.

"Go on," Linda urged him.

Larry gave a dismissive shrug. "When we, er—when we broke down the door, you know, and *found* the woman in the toilet—she'd shrunk."

"Shrunk," Linda repeated. Then, "Did you say shrunk?"

"That's right. She'd shriveled up, so she was scarcely any bigger than a child. She'd lost her half of her hair, and her skin was all dried up, and it was disgusting. She looked like one of those kids you see in those Ethiopian famine pictures."

"How long was she locked in the can?"

"That's the crazy part about it. Four, maybe five minutes at the most."

"How could anybody shrink up like that? And as *quickly* as that?"

Larry stood up. "I don't know. I never saw anything like it in my life. I mean, I've seen dead people. I've seen dried-up dead people, like mummies practically. But nothing like this. I need another drink."

"It's so bizarre," said Linda.

He opened the icebox door and took out another bottle of Verdicchio. "You're telling me? It was so Goddamned bizarre I didn't know whether to laugh my head off or run for my life."

He peeled the gold plastic from the top of the bottle, and dug in the point of the corkscrew. "She was shrunk, but she was still alive and she was vicious. Snapping and biting at everybody. We called the paramedics to take her away and she bit one of the paramedics."

"Where is she now?"

"SFG, under guard. I've asked Dr. Jensen to take a look at her. You know, the endocrinologist. Houston Brough thought she may have suffered from massive adrenal insufficiency. Like a huge blast of AIDS."

Linda watched him pouring wine. "What do *you* think happened?" she asked.

Without looking up, Larry gave a grim smile. "I don't know, sweetheart. I really don't. I'm trying not to believe what I saw with my own eyes. I'm trying to persuade myself that I'm suffering from overwork; or stress; or maybe even Manilow's Syndrome."

"Manilow's Syndrome" was what the SF police had dubbed a refusal to believe what was right in front of your nose.

Larry lifted his left hand again, and inspected his palm, as if he half-believed that the shadowy face would reappear. "Maybe you're right. Maybe it's something from the other side."

Linda said, "Do you want to go to Muir Woods *this* weekend?"

He glanced at her suspiciously. "This is a change of heart. Wild horses wouldn't have dragged you there yesterday."

She stood up, and hooked her arms loosely around her waist, and kissed his cheek. "I know. But maybe you need all that awe and nature and beauty."

He kissed her back. Every time he looked at her, he was amazed how pretty she was. *Really* pretty. Cute pretty.

"Well, okay, if I can spare the time," he told her. "The way things are going, this assignment is sprouting like mushrooms."

"Just one condition," Linda insisted. "We don't go to Basta Pasta."

"I *like* Basta Pasta."

"But I want to go to Monroe's."

"On my pay?"

"Ask for a rise. Tell them you won't catch the Fog City Satan unless they pay you another ten thousand a year."

He laughed, and kissed her. Right now, that was just the kind of silliness and affection that he needed.

But as he lay in bed that night, on a dark hill in a dark sea-circled city deadened by fog, he thought he felt an irritation in the palm of his left hand. He squeezed his hand into a fist, but the irritation grew sharper, as if somebody were clawing at the palm of his hand with ragged fingernails.

He reached across and held his hand close to the illuminated dial of his digital alarm-clock. Gray shapes and shadows were passing across his skin, forming blotches and shapes. He gripped his left wrist in his right hand to steady his palm, and stared at the shapes intently. They looked like floating birthmarks; patches and fragments and splatters. An uncanny Rorschach pattern, opening and closing in front of his eyes.

After a while, the shadows began to cling together, like skeins of wool and dust and cobwebs blown across a pale stone floor. Gradually they gathered themselves into the same face that he had seen on his hand in "Alphonson's Cantina". A placid, smiling, self-satisfied face, existing in some time or place that was beyond imagination. It looked almost as if the wind were ruffling his hair, as if there were sunlight behind him.

Time to feed, Larry's hand whispered.

He cupped it against his ear, and listened, like a child listening to a conch shell to hear the sea.

Time to feed, my friend. Time to feed.

He opened his hand; and instantly the briefest of blue-white flames flickered on his naked palm. He thought he could smell something bitter and aromatic; like burned grass. But the smell faded, and the darkness poured back into the room, and all he could hear was Linda's breathing, and the sounds of the night.

Foghorns, sirens. The cries of people with no place to go.

For a moment, he was tempted to wake Linda, and tell her what had happened. But then he rested his head back on the pillow and decided against it. Although he didn't understand why, he had the feeling that it was safer if she were not to know.

4

He met Dogmeat Jones on the corner of Valencia and Sixteenth. It was late morning, still foggy. Dogmeat looked as if he had been sleeping in his clothes. As usual, he was wearing his huge embroidered sheepskin jacket with its filthy matted fur and its clusters of buttons—"Impeach Nixon" and "Suramin Sucks" and "Horse Badorties For Ever." Beneath his jacket, his spindly legs were tightly encased in moth-eaten jeans of maroon velour, and he wore brown cowboy boots whose heels were worn down at such sharp diagonals that he walked bow-legged.

Originally a native of Crete, Illinois, Dogmeat had come to San Francisco in the first blooming of the hippie era and twenty-two years later he had left neither Valencia Street nor 1966. He was well over forty-five now, although his face was strangely boyish, almost angelic, like a brat-pack actor. He wore octagonal pink-lensed Byrds sunglasses and his gray hair was tied in a pony-tail at the back. He knew everything that was going down in the arts and crafts community, and Larry counted him as one of his most productive informants.

"Hungry?" he asked Dogmeat.

"I could sit and admire something Mexican, mon pal," said Dogmeat.

"How about 'La Cumbre'?"

"Nein, nein. The lines are always too long. Let's go to the 'Pancho Villa Taqueria' and entertain some burrito vegetariano with guacamole and whole beans."

"You're the boss."

They squashed into a table at the "Pancho Villa" next to a girl who was talking loudly about her last abortion and smoking something fragrant but illegal. Dogmeat began to get serious with his huge vegetarian lunch while Larry sipped without any appetite or thirst at a cup of strong black coffee. Larry hadn't slept well after that face had reappeared on his hand last night, and he was feeling jagged and frustrated, as if he had a hangover.

"Believe me something very heavy is about to manifest itself," said Dogmeat, with beans and guacamole churning around in his open mouth. "I hear it here, I hear it there. It's like birds, when there's a tremor on the way. Everybody's a-twitter. Everybody's *uneasy*, you know. It's all highly Selassie." Dogmeat had an idiosyncratic habit of using names as adjectives.

"And you think it's something to do with the Fog City Satan?" asked Larry. "What makes you think that?"

"Well, it's more of a rumor than a brass-plated reality," said Dogmeat. "It's more of a *buzz* than a specific warning, if you dig my meaning. More of a thickening sensation in the city's arteries, *n'est-ce pas?* A Muhammad in the alley. More in the way of *extra gravity*. Like there's thunder on the way; but nobody knows from where."

Larry set down his coffee cup. "Tell me," he asked, patiently.

"Two things. Thing the first, you know David Green the artist? He was painting last week when all of a sudden he turns around and sees a face on the window of his loft. A face, like a photographic negative, that's how he described it, like it's not outside looking in or anything, it's *in the glass*. Not only that, it's actually *moving* and staring at him, and he thinks he can hear it *talking*, too. Not just the Gettysburg address, either. It's saying those same words that the Fog City Satan said on the radio. All that shit about the other side and time to feed. Anyway what's the explanation? It may be that David's been overindulging in that new Colombian crack they've been shipping in. He was always a little cavalier with the nose candy. But he swears it's *vrai*; and what's more his lover Tim Terry disappeared the same day, vanished and never came back. Not even a phone call. Not even a *billet doux*. Left his cold cream, his tennis shoes, and his Commes des Garçons evening shirt, the one with the spots. At first David's not too worried. He reckons that a George in the hand is worth two in the Bush. But then he sees the face in the window twice more; once at night, which scares him totally *merde*less, and he goes to stay with Harry and Barry Kuzdenyi on Mission."

Larry said, "What about thing the second?" He did his best to keep his voice steady. *A face, actually moving, and he thinks he can hear it* talking, *too*.

Dogmeat wiped his mouth with the back of his hand and sniffed loudly. "Thing the second is at Hana's Restaurant, right, opposite the Japan center. Michael Leibowitz who is an engraver at the U.S. Mint is having dinner with his cousin from Seattle, Bill Freberg. He's drinking a bowlful of *yose nabe*, when all of a sudden he sees reflected in the soup this face which isn't his. He keeps staring at it but it's somebody else, he doesn't know who, and this face keeps smiling at him. He practically checks in to the Harp Hotel there and then, at table five.

"Anyway his cousin Bill Freberg takes him home and gives him a handful of sleeping-pills and Michael sleeps like he's dead. When he wakes up the next morning, though, Bill's gone; left all of his bags, but disappeared. Michael calls his folks, calls his ex-wife. He calls the cops. Nobody's seen him. And the rumble and the bumble is that this is happening all over. People keep seeing these faces where faces don't have any right to be. And people are disappearing like they're ants disappearing down a crack in the sidewalk."

Larry was tempted to tell Dogmeat what had happened at "Alphonson's Cantina"; but Dogmeat was such a wildfire gossip that by the time it was happy hour at the Cadillac Bar, everybody south of Market would know that even the SFPD were getting jittery about faces appearing where faces didn't have any right to be.

In an odd way, however, he was reassured. If other people had been seeing moving, living, talking faces, then perhaps the shadows on his hand were part of a natural and explicable phenomenon. Maybe it was some kind of hallucination induced by this unnatural August fog. Maybe it was something in the water.

Dogmeat pushed his plate away. "I could die for this stuff," he remarked. "If I didn't give me such bad gas, I'd eat it all the time. I mean, who needs meat? Did you know that they inject cattle with meat tenderizer *before* they kill them? They gravity-feed about a pint of some stuff made out of paw-paws right into their jugular vein. While they're still *alive*, man! Can you imagine the agony? No, you can't imagine the agony. Give me beans, give me beans; at least beans don't feel the perpetual punishment of perverse pain. Who said that? Spiro Agony."

"You want some dessert?" Larry asked him. dryly.

"For sure. As long as it never walked or flew."

Larry beckoned the waitress. Then he asked Dogmeat, "Do you know a woman called Edna-Mae Lickerman? Big woman, dark-haired, smokes little cigars. Runs a pottery store on Vallejo."

"Oh Edna-Mae, oh certainly," said Dogmeat. "Now Edna-Mae used to be something in the good old bad old days. She made wonderful roach pipes and all kinds of far-out stuff. She's not as old as she looks, as a matter of fact, but she had a *malheureuse* marriage and it told on her face. Her old man was Nathan Lickerman. He used to run the Lickerman School of Expressive Dance. It should have been called the Lickerman School for Underage Young Ladies to Get Their Muffs Touched Up by a Foaming Lecher. Nathan spent less and less time at home, and more and more time at the dance studio, adjusting the pantie area of his young ladies' leotards. At first Edna-Mae was heartbroken, then she took a lover to pay the nasty Nathan in his own kroner. Well, several lovers, as a matter of fact, but the grand amour of her middle-age was a guy called Julius Kwolek. He was solid tofu from ear to ear as far as I could make out. I mean, whenever he farted he turned around to see where the noise was coming from. But Edna-Mae was crazy about him. She and Nathan got divorced. A lot of hand-made pottery got thrown—and I don't mean on the wheel, neither. Edna-Mae and Julius planned to get married, but they came up against an insurmountable obstacle which was that Julius died of a massive coronary three weeks before the ceremony. Edna-Mae was never the same after that. She got into tequila and spiritualism and kelp, and believe me those three things can age you even more dramatically than two nights in Cedar Rapids, Iowa. I saw her, what, two or three weeks ago. She usually hangs around at some rundown Mexican joint on Front and Green. She bought me a cerveza. She seemed to have eased off the kelp, stepped up the tequila."

"When you say she got into spiritualism," asked Larry, "was this something she did alone, or with a group?"

"We-e-ell, she did both. She used to tell fortunes. She was good at fortunes. Tealeafery, crystal-ballery, and that. But mainly palms. Palms are great. A good palmist can track your life right down to the last minute, practically; and do you know that there's new scientific research that shows a *provable* correlation between your life expectancy and the lines on your hands. So stare at your hand and tremble, lieutenant. If your lifeline looks in the least bit branchy, you're in deep shit."

That remark was too close to the truth for Larry to laugh. "Tell me about the group stuff," he asked, his voice edged with glass.

Dogmeat said, "I'll have the Cisco Kid Surprise. That's all fruit, of course."

Larry finished the dregs of his coffee and waited. He was suddenly aware that Dogmeat was hedging.

"Do you have a problem with this?" he inquired.

"Maybe *un poco*," said Dogmeat, diffidently.

"Is this something you'd rather tell me in private?"

"I don't know. It all happened a long time ago. But it was all *mucho* unpleasant at the time, *versteh?* This was back in Edna-Mae's headshop days, when the world was young and Grace was Slick. A deeply heavy group of black-magic-type people hit town. They had a secret name that nobody was supposed to know, and everybody said that if you even so much as mentioned that they existed, they'd cut your throat all the way around. There was a lot of deeply heavy mumbo-jumbo going down, I mean you're talking *merde lourde* here. There was talk about Satan-worship, animal sacrifices, stuff like that. That was the time some young woman knelt right down in Union Square in front of the St. Francis Hotel and deliberately got herself beheaded by a cablecar. Edna-Mae was into this group for a while, although she never told me much about it. It all broke up afterward, who knows why, and nobody knew what happened to any of these heavy people afterwards."

"Did Edna-Mae mention any of this stuff recently?" asked Larry.

The waitress brought Dogmeat's Cisco Kid Surprise. He looked at it in disappointment.

"Something wrong, sir?" she asked him.

"It's not particularly *surprising*, is it?" he demanded.

She frowned at it, too. "I don't know. Maybe it would be more surprising if you were expecting something else."

"What do you think the Cisco Kid would have thought of it?"

"I don't know," the girl replied. "I don't even know there

was a Cisco Kid. I thought the dessert was like, you know, a San Francisco surprise for kids."

Dogmeat dug his spoon into the luridly colored fruit. "Thank God Duncan Renaldo can't hear you say that."

Larry watched him as he ate. "Did you ever hear of a spiritualist called Wilbert Fraser? I'm going to pay him a visit tonight, along with my mother."

Dogmeat nodded. "Sure I know Wilbert Fraser. He used to live on Valencia for years, before some adoring widow left him a heap of shekels and he moved to Nob Hill. He's the current guru *non-pareil* of the purple-rinsed seekers after truth, negotiable bearer bonds, and the world beyond the veil. He was all mixed up with Edna-Mae, too, in those days, but don't ask me how."

"Is he any good?" asked Larry.

"Rock back on your heels, but yes. Or so I've heard. I'll tell you who went to him to talk to her dead daughter, and that was—" here he leaned forward, and whispered into Larry's ear the name of a hugely wealthy San Francisco society matron.

"No shit," said Larry.

"No shit," Dogmeat told him. He scraped up the last of his Cisco Kid Surprise. He blew his nose on his crumpled-up paper napkin, and then said, "Well, then, what's all this worth?"

"You mean the buzz and the bumble, the faces in the *yose nabe?*"

Dogmeat sniffed, and nodded happily.

"I don't know," said Larry. "I guess it's worth a burrito vegetariano and a Cisco Kid Surprise."

"Oh, come on, man," Dogmeat protested. "This is highly

precognitive information I'm giving you here. It has to be worth a twenty at least."

"I want to hear more before I pay, okay? Any more faces, any more disappearances, tell me."

"Do you have some kind of personal interest in this?" asked Dogmeat, slyly, his eyes narrowing behind his pink sunglasses.

"Just don't forget to call me, okay?" Larry told him.

"All righty," said Dogmeat. "But next time it's a fifty. Otherwise, a curse on all your horses."

"It's 'houses', not 'horses'," Larry corrected him.

"Well, them too," said Dogmeat.

He returned to the Hall of Justice that afternoon feeling as if he had a hangover, even though he hadn't been drinking. He passed Dan Burroughs' office, room 400, and knocked on the open door. Dan was sitting in a haze of gray cigarette smoke, writing up his monthly report to the Commissioner. His yucca looked as if it were dying of asphyxiation, and the only decoration in his office was a faded color photograph of Dan shaking hands with Karl Malden and a poster for the Studebaker Museum in South Bend, Indiana. Dan had always believed that Humphrey Bogart was the last great American actor and that the Studebaker was the last great American car.

"How's progress?" he asked. "I've promised the Press a statement in time for the six o'clock news."

"Do you want the natural progress or the supernatural progress?"

"What the hell is that supposed to mean?"

Larry went into Dan's office and sat down in front of the desk. "There's something very weird about this investigation, Dan."

"Oh, yeah?" Dan challenged him.

"Did Houston tell you about the Lickerman woman?"

"Sure. But so what? She suffered some exaggerated form of endocrinal collapse, that's all. It's a common symptom of AIDS. The doctors are coming up against new symptoms everyday."

"An endocrinal collapse? In four minutes?"

"Who the hell knows? Leave it to the doctors. All I want you to do is find this guy."

Larry said, "What happened to Edna-Mae Lickerman is a part of what's going down here."

"Houston tells me you've staked out the cantina, in case he comes back?"

"That's right. Bill Glass is out there now."

"And what about the cantina's customers?"

"We've interviewed almost all of the regulars, and we've tracked down nine out of thirteen casual diners who were there Friday evening."

"And?"

"Some of them remember a big guy in a leather jacket making a phone call, most of them don't."

"Any identifications?"

"None so far. Not even close. We've made a particular point of showing them every felon that Joe Berry ever arrested—even if they're still in the slammer."

Dan sucked hard at his cigarette, then crushed it out in a

Goodyear tire ashtray that was already crowded with butts. "Somebody must know this maniac. He must have a lover, or a friend, or a landlord, or an employer."

"We should have an artist's impression ready for six o'clock, if that'll help," Larry told him.

"Okay, good. But I want to see some real cerebral detective-work here, Larry. I've promised Mayor Agnos that this guy won't be allowed to massacre one more Bay area family. Not one more."

"I just hope that's a promise we can keep," said Larry. "Believe me, Dan, there's more to this investigation than meets the eye."

"Like what? Like the incredible shrinking woman? Do me a favor, Larry, I want inspiration, not science-fiction."

"I'll send you up your artist's impression," said Larry, pushing back his chair.

Houston was waiting for Larry in his office. He looked as tired as Larry felt. He had been following up a report by a nosey landlady in the Mission District that her lodger had been behaving suspiciously "burning joss-sticks and chanting and this morning I found a cleaver in his kitchen, just thought you ought to know." Then he had spent two hours interviewing a twitchy young man with a faded Giants T-shirt and glaring red spots who claimed to be the Fog City Satan except that he couldn't remember any of the details of any of his killings, and on the night of the Berry killing he had been baby-sitting for his sister on Presidio Avenue.

"Any word from the hospital?" Larry asked him.

"Not so far," said Houston.

They sat in silence for a moment. Along the corridor, telephones were ringing, and nobody was answering. Out of the window, they could see nothing but gray gloom, and the shapes of familiar buildings made unfamiliar by the fog.

"Think this is ever going to lift?" asked Houston.

Larry shrugged. He picked up a pencil and turned it end over end. From the windowsill, Linda and Frankie and Mikey smiled at him out of a silver photograph frame.

"Where do we go from here?" asked Houston. "It seems like the only way we're ever going to catch this guy is by knocking on every door in the whole Goddamned city. Either that, or lucky accident."

"The cantina's a start," said Larry.

"What if he never goes back there?"

"Then we keep on asking questions and circulating his description and praying that he doesn't do it again."

Houston sat watching Larry for a long time, in silence. Then he said, "You think there's something occult in this case, don't you?"

Larry nodded. "I don't just think it, Houston. I'm convinced of it. You saw my hand. You saw Edna-Mae. Neither of those occurrences was natural or explicable, no matter what Dan thinks about it. And last night it happened again."

He raised his hand, palm flat. "Last night I felt my hand itching, and I saw the shapes moving across it, and I heard the voice whispering, too. And I'm not the only one. I talked to Dogmeat today and he told me that at least three or four other people have experienced a similar kind of phenomenon."

Houston's lower lip protruded. He looked unhappy and serious. "So what are you going to do about it?"

"I'm going to split this investigation into two. On one side, we're going to follow a totally routine and traditional investigation. Thorough, professional, but right by the book. On the other side, we're going to look into the supernatural aspects of it; and we're going to do that just as thoroughly."

"How do you think Dan's going to take to that?"

"Dan isn't going to know about that. Not unless you tell him."

"You don't *believe* that any of this was supernatural, though?" Houston asked him.

"I believe in what I see with my own eyes, Houston, whatever the hell you choose to call it. But the way I feel about this investigation right now is that if we stop at the threshold of what we can't understand, our boy is going to leave us way behind, stuck by our own lack of imagination in reality-land, and there are going to be more families murdered, and maybe a whole lot worse, and we'll never be able to catch him, never."

"Well, lieutenant," said Houston. "If that's what you want to do."

"Houston," Larry replied. "Last night I laid in bed and that face appeared on my hand and it spoke to me."

"Yes, sir."

"Now, do you think I ought to ignore that manifestation, put it down to overwork or too much linguine before bedtime, or do you think I ought to take it into careful consideration as a possible item of evidence?"

Houston looked down at his polished tan Oxford shoes, and then back up again. "I guess you could try to take a video-recording of it, lieutenant, next time it happens. Then maybe it wouldn't be so difficult for other people to believe."

"But you believe it? You saw it for yourself."

"I don't know. I *thought* I saw something, sure. But like you say—overwork, stress. Sometimes you can make yourself believe something just because you want to believe it."

"Houston," said Larry, getting up from his chair and sitting on the edge of his desk, "at least two other people in the city have reported similar incidents." He jotted their names down on his notepad, *David Green, Michael Leibowitz*. "David Green is an artist, he's crashing with the Kuzdcnyi twins. Michael Leibowitz works for the Mint. Go talk to them both. Find out what they think. Then find out what you think."

Houston reluctantly took the piece of paper and left the office. More phones rang. Larry remained seated on the desk after he had gone, thoughtful and more than a little anxious. He knew that Houston was a devotee of the Arne Knudsen school of scientific detective-work; but he wasn't quite sure where Dan Burroughs stood in the middle of this; or how closely Houston was reporting back to him.

The phone rang. Larry scooped it up and said, "Foggia."

"Oh hi," came a bright and cultured voice. "This is Fay Kuhn your favorite newshound. I'm interested in writing a profile on you for Thursday's magazine section. Do you think you could spare me a little time tomorrow morning?"

"Miss Kuhn, I'm right in the middle of a complex and serious homicide investigation."

"You spared an hour for Dogmeat Jones."

"How do you know that?"

"Oh, come on, lieutenant. Even burritos have ears."

"Well—" Larry swung his desk diary around. "I can

spare you fifteen minutes, tomorrow at eleven o'clock. But absolutely no longer. And I may have to cancel at short notice, depending on how the investigation is progressing."

"It *is* progressing, then?" asked Fay Kuhn.

"Ms Kuhn, I'll talk to you tomorrow."

"Thank you, lieutenant. And, lieutenant?"

A patient sigh. "What is it, Ms Kuhn?"

"Lieutenant, have you heard anything about faces appearing where faces oughtn't to be?"

Larry massaged the back of his neck. Stress, he could feel it. His muscles were tensed like ropes. He might have known that Dogmeat would gossip to the Press. He should have paid him the twenty. It wasn't worth compromising a complicated and critical investigation like this for the price of a couple of bottles of cheap wine.

"Ms Kuhn, what do you mean by faces appearing where faces oughtn't to be?"

"You tell me, lieutenant. Faces in windows, faces in Japanese soup. Maybe San Francisco is entering into a new era of magical weirdness."

"Maybe Dogmeat Jones isn't playing with a full deck."

"Maybe Dr. Howard Kaplan can't find out what happened to Mrs. Edna-Mae Lickerman."

"Well, well," Larry admitted. "You're good. I'll grant you that. But I won't grant you an interview tomorrow morning unless you keep all of this stuff to yourself, at least for now."

"What's Dan Burroughs going to tell us tonight?" asked Fay Kuhn.

"You can hear it along with everybody else. But if I were you, I'd leave some space open for a picture."

"Thank you, lieutenant. See you tomorrow. And by the way, our editorial secretary thinks you're cute."

Larry hung up. He waited for a long moment, then he picked up the phone again. It rang and rang for almost a minute, and then a laconic voice said, "Guido's Bar."

"I've got a message for Dogmeat," said Larry. "Tell him his benefactor called."

"Benny who?"

"His ben-e-factor, what are you, Chinese or something?"

"As a matter of fact, yes."

"I'm sorry," said Larry, "That was wrong of me."

"Don't worry about it," the laconic voice replied. "It takes all sorts. Hell—at least I'm not a Jap."

Larry said, "Could you tell Dogmeat his benefactor called him. Tell him his benefactor said that he's dogmeat."

There was a pause. Then, "Tell Dogmeat that he's dogmeat?"

"You got it," said Larry, and put down the phone.

He called for his mother at eight o'clock. The fog was beginning to clear, but the city still looked blurred at the edges, as if he were looking at them through steam-fogged spectacles. His mother wore a black Chanel summer coat and her hair was fastened back with a diamond-studded Chanel clip. She looked elegant and handsome and he was proud to take her out. He just wished they were going to the Washington Square Bar & Grill for dinner, instead of Wilbert Fraser's, for a conversation with dead people.

She had trouble climbing into his Toyota. "Your father

would never have bought a Japanese car," she complained. "For him, it was a Lincoln Town Car or nothing."

"My father wasn't a cop."

"God forbid he should have been."

They drove slowly to Wilbert Fraser's house. The fog lay thickly in the dips but the hilltops were almost clear. For the first time in days, Larry could see Coit Tower. For some reason, he had always felt reassured by the sight of Coit Tower. It was a reference point in his life; from the days when he was small and had watched its high lonesome light from his bedroom window to the days when he had dropped out and tuned in and believed that the only family was the family of peace, love and good grass.

He could still recite Gregory Corso's *Ode To Coit Tower* which had been his own particular psalm of rebellion.

"*O anti-verdurous phallic were't not for your pouring height looming in tears like a sick tree or your ever-gaudy comfort jabbing your city's much-wrinkled sky you'd seem an absurd Babel squatting before millions.*

"*Ah tower tower that I felt sad for Alcatraz and not for your heroes lessened not the tourist love of my eyes.*"

These days he wondered how he had managed to understand what any of that poetry meant. Had it meant anything? He had believed in those days that he had understood it. Maybe even Gregory Corso hadn't understood it.

In any case, those hippie days had faded like the sunshine had faded, and Larry had been left at the age of eighteen with the choice of returning to the bosom of his traditional and prosperous family—standing short-haired and respectful and dark-suited at his father's elbow at charity dinners, shaking hands with the Ben Swigs and the Louis Luries and the Mrs. Hans Klussmanns of this world—or of doing something else rebellious and different.

Eleonora said, "You don't have to drive too fast, my darling. Better to be late in this world than early in the next."

"Seems like tonight we've got the choice of both."

"You won't mock Mr. Fraser, will you? He's very sensitive to any kind of skepticism."

"Who said anything about skepticism?"

Eleonora directed him to a large Victorian frame house on Jackson; a shabby survivor of the great earthquake of 1906 and of countless lesser disasters since, not the least of which appeared to be its sale to Wilbert Fraser. Its shingles had slipped, the paint on its shutters was flaking like eczema, and its front yard was nothing but a pale tangle of thistles. Its front porch was heaped up with dry and flowerless wisteria, as if it were wearing a saucy but decayed toupee.

"Wilbert isn't rich," said Eleonora, as if that explained everything.

Larry cramped the front tires and locked the car. Then he followed his mother up the front steps with a sense of increasing reluctance. He had walked into the back room of a Chinese restaurant once, looking for an iced-out killer called Henry Kwo, and he had felt the same sense of reluctance then, terrible reluctance, as if a small child had seized hold of his ankles and he had to drag him across the floor with every step. The only difference was that when he was looking for Henry Kwo, he was able to draw his .38, and dodge from doorway to doorway. He wouldn't be able to do that here, at Wilbert Fraser's.

The front door opened before they reached it. There was a bright plain-glass lantern shining high up in the hallway ceiling, so that it was difficult for Larry to see anything of Wilbert Fraser but shadows. He could make out silvery greased-back hair, however, and a large loose-fitting sweater, and large-lensed designer eyeglasses.

"Mrs. Foggia, you don't know how good it is to see you again," he crooned, holding out his hand. Larry caught the quick needle-sharp twinkle of diamond rings. "And who have you brought along with you tonight? This can't be your son! I don't believe it!"

Larry grasped Wilbert's hand. It was like taking hold of a bunch of tepid, slippery, overcooked asparagus. "I'm Larry, how do you do," he told him. "Actually my mother is as young as she looks. It's just that I'm, well, very mature for my age."

"How do *you* do, I'm sure," said Wilbert. "You'd better come on in. It's still so foggy and my bronchitis, you know. Once I've caught it I wheeze for weeks."

"How many are you expecting tonight?" asked Eleonora clearly, as they stepped into the narrow hallway. "Mrs. Sheraton Jardiner isn't coming, is she?"

"She was going to, poor dear, but she had to cry off," said Wilbert, leading the way into the huge high-ceilinged sitting-room. "Mr. Jardiner had a climbing accident up at Yosemite. He went there with his secretary instead of her!"

"You're such a gossip, Wilbert," Eleonora told him; although it was clear to Larry from the apple-tart expression on his mother's face that she adored gossip; especially about those San Francisco society women who now looked down on her because her husband was long dead and his fortune had dwindled. There had been a time when all the Foggias were big time, don't talk about Ghirardellis or de Domenicos.

The sitting-room was relentlessly decorated in brown. Brown velour armchairs, brown velour couches, brown floral wallpaper, brown pictures, brown rugs, brown cushions. It had once been grand but it takes money to stay grand and now the velour was motheaten and the rugs had worn down to gray string patches. There was a smell of Safeway lavender room spray and Black Flag.

Five people had already arrived. Two of them Larry recognized immediately as friends of his mother's. A balding bespectacled man of sixty-six with the blueish complexion of a chronic angina sufferer. This was Bembridge "Bembo" Caldwell, who had once worked for Gene Autry as business manager for the Mark Hopkins Hotel, and who had overseen its decline in the mid-1950s into chronic Autryesque tackiness, with painted stallions on the walls, and the hideous slogan "Where Friends Get Together". A tall fortyish woman with an English accent, fraying ginger hair, and a wild cast in her eyes. This was Samantha Bacon, whose dazzling film career in the Swinging Sixties had taken her from London to Hollywood; and then from Hollywood to nowhere at all; and from nowhere at all to San Francisco, where she had been rescued from vodka and cigarettes and barbiturates by a kindly old man who owned a chain of delis and who had been almost unhealthily obsessed with her first picture.

Larry shook hands and tried to keep smiling. For some reason, he felt anxious and irritable, and the backs of his hands started to itch as if he had spent all afternoon tearing down poison ivy. The house seemed exceptionally stuffy and closed-in. Even though he could see that two of the living-room windows were half-open, no air seemed to penetrate, no drafts blew. The discolored net curtains with their patterns of birds and flowers hung motionless; shrouds; washing. Yet he could hear the noises of the street.

"Larry, it's been ages," said Samantha. She wore a red satin dress with flouncy sleeves that clashed with her hair. Her eyes clashed with everything.

Larry kissed her cheek. "How're you doing, Sammy?" he asked her.

"Do you know anyone in Traffic?" she said.

He smiled. "How many tickets do you have?"

"About a thousand. I'm not asking them to let me off: I just want time to catch up."

Larry laid a hand on her pale freckled shoulder. There were some women he liked to touch and some women he didn't. Samantha had always felt too chilly; as if her body had recently been trawled from the Bay.

"You can introduce me here," he suggested.

"Oh well surely," she gushed. "This is John Forth, he's an architect." Larry shook hands with a small evasive-eyed man of thirtysomething, with a bifurcated Karl Malden nose and no chin. "John redesigned the Garden Court at the Sheraton-Palace, but of course the city declared it an historical landmark and so they had to shelve his remodeling *ad infinitum*. I mean for ever."

"Hey, bad luck," said Larry. "But I always liked the

Garden Court, so, you know, maybe it all worked out for the best."

He was sure that he could hear John Forth grinding his teeth together, out loud. He was sensitive to things like that. He was also sensitive to the fact that Samantha had called the Palace the Sheraton-Palace. Born-and-bred San Franciscans still resented the takeover, even today, and called the hotel by its proper name.

A thin bustless woman in a very low-cut poppy-print dress came across the room and showed Larry her pearls and her horsey teeth. "Margot Tryall," she announced. "My father and your father used to play golf together."

"Oh, yes," said Larry, "Jack Tryall. How is he these days? How's the yacht business?"

"The yacht business is booming, thank you," Margot Tryall lisped. "But I'm afraid my father left us in January."

"He left you?" asked Larry, unsure what she meant.

"Yes, he—" and here she raised her eyes upward. Larry looked up, too, until he realized that Jack Tryall had gone even higher than the molded Victorian ceiling. Margot said, "That's why I'm here."

"Margot had quite a conversation with her father the last time we met," Eleonora explained. "They talked about all kinds of things. Yacht races, cocktail parties, how to trim the bushes."

"Good deal," said Larry, apprehensively.

The last guest was a man in his early forties; well built, obviously athletic; with hair that was partly gray and partly bleached by the sun. He had a self-confident idiot smile that Larry particularly disliked. He was the kind of guy who would football-tackle a plainclothes detective in the middle of making a bust because he mistook him for an armed mugger.

"Dick Volare," he said, grasping Larry's hand. "Understand we share some of the old Neapolitan blood. Hah, *gumba*?"

"How are you, Dick?" Larry asked him.

"Oh… business couldn't be better. I'm in oceanfront real-estate, that's me. Volare Views, Inc., maybe you've heard about us. You want to see the sea? Come down to Volare Views. We can fit you up good."

Larry nodded and smiled. "Usually, if I want to see the sea, I go down to the beach. But whatever."

Wilbert Fraser clapped his hands for silence. In the stark light of the living-room, Larry could see him clearly for the first time. He had a big fleshy nose, perforated with large pores; a sloped-back forehead, and hair combed straight back in that 1939 style that was universally favored by Poles and Rumanians and Czechs. His skin was age-speckled, the pale color of liverwurst casing, his lips were purplish and thick. But his eyes glittered like the diamonds on his fingers. In spite of his skepticism about seances, Larry felt that he was in the presence of somebody whose knowledge extended beyond reality, beyond things that you could touch and feel and squeeze and clap into handcuffs.

"I'd like to thank you all for coming tonight," said Wilbert Fraser, a little breathily. "Particularly those of you who have never been here before; and for whom this meeting will be their first adventure into the hallways of the spirit world." He turned toward Larry, and nodded, and Larry gave him a small wry smile in return.

"Unlike other spiritual mediums, I prefer not to use a

table," Wilbert Fraser explained. "I always believe that we should stand facing each other, open and unencumbered. Some of my more successful forays into the spirit world have been carried out when all of my guests were completely nude; but—" seeing the sudden alarm on Margot Tryall's face "—the way you are all dressed tonight, in your everyday clothes, simple and unpretentious, that's good, that will suffice."

He closed his eyes for a long moment—so long that Larry began to wonder if he had fallen asleep on his feet. But at length he opened them again, and nodded to each of them in turn, and then raised both his hands, palms outwards, and smiled.

"Don't you usually hold hands?" asked Larry.

Wilbert Fraser shook his head. "The mediums who insist that you all hold hands are doing so simply for their own safety. The power of the spiritual world is such that they are unable to control it at full strength—so they suppress it by with the mental and physical resistance of several human bodies linked together. It works in exactly the same way as an electrical resistor."

"But you prefer to work with the undiluted stuff, is that it?" Larry put in.

"Quite right," said Wilbert Fraser. "For me, there is nothing like dealing with the full, raw energy of the world beyond without any kind of muffling or suppression. You could say that I like to grasp the bare wires of the supernatural. That way, I can give you an experience of the spiritual world that you will never forget—not even when your life is over, and you yourself have joined those spirits in the hallway beyond."

"Wilbert, shall we be getting on with it, dear?" Eleonora suggested.

"Of course," Wilbert acknowledged. "I was simply trying to explain to your son that tonight I will be able to show him the supernatural with a clarity that no other medium in California can match."

"I've already told him how good you are, my dear," Eleonora interrupted.

"Well, since you have been so complimentary, you should be the one to start our adventure," Wilbert Fraser smiled. "I suppose you wish to see your husband again?"

Larry gave his mother a quick, concerned glance. He had realized, of course, that his mother came to Wilbert Fraser in order to get in touch with his father, but it hadn't occurred to him when he came out tonight that he might actually see his father for himself. The idea of it made the back of his neck turn cold with apprehension, and he could feel his wrists tingling—the same feeling that he had whenever he knew that he was going to see a particularly nasty dead body.

For some reason, he experienced an instantaneous mental flash of the time that he had forced open the trunk of a bronze Buick Riviera that had been abandoned in the darkest drippiest corner of an underground parking-lot for a month and a half until somebody complained about the stench. The trunk lid had groaned, and then crashed upward, revealing a trunk that was filled with pale green slimy balloons, and two eyes that swam amongst these balloons like lost oysters. The smell had been so bad that Larry had felt as if he were still breathing it and tasting it a week later.

Eleonora was intent on Wilbert Fraser when Larry first looked at her, but then she turned and smiled at him and caught his look of anxiety.

"Wilbert, dear, let's do Margot first, shall we? Larry's never been to a seance before... it might help him to accept his father more easily if he knows what to expect."

"Of course," Wilbert agreed. "We don't want anybody upset now, do we?"

He ushered them all into a circle in the center of the living-room. Before he joined them, he switched off all the lights except for a gloomy fringed standard-lamp in the corner next to the curtains. He gave a quick look around to make sure that the arrangement of the room was satisfactory—then he lifted his hands as before, palms outwards, and all of them did the same. Larry felt like a criminal putting up his hands at the point of a gun, until Wilbert said, "No, Larry, no. You're not under arrest. You must stretch your hands, push them against the weight of the cosmos."

"Push them against the what?" asked Larry.

"The cosmos, the weight of the world. Here—pretend that you're a mime, like Marcel Marceau, pushing the palms of his hands against an imaginary sheet of glass. *Push*, that's right; until you can feel the cosmos pushing back."

To be truthful, Larry couldn't feel anything pushing back, but he stretched the palms of his hands and pretended to be Marcel Marceau pressing his hands against a window, and that wasn't especially difficult. He looked at Eleonora and wondered if he ought to smile at her. Maybe there was some kind of special etiquette at seances, like nobody smiled. Margot Tryall sure looked serious; and Dick Volare of Volare Views, Inc., looked as if he had eaten some bad fish for lunch. Not the time or the place for cracking the joke about the clairvoyant who punched his friend for going to bed with his wife next Saturday.

"Very well," said Wilbert Fraser. "We will look first for Margot's father, Mr. Jack Tryall. Margot... would you care to step into the center, so that we can locate him for you?"

Quivering with pleasure, Margot Tryall stepped forward into the middle of their circle, and they arranged themselves so that they were standing around her at evenly spaced intervals, their hands still raised.

Wilbert Fraser lifted his eyes to the ceiling, and said, quite conversationally. "I'm looking for somebody who can help me to find Jack Tryall. I have his daughter Margot here with me tonight, and she's real keen to chat with him some more."

This didn't sound like seance-talk to Larry. He had expected the air to be heavy with incense, and Wilbert Fraser to recite mysterious and ancient litanies which would arouse the dead from their sleep on the other side. Well—even if he hadn't expected *that*, he had at least expected something a little more formal, something with a bit of *ritual* in it. Not this "howdy, anybody home?" kind of stuff. He began to feel increasingly skeptical and increasingly idiotic. He was glad that nobody downtown could see him like this, with his arms up, playing pat-a-cake with the cosmos.

Wilbert Fraser repeated, "I'm looking for somebody who can help me to find Jack Tryall. Is anybody willing to help?" He sounded as matter-of-fact as if he were calling the gas company on the telephone.

Larry cleared his throat. Already his arms were starting

to creak with the effort of holding them up for so long, and he promised himself that he would never again make prisoners stand for twenty or thirty minutes with their hands in the air.

He cleared his throat.

"Still looking for somebody to help me find Jack Tryall," Wilbert Fraser intoned. "Still looking for somebody to help me find Jack Tryall."

Suddenly, Jack thought he glimpsed a haze of blueish light, dancing around Wilbert Fraser's forehead like a crown, and then dwindling and vanishing. He kept his eye closely on Wilbert Fraser now, watching for the slightest sign that it would happen again.

"I can hear you," said Wilbert Fraser. "I can hear you very faintly. You sound like you're talking down the end of a cardboard tube." The blueish light flickered again, so quickly and so faintly that Larry almost missed it. Now he was sure that Wilbert Fraser wasn't talking to *them* any more, but somebody only he could see. There was a soft rustling sound somewhere behind Larry's back—soft, soft rustling in the shadows in the very darkest corner of the room. Soft as silk, soft as breathing, as if somebody small were creeping on silk stockings, playing hide-and-go-seek. Larry wanted to turn around to see who it was, but his mother widened her eyes and gave him a quick, severe shake of her head.

"I can hear you," said Wilbert Fraser, "but not too distinctly, I'm afraid. You are a young one, yes? You are just a child. Maybe you should find us a grown-up to take us to Jack Tryall."

The rustling behind Larry's back appeared to hesitate for a few moments. But then the blueish light around Wilbert Fraser's forehead began to brighten and dance even more excitedly, so bright that it reflected blue diamond points in his eyes, and gave his face a blue-white pallor, as if he were as dead as the souls that he was summoning.

"You're going to have to speak louder, dearest," Wilbert Fraser coaxed his spirit. "You're going to have to show yourself."

It took all of Larry's self-discipline not to turn around. Because behind him he could hear renewed whispering and rustling, and a singing magnetic coldness, as if somebody had opened a door to a refrigerated meat-store. He stared at his mother but his mother seemed quite calm, quite passive, and unafraid. Margot Tryall was standing in the center of their circle, her head thrown back, her eyes closed, her hands raised like all of the rest of them, but now her fists were tightly clenched. Dick Volare had his head bowed so that it was impossible for Larry to see his face, but he could tell by the creases on his cheeks that his teeth were gritted in a masklike grimace. Bembridge Caldwell's eyes were closed, and he was whispering something to himself. He was standing closest to Wilbert Fraser, so his face too was suffused in deathly blue; as if he hadn't looked sick enough already. Samantha Bacon was staring fixedly at Larry, her wide-apart eyes apparently unfocused. At least Larry *thought* that she was staring at him. She could have been staring over his shoulder, at what she could see behind him.

"Come on, dearest, you're going to have to show yourself," Wilbert Fraser coaxed his little spirit. "You won't be able to help us find the fellow we want unless you point out the way."

Larry heard more rustling. Then a sound like nothing he had ever heard in his life before. A sound like somebody breathing down the longest tunnel that he could imagine; somebody breathing closer and closer with every breath; yet still so very far away.

It gave him a chill of infinite fear, and he knew that he was going to have to look around.

But Wilbert Fraser hissed, "*Larry! Whatever you do, don't turn around!*"

"What?" asked Larry, bewildered.

"*Don't turn around! You'll upset the balance! You'll see her soon enough—yes, and your father, too!*"

The breathing grew quicker. Quick, quick, quick. The rustling changed to a pattering, and the pattering grew faster and closer, too, like somebody running in ballet-slippers. "*Faster, my dearest, faster!*" Wilbert Fraser urged her. "We're waiting for you here, in the real, real world! *Faster, my little darling!*"

The blue light around his forehead grew brighter, illuminating his face in grotesque and shadowy relief, like a death-mask. The light was almost dazzling now, like the sun through a winter fog, and Larry would have shielded his eyes with his hand if he hadn't been terrified of upsetting Wilbert Fraser's precious "balance".

Without warning, the blue light suddenly branched out, flickering from one outstretched hand to the other, hesitating, then abruptly jumping, until all of their hands were joined together by a twitching, hazy rope of intense energy.

"*Come on, sugar, come on, my little sugar*!" Wilbert Fraser urged her, although his voice wasn't much more than a harsh whispering slur.

Larry listened intently. He couldn't hear anything now, although he could still the coldness, he could still feel the draft touching his back. Then, in a rush of ice-cold air and taffeta, a small girl of about eleven brushed past Larry's elbow, actually nudging him, her taffeta actually scratching the back of his hand. She frightened him so much that he blurted out "*Ah*!" and took an involuntary step back.

Unless she had been hiding in the curtains, or had climbed through the window, there was no way that she have crept into the room while Larry was standing in the circle, and pushed past him without him knowing that she was coming. Larry had a sixth sense about people coming up behind him. He could feel their aura. He could feel the molecules of air that surged ahead of them as they approached. But this little child had come close enough to stick him in the ribs with a 90-cent kitchen knife, and he hadn't even felt a whisper.

"Don't be alarmed," Wilbert Fraser warned him. "Everything's fine. This little girl is going to do her best to guide us to Jack Tryall. Remember, it's not easy. It's not easy for you and it's not easy for her. Believe me, there isn't any pain worse than the pain of being dead, and separated from the people you love, and *knowing* you're dead."

Larry stared wide-eyed at the little girl's back. She had entered the circle and was standing facing Margot Tryall. Margot still had her head thrown back and her eyes closed and her fists tightly clenched; and it looked almost as if the little girl were *willing* her to open her eyes and take notice of her.

Larry couldn't yet see the little girl's face, but her dark wavy hair was twisted into braids, and she wore a bow on each side, over her ears. She wore a white taffeta party-frock, and white ankle-socks, and shiny white silk slippers.

Although there was no wind in the room, no draft, her hair waved and her party-frock ruffled, and Larry was conscious of a soft echoing screaming sound; the kind of sound you hear in subway tunnels, distorted, breathy, weird; a sound that could be distant voices or distant trains, or simply the wind blowing from one underground chamber to another.

"Hallo, sweetness," said Wilbert Fraser, apparently unafraid. "What's your name, hunh? Are you going to help us to find this lady's father?"

The little girl said something indistinct. Wilbert Fraser leaned forward, his hands still raised, and repeated, "Are you going to help us find this lady's father? Jack Tryall, that's his name. Are you going to show us where he is?"

"Dead," said the girl, in an odd hollow voice that gave Larry that neck-prickling feeling again. It sounded like someone speaking with their mouth pressed against an empty mug.

"Well, sure, sweetness, we know he's passed over, that's why we want to talk to him. We want to comfort him, see, let him know that he's not forgotten."

"He's dead," the girl repeated.

Wilbert Fraser stood up straight again, and looked at the little girl with an expression that was decidedly testy.

Larry was beginning to wonder if this spirit-manifestation were a clever hoax. Maybe this girl was Wilbert Fraser's niece, or a pupil from one of San Francisco's dozens of acting schools. Maybe the chill that he could feel behind him was nothing more supernatural than air-conditioning, turned right down. He couldn't explain the blueish light that still flickered from one outspread hand to the other; but maybe there was a simple scientific explanation for that, too. Maybe it was static electricity, created by some kind of Van der Graaf generator.

At this moment, the little girl turned around and stared at him, straight at him. In spite of everything, he shivered. She was probably a hoax, probably a child actress. But supposing she wasn't? Supposing she were really dead, and this was her spirit?

She had a plain, spoiled face with piggy little brown eyes and freckles, and a small mouth, small as a stab-wound in a week-dead belly. She sure didn't *look* like a spirit. She looked like any one of dozens of brats who sit sulking at theatrical auditions while their mothers endlessly fuss and braid their hair and carp about the opposition.

For a moment, Larry thought that the little girl was going to say something, but then she turned her back again. As she did so, Margot Tryall opened her eyes at last and looked at her.

"Are you my spirit guide?" asked Margot, in an awed whisper.

The girl nodded.

"Sweetness, you must show this lady where her father is," Wilbert Fraser insisted. "Do you understand that? You don't have to speak. All you have to do is nod once for yes and twice for no."

We could have done with a table, thought Larry. Knocking is a whole lot more decisive than nodding.

The girl lifted one hand and pressed it flat against the palm of Margot's hand. The room seemed to grow gloomier and colder, and the hazy blue light that connected the hands of everybody standing around begin to dim, and dance more epileptically, like a fluorescent tube about to flicker out.

Larry had a feeling of closely compressed anxiety. He turned to Eleonora again, but again Eleonora shook her head. *Don't upset the balance*, her expression told him. *Wait until you've seen before you say you don't believe.*

"We want you to take this lady to talk to her father," Wilbert Fraser repeated. "Do you understand that, my little sweetheart? One nod will do it. Just give me one nod."

The little girl hesitated, then nodded. Wilbert Fraser beamed in relief. "They all agree to do it in the end," he said, more to the little girl than to anybody else. "It's just that some are a *tad* more awkward about it than others."

Margot whispered, "Little girl, little girl. What's your name, little girl?"

"Roberta Snow," the girl replied.

Margot smiled with benign delight at everybody in the room. "Roberta, what a pretty name! I had a cousin Roberta! Roberta Somerville! She died when she was about your age, too! Maybe you've met her!"

"Come on, now, Margot, we may not have too much time," Wilbert Fraser interrupted. "We have to find your father."

The little girl stood still and silent for a moment. Then she lisped, "He's dead. Your father's dead."

"I know he's dead," Margot nodded, sadly. "That's why I want to talk to him. Can you find him for me?"

It was then that the room grew darker still, and the air felt as if it were quivering like a freshly scraped violin-string. Larry could hardly make out anything in the darkness, except for the little girl's wind-ruffled taffeta party-frock, and Margot Tryall's pale face, and Wilbert Fraser's diamond-glittering eyes.

He had the most unearthly sensation that, instead of standing in Wilbert Fraser's living-room, they were standing in a cathedral. He looked up, and he could see vaulted cathedral arches, and tall windows of blood-colored glass. He could hear the high-pitched singing of a choir, and the deep reverberation of a pipe-organ. He could feel the chill of the marble flooring; and all around him stone saints stood with eyes that were dead and hands that were frozen in gestures of love and compassion and holy censure.

Yet he could still just as clearly see Wilbert Fraser's living-room, and his mother, and Samantha Bacon, and Dick Volare, and Bembridge Caldwell. It was like standing in two places at the same time, one experience overlapping the other.

Hologram, he thought. *Just about the most technically flawless hologram that I've ever seen.*

He turned his head around to see if he could discover where the projector was hidden.

At that instant, the little girl Roberta whipped her head around and glared at him with unmitigated ferocity. "*You!*" she hissed, in a voice as cold as a snake.

"Larry!" Wilbert Fraser appealed. "Don't turn around! Don't upset the balance!"

The blue light suddenly flared and crackled; and blue sparks showered down from everybody's hands. Larry didn't know whether he was standing in a cathedral or a living-room. The floor was covered with a crimson-patterned rug, but at the same it was marble. Their voices were muffled by curtains, and yet they seemed to echo, too. The assault on his senses was like the effects of an earth tremor—when you look for stability and reassurance in the very walls and floors that are swaying and betraying you.

For one split-second he thought: *You're being tricked here, Larry. They've found a way to disorient you so wildly that you'll believe anything and everything.*

He thought: *Grab the little girl. This so-called "Roberta Snow". Then everybody will see for sure that this is a hoax.*

"Come on, little girl, my dearest little one, we have to hurry," Wilbert Fraser urged her. "We have other people to talk to tonight. Hurry."

"Just a minute, Mr. Fraser," said Larry. His voice sounded as if he had a pillow pressed across his mouth—so blurred that he wondered if anybody else had heard it. He took a single step forward and held out his hand toward the little girl.

The little girl turned her head and glared at him again. "*Keep away!*" she spat at him. He was about to snatch at her arm, but then something happened to her face, and he stopped in alarm.

Her hair unbraided itself and rose slowly into the air, waving as if she were lying back in a pool. Her face grew pale, with a faint greenish tinge, and her cheeks and her eyes puffed up. Still she continued to stare at him with hostility and resentment, although the pupils of her eyes milked over, like a boiled fish lying on a plate.

Wilbert Fraser said, "Larry! Please, back off! You don't know what damage you can do!"

Larry didn't know what to say; didn't know what to do. But from the swollen transformation of the girl's face, and the way in which her hair was slowly waving in the air, he was convinced now that he wasn't looking at a hologram. He was convinced now that what he was experiencing was real—even if it wasn't exactly what Wilbert Fraser was claiming it to be.

"Come on, sweetness," Wilbert Fraser murmured to the little girl. "Everything's fine; everything's dandy. Nobody's going to touch you. Nobody's going to hurt you. We're all your friends."

There was a moment of excruciating tension. Looking across at his mother, Larry saw that her eyes were wide with fear, and that her neck was tautened into sinews. Margot Tryall was quivering, breathing in shallow gasps. Bembridge Caldwell was grayer than ever, and sweating.

"Come on, sweetness," said Wilbert Fraser.

The little girl screamed. A high gargling scream that could have shattered glass. As she did so, thick green water gushed out of her nose and mouth, gallons of it, and splashed on to the rug. She stood gagging, choking, with tendrils of slimy weed hanging out of her nostrils.

Wilbert Fraser said, "Come on, sweetheart," and reached out his hand. But the little girl twisted away and pushed her way out of the circle. Larry turned to see which way she would go, but she ran directly toward the main window.

"For Christ's sake, stop her!" he shouted. "She's going to ju—"

He stopped; stunned. The little girl ran toward the window, her own reflection rushing toward her in the night-darkened glass. She took one slippered step on the brown sofa in front of the window, and threw herself into the window, her arms spread wide, her head thrown back. And vanished.

There was a long silence, punctuated only by the steady dripping of water. Larry was the first to walk toward the window and touch it with his hand. Cold, unbroken glass. Outside, nothing but the fog, and the night, and a drop so far to Wilbert Fraser's front yard that nobody, not even an acrobat, could have survived it without breaking a leg.

Larry turned back and stared at Wilbert Fraser and the rest of the guests.

"She disappeared," he said. "Did you see that? She jumped into the window and she disappeared."

Wilbert Fraser dryly rubbed his hands together. "Larry... I told you before we started that we were going to be dealing with the full undiluted energy of the world beyond."

On a sudden thought, Larry went back to the window, and tried to open it. Maybe Wilbert Fraser had worked out a way of opening and closing it so fast that you wouldn't realize what had happened. But it was a heavy Victorian sash window, and its frame had been distorted by years of earth-slips and settling, and what was more, it was stuck with cream-colored paint. He heaved at its two brass handles, but he couldn't budge it.

"Larry, darling," Eleonora pleaded. Her face was white. "I know that it's hard to accept the spirits, the first time you see them."

Larry returned to the circle. He pointed to the water on

the floor. "How did you do that?" he asked Wilbert Fraser, bluntly.

Wilbert Fraser said, "The little girl was drowned. When you challenged her reality, she had no choice but to show you that she was truly dead. You must remember that the spirits are very traumatized by what has happened to them. They are mostly very vulnerable. Especially the children."

Margot Tryall had tears in her eyes. "I could have seen my father, Larry," she told him. "Roberta could have taken me to see my father."

"Well, I'm sorry I spoiled things," said Larry. "Sorry for being so skeptical, you know. I'm embarrassed. It just looked to me like hocus-pocus."

"Do you want to make a search for hidden projectors and microphones and dry-ice machines?" asked Wilbert Fraser, sharply. "I really don't mind if you do."

"It's all right, forget it, I'm sorry," Larry told him. He was still hyperventilating from the experience of seeing the young girl. "I guess I suffer from Detective's Disease. I can't take anything on face value, even when it's right in front of my nose."

"Well, you're not the only one," Wilbert Fraser replied, a little more charitably this time. "I just hope I've managed to convince you that the other side is a reality."

Larry nodded. "I'm convinced, believe me."

But Dick Volare was seething that Larry had brought the seance to such an abrupt end. "Oh, at last you're convinced? I thought we Neapolitans had some imagination, you know? A little trust, a little faith. You can believe in the Holy Mother, right, and the Immaculate What's-it's-Name, and you can't believe in this? Let me tell you something, Larry, I'm glad I haven't been wrongfully charged with some felony or other, lieutenant, the amount of evidence that it takes to convince *you* of anything."

"That poor little girl," whispered Samantha Bacon. "She reminded me of me, you know, when I was young."

Bembridge Caldwell was too busy coughing phlegm into his handkerchief to say anything. John Forth kept breathing tight little breaths. He was obviously in minor shock.

"Well, there's no point in us continuing now," said Wilbert Fraser. "The spirit-world is far too unsettled. We might accidentally stir up a spirit that can do us more harm than good."

Larry frowned. "What kind of spirit would want to do us harm?"

Wilbert Fraser gave him a quick, dismissive glance. "Oh, there are many, Larry. Too many to mention."

"But what harm could a spirit actually do?"

"Plenty, I assure you. But let's not dwell on that."

"But spirits aren't flesh-and-blood, are they? If they don't have any material substance, how can they hurt us?"

Wilbert Fraser seemed reluctant to answer. Margot Tryall asked, "Couldn't we please have one more try at talking to my father? Just one more?"

"No," Wilbert Fraser told her. "When the spirits are unsettled, it can be quite dangerous to call on them again. Larry has asked why, and I suppose I ought to tell him. It's because many of them are capable of taking on actual physical shape, actual human substance. They do it in several ways. They can borrow or steal substance from the living. You've heard about ectoplasm, I expect? That's when a spirit borrows flesh from a living person—usually a medium—in order to make a physical appearance. The spirit literally grows out of the medium's body... sometimes no more than a head, occasionally an entire figure. You have to be very careful not to harm these manifestations, because they're made out of *you* if you hurt them you'll only be hurting yourself. There are dozens of authenticated photographs of ectoplasmic appearances. There was one in London in 1878, when the famous medium William Eglington produced the materialization of an Arab out of his own stomach. There was another in Lisbon at the end of the First World War, when there was a very frightening materialization of a subhuman-looking nun."

"But that little girl didn't grow out of any of us, did she? She just walked in."

"She was nothing but a ghost, Mr. Foggia. The sharply evoked memory of a tragic young child. She had no more substance than an actress on a movie screen."

"I'm sure I felt her dress."

Wilbert Fraser smiled and shook his head. "You felt what you expected to feel. There was nothing there. Nothing material, anyway."

"You said something about spirits *stealing* substance."

"Well... we don't want to talk about things like that," said Wilbert Fraser, looking around the circle and chafing his hands together. "I think we've all had quite enough excitement for one evening. A very clear manifestation... even though it came to such a sudden end."

"Please, tell me how spirits steal substance," said Larry.

Wilbert Fraser looked uneasy. "It's very rare," he replied. "And I'd be deeply upset if I deterred anybody here this evening from trying to communicate with those they love. But, yes, one does occasionally come across spirits who steal human substance."

"How do they do that?"

"They literally feed on the essence of the soul. They feed on your flesh, your blood, and worst of all they feed on your personality."

"And what would happen to you, if you fell victim to one of these characters?"

Wilbert Fraser tried unsuccessfully to smile. "You would most probably die."

"What if you didn't?"

"I really don't know. I never heard of anybody meeting a truly voracious spirit and surviving the experience."

John Forth put in, anxiously, "Do you mind if we change the subject?"

"Might you be *shrunk?*" asked Larry.

Wilbert Fraser stared at him directly for the first time. "Has this actually happened?" he asked, sharply. "I mean, here in San Francisco? Recently?"

Larry said, "Hypothetical case."

"It's happened, hasn't it?"

"Let's put it this way. We do have an inexplicable case of catastrophic endocrinal failure in SFG."

"How catastrophic?"

"Weight loss of well over a hundred pounds. One hundred forty-six down to forty-four."

"It's not anorexia?" asked Wilbert Fraser. "Anorexics occasionally have delusions of sinister spiritual presences, trying to force them to eat."

"It wasn't anorexia, Mr. Fraser. Or if it was, it was no

kind of anorexia that I ever heard of. She lost the weight in a little less than four minutes."

There was a startled gasp from Margot Tryall; and a "*four minutes?*" of disbelief from Dick Volare.

"Nearer three," Larry corrected him.

"I can't believe it," said Samantha Bacon. "That's some diet, don't you think? Maybe you could patent it. Lose Weight With The World Beyond."

"I don't think that's funny in the least," chipped in John Forth. "I think it's Goddamned hair-raising."

Larry didn't take his eyes away from Wilbert Fraser. "Could it have been?" he asked him, so softly that only Wilbert Fraser could hear.

Wilbert Fraser pursed his lips thoughtfully. Then he said, "I really don't feel qualified to answer."

"I don't even want a yes or a no," Larry persisted. "All I want is a well-informed maybe."

"I don't know," said Wilbert Fraser. "I wish I could. But not knowing the case—"

"Edna-Mae Lickerman," Larry told him.

From what Dogmeat had told him, Wilbert Fraser had been involved with Edna-Mae Lickerman in the mystical magical Haight-Ashbury headshop days. So he wasn't at all surprised when Wilbert Fraser's eyes gave that little defensive flicker that tells any experienced detective that he has touched a nerve.

"Doesn't ring any *immediate* bells..." said Wilbert Fraser.

Larry raised an eyebrow, didn't reply.

"She's the one who's lost all of this weight?" Wilbert Fraser asked.

Larry nodded.

"Well," said Wilbert Fraser. Larry knew that he was play-acting now; that in reality his mind must be racing with questions, racing with fears. "I guess her condition *could* have been caused by some kind of spirit-feeding."

"Spirit-feeding? Is that what you call it?"

"That's right. Some of the really ancient spirits are capable of gutting your whole being. Your heart, your soul, like gutting a fish. They can tear out of you everything that makes you what you are."

"And this could have happened to Edna-Mae Lickerman?"

"As I say, I don't have any way of knowing for sure. It's conceivable, I suppose—although if a spirit that was capable of doing *that* to anybody had reared its head in San Francisco lately, I think I'd be one of the first to be aware of it."

"What are we going to do now?" interrupted Eleonora, quite querulously. "Won't the spirits settle down? Maybe we could have a drink, and give them a little time to rest? It seems a pity to stop now, after such a *vivid* manifestation as Roberta Snow."

"I'm sorry, Eleonora," said Wilbert Fraser. "I'm really very tired, after all that effort. The spirits are always very demanding. Maybe you'd care to call me tomorrow, and we can arrange another meeting."

"Oh, Wilbert, won't you change your mind?" begged Margot Tryall.

"I'm sorry," said Wilbert. It was clear that what Larry had told him about Edna-Mae had upset him badly. "I'm really not in the mood any more."

"Well, thanks a lot, *gumba*," Dick Volare said to Larry.

Larry ignored him and held out his hand to Wilbert

Fraser. "It was good to meet you," he said. "And, believe me, if I hear any more news about Edna-Mae..."

Wilbert Fraser looked as if he were about to say something, but then he changed his mind. "Maybe another time," he said.

"Another time?" asked Dick Volare incredulously. "What's he going to do to the next spirit-guide, place it under close arrest?"

"Hey, *acqua in bocca*," said Larry.

"Keep quiet, he says," Dick Volare retorted.

Larry and Eleonora said goodnight to everyone and Wilbert Fraser showed them to the front door. Before they left, he laid his hand on Larry's shoulder and said, "Maybe soon you and I can have a talk."

"Of course," said Larry. "You want to discuss anything in particular?"

Wilbert Fraser made a *moue*. "This and that. The old days. You remember that night in the summer of '67, when they busted Rudolf Nureyev and Margot Fonteyn for smoking pot at that party on Belvedere Street? That was my party. Forty-two Belvedere Street. Seems like yesterday."

"Was Edna-Mae there too?" asked Larry.

Wilbert Fraser thrust his hands into the pockets of his sagging needlecord pants and stared around at the fog. "Your heart's in the correct place, Larry. Try to keep it there."

"Meaning?"

"Meaning there's some feeding going on, Larry; and maybe worse to come."

5

They drove back to Eleonora's house. Eleonora said, "I'm so sorry you didn't get to talk to your poppa."

Larry parked the car and helped his mother out. The fog felt like damp net curtains. "Maybe it was all for the best. That little girl scared the shit out of me. I don't know what I would've done if poppa had appeared."

"You don't have to use bad language. What would your poppa say?"

"I'm sorry," said Larry. Then he lifted his eyes heavenward and added, "I'm sorry, poppa."

He took her up the steps and opened the door for her. "Do you want a cup of tea?" she asked him. "I have some wonderful Orange Pekoe."

"I could use a drink as a matter of fact. And maybe I can telephone."

"Go right ahead. You know where everything is. Can you put the kettle on?"

Larry plugged in the kettle in his mother's diminutive pine-paneled kitchen, then went through to the living-room. "*Che violino! Che violino!*" screeched Mussolini. Larry went up to his cage and slammed it hard with the flat of his hand, making Mussolini scream and flutter wildly off his perch.

"One more insult out of you and you're parrot sandwich, you got it?"

He picked up the phone and dialed home. Linda answered immediately. He could hear rock music in the background, John Cougar Mellencamp, *Let It All Hang Out*. Linda only played rock'n'roll when Larry wasn't home.

"*Oh hi-i-i, darling, how was it?*" she asked him. "*Did you get to talk to your father?*"

"Don't laugh. I didn't get to talk to poppa but I saw a real spirit."

"*You saw a real spirit?*" She was using that voice on him, the same voice she used when she asked Mikey if he had genuinely seen a monster looking up at him from the bottom of the toilet.

"Linda, it was real. It was a little girl and it scared the shit out of me. I mean it scared me to death."

"*You're kidding.*"

"Do I sound like I'm kidding?"

"*No, maybe not. But you sound like you're on something.*"

"Be serious. Have I ever been on anything?"

"*The first night you took me out you brought about a kilo of grass.*"

"The first night I took you out I was nervous. Tonight I'm terrified. There's a difference. Anyhow, I'll tell you what happened when I get home. I have to tuck momma up and call Houston Brough."

"*What time do you think you'll get back?*"

"Midnight, no later."

"*I love you, you mad Italian.*"

He hung up, and dialed Houston Brough downtown. He was transferred to the Parkside Police Station between the Golden Gate Park and the Haight-Ashbury, where Houston had gone to talk to David Green.

"He came in late this afternoon and asked to be locked up in a cell. He said he was scared because somebody was out to tear him to pieces. He couldn't say who. I asked him if the person who was after him bore any resemblance to the person that he'd seen in the window of his apartment and he went apeshit. He collapsed. They'll be taking him to the hospital later."

"Could he describe the face in the window?"

"Sorry, I didn't get that far. He totally freaked."

"How about Leibowitz?"

"Not at home; and his neighbors haven't seen him or heard from him since Friday morning."

"Houston, I need to find him. I need some coherent descriptions. I need some facts. I need some Goddamned meat-and-potatoes."

"I'll keep trying, what can I say? I've got every fairy between here and Fairfax on the lookout for him."

"Less of the fairies, okay? Think community relations."

"I'm going back downtown, lieutenant, then I'm signing off. I'll catch you in the morning."

"Sure thing."

Eleonora came in with a tray of tea and a small home-baked *torta di noci*, freshly sliced up, and a glass of chilled Orvieto for Larry. She sat down beside him and laid her hand on his.

"Your poppa's proud of you, you know."

"Even though I turned my back on the family business?"

She smiled, and leaned forward, and kissed his forehead. "Your poppa knew more than most people realized."

Larry lifted his glass in a silent salute to his dead father. It was very gloomy in the living-room. Larry could almost have imagined that his father was still somewhere here— sitting in that high-backed chair, perhaps, staring at the fire, the way he always used to. He was almost tempted to get up and make sure that he wasn't.

"You feel his presence, too?" his mother asked.

Larry nodded. "It's strange, isn't it? Once you realize that dead people are still with us, you can practically reach out and touch them. I never even *guessed*."

Eleonora whispered. "They're here, all right. The night is *alive* with them. They're very stirred up, very excited."

"Well, I'm not surprised, after what happened at Wilbert Fraser's."

"Maybe we should talk to your poppa after all."

Larry looked at her cautiously. "What do you mean? You heard what Wilbert said. He was too tired and it was far too dangerous."

"Oh, it's *never dangerous*," Eleonora mocked. "That's only Wilbert's excuse for being temperamental. How can it be *dangerous* to talk to your father?"

"But Wilbert won't do it, will he? Not tonight?"

His mother arched her neck. "Who said anything about Wilbert? *We'll* do it, you and me, together!"

"Hey, hey. hey, wait up a minute! We're not mediums, are we? We don't even know how!"

"*I* know how. Your grandma showed me how. And she always said that I was very sensitive."

"I remember. I thought she was talking about your skin."

His mother laughed. "Come on," she coaxed him. "Let's try it! I can feel your poppa so strongly... I'm sure we'll be able to talk to him. Just a few words, Larry! Just to prove to yourself that it's possible! I promise you—it's wonderful! His voice, remember his voice? Remember the way he used to laugh?"

"I'm not too sure about this," said Larry. After his experience with the drowned girl, he wasn't convinced that seeing his father was such a terrific idea. Supposing his father were obliged to show him how he had died of a heart-attack, in the same way that Roberta had been obliged to show him how she had drowned? Supposing his father actually *spoke* to him—told him things he had never known before—things that he didn't want to hear? Supposing Mario Foggia turned out to be less of a giant than Larry remembered him? Not the great laughing Neapolitan folk-hero who could crack Christmas walnuts with his bare hands, but an ordinary man with a thin-clipped mustache and sloping shoulders and a dark blue three-piece suit?

Supposing they were surprised by one of those ancient spirits that could gut you like a fish—heart, soul, everything that made you what you are?

Eleonora said, "It's very easy, so long as you believe. We'll turn the lights low, and then we'll both think about your father, and then I'll call on somebody to guide us."

"I don't know, momma."

"Hush! You'll enjoy it."

She went around the room, switching off the lamps, until the only illumination came from a single small art-deco lamp with a mushroom shade of dark-yellow glass. She covered Mussolini's cage with its cloth, even though Mussolini protested vociferously. "*Pesci in fascia! Pesci in fascia!*"

She sat down again, and lifted both of her hands, palm outward, in the same way that Wilbert Fraser had done.

"Maybe we should hold hands... you know, insulate ourselves a little?" Larry suggested. "You know what Wilbert said about the full strength of the supernatural. Like holding bare wires."

"Oh, we'll be *fine*," his mother reassured him. In the darkness, he could hardly see her face, and the shadows of the furniture seem to have grown up the surrounding walls like huge ramparts of darkness. "Come on, dear, lift up your hands."

Reluctantly, Larry did what he was told. His mother closed her eyes and meditated for a while. Larry tried to think of his father, too. *Poppa, where are you now, poppa?* In this room it wasn't difficult. Every chair, every table, every picture, every drape—everything was deeply imbued with his father's lost presence and his father's life.

Larry closed his eyes for a moment, too, but the feeling of his father was so strong that he quickly opened them again. He had sensed for a split-second that there was somebody else in the room.

"Is somebody going to guide us to Mario Foggia?" asked his mother.

There was silence; although Larry thought he could feel the temperature dropping a little, and a sense that the atmosphere was somehow *thickening*, like cold clear soup with cornmeal stirred into it. Mussolini scratched irritably underneath his cover.

"Who's going to help us find Mario Foggia?" Eleonora urged. "Is somebody going to help us find Mario Foggia?"

Larry remembered to keep his palms stretched flat and to push against the cosmos. This time, he thought that he could feel the cosmos pushing back. Millions of teeming molecules, pressing against his hands. The chilly, busy substance of the night.

He closed his eyes again. Somehow it seemed less dark inside his eyelids than it did outside. He could feel his father's aura, for sure, but he found it difficult to picture his father's face. *Poppa, poppa.* But all he see was the dark pinstripe suit and the perfect cuffs and the fresh-picked carnation in the lapel. No face. Only that suit, and the smell of tobacco, and cologne. And he remembered laughing. A breezy day, and sunlight, and clouds that fled across the Bay like frightened sheep. And his father laughing.

"That man Lupone! Trying to act so high and mighty! And what does he say when he wants to go to the bathroom? Where is the *ubacasa*, Mario, that's what he says! Where is the outhouse?"

Why did he remember something so fleeting, something so irrelevant? He could smell cooking, he could smell *spaghetti al sugo di pesce*, spaghetti with fish-head sauce, which his father had always eaten for *i primi* on Friday evenings.

"You will always say *gabinete*, Laurence. You don't want to sound like slum-dweller."

He opened his eyes again. He thought he could see faint blue specks of light encircling his mother's head, like halo of fireflies. Then the light grew brighter, and began to flicker and dance, and he was sure of it.

Eleonora opened her eyes and looked across at Larry in

triumph. "I'm beginning to get something!" she whispered. "I can hear voices! Somebody's coming to guide us!" "For God's sake, momma, be careful."

The blue-white light danced around Eleonora's shoulders, and then suddenly branched to the palms of her hands—hesitated—and then jumped across to Larry's hands.

The sensation was electrifying—far stronger than the spiritual charge that Larry had felt at Wilbert Fraser's house. The instant that he was connected to his mother, he heard the same voices that she was hearing. Crying, sobbing, somebody calling. Very far away, like the cries of people on a sinking ship.

"They sound pretty upset," he told his mother. "Maybe we should leave them alone."

"They always cry like that," said Eleonora. "They're grieving for their lost lives. Don't worry, somebody will come to help us."

Larry was breathing slowly now to steady himself. The atmosphere in the living-room was chillier still, and deeply unpleasant. He began to feel that centipede-tickling on the palm of his hand, although he didn't dare to turn it around and look at it in case he broke the connection of flickering blue-white light.

"I'm still looking for somebody to help me find Mario Foggia," his mother repeated, quite testily. "Come on, now, who can help me find Mario Foggia?"

Eleonora sat in her chair with great composure, her thin hands raised. She looked almost beatific; and Larry thought what a brilliant mother she had always been, and how much he loved her. It was a strange feeling to look at a woman and to think that you had once lived inside her body, that you had fed inside her, warm and secure, and swum and turned and stretched and kicked, and slept and dreamed of greatness. Larry's grandmother had always said that sons never forgave their mothers for pushing them out into the daylight. They might love them beyond all loves, but they never forgave them.

"I need a guide," his mother was calling. "There are so many guides, I can feel you! I can feel you! Why are you shrinking away?"

The sensation in the palm of Larry's hand grew sharper, like scratching fingernails. At the same time, the blue-white light began to shudder uncontrollably, and flicker from one of Larry's fingers to the other with the crackling, fitful noise of electrical static.

Larry began to feel that the tension in the living-room was rising; while the temperature plummeted like a stone dropped into the sea.

"It's cold," he told Eleonora.

"A sure sign of spirits," Eleonora responded. "They're here, they're very close, but for some reason they're keeping their distance."

Suddenly, the blue-white light died away; and the room was gloomy again, with nothing but the dim marmalade-colored lamp to illuminate it.

Eleonora twisted around in her chair, straining her eyes in the darkness. "There's something wrong here, something wrong," said Eleonora. "That light is our beacon. That light draws our guides towards us. It's benign and it's helpful and it's never done anything like this before."

Larry said, "Maybe we shouldn't have tried to do this tonight. Come on, let's call it a night."

But Eleonora didn't answer. She stayed stock-still, listening, listening.

"There's something here," she breathed. "*There's something here.*"

"Is it poppa?" asked Larry, dry-mouthed.

"I'm not sure. But it's very strong. Can't you feel it for yourself?"

The scratching in Larry's hand was becoming unbearable. Harsh, regular scratches, over and over again. He turned his hand around and looked down at his palm. The blotchy shadows were moving across it, the shadows of the clouds beneath which his father had once laughed. His dead father. His *dead* father, whom they had called for tonight.

"Momma—" he said; but Eleonora hushed him again.

He looked back down at his hand and the shadows were already skeining themselves together into the distinctive features of a man's face. The man had his head partly turned away, as if he were talking to somebody behind him. Larry could see him moving his lips, and smiling, and nodding. He looked like a character in a tiny movie.

"Momma, take a look at this," he begged her.

"Hush, Larry, please." Eleonora's voice sounded irritable and strained.

"Momma—"

"*There's something here,*" she whispered. She turned and stared at him and all the blood seemed to have dropped from her face, leaving it white as chalk, with features chiseled out of chalk, and a mouth chiseled out of chalk.

"Is it poppa?" asked Larry.

Eleonora hesitated, and then quickly shook her head.

Larry squeezed his fist tight. He could still feel the crawling sensation on his skin, but he didn't want to look at it.

Eleonora said, "*Something's in father's chair.*"

Larry glanced quickly toward his father's high-backed chair. For one heart-lurching instant, he thought he could see a sleeve protruding from the side of the chair, but then he realized that it was his mother's discarded black coat.

"Momma... there's nothing," he said.

"Oh Blessed Mary Mother of God there's something there."

Larry stood up. "Momma, relax. Calm down. There's nothing there. I'll show you."

"*No!*" screamed his mother; and he had never heard such terror in her voice before.

This had to stop now. Larry circled around the chair and there lay his mother's black coat, just as she had dropped it, sleeves hanging, collar turned up.

He tried to smile at her. "It's your coat, that's all. It's only your coat."

He lifted it up to show her. But still she shrank back, staring at it as if it were alive.

"Momma—" he said, growing impatient, and walked toward her, still holding up the coat.

"Larry! No! Take it away! Larry!" his mother babbled at him. "Larry!"

"Momma, calm down," he told her. "It's only a c—"

But then he realized with a stroke of pure fear that the coat was more than a coat.

It was standing on its own.

It had bulk and weight, and its own rumbling darkness. It was filling itself with substance, it was filling itself with strength. It grew larger and taller and heavier; a massive headless creature of black fabric.

Larry, stunned, tried to take his hand away. It was only then that he understood what was happening. Out of the palm of his hand, a thick gray-white gel was pouring. It poured swiftly and relentlessly into the open sleeve of the coat, so that the coat billowed larger with every second that passed.

Ectoplasm, that's what Wilbert Fraser had told him. *Some spirits borrow it, some spirits steal it. Some spirits can gut you like a fish.*

The coat was taking his own spiritual substance to give itself life.

Larry wrenched his hand away. The ectoplasm tore like gelatinous wallpaper-paste. He stumbled back, knocking over the tea-tray, colliding with a table. He stared up at the dark thunderous shape of the spirit, panting, not knowing what to do. The room felt as if it were collapsing underneath its own weight.

"Momma..." he choked, grasping her stiffened shoulder. "Momma... get rid of it! Send the damn thing back where it came from!"

Eleonora Foggia was trembling. "I can't," she said, in a dust-dry whisper. "I don't know how."

"It's not poppa, is it?"

She shook her head. "I don't know what it is."

The coat showed no signs of moving. It remained where it was, only three or four feet away from them, black, headless, blind. But it gave off a penetrating chill, and all around it a soft and doleful wind seemed to blow, making the velvet drapes gently thunder as if there were somebody hiding there.

"What do you want?" Larry asked it.

The coat-creature appeared to ripple; but that was all.

"What are you? What do you want?" Larry demanded.

"You must go!" Eleonora shrilled at it. "You must go back to the other side!"

Still the coat-creature swayed in its own cosmic wind; and still it gave no indication of what it was looking for; or what it was; or why it was here.

"Jesus, I'm calling Wilbert," said Larry. With hands that would barely obey him, he opened the address-book on the telephone table and found FRASER, Wilbert, and dialed the number. All he could get was a steady, harsh crackling sound, as if Wilbert had dialed somewhere remote and then left the phone off the hook.

He hung up. As he did so, his mother said, "Larry," in a very different tone of voice.

He felt a low resonance, not like an earth-tremor, more like the sound of the rapid transit train rumbling eerily through the tube that lies on the bottom of San Francisco Bay. The single lamp began to dwindle and dim. Then, for a long and terrible moment, they were swallowed in complete darkness.

"Momma?" Larry called her, reaching out with both hands.

Eleonora Foggia didn't answer.

"Momma," cautioned Larry. "Momma, don't move."

The room was chilly and quiet. Only the soft, soft soughing of that impossible wind. The blackness was utterly seamless. Not even a hint of reflected light from Eleonora's collection of mirrors.

"Momma, you okay?" Larry asked her, reaching out cautiously into the dark.

He heard a dragging, bumping sound. Then a reed-hollow *oohhhhhhhh* like somebody sobbing in pain and desperation.

He edged forward, until his knee made contact with the side of his mother's chair. He reached out sideways, trying to feel her, but she didn't seem to be there.

"Momma, where are you? What's happened?"

There was a second's long silence. Then he was suddenly dazzled by a shattering light—a light that flooded the room with flattened shadows and turned reality into blinding-white theater. The coat-creature was transformed from a creature of total darkness into a huge horned apparition of unendurable brightness.

Larry shielded his eyes. He heard his mother shriek at the top of her voice. She was crouched on the floor at the creature's feet, her shoulders hunched, her fists clenched, her face distorted into an expression of absolute agony.

"Back off!" Larry yelled at the creature. He took a rash step forward, but instantly the huge bright foggy figure turned around and swept him back with a force that was chillingly physical; and yet mental, too, as if it had breathed cold breath on his naked brain.

He heard a terrible wrenching, bone-crackling sound—a sound like sinews being stretched and skin being torn and nerves being twisted. Eleonora grasped the sides of her mouth in her hands and clawed it wide apart, choking and gasping for breath. She stamped at the floor with one high-heeled shoe in a desperate attempt to communicate her pain and her fear and her suffocation, and she began to shake all over.

"Leave her alone!" Larry roared at the creature. "Leave her alone, or I'll drop you!"

He tugged out his .38 and raised it in both hands. "Leave her alone!" he repeated.

The figure ignored him. Maybe it couldn't really see him. Maybe it didn't understand what a gun was. Maybe it knew what a gun was but didn't care.

Larry edged closer, nudging at the figure's outline with the .38's muzzle. "Whatever the hell you are, back off! Do you understand? Back off!"

Still the figure ignored him. Larry was ready to fire when he suddenly thought of Wilbert Fraser's words. "*Of course, you can't harm them, because they're using you to give themselves shape. They're made of you. If they get hurt, you get hurt. If they die, you die.*"

Eleonora gargled and retched in agony. Larry hesitated, desperate, still holding the gun, but much less confidently now. Supposing Wilbert Fraser had been wrong? He had seen the ectoplasm sliding out of his hand, but how could this huge figure of light and fog really be made out of *him*? And even if Wilbert Fraser had been right, how could he let his mother be hurt like this, just to save his own skin?

Before he could think what to do, his mother was jerked up into a kneeling position, her back painfully arched, her mouth still stretched wide open. She tried with one half-paralyzed arm to reach out for Larry, her eyes bulging, frantic, but Larry didn't know whether to shoot, or to run, or to wrestle this dazzling creature to the floor, or whether to stay still and watch his mother in horror and pray that it couldn't really harm her, after all.

"You're not real!" he screamed at it. "You're not real, you can't harm anybody!"

But whatever it was, whatever hallways of psychic darkness it had appeared from, the figure was real.

Larry heard his mother gag. Her ribcage convulsed. Then a huge tide of blood and light and noise and flickering images came pouring out of her mouth.

He stood frozen, unable to move, unable to speak. He had never imagined what anybody's soul could look like— how their actual *being* would appear, if only you had the means to drag it out of them.

Now he knew. It looked like a torrent of everything that his mother had ever done, or felt, or thought, or experienced. The figure had made her vomit not only everything that she had ever eaten, but her entire life.

He saw blood, flesh, half-chewed fish, neon lights, babies, faces, rainstorms, lightning, bicycles, pillows. He heard screaming and singing; pianos and orchestras. He heard running feet, running feet, and doors slamming again and again. He heard laughter that was drowned by the ocean. He heard hundreds of clocks chattering, then chimes and chimes and chimes. He smelled home. He smelled cooking. He smelled perfumes and flowers and freshly-baked bread.

Then, with a last effort that wrenched and twisted his mother's diminished body like a rag-doll, he saw pints more blood, and his father's face, plastered in blood and something else, something that he didn't understand—another man's face, secretly smiling, crossed by a fleeting burst of sunlight.

All of this chaotic tangle was dragged into the dazzling light of the figure's form, and absorbed.

There was a deafening shout; and a cracking noise like a mine-prop collapsing. A dried dwarf-like Eleonora fell on to her side on the rug, keening and shivering and convulsively jerking her leg.

Larry crossed himself. In the name of the Father the Son and the Holy Ghost this is it, oh Christ protect me. He lifted his gun with both hands and aimed it at the very heart of the blinding light.

But he didn't have the nerve. Supposing he fired, and killed himself? Who would hunt down the Fog City Satan then? Houston Brough? Or Arne, with his endless analyses, and his computer printouts and his forensic tests?

Besides, the tall ectoplasmic figure was dimmer now, much dimmer; and it seemed as if the soft cold wind that it had exuded was now reversed, and was being sucked back to the center of its being.

"What are you?" he demanded, his voice harsh.

The figure nodded its dark, huge head.

"*What are you?*" Larry screamed at it. "*What do you want? What have you done to my mother?*"

The figure didn't reply, but was now so dark that it was blacker than the blackest shadows. For a second, the cold wind that blew toward its center grew fierce and freezing, then it died away altogether.

His mother's black coat dropped empty to the floor.

Larry cautiously approached it, and picked it up. For the

briefest of moments, he heard the music of a steam calliope, and saw a will-o'-the-wisp of brightly-colored light. He thought he heard laughter, and the sound of cheering. He thought he smelled popcorn and that distinctive aroma of cotton-candy.

Then it was gone.

He stood up, still shocked, but deeply emotionally moved, too. Behind him, on the floor, he heard his mother cough. He knelt down beside her and lifted her heavy trembling head and tried to comfort her. She looked the same way that Edna-Mae had looked: her scalp tufted and blotchy, as if she had eczema, her cheeks collapsed, her limbs thin as sticks. Her clothes hung around her, and her rings lay scattered on the floor where they had dropped from her skeletally thin fingers.

"Momma... momma, it's Larry. Listen, momma, I'm going to get you to the hospital."

Eleonora's eyes rolled wildly. He lifted her carefully up in his arms. She weighed no more than a run-over cat, and her feet swung as he carried her out of the door and along the hallway and out into the fog.

She made no sound; but her rolling eyes told him that she wasn't dead.

He eased open the passenger door of his Toyota with his knee and lowered her into the seat. He carefully tightened her seatbelt so that it fitted closely around her bony, protruding hips. She stirred and trembled, and a thin string of glistening saliva slid from her lower lip. Her eyes were open and she kept looking at him, but she showed no sign that she recognized him, or that she understood what had happened to her. Larry was more shocked than he liked to admit, and when he sat down beside her, his hand was juddering so wildly that he could scarcely jab the key into the ignition.

He started up, and pulled away from the curb. A taxi blasted its horn at him because he had forgotten to switch on his lights, and he had pulled away without making a signal. "I'm sorry! *Scusi!* I didn't see you!" he called.

"Forget it!" the driver shouted back. "I never expect assholes to have eyes!" If Larry hadn't been so distressed, he would have taken his number and reported him. But right now, all he cared about was getting this collapsed crow's-nest that had once been his mother off to the hospital.

He clamped his flashing red light on to the roof of his Toyota and drove at full throttle. The car bucked and bounced as he drove across Larkin. The fog was so thick that all he could see was blurred lights, ghostly fluorescent signs.

"Mario!" his mother croaked, swiveling her head around.

"Momma, everything's okay, just keep quiet!" Larry reassured her.

"*Mario!*" his mother screamed.

"Momma, everything's okay. This won't take long. You had an accident, that's all."

But his mother twisted around to stare at him and her eyes were crammed with hatred. "Mario, you bastard, you betrayed me, you bastard."

"Momma, listen," said Larry, laying his hand on his mother's arm. "This is Larry. You had an accident. Everything's going to be fine. Just take it easy, everything's going to be terrific."

His suspension slammed as he drove across Polk. His

mother was almost thrown out of her seatbelt. A red bread truck pulled in front of him in the fog, Lasorda's Pane Integrate, a fucking Italian bread truck, and he swerved and leaned on the horn.

"Police!" he screamed out of the window. "Get out of the fucking way!"

The driver couldn't hear him over the bellowing of his rig, and simply waved.

He skidded, spun the wheel, and almost lost the Toyota on the intersection with Van Ness. His mother's tufted head knocked against the window, but she continued to rant and babble and curse.

"You went with that girl, you went with that girl, and you took her to bed, didn't you, on our anniversary, our silver anniversary, and all the family waiting for us and you were late, and they *knew* where you'd been."

"Momma, calm down," Larry told her. "We're almost there, okay?"

"You know nothing," his mother spat; and convulsed.

"Momma, please hold on. Three minutes, we're there."

"*You know nothing*," she raged.

"Come on, momma, you know what grandpa always used to say. *Giovane potesse, vecchio sapesse*. The young people got the energy, the old people got the know-how."

"*You know nothing, you bastard*," his mother screeched. "*You humiliated me, time and time again, in front of your family. You made me feel so small.*"

"Momma, I don't know what the hell you're talking about."

His mother arched backward in her seat, trembling

and muttering. Larry was almost hysterical. *What the hell have I done?* he thought. *I've destroyed my own mother, destroyed her. That elegant witty woman I loved so much. Holy Mother, look at her now, look at her now!*

Like some shabby malevolent dwarf. Swearing, drooling and rolling her eyes. *Sancta Maria, ora pro nobis.*

"Momma, for God's sake, hold on."

But then, halfway between Willow and Eddy, his mother started throwing herself from side to side, her thin arms flailing, her feet kicking. She forced herself in front of Larry and snatched and bit at his hand.

The Toyota swerved across the street and collided broadside with a slowly moving truck. Pieces of trim and smashed plastic glittered in the fog. Larry spun the wheel but his mother clawed at his face and bit at his ear and his scalp. He forced her away, but she came back at him with even great ferocity, screeching and panting and spitting. It was like trying to fight off a demented cat.

"Momma, for the love of God!"

She bit at his face, and he felt her teeth crunch against his cheekbone. The Toyota skidded, slewed end-over-end, hit the curb backward and slammed against a hydrant. The windshield dropped out in a hailstorm of toughened glass. Larry's head knocked against the steering-wheel and he felt his back twist against the seat.

Still screeching, his mother scrambled out of the open windshield and on to the glass-strewn hood. He tried to snatch at her ankle, but she was far too quick for him. "*You!*" she kept screaming at him. "*You betrayed me! You humiliated me!*"

Half-hopping, half-falling, she jumped down from the car and into the road.

Even Larry didn't see the huge green tractor-trailer that was bellowing up Van Ness on its way to the Golden Gate. He was too shocked, the fog was too thick. For some reason, he didn't even *hear* it.

But just as his mother limped crabwise across the road, the rig emerged from the fog with its klaxons blaring.

"*Momma*!" Larry yelled; although she was scarcely his momma any more.

The tractor's wheels missed the crouched little creature by inches; but she tried to dart in front of the trailer's wheels, right underneath the rig. One huge tire crushed her on to the road-surface as if she were nothing more than sticks and rags. The brakes locked. The tires howled in a long agonized chorus. Eleonora Foggia was jammed right beneath the wheel, and it dragged her along for nearly thirty feet, so that she was nothing more than a wide scarlet smear on the pavement, gruesomely decorated with smashed fragments of hair and bone and ripped-apart fabric and glistening pig's-caul intestines.

Larry lowered his head. His knees ached where they had collided with the underneath of the dash. His chin was wet with blood. He didn't know what to do next, whether to sit here and wait for somebody to help him; or whether to pretend that he wasn't here at all.

A black man in a windbreaker stared into the open windshield. "How're you doing, man?" he wanted to know.

"Good. Good. I'm doing good," said Larry.

"That your kid got run over?"

Larry shook his head. "It wasn't a kid, it was—" He

touched his eyes with his hands and realized that he was weeping. "Shit," he said, annoyed at his own weakness.

"I was the first here, wasn't I?" the black man asked him.

"Sure," said Larry. He picked up his r/t and miraculously it still worked. While the black man stared at him in fascination, he called police headquarters and asked to speak to Houston Brough. Houston was supposed to have left for home, but Glass said that was probably over on 24th Street, interviewing a man who said his neighbor had been chanting and burning incense all night. Larry's voice kept trembling, and he had to stop from time to time and take deep breaths to control himself.

"Houston? I've had a traffic accident on Van Ness. Between Eddy and Willow. It sounds like the cavalry's already on its way. Listen, I'm fine, I'm not hurt, but my mother was, um, killed."

"*Jesus, Larry, I don't know what to say.*"

"Listen, Houston, she wasn't quite what she used to be. She—she'd changed, like Edna-Mae."

"*She'd* what? *I didn't catch that.*"

"She'd changed, like Edna-Mae Lickerman. I don't know, shrunk. She went crazy in the car and tried to scratch me to pieces."

"*What are you going to do now?*"

"I'm going to talk to Wilbert Fraser. Then I'm coming back to Bryant Street. What's the time now?"

"*Ten, a little after.*"

"Okay, I'll meet you at eleven-thirty. And, do me a favour, will you? Call Linda and tell her what's happened. Tell her my mother couldn't have felt a thing. Tell her I'm fine, no problems. Tell her I'll call her later."

"Ten-four, lieutenant."

By now, two patrol cars and an ambulance had arrived at the scene. Across the street, a Chinese police officer had caught hold of the arm of the truck driver, who had climbed down from his rig and was walking around in a circle. Larry wrenched open the distorted door of his Toyota and climbed stiffly out. A young cop came up to him and said, "Are you okay, sir? You shouldn't try to move just yet awhile. I'll have the paramedic check you over."

Larry produced his badge. "I need a ride," he said, in a woolly voice. "Check with your partner, then get me over to Jackson Street."

"Sure," said Larry. "Whatever."

"Just give us some time, lieutenant. We're going to have to take down some details. You know what I mean? Paperwork."

He waited beside his wrecked car, smearing the blood from his face with Kleenex. He didn't look over at the tractor-trailer or the dark shining smear on the roadway that used to be his mother. The red ambulance lights flashed on his face; and on the face of the curious black man, who stood beside him respectfully and almost proprietorially. "I was the first here, wasn't I?" he asked again.

Larry nodded. "Sure you were. No question about it."

The last of Wilbert Fraser's seance guests were just driving away as Larry arrived back at Jackson Street. Samantha Bacon, wrapped in a white fluffy fun-fur coat (no actress, not even an almost-forgotten face like Samantha Bacon, could afford to wear anything environmentally unsound.) Bembridge Caldwell, looking blue-gray and profoundly unwell.

Larry thanked the young police officer for the ride, and climbed out. As he came limping up the steps, Wilbert Fraser was waiting for him by the open front door.

"Larry! My God! What's happened?" he asked. "You look like you've been in a car wreck."

"Very astute of you," said Larry. His lips felt like cotton wadding. "We had an accident on Van Ness. My mother's dead."

"She's dead? Eleonora's dead? You're not serious? *Eleonora?*"

"I'm sorry, but I'm totally serious."

"Oh, dear. Oh, God. Oh, dear, I don't know what to say." Wilbert Fraser bit his lip. Larry could see the tears sparkling in the corners of his eyes, and prayed to God that he would have the strength not to cry, too. Not just yet, anyway. *Let me cry in private, when this is all over.*

"I need to talk to you," he told Wilbert Fraser.

"Of course, of course, anything. Come in. Do you want to wash up? I can lend you a clean shirt. Oh, your poor mother! Dear, dear Eleonora! How did it *happen?*"

Wilbert Fraser closed the front door behind them, and led Larry through to a large bathroom with a marble basin and mahogany paneling and prints of naked boy snake-charmers being admired by hawklike Arabs. "You can wash up in there. Don't worry if you get blood on the towels. Would you like some coffee?"

"I need something stronger than coffee, Mr. Fraser."

"Please call me Wilbert. I was named after my great-grandfather. You know, Wilbert Bullock? He had the power too. It almost undid him."

Larry was startled when he saw himself in the mirror. His face was swathed in dried blood and there was an ugly bruised lump on his right cheek where his mother had bitten him. His hands were covered in bites and scratches too. His hair was white with dust and sparkled with powdered glass.

Slowly, carefully, he filled the basin with hot water and washed himself. The water turned rusty with blood. Then he limped across to the living-room, where Wilbert was waiting for him with a bottle of Jack Daniel's and two cut-crystal glasses.

"Please, sit down," said Wilbert.

Larry sat in a large brown-velour armchair, and took a large mouthful of whiskey. He shuddered as he drank it, and it burned his throat; but it warmed him up, and relaxed him, and overwhelmed that dreadful thumping heart-attack feeling caused by too much adrenalin surging round his system.

Wilbert said, "I don't really understand why you want to talk to *me*."

"We held a seance of our own," said Larry.

"I don't follow."

"We went home this evening, my mother and me, and we held a seance of our own. My mother was sure that she could handle it. She used to hold seances all the time with my grandmother."

Wilbert said, "Damn." Then, "Damn, damn, damn." He looked up. "She wanted you to talk to your father, I suppose?"

Larry nodded. "She was so excited that I saw that little girl tonight. She was so excited because I actually *believed*."

"What happened?" asked Wilbert gravely, taking off his spectacles and folding them. "The spirits were *very* unsettled tonight. Dreadfully unsettled."

"We held up our hands, same way we did when we were here. I know, I know. I know what you said. It takes a really powerful medium to handle that kind of a seance. I did try to remind her. But she wanted to do it the same way as you. Bare wires, know what I mean?"

"Of course," nodded Wilbert. "But incredibly risky."

"You're not kidding. The lights went out... then my mother's coat dragged all of this ectoplasm out of my hand. Well... I guess it was ectoplasm. We had a coat that stood by itself."

"Oh, God," Wilbert despaired. "Didn't either of you have the least idea of the *danger?* I mean, communicating with the spirit-world is usually safe, just like flying in a 747 is usually safe. But you wouldn't let a three-year-old kid fly a 747, would you? Well, *would* you? Any more than you should have allowed somebody as inexperienced as Eleonora to contact the dead!"

"I didn't realize," said Larry. "I told her to be careful. I told her to hold hands."

"It wouldn't have made all that much difference, holding hands, if you were up against a spirit who could drag that much ectoplasm out of you."

"Oh," said Larry, feeling worse than ever. He swallowed more whiskey.

Wilbert looked at him thoughtfully. "Your *hand*, did you say?"

"Excuse me?"

"You said it took the ectoplasm out of your hand?"

"That's correct. Anything wrong?"

"No, no. Of course not. But it's very unusual. Most of the time the spirits take it out of your side, or your stomach, or occasionally your head. You don't often hear of ectoplasm appearing out of your hand. Let me take a look at it, would you?"

Larry sat forward in his seat and held out his hand. Wilbert took hold of it and turned it around, carefully scrutinizing the palm. Then, still holding it, he raised his head and looked directly into Larry's eyes.

"You're one of them?" he asked, in disbelief.

"One of who?"

"You know what I'm talking about. Jesus! The moving hand."

Larry abruptly took his hand back. "You know about this stuff?"

"For sure. You're one of the Black Brotherhood. No wonder my seance with Margot Tryall went so haywire."

"The Black Brotherhood? What the hell is the Black Brotherhood?"

"You have the moving hand and you don't know what the Black Brotherhood is?"

"Should I?"

"The Black Brotherhood was one of the most powerful occult groups that San Francisco ever knew."

"Dogmeat Jones mentioned something about that."

"They were fearsome—truly fearsome," said Wilbert. Then, changing the subject, "Is Dogmeat still around? I haven't seen Dogmeat in a long, long time."

"You haven't seen Edna-Mae Lickerman in quite a while, either," Larry added.

"No," Wilbert admitted, with embarrassment. "Of course, yes, I was just pretending that I didn't know her. As a matter of fact I knew her real well. I'm sorry I didn't fess up to it this evening: I was being defensive. I have an aversion to policemen who can't stop being policemen, even when they're off duty. It tends to make it difficult to be totally open with them."

Larry finished his whiskey. "As a matter of fact, Wilbert, tonight I *was* on duty. I'm assigned to the Fog City Satan."

"I see. You didn't think that anybody *here* could have—"

"No, no, of course not. But the Fog City Satan keeps on giving this warning. Something terrible is going to come over from the other side with the express intention of eating San Francisco for lunch. To *feed*, that's the word he keeps using. Up until tonight, I didn't know anything about the other side, except what my mother had told me, and that's why I came. Now, well, shit. I wish to God I hadn't."

"I'm sorry, Larry," said Wilbert. "You don't know how much."

"What I need to know is—is there any possibility that some kind of spirit can come *back* from the other side?" asked Larry. "Sort of, like, come back to life?"

"You're talking about resurrection? Genuine resurrection?"

"I guess so."

"Well... there are myths and legends about it," Wilbert replied. "There are several rituals, too. But whether these rituals work or not..."

"This Black Brotherhood… is that the kind of thing that they were into?"

Wilbert gave him an evasive shrug.

"Could the Black Brotherhood have anything to do with the Fog City Satan?" Larry persisted. "I'm trying to establish a link here, Wilbert. I'm trying to get a toehold."

"You tell me, Larry. You're the man with the moving hand."

Larry held his open palm close to Wilbert's face. "I told you. I got this by accident, Wilbert, not by design. If I knew how to get rid of it, I would. Now I need to *know*, Wilbert. I need to know everything whether you think it's relevant or not. Who were the Black Brotherhood, for instance? And what do *you* think's going down?"

"Well, I'll *try* to explain it." said Wilbert. "It's difficult to *believe*, that's all."

"After tonight, I think I can believe pretty well anything."

"Well…"said Wilbert. "This all goes back a long, long way. And a lot of it is rumor, and conjecture, and downright superstition."

"Just tell me what you know," Larry interrupted. "We can sort out the facts from the superstition later."

"The way I got into the occult was more or less by chance," Wilbert explained. "Although most of the members of my family have always had a strong psychic gift, particularly on my mother's side, I took it for granted most of my life. When I was a kid, I thought that *everyone* could hear voices and smell smells and see spirits walking around. It never frightened me. I knew these people that I was talking to were dead; and I knew that they couldn't hurt me. Most of the time I felt sorry for them. I mean, some of them were deeply shocked and traumatized by dying—especially if they'd died violently, like that little girl Roberta we saw tonight.

"At one time I actually toyed with the idea of setting up a Spiritual Therapy business... counseling people's dead relatives, helping them to adjust to the reality of being dead. I mean, people get very lonely and bewildered when they die... they miss their families and their friends, they miss the plain and simple pleasure of being alive. They miss the tastes, the feelings, the kisses, the love. One young boy described being dead as the difference between color television and black-and-white."

Two or three hours ago, Larry would have dismissed Wilbert as a complete crazy—only one step saner than Mad Jack McMad, the Winner of the All-America Mr. Mad Contest. But now that he had seen for himself the little drowned girl in the taffeta party-dress—now that he had witnessed the ferocity of the creature that had destroyed his mother—he believed with a kind of masochistic doggedness in every word that Wilbert said. *I was wrong and Wilbert was right. There are spirits and there are ghosts and there is a face that moves on the palm of my hand.*

Wilbert said, "I came across the Black Brotherhood pretty much by accident. That was about 1964, 1965. In those days, I was working for the San Francisco Museum of Modern Art. I was a picture framer, although I always told people I was an artist. I was living with a friend called Almo Stemti over a beatnik coffee-bar on Valencia. You should've seen me. Sloppy-Joe sweater, beard, beret. Every sentence beginning with 'like'. Like, the whole beatnik bit."

"Sure, sure," said Larry, testily. He was beginning to shake from the shock of his accident; and in the same way that he had seen police officers gradually become aware of having been shot, he was gradually beginning to understand that his mother was dead, that she was truly and absolutely dead, and that what had happened tonight wasn't a masquerade, or a horror-movie. No latex, no fake blood. No Freddie.

His elegant handsome beloved mother had been physically and emotionally desiccated by a blinding white light, and then crushed in front of his eyes into a paste of plasma and hair and bone. Larry knew that before the night was over, he was going to have to confront the total horror of it; the grinding grief; and that for a while he would probably go over the edge.

Right now, though, he had an urgent job to do; and the horror and the grief would have to stay where they were— lid on, screwed down tight.

Wilbert finished his whiskey and poured himself another one. His eyes never quite caught Larry's eyes; as if he were afraid or ashamed. "The Black Brotherhood? One day they weren't around and then they were. It was like that song '*First there is a mountain, then there is no mountain, then there is.*' Or a Western, when the bad guys suddenly ride into town. There were four or five of them, and they always seemed to be everywhere. You'd go for a coffee and there they were, two or three of them anyway, sitting in the corner in their tiny black shades and their black shirts and all of those *ankhs* and crucifixes they used to wear. Except for one of them called Leper who was so thin you couldn't look at him, they were all huge guys, physically huge, with a really threatening presence. One of them looked Latino, but the rest were definitely white. Everybody on the scene began to get real tired of them, because they were always around, and somehow they always cast like a *pall* over everything, do you know what I mean? Conversation died, nobody laughed.

"Anyway the word got around that they were into the black arts. And some people started hanging out with them. Just to look brave, I guess. I mean in those days cool was everything, and if you weren't afraid to hang out with these guys, then you were *cool*. The girls used to find them fascinating. Edna-Mae loved them. She'd sit real close to them, even if they never spoke to her for hours, even if they totally ignored her. She sat there watching them drink, watching them smoke, watching them *breathe* for Christ's sake. They had charisma, although we didn't call it charisma, back in 1965.

"Then—in the early summer of '66, people started to die. There were some bad murders in the Haight-Ashbury and the Mission District. In fact those murders killed the peace-and-love movement before the tourists even got here. People stopped loving, people stopped trusting. I mean you're going to turn on and tune in with somebody who might happily saw your legs off when you're tripping? No way, no way at all.

"Of course we didn't connect the killings with the Black Brotherhood, not at first. But they began to boast about them, indirectly; and everything started to get weirder. Some of the girls actually slept with these guys, but I never heard of any girl sleeping with them twice. In the middle of the night the girls said they were woken up by voices that weren't even human voices. Like, tiny *gnarled* kind of voices. And they'd seen faces and clouds and stuff, moving across these guys' hands. Then—after a while—it spread. People started seeing faces on their TVs when their TVs were switched off; and faces in mirrors when there was nobody looking; and faces in wallpaper."

Larry said, "Nobody thought to call the cops?"

"Oh, come on, lieutenant. Everybody was dropping so much acid in those days, it could have been real, it could have been one huge collective hallucination. You know, a kind of Jungian trip, involving the whole neighborhood. Besides, nobody *ever* called a cop in those days. Cops had an unpleasant tendency to overstay their welcome. Maybe the guy upstairs kept pissing from his sixth floor window into your fifth-floor window-box, but what would happen if you called the cops? Two fat-assed kids with badges and boils and .357 Magnums would strut around your apartment like they owned it, and then try to slide their hands into the front of your girlfriend's bathrobe, and the next thing you knew, *abracadabra*, you'd be charged with obstructing a police officer in the course of fondling your girlfriend's pussy, and possessing a lid of stale grass that the cops been carrying in their glove-box since grass was first invented."

Larry wasn't amused. "It sounds to me like we're experiencing the same thing all over," he told Wilbert. "The killings, you know. The faces."

Wilbert nodded. "Yes, it does. I was hoping that it was something else, but it has the same ring to it. Same resonance. Flowers in the hair revisited...."

"You haven't thought of talking to the police about it before?"

Wilbert shook his head. "I've had some difficult times with the police in the past, Larry. Besides, I wasn't sure."

Larry lifted his hand. "I'm not the only one. The faces have been seen all over the city."

Wilbert lowered his glass. He looked deeply unhappy. "I've heard stories. I've felt the vibrations."

Larry said, "People have been seeing them in windows. In *soup*, even."

"How about your hand? Does your hand—talk to you?"

Larry self-consciously squeezed his fist tight, and nodded.

Wilbert sipped, swallowed, thought. Then he said, "I held a seance. You know, back in '67, when the Black Brotherhood started getting out of control. A girlfriend of mine had slept with one of them. It wasn't Leper, it was another one called Mandrax. Big, silent Latino. Scarred skin, looked like the moon. Anyway, this girlfriend ended up with a moving hand, just like yours. She tried to get Mandrax to get rid of it, wipe it off, but he wouldn't. Maybe he didn't know how. You wouldn't have called any of those guys super-intelligent. In the end she asked *me* to get rid of it. She used to lie awake at night and it used to talk to her. Quite understandably she was going crazy. She was neurotic enough to begin with. She used to be a friend of Natalie Owings."

"That's what my hand does," said Larry. "I see clouds, and a face, and then it talks."

Wilbert shrugged. "I don't know exactly how it's done. I never did figure it. But a few years ago I talked to an old medium in Berkeley, and he said that any powerful spiritual force can manifest its own image on windows or mirrors or any reflecting surface. And on hands, too, because the hand is the mirror of the human soul... even more than the eyes. That's why palmists read palms. That's why Red Indians lift their hands to each other and say 'how'. Here, look at my soul, I'm not hiding anything."

Larry asked, "What happened when you held that seance back in '67?"

Wilbert blew out his cheeks. "Fwoof! What didn't happen? That seance was hell let loose, hell let loose. That seance was one of the reasons I was praying that this Fog City Satan business wasn't anything to do with the Black Brotherhood. We held it in my apartment on Belvedere, and there were seven of us there, I deliberately chose seven because that gives you plenty of psychic attraction without being as overpowering as thirteen. Thirteen can bring the roof down. Anyway, the girl with the moving hand was there. Her name was Shetland Piper. And another medium was there... George Menzel. I was much less experienced, of course, in those days... so I went through all the mumbo-jumbo, incense, chanting. But before I'd finished, Shetland started to scream, because this huge bubble of ectoplasm was swelling out of her hand.

"She held her hand, palm upward, flat on the table, and we saw a head and half of a face. It was the most frightening manifestation I'd ever seen in my life. The head looked like it was tom in half, like a photograph torn in half, and it was so bright that none of us could work out if it were human or not. There was a terrible stench, too, like sewers or rotting meat; and several of us started to barf.

"I managed to ask that manifestation just three questions. The first was *who are you*, and the thing spoke to me and said, *The Worthiest One*. The second was, *what are you?* and the thing said, *Master of Truth*. The third one was, *what do you want?* and the answer was *Peace*.

"Then a hell of a storm broke out, and everything in my apartment went flying. Ornaments, pictures, chairs, tables. One of the girls was hit by a piece of broken glass and almost lost her eye. The ectoplasm itself flared up into a hot roaring flame. Shetland burned her hand badly—and, of course, she never regained the ectoplasm that the spirit had taken out of her. When they weighed her at the hospital she was three pounds lighter."

"But I didn't get my ectoplasm back, either," Larry put in.

"Then weigh yourself, and you'll see just how much the spirit took out of you. It wouldn't have needed pound-for-pound. An ectoplasmic manifestation is more light and energy than actual flesh. But it wouldn't surprise me if you'd lost nine or ten pounds."

Larry felt his arms and his thighs and his stomach. Wilbert was right. He did feel thinner. He *was* thinner.

"What happened after the seance?" he asked Wilbert.

Wilbert was quite drunk by now. "After the seance—after we'd taken Shetland and Suzie to the hospital—I went back to George Menzel's home in Sausalito and we had a long talk about what had happened. George was almost seventy then, and he'd been raising spirits since before the war, in Vienna. He was in Dachau during the war, and he spent his time holding seances for the Germans; that was how he survived. He also studied all the spirits, and the demons, and God knows what else.

"He said that he was sure that the Black Brotherhood were acolytes of an ancient Old Testament beast called Belial, the King of Lies. Belial was supposed to have been one of the first angels to be cast down from Heaven, but George was a little more down-to-earth about him than that. He said that there are certain supernatural manifestations which are created out of human passions and human weaknesses. Just like we create concentrations of smog or acid rain or oil-slicks out of environmental misbehavior; we also create concentrations of cruelty and hatred and callousness. Disease, too. The demon Pazuzu in *The Exorcist* was not actually a demon in the sense of being a little devil with a forked tail, it was a concentration of human unhealthiness. You know how you can walk into a certain house or a particular town or even a whole city and feel immediately and instinctively that it's a bad place. That's when you're aware of one of these demons, one of these concentrations, one of these so-called fallen angels."

Larry eased himself back in his chair. "But you asked this manifestation who it was, and it said *The Worthy One*. And you asked it what its name was, and it said *Master of Truth*."

"*Of* course. That was what convinced George that it really was Belial, or some kind of form of Belial. The name Belial in Hebrew mean 'worthless' and Belial was always known as the Master of Lies. He was created out of centuries of black lies and devious fraud and poisonous deceit. He was incapable *ever* of telling the truth."

"So... you and George Menzel decided that this was Belial."

"Yes," said Wilbert. "And more than that, we decided that the Black Brotherhood were trying to bring him back from the other side. We weren't sure how; but George had read someplace that Belial could only be resurrected by ritual sacrifice. We decided without any concrete evidence that the Black Brotherhood were probably responsible for all the killings in the Haight-Ashbury and Outer Mission."

"And still you didn't tell the police?"

"No."

"So what *did* you do?"

Wilbert took off his spectacles and pinched the bridge of his nose as if he had a headache. "George and me decided that somebody had to do something drastic. According to the Dead Sea Scrolls, Belial feeds first on your mind and then on your flesh; and he's a voracious eater. Imagine a Great White shark as a land creature; as a *man*, almost; and then imagine that man let loose in a city like San Francisco. They talk about killing machines: Belial is the ultimate killing machine. He lives to kill. He has an insatiable greed for flesh and blood and human experience. He has no humanity himself, but he's ravenous for *our* humanity. He wants to be king. If he can't rule in heaven, then he's determined that he's going to rule on earth."

Larry said, "You're taking me too far, too fast. I believe what I've seen tonight. I believe in the other side. But I can't say that I believe this. Belial, the fallen angel, the Master of Lies? Come on, Wilbert, let's get serious here."

But Wilbert wouldn't be moved. "Larry," he said, "I believed it back in '67 and I believe it now. The Black Brotherhood came to San Francisco with the specific intention of resurrecting Belial."

"But what was Belial the fallen Old Testament angel doing in San Francisco in the first place?" Larry retorted.

"I don't know. I can't even begin to answer that. But George and me thought that he was; and I *still* think that he was; and judging from what's been happening here lately, I'd stake my life on the fact that he still is."

"What did you do about it, Wilbert?" coaxed Larry, in the voice that he always used for suspects whom he knew would confess, so long as they were allowed to do it with dignity. College professors who had strangled their nagging wives. Frustrated executives who had shot their bosses. Beaten women, abused children, vigilantes, eccentrics.

"It was George. He burned them."

"George *burned* them?"

"That's right. We discussed it first, then we went ahead and did it. George was telekinetic. You know, he could make pieces of paper fly around, and move paperclips from across the room, and once I saw him turn eight successive pages of Webster's Dictionary, just by using his mind. The thing that he found easiest was starting fires. All he had to do was think about that hot-spot you get when you use a magnifying-glass to concentrate the sun's rays... and bingo! He'd start a fire.

Larry thought about Frankie and Mikey, taking their magnifying glass to Kirby Cove. Wilbert could see that he had momentarily lost his attention, so he leaned forward with the Jack Daniel's bottle, and asked, "Drink?"

"No... no, thanks. Just tell me what you did."

Wilbert thought for a moment, then, flatly, he said, "The Brotherhood owned a big black Delta-88. They used to ride around in it together, but very seldom did you see all of them in it at one time. George and I waited at the intersection of 16th and Mission for nine solid days, until one morning they pulled up right in front of us, all of them. I'd never seen George start fires before, but he placed one finger on his forehead and said, *There came three angels out of the east. The one brought frost, the two brought fire. Out frost; in fire. In the name of God, amen.*

"And do you know what happened? That car exploded, just as it was starting to move. Exploded, and burned out. It was in all the papers, on TV, too. But nobody ever found out that it was George who did it, and nobody could ever have proved it, either."

Larry was very solemn. "I think I remember that happening. Didn't they have some kind of safety inquiry? Ralph Nader came to San Francisco and examined the wreckage."

"That's right. But there wasn't any question about how effective it was. The faces stopped, the killings stopped. George and me wiped out the Black Brotherhood single-handed."

"But now they're starting again," said Larry.

"Yes," agreed Wilbert, despondently.

"So you think the Black Brotherhood's back?"

"Who knows? I don't get involved with that stuff any more. I let rich women talk to their dead husbands. I let grieving widowers talk to their dead wives. I even arranged for Mrs. Chauncey Middleberg II to walk her dead poodle."

"If you don't know, then who does know?" Larry asked him. "How about this George Menzel character?"

"Died last fall. You'll find him in the Jewish cemetery."

"Maybe you can raise him for me."

Wilbert said, "No, I can do better than that." He stood up, and walked unsteadily across to his desk. He dragged out his chair, unscrewed his fountain-pen, and wrote a name and address on an index-card. Flapping it between finger and thumb to dry it, he brought it back and handed it to Larry as if he were handing him a business-card.

"Tara Gordon," he said. "She runs the Waxing Moon on Jessie Street. It's a what-d'you-call-it, an occult store. She knows everybody and everything when it comes to the fey and the far-out. If the Black Brotherhood are back, she's your woman. She'll help you."

"Thanks," said Larry. Then, more quietly, "Can you get rid of this moving hand for me?"

Wilbert blew out his cheeks a little. "I guess I could try."

"You did it for Shetland Piper."

"Shetland Piper got her hand burned. Shetland Piper was never the same again."

"All the same… could you get rid of it for me?"

"Okay… I'll think about it. I can't do it tonight. It needs full-scale psychic energy; and a whole lot of balls; and quite frankly those are two commodities I'm kind of short on tonight."

Larry stood up. "Thanks for everything," he told Wilbert. "I appreciate it."

"Just be careful," Wilbert warned him. "And just remember that Belial will never tell you the truth, *ever*. The only thing you can rely on is that everything he says to you will be a lie."

"Goodnight, Wilbert," said Larry, and shook his hand. It was just as clammy as it had been before. Wilbert came to the door with him and watched him hobble his way down the steps. A taxi passed by almost immediately, and Larry hailed it. As he drove away, he could see Wilbert standing in the lighted doorway, his arms by his sides, looking defeated and tired. He had been exploring the world beyond the veil so often that he was probably ready to go there himself. Larry could remember his grandmother sitting in her sunlit morning-room, saying that she was ready to die. "Every time I travel to the spirit-world, I leave a little of myself behind. Soon there will be more of me on the other side than there is on this side; and that is when I shall leave you."

6

Linda was waiting up for him. Without a word, she held him tight and hugged him, and he could feel her tears through his shirt.

"I'm okay," he reassured her. "It hasn't really sunk in yet."

"Oh, but Larry! Your poor mother!"

"I don't think she really knew what hit her."

"What were you doing on Van Ness? I don't understand it."

Larry went through to the kitchen, took down a bottle of whiskey from the cupboard and poured himself half a glassful. He swallowed almost all of it in three large gulps.

Linda said, "*Larry!* You're going to have such a *hangover.*"

"Thank you for your consideration, my mother died tonight and I have a hangover already."

"Are they going to charge the truck-driver?" asked Linda.

"What with? It wasn't his fault. She ran out in front of him."

"Oh, Larry, I'm so sorry."

"Sure. Me, too."

"I haven't told the boys yet. I thought it would be better, coming from you."

Larry nodded. He didn't want to discuss his mother any more. He had thought that—when he got home—he would be able to tell Linda everything that had happened, talk it all out. At least if he started to talk about it, he could begin to absolve himself of some of the guilt. But now he was here, he felt strangely secretive about it; strangely defensive. He still had to work it out inside his own mind before he could tell Linda about it. He believed it himself because he had seen it with his own eyes, but he didn't feel like persuading Linda to believe it.

He could see everything that had happened tonight in the sharpest of detail. The little girl with pondwater gouting out of her mouth. His mother's life, vomited up in front of him. His mother's black coat, dropping empty to the floor. The tractor-trailer, desperately trying to brake. His mother's blood, his mother's lungs. Two yellowish balloons, glued to the pavement; like jester's bladders.

"The best thing you can do is get some sleep," said Linda, laying her hand on his arm.

"Sure thing," he told her. He finished the last of his whiskey, and she took the glass away from him and kissed him.

He went to the bathroom and stood on the scales. One hundred and seventy-three. He'd lost thirteen pounds. Samantha Bacon had been right. Lose Weight With The World Beyond.

He washed his teeth. Afterwards, he hesitated, then picked up the nailbrush and scrubbed at the palm of his left hand until it was sore. He stared at it closely. Unless the shadows started moving across it, there was no way of telling whether he had managed to erase the moving pictures or not. Just for good measure, he chafed his hand with a pumice stone, until he had abraded a whole layer of skin, and his hand felt as if it were on fire. Then he went to bed and switched off the light. But he couldn't sleep. He kept hearing Linda in the kitchen, clearing up the dishes, and the sad lost sounds of foghorns in the Golden Gate. His hand kept burning. Tomorrow he was going to have to start hunting again—trying to track down whoever it was who was trying to bring Belial back from the other side.

The trouble was, the idea of somebody resurrecting an Old Testament angel in San Francisco in 1988 seemed so Goddammned preposterous. Why here? And why now? And *how*?

He felt Linda climbing in to bed next to him. She put her arm around him and cuddled close and kissed his cheek.

"Are you still awake?" she whispered.

"Sure."

"Are you okay? You're terribly quiet."

"I'm okay."

"How was the seance? Did you manage to find out anything?"

"Not too much." *(Tell her, why don't you?)*

"So Wilbert Fraser's not much of a medium?"

"Not much." *(Tell her, for Christ's sake. Tell her about Roberta Snow. Tell her about the coat. Tell her about the ectoplasm.)*

A long silence. Then Linda said, "How about a couple of Nytol?"

"No, thanks. I'm okay. My brain's racing, that's all."

He switched on his bedside lamp and took yesterday's

Chron out of his side-table. Ten minutes of cryptic-crossword-solving would relax him. While Linda turned over and wrapped herself up in the quilt, he looked through the clues and tapped his ballpen against his teeth.

7 Across: Doesn't stand for deception (4). Larry wrote in LIES.

3 Down: He commands sailing-vessel (6). Larry wrote in MASTER.

11 Across: Iron rations Edward has for lunch (4). Larry thought for a moment and then realized the answer was a combination of Fe for Ferrous and Ed for Edward. FEED.

21 Down: Fill out muscle (5). FLESH.

Larry stared at the crossword in slowly-growing apprehension. LIES, MASTER, FEED, FLESH. This was too much a coincidence to be true. Something mischievous was at work here: something deceitful. But how could a spirit change the crossword in a newspaper? Were the clues the same in every copy, or just in his? Maybe he was hallucinating. Maybe he was dreaming. Maybe he was still back at his mother's house, in the dark, and none of this was happening.

Linda turned over and frowned at him from out of her nest of quilt. "What's the matter? You keep jumping around."

"It's nothing. I think I have to make a phone call."

"What, *now?*"

"Yes, now, or else I won't be able to sleep."

He went through to his study and punched out Houston Brough's number. The phone rang and rang but Houston wasn't at home. Eventually Houston's answer-phone picked up

"*You have reached the home of Houston and Annelise Brough...*"and Larry left a message. Then—still sleepless, still frustrated—he rang the *Chron*.

It took almost five minutes for the switchboard to find him a cross and sleepy reporter. It took another two minutes for the cross and sleepy reporter to find the crossword for him. "I want the clues for 7 across, 3 down, 11 across, 21 down," Larry told him.

There was a lengthy pause. Then the reporter said, "Seven across is 'dispose of that hut'. Three down is 'down for the night'. Guess that's 'bedded'. Eleven across is—let me see here—"

"Don't worry, that's enough," said Larry.

"Are you sure? Eleven across is 'sounds as if it's required when making bread.' That could be 'need', yes?"

"Yes," said Larry. "That could be 'need'."

He hung up. He felt as if the whole of his life were sliding away from underneath his feet. Same paper, same day, different crossword. A crossword that had been changed especially for him. LIES, MASTER, FEED, FLESH. The beast was aware of him, no doubt about that. It was mocking him, too. *I can shrivel your mother. I can shrivel anybody I want. I can change your newspaper, right in front of your eyes. And you think that you can catch me?*

He sat in the dark in his study for nearly twenty minutes. Then he returned to the bedroom and eased himself back into bed. Linda was sleeping. She was used to him coming and going in the night. A man needed a disturbed mind to be a good detective; and Larry was a good detective; and his mind was disturbed. All day long, all night long, his mind was churning like a concrete-mixer. LIES, MASTER, FEED, FLESH.

He curved his hand around Linda's bare hip and closed his eyes. He couldn't remember the last time that they had made love. Either she was too tired or he was too tired or they were both too drunk; or else the grisly events of his day's work made it impossible for him to think of anything but blood and intestines and eyes that stared in the last desperation of death. They were dead, but their faces were still pleading, *Please don't kill me.*

And, after tonight, he didn't even have the consolation of knowing that they were safe and happy with God.

He pressed his face against Linda's smooth warm back. He loved her so much that he felt like waking her up just to tell her. *I love you. I love you. I always will.* But it was almost 2:00 am now, and she needed her sleep. He let his hand stray down, and gently wind the curls of her pubic hair around his finger. How was it possible to love anybody so much?

He slept from sheer exhaustion. Then he opened his eyes again, because he thought he heard a rustling noise on the opposite side of the bedroom, and for one heart-stopping moment he imagined his robe was beginning to fill and ripple and rise up from the chair.

He stared at it, holding his breath, but it stayed where it was, where he had left it, one sleeve hanging, the collar twisted open.

He lay back on the pillow again, as carefully as he could, trying not to wake Linda. Now he knew why he hadn't told her about the seance; and what had really happened to his mother. The horror of it ran too deep, and roused too many primitive fears. It was like being a child again, terrified of the dark. Larry knew that he would never forget that coat as long as he lived, and he didn't want Linda to experience that fear even half as starkly as he had.

He tried to sleep some more, but sleep had deserted him now. He eased himself out of bed and went to the study, and switched on his desklamp. All Arne's dossiers and photographs lay spread out in front of him. The Tesslers, whose legs were sawn off. The Wursters, whose tongues were cut out. The Yees, whose forearms were chopped off. The McGuires, whose ears were severed. The Ramirez', who were blinded. Then the Berrys, who had been nailed down hand and foot.

He supposed there was some kind of pattern to all these killings, in that a different part of the body had been mutilated in each. But it wasn't a pattern that appeared to relate to anything in particular.

It could have something to do with "hear no evil, see no evil, say no evil." But where did the legs and the arms come into it?

He thought about Wilbert Fraser and the Black Brotherhood. He thought about the faces that people had been seeing in windows and mirrors. He thought about Edna-Mae Lickerman; and his mother, too. He thought about everything that had happened since he had taken over this investigation, and his thoughts hurt. It was like a jelly-jar, smashed on a supermarket floor. Sticky and messy and full of vicious fragments of broken glass.

He held out his hand, palm upward, and stared at it. Somehow, *he* came into this investigation, too. He had the moving hand, although he didn't understand what that really meant, or how dangerous it might be, or how he was ever going to get rid of it.

He thought about Belial. Was there really such a beast as the Master of Lies?

LIES, MASTER, FEED, FLESH. The proof, as far as Larry was concerned, was incontrovertible. Only his paper had carried that message. It had been meant especially for him. The beast was not only powerful enough to steal his ectoplasm, it was sentient, too. It knew him, and it had him marked.

As he stared at the palm of his hand, he saw the clouds beginning to glide across it. He remembered what Houston had said, and he crossed the study to the closet, opened the louvred doors, and took out his Sony video camera. He sat back at his desk, focused the camera manually, so that he could get pin-sharp focus, and switched it on.

The clouds swirled and snagged and began to form a picture. That face again, smiling and unruffled. And then that voice, tiny but clearly distinguishable.

Almost time to feed, my friend. Almost time!

"Feed on what?" Larry demanded.

There was a very long silence, as if the face were surprised that Larry had answered it back. But eventually it said, *On that which was promised. On my earthly reward.*

"What was your earthly reward?"

A thousand thousand, that was what was promised.

"You mean *people*? A thousand thousand *people*?"

That was my earthly reward.

"Who promised you this reward?"

Those who called me.

"But who were they?"

If you hear a voice in the darkness, do you care whose voice it is? Besides, their names are nothing to me. I would feed on them, too, if I could.

"Why did they call you? Did they say why? Did they say what they wanted?"

"What does any man want? Power over other men; wealth; and immunity from guilt."

"When did this happen? When did they call you?"

Much longer ago than you could ever remember, my friend. And I've been waiting ever since. Not patiently, either. But now my time has come. Now it's time for me to feed.

Larry crushed his fist tight shut, and kept it shut. All he wanted to do was to squeeze the life out of the creature that had marked his hand. Asphyxiate, break its bones. He kept his fist so tight for so long that he began to tremble with the effort.

Blood slid out between his knuckles, three darkly-glistening runnels of blood, and dripped on to the photograph of the Tessler family on the desk.

"Bastard bastard bastard," Larry grimaced. "I'm going to do to you what you did to them, what you did to all of them, but to you I'm going to do it twice as slow."

"Larry!" said Linda.

Larry looked up. Linda was standing in the study doorway naked. Her hair was fluffed up and she looked sleepy and startled.

"Larry, what are you *doing*? Look at your hand!"

Slowly, Larry opened his fingers. His palm was filled with blood. But there were no clouds, no pictures, no faces.

"I guess I—" he began. But then he realized that there was no way of explaining what he was doing without telling Linda everything; and right now he didn't want to tell her everything.

"I guess I was trying to get a grip on myself," he added, weakly.

Linda came over and took hold of his hand. She reached across the desk, tugged out several kleenex, and mopped up the blood.

"You were *filming* yourself, too!" she said.

Larry gave her an awkward shrug. "I don't quite know what I was doing. It's the shock of momma's death, I suppose. I was just trying to understand what pain was like."

"I would have thought you knew that already, in your job."

"I mean, what pain *feels* like."

She kissed his forehead. "Come wash your hand in the bathroom. There's no cut or anything. If you can't sleep I'll make us some tea."

Larry switched off the video camera and wearily rose from his chair. "I'm sorry," he said, putting his arm around her. "Sometimes it must be like living with a crazy person."

She kissed him again. "What do you mean 'sometimes'?"

He woke Frankie and Mikey at seven o'clock and made them breakfast, pancakes and crispy bacon and maple syrup. They sat at the breakfast bar in their Fred Flintstone pajamas swinging their bare feet. Frankie was trying to teach Mikey the Declaration of Independence, without much success.

"When in the course of human events it becomes necessary for one people—" Mikey began; then stopped and said, "That's wrong!"

"What do you mean it's wrong?" asked Frankie.

"You can't say one *people*. It's one *person*."

"But it's people like in millions of people."

"It's still wrong," Mikey insisted.

"It's in the Declaration of Independence, it can't be wrong."

"Go on, Mikey," Larry coaxed him. "Frankie's right."

"Okay, okay. For one people to dissolve. How can people dissolve? That's silly! How can people dissolve?"

Larry drove them in Linda's wagon to their Cub Scout gathering on Lombard Street, where already most of their troop had assembled, ready for the bus.

"You take care, you guys," Larry told them, and kissed them goodbye. The streets were filled with hazy sunshine, and although he hadn't slept for most of the night, Larry was beginning to feel more optimistic. The events of yesterday evening hadn't lost any of their rawness or strangeness, but at least he had some idea who he was looking for, and what he was up against.

Houston Brough was waiting for him in his office, drinking strong black coffee.

"You all right?" Houston asked him.

"Surviving."

"El Chiefo wants to see us. The Press have got wind of the fact that we're investigating the supernatural. He doesn't like it one bit."

"Anything published yet?" asked Larry.

"Not yet, but they've been asking."

"I'll slaughter that Dogmeat," said Larry.

They walked along the corridor to Dan Burroughs' office. Houston said, "I checked up on Edna-Mae first thing this morning. She's under restraint, but reasonably stable."

"Is she coherent?"

"She's asleep most of the time."

Dan Burroughs was standing by the window, his hands in his pockets, smoking furiously. He didn't turn around when Larry and Houston knocked on his door and walked in, but it was obvious from the set of his shoulders that he knew who they were.

"That Fay Kuhn woman was on to me this morning," he said, harshly. "She wanted to know if it were true that the investigating officer in the Fog City Satan case had attended a seance on Jackson Street last night."

"I'm seeing Fay Kuhn at eleven," Larry replied. "I can talk about it then."

Dan Burroughs turned around. The sunlight shone through his cigarette smoke. "So it's true, you did go."

"Sure it's true. I'm looking into every possibility, natural and supernatural."

"Joe Berry wasn't nailed to the floor by a spook, Larry."

"I didn't say that he was. But whoever *did* nail him to the floor did it for a reason, and that reason could have been connected with the supernatural. People kill for religious reasons… you wouldn't give me a hard time for checking out the churches, would you?"

"Don't get smart, Larry. Religion is one thing. The supernatural—the occult, whatever, that's another. It makes for bad publicity."

"I don't give a two-toned shit about bad publicity, Dan,

I'm looking for a man who saws people's legs off and sets fire to small children. If I feel the need to check out the supernatural, I'll check out the supernatural."

Dan Burroughs came away from the window and circled around Larry and Houston like a school principal who had caught them drinking beer behind the bushes. "I don't want to hear one more word about the supernatural in connection with this investigation. This investigation is going to be carried out by the rules of orthodox police procedure; and when you arrest the perpetrator, which had better be pretty damned soon, you are going to make sure that your evidence is complete, watertight and non-wacky. Do you understand me? I want to take this maniac into court and I want the prosecutor to have all the information necessary to prove beyond a shadow of doubt that he killed all of these people, and I want to see him convicted and sentenced and gassed.

"If you screw up because you've been obtaining evidence from ghosts or ouija boards or crystal balls, then believe me, Larry, I'll never forgive you."

Larry said nothing. Dan laid his hand on his shoulder and looked at him with one eye open and one eye closed against the smoke from his cigarette.

"By the way," said Dan, "I heard about your mother. I'm truly sorry. She was a fine woman. Fine, fine woman."

"Yes, she was," Larry agreed. "Is there anything else?"

"The mayor's office keeps calling. I'd just like to know how close to our boy you think you are."

"Getting closer every day, Dan."

"But no ghosts, please."

"Give me some space, Dan. You'll get your gassing."

Dogmeat met him on Fisherman's Wharf. The fog had completely lifted now, and the bay was glittering and bright. Larry had borrowed an '82 Le Sabre with a whining transmission from the police car pool. He parked opposite Pier 39, and climbed out, putting on his sunglasses as he did so. Dogmeat was perched on the railings in his shaggy jacket and his skinny velvet pants like a huge tattered vulture.

"*Buongiorno, mon ami*," he said, flicking away the roach that he had been smoking, and breathing out grass fumes.

"Good morning, you blabbermouth," Larry replied. "If I can't get you for possession, I can get you for littering."

"Hey, hey, *pourquoi* so short-tempered?" Dogmeat asked.

"Because every time you and I have one of our little conversations, I don't expect you to go running to the nearest telephone to tell Ms Fay Kuhn what we've been chewing the fat about, that's *pourquoi*."

"Oh, come on, man, I have to make a *croûte*. Time was, the police department paid regular and good. These days I have to top up my income from the media."

"Time was, your information was regular and good."

Larry walked along the pier with Dogmeat hobbling along behind him on his worndown heels. It was still too early for tourists, although the wind was warm and the sun was dazzling, and the Bay was at her best. Larry leaned on the railings and looked down at the small boats bobbing like ducks at their moorings.

"This time I've got something Grade-A," Dogmeat told him. "But I have to see some Johnny Cash up front. Even an artist has overheads. Rent, tamales, guitar-strings, grass."

Larry opened his billfold and took out three twenties. Dogmeat held them up to the light one at a time. "Cops pass more counterfeit cabbage than anybody," he sniffed.

"So what's this Grade-A information that you've got for me?" asked Larry.

"I was talking to John de Villescas, he's a set-designer and mask-maker, works for the Curran Theater. Kind of an oddball... doesn't speak to anybody much. Believes that words are valuable, not to be wasted. Lives in this *turret* on Union Street. He's not gay which is a huge rarity, but somebody once told me that he had a thing for sheep which was probably a vicious lie. Sheep are so *passé* and John is avant the avant garde. Now if they'd said *llamas*."

"How about getting around to the point?" Larry suggested. "I have an interview in twenty minutes."

"For sure. To schneiden a long story short, John was asked in January to make a mask. Like, it was a private commission, not for the stage or anything. But it was *trés trés* weird, a huge black full-head mask like a monster stag-beetle, with horns, and eyes, like nothing you ever heard of before. The guy commissioned it on the phone, and sent John used cabbage in the mail. Well... he was paying seven hundred fifty dollars for it, and John wasn't going to tell him no. Seven hundred fifty dollars equals a lot of burritos, *n'est-ce pas?*"

"How did your friend know exactly what kind of a mask the guy wanted?" asked Larry.

"Oho, he was real particular. He sent an engraving in the envelope, along with the cabbage. Very detailed in every wayland jennings."

With a flourish, Dogmeat produced from the pocket of his ratty Afghan jacket a soiled and dog-eared sheet of paper. Larry took it, and unfolded it, and there it was. A detailed steel engraving of a huge figure in a black cloak, with the black horned head of a stag-beetle. Behind the figure, in the shadows, hundreds of naked bodies writhed like maggots, and lightning was crackling out of the clouds.

He knew at once who the figure was. He didn't even need to look down to the bottom of the illustration and see the name *Beli Ya'al, Master of Lies*.

"Dogmeat," he breathed. The engraving flapped in the bright morning breeze. "Dogmeat, you're some kind of genius."

"Maybe worth genius money, then?" Dogmeat suggested.

Larry nodded, and handed him another two twenties. Dogmeat scrutinized these two fresh bills with his usual suspicion. "You have to ask yourself, where does all the counterfeit money *go*, after a bust? Don't tell me you burn it. Just like all that pornography and all that dope and all that unaccounted-for jewelry and stuff."

"What made you think I'd be interested in this?" Larry wanted to know.

"You *are* interested in it, then?"

"Oh, for sure. This is the first piece of solid evidence I've had that I'm not losing my marbles."

"What are you trying to do?" Dogmeat asked, with

exaggerated bewilderment. "Catch this killer or prove your sanity?"

"I just want to know what made you think I'd be interested in this engraving."

"Because of the guy who commissioned it, *naturlich*."

"Don't speak in riddles, Dogmeat, I'm not in the mood."

Dogmeat rummaged in his fringed hippie-style satchel and produced a fat, half-burned joint. "You don't mind if I jolt, *monsieur?*"

Larry watched him light up, and sharply suck the smoke through his teeth. "Ah... grass is not what it was. Gone is *l'âge d'or*. Can you smell this stuff? It's like smoking your grandmother's hedge."

Larry patiently waited for him to finish posturing, and then said, "Come on, Dogmeat. Tell me what happened."

"Aha!" said Dogmeat. "What happened was, the guy came to collect his mask in person. He said he wanted to make sure that it fitted good before he shelled out the necessary clams. John told me that the guy was already wearing a dark green ski-mask when he appeared on the doorstep, with nothing but holes for eyes. He came in, he took a look at the mask, he took it into the bathroom and tried it on. *Avec* the door locked, so John couldn't watch him. But he came out of the bathroom and said that he liked it; and he paid the money, and split."

"He didn't give your friend any indication where he lived, where he hung out, what his name was?"

"Come on, lieutenant! What do you want, boysenberry jelly on it?"

"Could he describe him?"

"For sure. Huge, Caucasian, dark hair, mid-forties, huge."

"Sounds like our boy," said Larry.

"There's something else," put in Dogmeat.

"Is this for free?" asked Larry.

"Was the rest of the information worth paying for?" Dogmeat retorted.

"Yes, it was, as matter of fact."

"Then this is worth paying for, too."

With a show of reluctance, Larry took out his billfold and stripped off another forty dollars. Dogmeat made them vanish faster than David Copperfield. "The point was..."he said; "John has a convenient peephole in his bathroom wall, left over from the time when the apartment was let by some voyeuristic weirdo to any girl with a good buster keaton. So, when the guy was trying on the mask... John took a look."

"Pity he didn't have the presence of mind to take a photograph, too."

"You don't even need a photograph to nail this chump, lieutenant. When he took off his ski-mask, poor old John practically lost his Magic Pan brunch on the spot. The guy's head was shriveled and disfigured, with raw bits and leathery bits and patches of skin and sprouts of *cheveux*. His nose was all tilted up, his eyes were half-closed. Typical victim of our old friend Major Burns."

"He was *burned*?" asked Larry, suddenly alert. *It was George. He burned them. That car exploded, just as it was starting to move, Exploded, and burned out.*

"Not like Freddie Krueger. Properly burned. Brown and scarlet, thick scar-tissue, face like a leather football."

Larry said, "The Black Brotherhood were burned."

Dogmeat's eyes darted quickly and worriedly around the pier. "You—unh—found out their name, then?"

"Wilbert Fraser told me their name."

"Well... let me tell you this, lieutenant. They never liked people mentioning their name back in the ' '60s; and so I never do now. In my line of work, discretion is the better part of having your fries removed, *comprende?*"

"Do you think that any of them could have survived?" asked Larry.

"Who knows? A burned guy commissions a mask that could be connected with ritual-type killings... it's a lead, *n'est-ce pas*, as one electrician said to the other."

"I'm going to find this joker," said Larry; much more to himself than to Dogmeat.

"Sure you're going to find this joker," Dogmeat agreed. "You know what happened to the queer king who got shipwrecked on a desert island with his court jester? After a month he was at his wit's end."

Larry replaced his Ray-Ban Aviators and grasped Dogmeat's bony fingers and gave him a crushing handshake. "I'll be in touch, okay? Meanwhile keep your eyes open. Anything, *anything*, and I'll pay you extra. Tell your pals to look out for burned guys, guys in masks, guys with heavy face-paint. Tell them I'll pay them, too."

Dogmeat sucked at his joint. "This is a heavy one, *es correcto?*"

"*Hasta luego,*" said Larry, and walked away from Pier 39 under a bright sky like broken mirrors.

★

Fay Kuhn was waiting for him at the Hall of Justice. She looked relentlessly smart in a beige suit with angular shoulders and a short skirt. An identity badge was already fastened to her lapel next to an enameled pin of Swee' Pea. Larry jerked his head to indicate that she should follow him up to his office, and she did, heels sharply rapping.

Houston Brough was waiting for him, too. It was obvious that he wanted to tell Larry something urgent, but when he saw that Fay Kuhn was closely behind him, he gave Larry an awkward smile and a shrug and said, "Okay—it's okay. I can see that you're all tied up. It wasn't anything special."

Larry said, "Sit down," and Fay Kuhn sat down, crossing her legs. She took out a notebook and pencil, which was rare. Almost every reporter used a tape-recorder these days.

"You write shorthand?" he asked her.

She smiled. Glossy scarlet lips, painted in perfect bows. "I was taught journalism by old men who knew how to compose sentences and how to take a proper note."

"Tom Wolfe?" he asked her.

"Shit," she replied.

"Hunter Thompson?"

"Shit."

"Good," he nodded. He had suffered enough at the hands of gung-ho journalists. "What do you want to know?"

"I want to know whether you're investigating every possible avenue in your hunt for the Fog City Satan. Or 'so-called' Fog City Satan, to quote Dan Burroughs exactly."

"Of course." Larry leaned back in his chair and steepled his fingers. "Every possible avenue."

"Including the supernatural?"

"I'm sorry?"

Fay Kuhn crossed her legs provocatively and impatiently. "Are you denying that you have any suspicion that the Fog City Satan may not be altogether earthly?"

"I'm not sure what you mean, Miss Kuhn."

"If you're not sure what I mean, why did you attend a seance held by the well-known Nob Hill medium Wilbert Fraser last night?

Larry eased forward in his chair and drummed his fingers on his desktop. Linda and Frankie and Mikey were grinning at him out of their photograph frame. Unconsciously, he grinned back at them.

Larry shrugged, didn't know what to say.

"I've heard the rumors," said Fay Kuhn. "People are saying that there's some kind of—I don't know, what can you call it?—some kind of *psychic disturbance* in the air."

"I'm not sure what you mean by that, either," said Larry.

"Lieutenant, we live in San Francisco. We live on the fault line. We're sensitive to every kind of disturbance—climatic, seismic, political, emotional or psychic. We're like human seaweed."

Larry stood up and circled around his office. Throughout the building, unanswered phones rang as if they had been orchestrated. Laurence Foggia and his Singing Telephones. He decided to take a long shot with Fay Kuhn. She wasn't any kind of idiot—and no matter what Dan Burroughs thought about talking to the Press—she could conceivably be helpful.

"There have been incidents of psychic disturbance, yes," he agreed.

Fay Kuhn looked up at him sharply. "Faces?" she asked.

"Yes," said Larry. "Faces."

"Can you give me more specific details than that?"

Larry shook his head. "Not at this time. I haven't yet investigated any of the reports personally, so I'm unable to verify them. But there have been an unusual number of incidents which appear to have no rational explanation. They may be connected with the Fog City Satan case."

"Very discreet of you, lieutenant," smiled Fay Kuhn. "But I think they *are* connected with the Fog City Satan case. In fact, I'm sure they are."

He looked at her narrowly. "Go on."

She reached into her shoulder-bag and took out a musty-looking library book with a tattered jacket. "I found this," she said. "*The Day Before The Earth Shook*, by Doris Kelville. It's a detailed portrait of San Francisco on Tuesday, April 17, 1906... right up until that moment just after five o'clock the following morning when the earthquake occurred."

Larry returned to his desk. "What led you to research back that far?"

She was flipping pages. "Oh... I was looking for something else altogether. A story about those long-lost city archives that were turned up in the basement of City Hall. Here we are—look."

She handed the open book across Larry's desk. Five long paragraphs had been marked in red felt-tip pen.

"Shortly after midnight on Wednesday morning, a woman was arrested while attempting to dig up the pavement at the intersection of Front and Green Streets. She had done no serious damage, but her manner was so "unGodly and abusive" that she was taken to the Hall of Justice (in those days on Kearney Street). She turned out to be the city's most celebrated clairvoyante and palmist, Edith Nielsen, who the previous year had publicly warned the twenty-six-year-old Chief of the Fire Brigade, Dennis T. Sullivan, that he would be killed by "a bolt from the blue."

"Mrs. Nielsen said that she had discovered the 'real perpetrator' of six appalling mass-murders which had taken place in San Francisco during the latter part of 1904 and the early months of 1905; and that she was digging up the pavement in an attempt to forestall a seventh. She would not apparently say how, or why.

"The mass-murders were known at the time as the Blue Letter Murders because after each killing the murderer would send a letter on azure bond to the editor of the *San Francisco Morning Call*, boasting about his horrific activities. (For a detailed account of the Blue Letter Murders, *vide* Arthur Strerath's *Murder On The Brink Of The World*, Putnam, 1935.)

"In a statement to the police, Mrs. Nielsen said she had been warned by friendly spirits that San Francisco faced 'a great catastrophe' and that the murders had been simply a prelude to it. For weeks, she had seen ghostly faces in windows and mirrors and on the palms of her clients' hands, and this was 'a sure sign' that 'some terrible disaster' was imminent. At least a thousand people would die in one day, she said.

"As it turned out, the earthquake and the subsequent fire left only 478 officially dead. But fire chief Dennis T. Sullivan was the first man to be killed by the first chimney-pot that fell down. Actually that was one of the reasons the city was so badly damaged by fire… the fire crews had lost their leader."

Larry handed the book back. "What led you to connect this incident with the Fog City Satan?"

Again Fay Kuhn rummaged in her bag. This time she produced a sheaf of glossy, acrid-smelling photostats. "I couldn't get a copy of the original book on the Blue Letter Murders, but a member of the Mystery Writers of America sent me these, from his own private collection."

Larry leafed quickly through the pages. "Six ritualistic mass homicides. Okay… I see the parallel. But these happened more than eighty years ago. You're not suggesting the same perpetrator is still alive and killing after eighty years?"

"Of course not. But take a look at what was done in each of these cases. In the first one, a family on Hayes Street had their feet cut off. In the second, three people on Dolores Street had their throats cut. In the third, the victims had their hands severed. In the fourth, in Chinatown, a husband and wife had molten type-metal poured into their ears, hot lead and antimony. And so on."

Larry re-read the photostats more carefully. There was no doubt that the 1906 killings followed a similar pattern to the Fog City Satan's attacks. In fact, they followed the *only* pattern that Larry had been able to discern. Each killing had included the very specific maiming of a different part of the body.

"How long have you had this information?" asked Larry.

"Three weeks already."

"Didn't you show it to Lieutenant Knudsen? You might have convinced him that your report was worth looking into."

"Of course I showed him. But he simply said that it wasn't scientific. He said that if *he* had never heard of any of these killings, it wasn't very likely that the Fog City Satan had, either, so the chances of your boy being a copycat killer were—how did he put it?—about one in a grillion."

"That's one more chance than none in a grillion."

"Oh, for sure. But try telling that to Know-it-All Knudsen." She pronounced both "Ks". "'Not scientific, I'm afraid,'" she quoted.

"It's scientific if you believe it."

"Do *you* believe it?" asked Fay Kuhn, cautiously.

But at that moment, there was a casual, loose-wristed knocking at Larry's open door, and Dan Burroughs stepped in, with a cigarette hanging from his lip. "Good morning, Ms Kuhn," he greeted her. Then, "Larry... when you have a moment."

"We won't be long," said Fay Kuhn, without turning around. "I just have to ask Lieutenant Foggia few personal questions."

Dan came into the office, circled around Larry's desk, and picked up the photostats about the Blue Letter Murders. "You're not still harping on about this, are you, dear?" he asked Fay Kuhn.

"I thought the lieutenant might be interested to see it, that's all," Fay Kuhn retorted. "After all, I gather that you assigned him to the Fog City Satan to get a different view on the case."

Dan Burroughs coughed, and sniffed. "I've already taken a look at this material, Ms Kuhn, and not to put too fine a point on it, it's all a fairy-story. We do occasionally work by hunch and inspiration... that's one of the reasons that Lieutenant Foggia was given this assignment. It's a weird case, and he's a very inspirational detective. But at the end of the day we have to come to court with proof, Ms Kuhn. And not just any old proof, either. *Believable* proof. The kind of proof that's going to make it cast-iron certain that twelve good but retarded civilians are going to send the maniac who's been committing these crimes to the gas chamber."

Fay Kuhn hesitated, then she reached across Larry's desk and collected up her papers. "I'm sorry to have bothered you," she said. "Maybe we can finish up the personal details later."

"Whatever you want," said Larry. "You know where to reach me." He wanted to say, "I believe you. I believe you totally. Take a look at my hand." But he was too conscious of Dan Burroughs' hostility to Fay Kuhn; and to any suggestion that there was anything supernatural about the Fog City Satan.

He walked Fay Kuhn to the end of the fourth-floor corridor. "You'll have to make allowances for Deputy Chief Burroughs," he said. "He's very procedural."

"Sometimes people act very procedural in order to disguise the fact that they're up to something highly non-procedural," Fay Kuhn remarked.

They stopped beside the elevators. The doors opened and two officers came out with a huge black teenager in a lurid pink track suit. "Who you calling a black faggot you white shrimp?" the teenager was protesting.

Larry held the elevator doors. "Am I supposed to infer anything in particular from that comment?" he asked Fay Kuhn.

"You can infer what you like. Deputy Chief Daniel Hadrian Burroughs is a man of many interests. I just think that you ought to watch your back. Not to mention your front and your sides."

"All right, if you think it's wise."

"I think it's wise. Particularly in this case. And there's something else, too."

"Oh, yes?"

"What was Edith Nielsen trying to dig up on the corner of Front and Green?"

"How should I know? Do *you* know?"

Fay Kuhn gave him a little shrug. "I don't have any idea. But she did say that she was trying to forestall a seventh mass killing. Now, how do you suppose she was going to do that?"

"I don't know that, either."

"Well, there we are. We're both as ignorant as each other. I'm just suggesting that it might be worth your while to find out."

Fay Kuhn stepped to the back of the elevator. Larry held the door for just a moment longer, looking at her with both curiosity and appreciation. Then he let the doors go, and she disappeared from sight, still with that faint acidic little self-satisfied smile on her face.

Larry decided as he walked back to his office that he liked her.

7

After a quick take-out Chinese lunch with Houston Brough, and an update meeting with detectives Jones and Glass, Larry drove to his mother's house to collect Mussolini. He didn't intend to keep the parrot himself; but one of the young patrolmen in the bunco squad was something of a bird-fancier, and Larry had promised to give it to him.

The old house stood quiet in the afternoon sunshine. Larry unlocked the door with the same key that his father had given him on his thirteenth birthday. Inside, the hallway smelled of cooking and dust. The sun angled through the stained-glass skylight above the front door and cast a pattern on the wallpaper like an old monk with his face hidden by his hood. He remembered that figure from his childhood, and how much it had frightened him. So much, in fact, that he hadn't liked to venture alone into the hallway on summer afternoons, because he knew that the faceless monk would be waiting for him.

He opened the door of his mother's living-room, and a score of reflected images of himself opened the door, too. He stood still, looking around. The drapes were still drawn, the table was still lying on its side, the teacups overturned.

The coat, too, was still lying where it had dropped. Larry hesitated for almost a minute, listening, then walked across and picked it up.

It was just a coat. He stroked the collar two or three times. It still smelled of his mother's perfume; as if she were still alive. He folded it over the back of the chair, and then hunkered down and picked up the teacups and all the scattered sugarlumps. When he was very small, his mother had given him sugar-lumps for a treat, so long as he swore on the Bible that he wouldn't tell his father.

Mussolini's cage was still draped in its black cloth. He had heard the parrot's claws scratching on its perch when he first came into the room; although it hadn't screamed anything rude at him. At least the poor creature was still alive. Maybe a day's dieting had done it good. Larry had always thought that his mother spoiled it. She used to give it pecans and macadamia nuts and Japanese cuttlefish bones. No wonder the Goddamned bird was so arrogant.

He heard Mussolini scratching again, and he called out, "All right, you housebound buzzard, I'm coming!". He picked up the last of the dried-up lemon-slices that had fallen under the couch, and dropped them into a broken tea-cup.

He crossed the living-room and approached Mussolini's cage. He was just about to tug the black cloth off it, when something stopped him. Some feeling. Some odd, left-field, unsettling feeling. Why hadn't Mussolini said anything, when he first came into the room? And why was he scratching so much? *Scratching*, as if he were sharpening his claws.

"Mussolini?" he called. "Is that you, Mussolini?"

Skkrattchch, skkrattch, skkrattch, from underneath the domed black cloth.

This is ridiculous, you can't be scared of a bird. It's nothing but a tattered old parrot, sitting in its cage. It's probably half-starved and dying of dehydration, and you're *scared* of it? He pulled at the cloth but the cloth snagged on the ring at the top of the cage and he couldn't disentangle it.

"It's okay, Mussolini. Uncle Larry to the rescue."

"*Time to feed,*" rasped the parrot.

"That's right, Mussolini, time to—

He stopped in mid-sentence, his arms upraised, still trying to pull the cloth free.

"*What* did you say?" he asked, with a tight cold tangle in his stomach.

"*Time to feed,*" the parrot repeated. "*Time to feed. Time to devour the thousand thousand.*"

Larry backed away. He checked the palm of his hand; but it was clear. No clouds, no sunshine, no smiling face. It wasn't his hand that was whispering to him. It was Mussolini. Or what he *assumed* was Mussolini, underneath that twisted black cloth. He didn't know what to do next. Whatever it was, it was caged, and he guessed that it couldn't get out; or it would have gotten out before. But all the same, he wasn't sure that he wanted to see what it was. Its voice sounded quite like his mother's, high and brittle and breathy. Maybe Mussolini's voice had *always* sounded like his mother's, without him noticing it. After all, his mother had taught it to talk. But for some reason it put the fear of God into him.

"Mussolini?" he called again. No answer. He reached

into his shoulder-holster and lifted out his gun. The simple answer would be to blow six .38 holes through the cage, and *then* see what was in it.

He eased back the hammer.

"Mussolini?" he repeated, very softly. "Is that you, Mussolini?"

God you must look like a total wacko holding a gun on a parrot's cage. He's a bird, that's all. Just because he talked about feeding, what does that mean? Your mother was always feeding him. All he knows is food and Italian insults.

"Mussolini, you'd better be Mussolini or else it's ventilation time."

"*Che violino!*" the parrot squawked. "*Che violino!*"

Larry lowered his gun. How could he have allowed one scrawny ridiculous parrot to frighten him so much? It just showed how tightly his nerves were stretched; and how this whole assignment had undermined his confidence in what was real and what was imaginary. By the time he had caught the Fog City Satan, he would probably be ready for the basket-factory.

He dragged the cloth from Mussolini's cage, wound it up, and dropped it on to the floor. Mussolini had his back to him, his head lowered.

"Come on, Mussolini, you and me are going for a ride."

Mussolini turned around on his perch. And it was then that Larry saw the huge white bulge that swelled out of one side of his head and neck. It had stretched the parrot's skin so that one gray-lidded eye was blindly closed, and half of his beak was twisted. What was so heart-stopping, however, was that *the bulge was a misshapen parody of the left side of Larry's own face.* It had a half-formed nose, a drooping wattle-like lip, and a dark brown eye that stared back at him with all the brightness and intelligence of his own.

And the cage door was open. All that had prevented Mussolini from escaping up until now was the tightly swathed cloth.

Larry stood frozen. His mind simply didn't know how to react—and even if it had, his body probably wouldn't have known how to obey.

He watched the parrot scratch its ungainly way across its perch, with that one dark-brown eye still staring at him fixedly. The added weight of its grotesque disfigurement had unbalanced it, and it hobbled like a hunchback.

"*Time to feed*," it whispered, in an almost-human voice.

"What are you?" said Larry. His throat was so tight with fear that he could hardly get the words out.

"*Everything you desire. Everything. But they promised me one thousand thousand and one thousand thousand is what I shall have.*"

"Are you—Belial?"

"*I am nobody you know.*"

"Belial, the Master of Lies. Is *that* who you are?"

"*I am everything you ever dreamed of. There is no angel sweeter than I.*"

The parrot sat staring at him for a long moment. Larry said, "Easy now… take it easy."

He took a step forward. If he could close the cage-door, then he would have this monstrosity trapped, and maybe he and Wilbert could—

But without warning, in a terrifying burst of fluttering and scratching, the parrot-creature scrambled for the door of its cage. Larry tugged his gun back out of its holster, but he was a fraction of a second too late. The bird exploded out of the cage and flew wildly and eccentrically around the living-room, screeching and crying as it flew.

Larry ducked again and again as the parrot flew over his head. Once it clawed at his hair, and he had to knock it away with his gun. "*Feed!*" it shrilled. "*Feed! Feed! Feed!*"

Off-balance, he tried to shoot at the parrot. He let off one shot which almost deafened him, and brought a huge lump of plaster cornice showering down. But then he thought: *supposing there's somebody upstairs—one shot through the ceiling could kill them. And what if the parrot looks this way because it's taken the one thing that I left behind when I left her with momma. My ectoplasm. Myself. If I kill or injure this parrot, the same thing could happen to me.*

Screeching and fluttering, the parrot flew around his head again; then perched on the chandelier, making it glitter and tinkle. Mussolini stared at him with his single brown human eye and his single gray parrot eye. His neck was swollen with the weight and the effort of carrying around half of a human face.

"Mussolini, you hear me?" called Larry.

"*I hear nothing but humanity. Delicious humanity.*"

"Mussolini, Belial, whoever you are… listen, calm down."

"*I want to go free,*" hissed the parrot/man.

"Is that another lie?"

"*You can think of it anything you wish, True, false— what's it to you?*"

Now Larry knew why he recognized the parrot's voice. It wasn't his mother's. It carried a similar accent, and a very similar intonation. But the difference was obvious. It wasn't his mother's voice, it was his own—reduced in timbre and resonance by the parrot's small body-frame. His own voice, shrunk. He was sure now that his ectoplasm must have left his mother's coat and concealed itself in the only living being in the room that was capable of escape. Mussolini the parrot. The only trouble was, it looked as if Mussolini hadn't been capable of absorbing all that ectoplasm. His own face still bulged from Mussolini's neck.

He glanced quickly around the room. His mother's shawl was still draped over the side of the sofa—the black tasseled Tuscany shawl that his father had given her, so many years ago, when life had been summery. Carefully, he sidestepped across the room and picked it up. The parrot/man watched him with odd and baleful eyes, like Edgar Allen Poe's raven. Its claws scratched uneasily on the branches of the chandelier; and again the chandelier glittered and tinkled.

Left-handed, Larry swung the shawl behind him. The parrot/man spat at him, "*I want to go free. I shall go free.*"

Larry hesitated for one more moment, then bounded up onto the seat of the sofa, and whirled the shawl so that it fell over Mussolini's perch and caught the creature inside. Then he snatched the bottom of the shawl and tried to twist it around so that the Mussolini would be trapped.

The parrot/man screeched and thrashed in hysterical anger. For nearly a minute, it lobbed itself from one side of the shawl to the other, beating its wings and tearing with its claws, and it was all Larry could do to keep hold of it.

But then it exploded out of the shawl in a burst of feathers and fury, and flew around the room, around and around, colliding with the walls and the ceiling and the chandelier. Larry went after it, swinging the shawl, but the room was too high for him to be able to throw it over Mussolini from the floor—even if Mussolini had stayed still for a couple of seconds.

Mussolini struck the windows so violently that he began to leave splashes of blood on the glass; and it was then that Larry realized he had no alternative but to let him go. If he didn't, Mussolini would beat himself hysterically to death—and God alone knew what would happen to his own ectoplasm if Mussolini did *that*.

He dropped the shawl and backed quickly toward the living-room door, still keeping his gun raised. He opened the door wide and then stood well away.

"All right you ugly fuck! Get the hell out of here!"

Almost immediately, Mussolini stopped his suicidal fluttering, and clawed and jangled back onto the chandelier. It sat there, swaying slightly, its wing-feathers matted with blood, and the sloping, inhuman expression on its face made Larry feel as if he were right on the brink of losing control.

"Go on!" he yelled at it, harshly. "Get the hell out of here!"

But the parrot stayed where it was; still swaying.

"C'mon," Larry urged him. "Shoo!" But then he realized that the front door was still closed, and that the parrot wouldn't fly out of the room until he was sure that he had a clear route of escape.

"All right, you shit," Larry growled at it. He could stand a deformed bird. He could even stand the idea that its deformity had been caused by stealing part of *him*. But what he couldn't stand was his own eye, staring at him with such malevolent curiosity, as if the parrot were wondering what it was really like to be whole and human, instead of some half-formed monstrosity from somebody else's nightmare.

Larry went to the front door. The blue monk was still shining on the wall, but it had become elongated now, because of the setting of the sun. It looked even more alarming and attenuated than ever—a monk who could stretch to impossible heights. A monk who could come in the dark, and stand over you, when your sleep was at its most disturbed.

He opened the door. Outside, sunlight, and Belvedere Street, and sparkling airplanes circling around to SFX. He turned, and at that instant the parrot creature screeched past him with a lashing of wings and feathers, and rose into the sunshine, and angled away. Mussolini had gone, and taken part of Larry with him.

Larry tried to see which direction the parrot had taken, but the air was too hazy, and the city skyline was too complicated; and when he saw a flying shadow it was nothing but a sheet of newspaper, tumbling in the breeze.

He felt bereft. Something had been stolen from him. Some look, some memory, some essence; but he didn't understand what. All he knew was that he felt diminished—less of the Larry that he used to be.

He returned to his mother's living-room. He walked around it, staring into one mirror after the other. *Who are you now? What have you lost?*

He couldn't tell. He picked up a silver-framed photograph of his father and looked at it for a very long time. Somehow he felt no affection for his father any more—almost as if he didn't belong to him. Almost as if they weren't related. He replaced the photograph on the table and thought: *something seriously bad is about to happen. I wish hell I knew what it was.*

*

Wilbert Fraser had been shopping at the Victoria Pastry Company on Stockton Street which was the only patisserie that made meringues exactly the way he liked them, and the Nature Stop on Grant Avenue, which was the only health-food store that stocked the dried seaweed that helped his psychic energy. He cramped the tires of his ageing black Lincoln Continental against the curb outside his house, and balanced the large white cardboard box of meringues up the steps.

"Nice day, sunny for a change!" called Mrs. Wente, who was leaning out of the next-door window, tending the geraniums in her window-boxes. Wilbert gave her a nod and a wave. He hated her. He particularly hated her cats, which always came over the fence and scratched up his garden.

He unlocked the door and went into the house. He hesitated for a moment. He thought he could sense something. Maybe something psychic. Maybe no more than the faintest of smells, tobacco, aftershave, sweat, as if an intruder had entered the house. Wilbert was highly sensitive to smells.

He called out, "Hello?" and waited, and listened, but there was no answer. No sound at all. He walked cautiously through to the pine-furnished kitchen, and put down his groceries, still listening. He was sure that there was somebody here. Somebody whose psychic aura was extraordinarily powerful; and unpleasant, too. *Sour* was the word that Wilbert would have used.

Still listening, still alert, he opened his old-fashioned dome-topped Westinghouse icebox, and put away his meringues. Just as he was closing the icebox door, he thought he heard a soft, suppressed creak, like somebody heavy treading on a floorboard and trying to suppress it.

"I know there's somebody here!" Wilbert called, starkly.

Silence. Nothing at all. Then suddenly the bang of Mrs. Wente's sash-window coming down, which started Wilbert's heart racing.

As quietly as he could, he tiptoed to the kitchen door. *I know there's somebody here*, he mouthed to himself. He stood listening so long his knees began to creak. On the opposite side of the corridor, a steel engraving of St Sebastian stared at him, naked and baleful, his torso pierced with thirty-five arrows (Wilbert had counted them), his penis generously swollen by an artist whose interest had obviously been more homoerotic than religious.

"Somebody's here! I know it!" shouted Wilbert again, and this time it was almost a scream.

He stepped into the corridor, and balanced his way along to the living-room like a steward balancing his way along the tilting companionway of an ocean-liner. In the living-room, the heavy brown furniture stood heavy, brown and silent. In fact the furniture was almost sullen, because Wilbert had been out for most of the day, shopping. Houses, like people, could resent being left alone. Wilbert had once been called to exorcize a house on Vallejo because it used to vandalize itself to the point of total destruction whenever its owners went on long vacations. Most of the time, people attributed wanton and inexplicable damage to poltergeists. But most of the time, it was the house itself that was behaving resentfully.

Yet… Wilbert could sense something more than a sulky

house. There was somebody else here. Somebody dangerous, and strong, too. He balanced his way from room to room, listening, pausing, occasionally calling out. Who's there? *Who are you? What do you want?*

Then, *breathing*.

Thick, coarse, irregular breathing. Not far away, either. Not in the kitchen, surely! He'd just left the kitchen. What about the bathroom? Trembling, jittery, he pushed open the bathroom door, but there was nobody there. Just Arabs, staring lasciviously at naked boys; and little baskets of perfumed soap; and dried flowers; and tissues. *Where are you going and what do you wish the old moon asked the three. We have come to fish for the herring fish that sail in this beautiful sea.*

What what what what.

"Where are you?" shrilled Wilbert.

But all he could hear was breathing. Breathing, and the sweaty smell of somebody near.

He stepped out of the bathroom and into the corridor and the man was standing right in front of him. Tall, heavy, *huge*, with a massive black nodding helmet which completely covered his head. His bare chest was glistening and smeared with red. He wore tight black leather jeans, hung around with chains and belts and silver skulls and studs. He stank strongly of sweat and engine-oil and something *herbal*, like burning fennel-sticks.

Wilbert stood speechless. The man took one step toward him, and grasped him by the shoulder of his pale green seersucker shirt.

"Well, my friend, you haven't been behaving too sensible, have you?"

Wilbert swallowed, and desperately asked, "What?"

"You've been talking to people you shouldn't have been talking to. Naming names you should have kept to yourself."

"I don't know what you're talking about."

"Of course you know what I'm talking about. Lieutenant Larry Foggia, that's what I'm talking about. Didn't you learn your lesson back in '67? Surely you remember what happened to Sean Thomson and Danny Rowano?"

"Listen," Wilbert stammered, "I haven't told anybody anything."

"You talked to Lieutenant Foggia."

"Of course I talked to Lieutenant Foggia. His mother was a friend of mine. She died this week in a traffic accident. How could I *not* talk to him?"

"It wasn't the fact that you talked to him," said the man in the mask, his voice muffled. "It was what you said."

"I didn't say anything. I just said, I'm sorry about your mother. That's all."

"So you didn't mention the Black Brotherhood, or Leper, or Mandrax, or any of the others?"

"Of course not! Why should I?"

The huge man gripped Wilbert's shoulder so tightly that Wilbert heard the sinews crackle. "You didn' say anything about Beli Ya'al... the great Beli Ya'al, whose day has now come at last?"

"Of course not!"

"*Liar!*" the huge man screamed at him. "*You told Foggia everything!*"

"For God's sake!" cried Wilbert. He tried to twist his shoulder away but the huge man slammed him up against the corridor wall and winded him.

"Not for God's sake, not for your sake, not for anybody's sake," the huge man hissed. "You kept your peace for twenty-three years, but now you've opened your mouth and now you're going to be punished."

Wilbert gasped, "Let me go, let me go. I swear, I *swear* to you I didn't tell him anything. Nothing at all."

"Ah…"said the huge man, much more softly this time. "But I know for a fact that you did."

"You're crazy, let me go."

"Crazy? You think I'm crazy? That's not nice. That's not nice at all."

"Just let me go, please. I've got cash in the study, you can have it all."

"I intend to have it anyway."

Wilbert took a deep breath and screamed out, "*Help! Somebody help me! Help!*"

Without hesitation, the huge man punched him in the face and broke his nose. Blood gushed down Wilbert's shirt and spattered on the floor. His nose hurt so much that he let out a mournful bubbling whoop like a peacock.

"Didn't you hear what I said?" the huge man asked him. "You have to be punished. Surely you accept the fact that you have to be punished."

"*Help!*" Wilbert gargled, spitting out blood. "*Somebody help me!*"

The huge man punched him in the nose again, and this time Wilbert felt bone crush and cartilage crack.

"I said, 'Surely you accept the fact that you have to be punished,'" the huge man repeated, like a patient parent talking to a wilful child.

Wilbert choked, coughed, and tried to nod. He had never

266

felt so frightened and helpless in his life. The huge man gripped his arm and dragged him along the corridor to the kitchen. There, he swept Wilbert's newspaper and coffee-mug off the large deal table on to the floor, and forced Wilbert backward, so that he lost his balance and had to lie flat on his back on the table-top.

Wilbert felt blood flowing thick and warm down the back of his throat. It tasted disgusting, and almost suffocated him. He retched, and tried to spit some of it out.

"What are you going to do?" he coughed. "Please—please don't hurt me too much. I can't stand pain. I never could stand pain. Not even the dentist."

"Oh, you'll like this," the huge man said, his black horned helmet nodding. "This will hurt you so much, you won't even feel it. This will be beyond pain."

Without any hesitation, he banged a huge triangular kitchen knife clean through Wilbert's right shoulder, just above the collar bone, and pinned him to the table. Wilbert screamed, and tried to snatch at the knife-handle, but the huge man pushed him down and banged another knife through the left side. Then, with two smaller paring-knives, he pinned his wrists to the table.

Wilbert tried to struggle, but the pain was intolerable. He could bear it more easily if he lay quite still, shivering, his face smashed, praying praying praying that this maniac wasn't going to kill him.

"You want to pray?" the huge man asked him. "You really want to pray? Then pray for Beli Ya'al, because Beli Ya'al is coming to feed, and soon he's going to feed on *you*."

"Please let me go," Wilbert whispered.

"Oh, don't you fret," the huge man told him. "You're going to like this. This is just your scene."

With another huge Sabatier knife, he cut the leather belt of Wilbert's pants. Then he sliced open the waistband of the pants themselves, and tugged them off, with one harsh jerk after another. Wilbert whimpered with pain with every jerk. He felt as if he were dying. How much blood was he losing? He was swallowing pints of it, and he could feel it soaking the shoulders of his shirt. I'm dying, I'm being murdered. Oh God don't let him hurt me.

"Cute shorts," the huge man remarked. "I always liked candy-stripe." He cut the elastic of Wilbert's shorts, and pulled them off.

Oh God don't let him castrate me.

The huge man leaned over him and all that Wilbert could see was the black glossy enormity of his mask.

"You should have kept your secrets to yourself, my friend. You should have remembered what happened to all those guys in the old days. Now it's going to happen to you."

Wilbert said, between grinding teeth, "I know you."

"Oh, you know me? Well, good for you."

"I know you, you cheap pathetic *démodé* hoodlum."

"Oh, yes?"

Wilbert took a deep quivering breath and said, "Mandrax! That's who you are! Mandrax!"

Without a word, the huge man took hold of Wilbert's penis and pulled it upward as if it were a scrawny young chicken that had dropped out of its nest. He squeezed it hard, so that the purple glans bulged out of the top of his fist.

Wilbert closed his eyes. He was sure now that he was

going to die. He didn't move, he didn't breathe. All he did was swallow from time to time to prevent himself from choking on the blood that was still sliding down the back of his throat. *Please make it quick.*

"Beli Ya'al is almost with us," the huge man said, almost singing the words in the muffled confines of his mask. "Praise be to Beli Ya'al. And pain and punishment to all of those who try to confound him. All those who betray his holy secrets must die; even as those who give him life must die."

"Please," said Wilbert, in a thick voice.

Very slowly, the huge man sliced into Wilbert's penis with his carving-knife, just behind the corona, so that he was cutting off the entire glans, like a plum. Wilbert felt agonizing coldness. The glans was so rich in nerve-endings that the slightest movement of the knife-edge was painful beyond anything that Wilbert could have believed possible. He went blind with pain. All he could see was scarlet, then black. He didn't even feel it when the huge man had sliced all the way through, and the top of his penis was off, leaving the headless shaft pumping out blood, pump, pump, pump, dark and red with every heartbeat.

The huge man bent close to his ear. "You see? The finest pain you'll ever feel. And now you'll die. Because nothing can stop that blood pumping. And I can take this little piece of you back to the master, as a souvenir. What do you call it? A trophy. So, good day to you, friend. It's been fun."

Wilbert, lying spreadeagled on the table, his thighs splattered with blood, thought: *he's killed me. The bastard's killed me.* The feeling of terror and helplessness was enormous. Already he felt colder, already he felt the darkness drawing in. But at the same time he was acutely conscious of the knives that had been driven through his upper chest, and through his wrists; and of the warm, repetitive hosing of blood which came from his mutilated penis. Pump, pump, pump.

He saw the black mask bobbing and dipping out of sight. He heard the door close. He thought: *He's gone. He's left me to die by myself. He's left me to die without even an enemy to curse.*

The blood ran noisily off the kitchen table, and ran on to the Mexican-tiled floor; and he still he pumped out more. The pumping was unstoppable, not that Wilbert wanted it to stop. He preferred to die than to live with a mutilated penis. He preferred the coldness, and the encroaching darkness, and a strange other-worldly feeling that began to envelop him, as if he weren't really here at all.

"Can somebody guide me?" he asked. "I'm dying. Can somebody guide me?"

Nothing. No response. The spirit world was strangely quiet, like a bar when a hostile stranger walks in.

"I'm Wilbert Fraser, I'm dying," he repeated. "Can't somebody help me?"

He thought he saw a faint blue light flickering, but he wasn't aware that he had managed to summon any of the spirits. It was only when he opened his eyes and saw a young girl's face smiling down at him that he realized that his call had been answered. It was Roberta Snow, the same girl that had appeared at his last seance, looking pale, blurred, but comforting, too. Wilbert felt that if *she* had already died, and could be helpful and happy; then *he* could be helpful and happy, too.

"I'm bleeding to death," he told her. His voice sounded remote, like a radio in an upstairs apartment. "I'm dying."

Roberta came close to him and held his hand. She appeared not to mind that his penis was exposed, jetting out thick warm gouts of blood. Once you'd died—once you'd met so many others who had died—maybe your physical manifestation wasn't very interesting any more. Maybe blood and maiming and crushing and flesh were all irrelevant; so long as the spirit survived.

"It's all right, Wilbert," she consoled him, and each word resonated like a bell on a summer's afternoon. "You have friends here, so many friends."

"I don't want to die. Can't you help me?"

She smiled, as if she thought he was teasing. "When you have to die, you have to die. You don't have any choice. Do you think I wanted to drown? My father was drunk, I couldn't get out of the car. I saw somebody's face, outside the window, he must have dived in to save me. But the doors were locked and he couldn't break the window. We stared at each other through the glass. I screamed and then I breathed in water. I looked at the man and the man looked at me. I pressed my hand against the glass and he pressed his hand over mine. Then he touched his hand to his lips and he blew me a kiss. That was all he could do. I loved him for that."

Wilbert was beginning to feel icy and distant. "Roberta... promise me something."

"What?" she asked him. "Anything."

"Tell Larry Foggia what's happened to me... please."

Roberta frowned. "I don't know whether I can do that. I'm dead, and he's still alive."

"Please, find a way. He has to know."

"But I'm dead and he's alive. He won't hear me, unless he's like you."

"Try your best. Find some way to tell him what happened. Tell him it was Mandrax."

Roberta leaned over Wilbert as he bled to death and kissed his icy-cold lips with lips that were icy-cold. Wilbert didn't want to rise from the table. He preferred to die where he was. Peace, perfect peace. And to die like this, in the arms of a girl who was already dead; that was more than he could have asked for. He had been familiar with the spirits since he was little. Now, as an adult, they were bearing him away.

"You are kindness itself," he told Roberta. Her hair waved in the water in which she had drowned, her eyes were pale green. Daddy daddy I can't get out. Daddy I can't get out.

Wilbert died of loss of blood at 5:27 that afternoon. The little girl in the taffeta party dress stood watching him, as the blood wrinkled and congealed on the kitchen floor. She was barely visible to the naked eye. Some people wouldn't have been able to see her at all. Others would have seen two dark smudges that were eyes, and the ghostly outline of a white party frock, and the kitchen units beyond.

In fact, nobody saw her, because she faded, like a photograph exposed to sunlight, and then there was nothing in the kitchen but Wilbert's body, pinned to the table by triangular knives, his thighs blackened by congealed blood. And then his wall-clock chimed half after five, and it was all over.

*

Larry walked into the Waxing Moon and he was surprised how high-tech it all was. He had been expecting one of those gloomy occult stores that you always see in movies, with ancient leather-bound books containing the hidden secret that everybody has been looking for since Reel One, and hideous demonic sculptures, and crucifixes, and paperback copies of the *Cultes des Goules* by the Comte d'Erlette, and *De Vermis Mysteriis* by Ludvig Prinn "and many other tomes hoary with age, having to do with thaumaturgy, demonology, cabalistics, and the like."

Instead, he found himself in a sparse, air-conditioned designer store, with brightly-illuminated display-cases of silver jewelry, and artistically arranged shelves of new occult books. The walls were lined in black felt; the floor black-carpeted; the railings up the stairs were chromium-plated and shiny. A hidden stereo played vaguely Indian music that Larry would have categorized as Ravi Shankar On His Day Off. In the far corner, a young girl in a pre-Raphaelite beret was sorting boxes of incense.

He picked up a weighty silver bust of a devil's head, on a polished onyx plinth. Almost at once, he was approached by a tall white-skinned woman with long brown perfectly cut hair. She was wearing a short black V-necked velvet dress, which exposed the globes of two white breasts, with a silver *ankh* jostling in between them; and black pantyhose; and stacked black shoes. She looked like Roger Corman's idea of an Egyptian princess.

"What *you're* looking for, you won't find here," she

announced. She had a hoarse, distinctive accent. Southern, but not lazy deep-down dirty Southern. More like Kansas City, Missourah.

Larry carefully replaced the devil's head on the polished glass shelf. "I'm looking for Tara Gordon," he said.

"And what else?"

"Why should you think that I'm looking for anything else?"

"Because anybody who's looking for Tara Gordon isn't just looking for Tara Gordon. They're looking for help, or enlightenment, or any one of those million things that can't be bought for money."

"Is that right?" Larry asked her. She had the most extraordinary eyes—hooded, slanted, with irises the color of Virginia dayflowers. Her breasts were so white that he could see the tracery of pale blue veins. He found her disturbing; almost intimidating.

"You're having trouble with your mother-in-law," she said. "Maybe you're looking for a fetish doll, to stick pins in."

Larry shook his head. "If I stuck pins in my mother-in-law, she wouldn't feel a thing. She wears a girdle that makes a vest look like a paper sack."

"You're a cop," she said. "There's been a weird crime, a very weird crime, and you think it's something to do with black magic."

He stared at her.

"Admit it," she said. "You're a cop."

He took out his badge, flopped it open. "All right. I'll come clean. My name's Foggia. I'm a cop. How did you know?"

"Only cops call a bullet-proof vest nothing but a vest. Everybody else in the world calls it a bullet-proof vest. How do you do, Lieutenant Foggia. My name's Tara Gordon."

Larry shook her hand, slowly. "You're very acute," he told her.

"Not acute," she corrected him. "Sensitive. I'm a sensitive."

He looked around. "I'm impressed with your store. I expected one of those dusty junkheaps they show you in the movies... you know, when Harry Erskine goes looking for the Manitou, that kind of thing."

"For goodness' sake, lieutenant, the occult is big business these days. We sell more copies of the *Necronomicon* than we can stock. And most of our tail of newt and eye of bat is gone way ahead of the best-before date."

Larry said, "Is there someplace private we can talk?"

Tara Gordon looked around. "I guess. Natasha! Would you mind the store for a while?"

Without hesitation, she led Larry across the thick black carpet to a small office stacked with books and mail-order envelopes and catalogs. On the wall hung a large poster for the World Fantasy Convention 1988, and a photograph of Stephen King without his glasses. She cleared away a stack of horror magazines and offered Larry a black leather-and-chromium chair.

"You were recommended by Wilbert Fraser," said Larry.

"I don't know whether to be flattered or insulted," said Tara Gordon.

Larry gave her a dry smile. "Wilbert said that you were highly *au fait* with the world beyond, and its practitioners."

"Very complimentary of Wilbert, for a change."

"You don't like him?"

"He's the biggest bitch in the business."

"That's dangerous talk for *this* city."

Tara Gordon laughed. "It takes a bitch to know one."

She went to a small black shiny icebox at the back of the office and knelt down to open it. Larry found himself looking at the glossy black curve of her inside thigh, and the way that her white breast was pressed in a swelling crescent against her upraised knee. She produced a bottle of Polish buffalo-grass vodka and two chilled glasses. Without asking Larry if he wanted any, she poured them each a generous measure and said, "*Prost!*"

Larry shrugged, and said, "*Prost!*" and swallowed. His head ached so much from yesterday's drinking that he was glad of a hair of the dog.

"I suppose this is something to do with the Fog City Satan," Tara Gordon remarked, sitting in her office chair and ostentatiously crossing her long legs.

"How did you guess?"

"What else would bring a police lieutenant into a place like this?"

Larry thought about it, and then said, "I guess you're right. Yes, come to think of it, you're right. I could use an analytical mind like yours on the squad."

"Well... it wasn't entirely analysis," said Tara Gordon. She raised her hand, her palm flat towards him, and circled it in the air, as if softly polishing a window so that she could see out of it. "You carried something in with you. Something strange. Something quite strong. Something very unpolicemanlike."

"What do you mean?"

"I'm not quite sure. But your aura is quite disturbed. Actually, *most* people's auras are quite disturbed these days, and policemen's auras are usually more disturbed than most... but yours especially. It reminds me of something... something violent; something dark. That's why I guessed you wanted to ask me about the Fog City Satan."

"Do you have any theories about it?" Larry asked her.

"I've been following the news. But then, who hasn't?"

"Listen," Larry told her, "I've been going out on something of a limb with this one. I've been following up the occult side of the case as well as the more conventional aspects. That's why I went to see Wilbert."

"And what did the lovely Wilbert have to say about it?"

Larry swallowed more vodka. It was peculiarly aromatic, like drinking wet hay, but he had to admit that he liked it. "Wilbert came up with the theory that one of the Black Brotherhood might have survived; and is trying to stir up the same kind of trouble that they did in the '60s."

Tara Gordon stared at him. "The Black Brotherhood?" she repeated.

"You *have* heard of them?"

"Of course I've heard of them. Everybody in this business has heard of them. But nobody goes around talking about them. Nobody even mentions their name."

"Really? What are they so scared of?"

"Probably nothing, these days. Although if one of them had *really* managed to survive—well, that would be different."

"Have you heard any rumors? Seen anybody who sticks out of the crowd? This guy is physically gigantic, anything up to six-four, and built like a reinforced concrete outhouse.

What's more, Dogmeat Jones reckons he knows an artist who's seen him, and his face and head may be badly burned."

Tara Gordon smiled, and shook her head. "I think I would have remembered anybody like that, don't you?"

Larry reached into his pocket and unfolded the engraving of Beli Ya'al that Dogmeat had given him. "Did you ever see this before?"

Tara Gordon examined it closely, then nodded. "Yes, I have. It's one of the illustrations from the *Pan Demonium* by Vadlek Nascu. In fact..."

Sharply, she put down her vodka, opened the office door, and walked across the black-carpeted store to an are marked *Reference Section*. Larry stood in the open office doorway watching her as she leafed through a large leather-bound book. Eventually she came stalking back, carrying both book and engraving.

"This engraving was tom out of *my* book!" she declared. "Look—the edges match perfectly! I'm furious! This book is worth more than six hundred dollars!"

Larry examined the torn page and the damaged spine of the book. "Hm..." he said, handing them back.

"That's all you're going to say? A two-hundred-year-old book has been vandalized and all you're going to say is 'hm'?"

"Do you have any recollection of anybody taking this book out to read?"

Tara Gordon angrily banged the book on to her desk. "I wish! I'd scalp him!"

"If it's the guy I think it is, you wouldn't have to."

"I don't remember anybody in particular," said Tara Gordon. "Nobody like the man you mentioned. Any of our customers is welcome to come browse. Mind you—they're certainly not welcome to come rip out pictures."

"Well… think about it over the next few days," Larry suggested. "Sometimes it's amazing what you can remember if you just give yourself some time."

Tara Gordon held the engraving of Beli Ya'al up between finger and thumb, as if it were soaked in something unpleasant. "Beli Ya'al," she repeated. "Who on earth would want to steal an engraving of Beli Ya'al? That's worse than stealing a picture of Hitler."

"It was probably used as reference to make a mask of Beli Ya'al," Larry explained.

"That sounds ominous."

"It *is* ominous. The guy wore the mask when he was carrying out most or all of his ritual killings."

"Well…"said Tara Gordon. "I wish I could help you, lieutenant, but I don't really think that I can. I haven't seen anybody fitting that description, and I *certainly* would have known if any of the Black Brotherhood had reared their ugly heads. I'll keep my eyes peeled, but the Black Brotherhood were always very secretive, from what I hear, and they meted out pretty damned unpleasant punishments to people who betrayed them."

"So I gather," said Larry. "I guess I'll just have to keep on looking. Shall I give your regards to Wilbert?"

"You can give him a limp-wristed wave, if you like. You're not using him as your adviser or anything, are you?"

"Any reason why I shouldn't?"

"Not really. But there are better sensitives than him."

"Like who?"

"Like me, for example."

"Well, good. I'll remember that, if I have urgent need of a better sensitive. Right now, I could use some solid, non-supernatural clues."

He finished the last of his vodka, shivered with the coldness of it, and stood up. "It's been a pleasure," said Tara Gordon. "If you weren't a cop and you weren't married and you were five years younger and you weren't Italian and your eyes were a different color and you didn't have that habit of rubbing the side of your neck whenever you ask a difficult question, I could quite like you."

She opened the office door again, and Larry laid his hand on her shoulder to usher her through. Instantly, she cried out, "*Ah!*" and jumped away from him. A wisp of grayish smoke rose from her black velvet dress, and a small patch of bare skin was reddened, as if she had burned it.

She stared at Larry in horror. "My dress! Jesus! You've burned my dress!"

Larry helplessly held out his hand. "I don't even know what—"

At once, Tara Gordon took hold of his wrist, opened his fingers, and stared into his palm. She touched it lightly here and there with her fingertip, and each time she did so, there was a tiny crack of static discharge, and a small wisp of smoke.

"Your *hand*—" she said. "I *thought* I sensed something like this."

Larry took it away, almost primly and closed his fingers. "Wilbert said it was called the moving hand. It's something to do with the Black Brotherhood and Beli Ya'al. I don't know how I got it, but Wilbert's going to try to exorcize it for me. I tried scrubbing it, nothing happened."

"You've had a *face* on it, too?"

Larry nodded.

"And have you heard about people in the city seeing faces in strange places?"

He nodded again.

Tara Gordon looked closely into his eyes. "You're a believer, aren't you?"

"A believer?" said Larry, sardonically. "I can't help it. I've seen too much evidence not to be. I've seen my own mother shrunk down to the size of a child. I've seen an overcoat walking on its own and a drowned girl who could talk and a parrot with my own damned head on it."

Tara Gordon reached up and brushed Larry's hair back from his forehead, an extraordinarily intimate gesture from somebody he had only just met. It was as if she were accepting him, and agreeing to take care of him.

"You're a rare man, lieutenant. When it comes to the occult, most people refuse to accept the evidence of their own eyes."

She turned back to her desk and picked up the leather-bound book. "You ought to read the chapters on Beli Ya'al. He was the first angel to be thrown down from heaven because he lied so much. Even when God gave him an opportunity to admit to his sins, he lied."

Larry said, "Wilbert thinks that Beli Ya'al may be here in San Francisco. He doesn't know why, or how. But it's looking more and more likely that the Black Brotherhood are back, and that they're trying to resurrect him, wherever he is."

Tara Gordon tentatively touched Larry's hand again. "If you must know, the whole occult community has been afraid of something like that for months—ever since the first of the ritual killings. The faces are the giveaway. According to this book, and according to legend, Beli Ya'al uses the images of people on whose lives he has fed to search for yet more lives to feed on. He's a trencherman of human lives. He likes long lives—lives with plenty of passion and variety and sex and violence.

"The images of these people can appear almost anywhere. In mirrors, on shiny tables—any one of those surfaces which normally act as windows for transient spirits. But of course the most potent window for the spirit is the palm of the hand. Has it ever occurred to you why people press the palms of their hands together when they pray? It comes from the days when they were afraid that their spirits would be so attracted by the nearness of God, that they would leave their bodies through the palms of their hands, and they would die."

Larry said, "I filmed it."

Tara Gordon put down her glass. "I'm sorry?"

"Last night... I filmed the image in my hand, with my video camera."

"You *filmed* it?" she asked, her eyes bright. "Did it register?"

"Sure. I've only looked at it briefly. I was taking the cassette down to the Hall of Justice to have our technical experts go over it."

"Can we see it now? I have a video-recorder in the back of the store."

"Do you think it could help?"

"I don't know for sure, but it's possible."

Larry went out to the car and took the video-cassette

out of the glovebox. The evening was warm and golden, one of those evenings when San Francisco is bathed in marmalades and yellows and terracottas, and Larry could genuinely feel that it was the city at the end of the rainbow. He was locking his car when he was sure that he heard somebody faintly whisper, "*Larry*," close to his ear. There was something else too—the slightest of distortions in the air, and a feeling that the back of his hand had been lightly scratched by the softest of netting.

He hesitated on the sidewalk, until a large woman in a maroon fringed Mama Cass-style dress said, "Pardon me, friend, a body wants to get through here," and he had to step out of the way.

Tara Gordon had already switched on the television when he returned to the store. He handed her the cassette, and she pressed *play* on her remote control. The first image that came into view was Frankie and Mikey, pulling faces at each other, and giggling. They must have appropriated the video-camera when Larry was out.

"Pretty scary, hunh?" Tara Gordon remarked.

"My boys," said Larry, in pride and embarrassment. "That's Frankie with his eyes crossed; that's Mikey with his fingers up his nose."

"They're probably beautiful," said Tara Gordon.

She fast-forwarded the tape until it darkened and blurred and Larry recognized his own hand, resting on his desk at home. At first the picture was out of focus, but when he moved his hand into the light, the focus sharpened up.

It took a while, but at last they saw gray clouds drifting and tangling across his palm.

"This is fascinating," said Tara Gordon. She was leaning

forward so that Larry could see the full pale curve of her breast, with the silver *ankh* resting against it. "You see these patterns that look like clouds in the wind? They're highly characteristic of spirit manifestations. We call them skeins. Nobody knows quite what they are. Von Budow said they were human longing, unraveled into the raw material of the spirit world. Some people think that they represent 'the veil' which separates this side from the other side."

"And what do you think they are?" asked Larry.

"I personally think that it's obvious. They're unformed psychoplasma."

"Oh, that tells me a lot."

"No, no. It's not difficult to understand. They're like spun-sugar in a cotton-candy machine, that's all. They don't take on any recognizable shape until you wind them around a stick."

Gradually, the "spun-sugar" on the palm of Larry's hand began to clot and tear and form itself into the recognizable shape of a man's face. Tara Gordon said nothing, but watched in fascination as the face began to move, and to turn, and to talk. The voice sounded tinny and distant; like a far-away radio.

Almost time to feed, my friend. Almost time!

"My *God*," breathed Tara Gordon. "You can hear it! You can actually hear it!"

"*Feed on what?*" Larry's voice boomed.

On that which was promised. On my earthly reward.

Enthralled, Tara Gordon watched and listened until they heard Linda saying, "*Larry! Larry, what are you doing? Look at your hand!*"

She rewound the tape, and replayed the moment when

the face first appeared. Then she pressed *freeze*, and they were confronted by the fluttering image of a good-looking, smiling man, the strong angles of his face illuminated by sunlight; half-turned away. He looked genial and relaxed; and there was no doubt that what he was saying didn't synchronize with the throaty, echoing threat that it was *time to feed*.

Tara Gordon sat in front of the television screen for almost five minutes, her chin in her hands, staring and saying nothing.

Larry said, "Maybe we could—" But Tara Gordon flapped her hand at him to tell him to keep quiet.

"Jesus," he said, under his breath.

Tara Gordon at last sat back. "I think I know who that is," she said.

"You *recognize* him?"

"It's hard to be one hundred per cent sure. But it looks like Lieutenant Sam Roberts."

"Who the hell is Lieutenant Sam Roberts? I thought I knew every ranking police officer there was."

"Well, you probably do," said Tara Gordon, standing up. "But you don't know your San Francisco history very well."

"Ms Gordon—"

"Please call me Tara. Or if you can't manage that, Mistress Tara."

She crossed the store to the Reference Section, and without hesitation pulled out a large book entitled *The Lawless Years: San Francisco 1845–1850*. While Larry stood behind her, she ran through the index until she found what she was looking for, and opened the book at a section of black-and-white photographs.

"There he is," she said, triumphantly. "Lieutenant Sam Roberts, one-time Bowery Boy, one-time member of the company that was brought out to California by Colonel J.D. Stevenson to fight the Mexicans; one-time volunteer policeman; one-time bounty-hunter and scavenger; one-time murderer, arsonist, rapist, thief and vandal."

Larry peered at the engraving closely. It showed a man with a genial, distinctive face. Broad forehead, thick eyebrows, and hair brushed firmly to one side. Larry glanced at the TV, where the freeze-frame picture still trembled, and there was no doubt in his mind at all. The man on his hand was the same man.

"I'm amazed," Larry admitted.

"Don't be *too* amazed," said Tara. "I've been studying the magical history of San Francisco for years. I've been writing a book which is two years behind schedule, at the very least."

"All right, then," said Larry. "I admire that. I couldn't write a book to save my life. Tell me the title."

"I can't possibly. It'll bring bad luck. Besides, I don't think I can ever finish writing it, so I'd save your admiration if I were you."

"But this Lieutenant Sam Roberts is in it?"

"That's right. He was a very strange guy, by all accounts. He used to hold occult meetings and tell his friends that he could talk directly to Satan. In 1849 he formed a group of so-called police officers who were supposed to keep law and order, but in fact they did nothing but rob and rape and burn down people's shacks and persecute non-American immigrants. They called themselves the Regulators, or the Hounds.

"In July of 1849 they attacked Little Chile. They shot the Chilenos indiscriminately. They raped women. They set fires. They tore down shanties.

"That was too much, even for the easygoing folks of San Francisco. The Hounds were hunted down by a Law and Order Party that was organized by Sam Brannan and Mayor Thaddeus Leavenworth. Some of the Hounds were caught and imprisoned, most of them escaped. A few of them drifted down to the waterfront. Nobody knows what happened to Lieutenant Sam Roberts, but about a month later he sent the people of San Francisco an open letter swearing his revenge on them.

"He said he was going to bring down a punishment on San Francisco that would be more terrible than anything they had ever known."

Larry stared at the palm of his hand. "And this maniac's appearing on my hand?"

"It sure looks like it."

Larry said, "Wilbert Fraser said he would exorcize it for me."

"There's no harm in letting him try."

"Is it something that *you* could do?"

Tara Gordon shook her head. "I don't get into that stuff any more, the other side, the world beyond the veil. Even a fair-to-good sensitive like Wilbert Fraser doesn't know half of what he's getting himself into. It's a whole different world, lieutenant—higher and deeper and wider than we can possibly know—where the laws of gravity and sanity and logic don't apply. A very dear friend of mine spent seven months in a coma once, after a seance, and then died; and God knows he didn't die happy."

Larry thoughtfully removed the video-cassette from its slot. "So what do you think I ought to do now?" he asked her.

"You're the detective."

"Don't you have any idea at all where this Fog City Satan might be hanging out?"

"All I can do is keep my eyes open."

"Okay... thanks," Larry told her. "And thanks for the information on Sam Roberts, whatever good *that's* going to do me."

"You're welcome. At least you *believe*."

"Believe? Believe me, I wish I didn't."

"Knowledge is a responsibility," said Tara Gordon, pouring herself another large buffalo-grass vodka. "Belief is a cross."

Larry left the Waxing Moon and crossed the busy sidewalk. When he climbed into his creaking Le Sabre and slammed the door and the whole interior smelled of Ralston because Fay Kuhn was sitting primly in the passenger-seat waiting for him.

"You're being unfaithful to me," she needled him.

"I'm carrying out an investigation."

"With Tara Gordon? Tara Gordon is the biggest vamp since Sally Stanford."

"Tara Gordon has behaved with complete propriety."

"Sure. I can smell it on your breath."

"As a matter of fact, Ms Kuhn, Tara Gordon has convinced me that what you've been saying about the Black Brotherhood is true... and that what Wilbert Fraser has been saying about them trying to revive the fallen angel Belial is true... whether any such thing as a fallen angel exists or not… and that what we have going down here is probably the most serious psychic disturbance in any American city since the Salem Witch Trials."

"Can I quote you?"

Larry hesitated. If he came out in print with the opinion that the Fog City Satan case had real connections with the supernatural, Dan Burroughs would just about detonate. On the other hand, he was now totally convinced that the answer to these six ritual slaughters lay in the spirit world; and that only those who believed in the after-life and the other side and the world beyond the veil would be able to help him.

There was another convincing reason for going public: the Fog City Satan would know for the first time that Larry was on to him, and that Larry was prepared to pursue him on an occult level as well a procedural level. Maybe that would unnerve him, put him off balance, flush him out of hiding. All of his threats had been arrogant and boastful. Maybe Larry could taunt him into boasting just a little more openly, and reveal what he planned to do next, and where. One handle was all he needed.

Fay Kuhn said, "Whether you allow me to quote you or not, I'm going to run something on the supernatural side of this investigation. I have to. The *Chron's* on to it, too."

"I'm pretty much in two minds about it," Larry admitted. "I'm going take a lot of flak from Dan Burroughs; and probably the mayor's office, too. But I guess on the whole it's better to bring it out into the open."

"All right, then," said Fay Kuhn, taking out her pencil. "Let me ask you first what led you to suspect that the Fog City Satan might be more than your common-or-garden sociopath?"

Larry cleared his throat. He was aware of the political gravity of what he was doing, but in the end—what the hell, the investigation was more important than the politics. "The thing was, in his broadcasts, the Fog City Satan kept mentioning 'the other side'. Meaning the other side of death, you know?—the spirit world. So at my wife's suggestion I went to a seance, to check this 'other side' out. I went there open-minded with no preconceptions. To be quite honest, I didn't expect anything to happen and I didn't expect it to lead anywhere."

"Okay... that was at Wilbert Fraser's?"

"That's right. And when I went to that seance, I discovered to my amazement that there *is* an 'other side', for real. No tricks, no hidden cameras, no bullshit. Well, don't write 'bullshit'. I've seen it, I've experienced it. And if it's real enough for a police officer to see and experience, then it's real enough to warrant serious investigation. Particularly if it's going to help me put this lunatic where he belongs, in San Quentin, on Death Row."

He talked to Fay Kuhn for almost a half-hour. She wrote an even, flowing shorthand note, turning over page after page of her springback notebook. She was almost through when Larry's radio crackled, and a voice said, "Car twenty-two, car twenty-two."

"Twenty-two responding."

"Is that you, Lieutenant Foggia? We have an urgent call for you from Sergeant Brough. He says to attend SFG as soon as possible. Floor nine. Edna-Mae Lickerman's acting up."

"Acting up, what's that supposed to mean?"

"How should I know? Sergeant Brough didn't tell me any more than that."

"On my way," said Larry, and reached for his red roof light.

Fay Kuhn said, "Can I come with you?"

"Technically, no."

But without any hesitation, Larry U-turned the Le Sabre through slow-moving traffic, and sped toward San Francisco General before Fay Kuhn had any opportunity to get out.

"I'm parked on a red," she told him. "I hope you can take care of it for me."

"Why do I seem to spend my whole life doing nothing but favors for Fay Kuhn?" he retorted.

"Because Fay Kuhn is going to do you plenty of favors in return."

"Hmh! We'll see about that when Dan Burroughs reads tomorrow's front page. What's your headline? FOGGIA FINALLY FLIPS?"

"I don't write the headlines. I simply report the facts as I see them."

"Well, come take a look at Edna-Mae Lickerman. Let's see how factual you can be about her."

Houston Brough was standing stiffly in the corner. His gun was drawn but he was holding it up tight to his chest.

In the center of the room stood a young white-clad nurse; a pretty red-headed girl of about twenty-two. Her blue eyes were wide open, her freckled face was drained white with terror and disbelief. Behind her, floating in the air, unsupported, so that she was even higher than horizontal, was the shriveled form of Edna-Mae Lickerman, with her tufted skull and her milked-over eyes and her wrists as thin as a bird's claws. She wore a hospital robe which rippled and trembled in an unfelt wind.

At the girl's throat, she held a large curved slice of broken glass.

She blindly smiled, and crooned, and floated behind the nurse as easily and as happily as if she were floating in the ocean.

"How can she *do* that?" whispered Fay Kuhn. "She's suspended in mid-air! How can she *do* that?"

Larry said, "Stay back. This could be very dangerous."

"But you said I could come along."

"I said you couldn't."

"But you brought me, all the same."

Larry didn't stop to argue. He edged his way into the room, sliding with his back to the wall until he reached the corner where Houston was standing with his gun drawn.

"Can you believe this?" said Houston. He sounded more annoyed then alarmed. "A homicidal psychopath who can fly."

"Has she said anything?"

"She keeps singing."

"Has she threatened the nurse's life?"

"Not verbally. But I wouldn't consider that piece of glass to be much of a goodwill gesture, would you?"

"Could you hit her from here?"

"Oh, for sure. But would she die? And even if she *did* die, would she die before she could give that nurse an extra mouth?"

Edna-Mae continued to float eerily in the air, her shriveled toes almost touching the drapes. She smiled to herself, and sang, as if she were the happiest person alive, as if this was the day to which she had been looking forward all her life.

"*By the meadow, sweet with hay…*

My love and I we walked one day…"

"Christ almighty, what the hell *is* this?" said Larry.

"She's been singing like this ever since I got here," Houston told him. "Same song, over and over."

"*By the bay, by the city*

He so handsome, I so pretty…"

Larry slowly unholstered his gun. "Edna-Mae?" he called out. "Can you hear me Edna-Mae? It's Larry Foggia. Lieutenant Larry Foggia. Remember I met you down at Alphonson's, on Front and Green."

"*He took my hand, he took my heart*

He promised we would never part…"

"Edna-Mae," Larry repeated, and took two cautious steps forward. Edna-Mae lazily turned in the air, so that she was further away from Larry than before; and she lifted her eyes and stared at him, although they looked so opaque that Larry didn't know whether she could see him or not.

"Edna-Mae, that nurse hasn't done you any harm. Don't you think you ought to put down that piece of glass?"

The nurse stared at Larry in desperation. She looked for a moment as if she were about to say something, or try to tug herself away, but Larry gave her a quick shake of the head. One slice with that piece of glass and Edna-Mae could sever her carotid artery, and even with all of these medics present, there was too much of a risk that she would bleed to death before anyone had a chance to get to her.

She was too young, too pretty. Even Larry wouldn't have taken the risk.

"Edna-Mae, why don't you give this young girl a break? She hasn't done anything to you except take care of you, try to nurse you back to health."

"He gave me babies, gave me four
Gave me five, then gave me more."

Larry stepped back to the corner. "I want a marksman here, fast. I want somebody who can shoot a heavy load with one hundred percent accuracy at close range."

"Rickenbacker's your man for that," said Houston. "He can shoot out your nosehairs with a .45 without even making you sneeze."

"Then get him."

Edna-Mae kept on swaying in the air and crooning to herself. With cold prickles around his scalp, Larry heard her sing

"See the little babies cry
Eat the meat and hope to die."

He edged back to the doorway. Fay Kuhn was waiting there, looking distressed.

"What are you going to do?" she asked him.

"Any bright ideas? I've sent for a marksman, that's about the best I can think of. Maybe I ought to send for a priest, too."

"See the little babies burn," sang Edna-Mae.

"See the way they twist and turn."

Larry turned back to Edna-Mae. He kept his gun behind his back, and raised his hand to her to show her that he meant her no harm. "Edna-Mae, you have to let that girl go. You know that, don't you? You don't have any right to threaten that girl. You don't have any right to hurt her in any way."

Edna-Mae spat at him. "She said the name. She said the name."

"What name, Edna-Mae?"

"She said the name she had no right to say."

"Maybe she can say she's sorry. I'm sure she didn't say it on purpose."

"Once a name is spoken, a name is spoken. She had no right. Not to mock him like that."

"Edna-Mae, this girl is a trained nurse. I'm sure she had no intention of mocking anybody. Now, please... think what you're doing. Let her go."

Edna-Mae said nothing, but smiled to herself as if she were dreaming, as if she were thinking of beautiful days gone by. Larry didn't know what to say next. The shining curve of glass was less than an eighth of an inch away from the nurse's bare neck, and even if he had managed to aim and shoot and hit Edna-Mae, too, he still couldn't be certain that she wouldn't have time to slice the girl open from ear to ear.

"Edna-Mae..."Larry said again. He wondered if he risked stepping nearer. But then a slight movement to his right-hand side caught his eye. He stopped, his hand still raised, and turned his head. Houston Brough saw him turn his head, too, and looked around to see what had attracted his attention.

On the lower right-hand pane of the window he could distinctly see a face. Although it was no more than a breathed-on outline, there was no mistaking eyes and nose and slightly smiling mouth. The sun gilded it for a moment and then it began to fade, but Larry was convinced of one thing: it had been the same face that kept appearing on his own hand, the face that Tara Gordon had identified as being that of Lieutenant Sam Roberts, the Regulator, the Hound.

He glanced at Houston Brough, "Did you see that?" he asked him, but Houston Brough simply shrugged, as if he couldn't understand what he was talking about. Larry turned back to Edna-Mae, and to the nurse, who was looking unsteady on her feet now, as if she were about to collapse.

"Edna-Mae you have to let that girl go," said Larry.

"Of course," said Edna-Mae, in a voice that was unexpectedly thick and coarse. "But not before she's nursed me back to health."

"Let her go *now*, Edna-Mae!"

But Edna-Mae suddenly stretched open her mouth and roared at him, a terrifying baleful roar that made him take two or three steps backward and raise his gun.

"*It is almost time for me to feed!*" she bellowed. Her blind eyes bulged with fury and greed.

Dazzling white light abruptly burst out of her eyes and ears, turning her head into a human Hallowe'en pumpkin. The blinding light of heaven, or the blinding light of hell. She opened her mouth in a hideous grin, and light streamed out of that, too, silhouetting her teeth. The nurse screamed, and tried to wrestle herself free. The curved piece of glass fell from Edna-Mae's hand, tumbled over and over, smashed on the floor.

Both Larry and Houston raised their guns, but Edna-Mae turned in the air like an underwater swimmer, and wrapped her bony legs tightly around the nurse's waist, so tight that neither of them could get a clear shot.

"Pull her off!" Larry yelled at Houston, and Houston vaulted the bed and tried to snatch at Edna-Mae's back. But Edna-Mae thrust her bony hands into the nurse's eye-sockets and screamed, *If you lay one finger on me, you whelp, I'll throw her eyes at you!*

Houston shouted back, "Fuck you!" but Larry said, "Houston! Houston, back off!"

For a moment, the nurse and Edna-Mae were involved in an awful parody of a loving embrace. The girl stood rigidly upright, shivering as if her fingers were locked into an electric socket. Edna-Mae clung around her like an ageing and shriveled monkey clinging to a tree, all claws and bony fingers. The light from her eyes was intense, and illuminated the girl's red hair like an angelic halo. Edna-Mae took hold of the nurse's head and pushed it back, as far as it would go, until she was staring the girl directly in the face, almost nose-to-nose.

Larry lifted his gun again, and took aim at Edna-Mae's head. But Edna-Mae turned to him and gave him a grin that almost blinded him, and said, "Fool! She and I are one now! If I die, she dies!"

Larry thought: *do it. The girl's going to die anyway*. But nobody back at headquarters would believe him. Reluctantly, fearfully, he lowered the gun and stepped back.

"Lieutenant?" asked Houston, confused.

"Just keep away," Larry warned him.

"What's she *doing?*" asked Fay Kuhn, in a stage-whisper.

Slowly, with a fatty crackling noise, Edna-Mae stretched wide the nurse's mouth. Then she stretched her own mouth as wide as she could, and lowered it so that it was no more than four inches over the nurse's mouth.

For almost half a minute, nothing happened. But then the girl's trembling grew stronger and wilder and more convulsive. Her fingers splayed and stiffened, and she rose up on to her toes, as if she were trying to lift herself into the air by sheer willpower, as if she were trying to rise to meet the wide-open mouth of the desiccated hag who clung to her shoulders.

Or as if she were trying to prevent her whole youthful existence being dragged out of her.

"*Larry?*" asked Houston. "What the hell do we do?"

But it was already too late. Out of the girl's outstretched lips appeared a soft glistening shape, pinkish-gray, smeared with blood and mucus. At first Larry could still hope that it was nothing more than her tongue. But he had seen his mother come face-to-face with the same blinding light and he knew what was going to happen; and that there was nothing he could do or say to stop it.

It was her life, coming out of her mouth.

It came trembling upward, the very first day of her existence, and Edna-Mae reached out with a long curving tongue to welcome it. The moment of the nurse's birth rose silently, silently, shining with light and unformed flesh and mucus, and Edna-Mae coaxed it into the dazzling hollow of her mouth.

None of the watchers said anything, nor moved. They stared in horrified fascination as the nurse's existence slid upward, out of her mouth, faster and faster, and vanished into Edna-Mae's insatiable maw. Light, color, music, tangles of flesh, faces, fingers. It looked like a long slithering umbilicus, a rope of human experience and growth and happiness. As it rushed upward, Larry heard snatches of voices, snatches of music, like a cassette-tape being wound forward too fast.

"—*Mommy's girl then—what?—that's the way, that's the way—no! you mustn't!—loves you, yeah, yeah, yeah— bicycle—saw him at school—six sevens are—love you love you—inside the—sound of breaking glass—love you—call me—aahhhhhhh!!!!!*"

As the nurse's soul was dragged out of her, a grotesquely logical thing happened.

Edna-Mae's body began to swell.

Her belly first, rising beneath her hospital gown as if she were hugely pregnant. Then her breasts bulged, and her arms and legs began to enlarge, with a high, squeaking stretching noise that reminded Larry of an over-inflating balloon. Her paper gown tore open at the back, baring white buttocks that boiled with swelling knots of cellulite. Her thighs filled like muslin bags being filled with thick cottage cheese. She wasn't taking on her previous shape. No cleavage; no curvy curves or elegant ankles. Even her head looked like nothing more than a misshapen bag, a receptacle for holding the life and soul of another human being.

She gripped the girl tighter and tighter, squeezing out the very last of her spirit. Fall days at med school, bicycle rides. love, quarrels, singing, and the painful acceptance that some of her patients had to die, no matter what she did for them.

The nurse shrank and dwindled and collapsed in the arms of the bulging human cuckoo who had stolen everything she was; and everything she might have been. Her clothes collapsed. A hand as thin as a turkey-claw disappeared inside a falling sleeve. Her curved paper cap fell, and rolled on the floor, backwards and forwards. Her red hair had turned to gray, and showered softly down inside her collar, on to a patchy, blistered skull.

Edna-Mae let her fall, and she fell with the saddest of rustling sounds. The room was utterly silent. Larry raised his gun in both hands but he knew that it could destroy any chance of recovery that the young nurse might have, if he killed or injured the woman who had taken her spirit.

"Larry?" whispered Houston. "Larry, do we shoot, or what?"

The light in Edna-Mae's eyes flickered and dimmed. The room suddenly seemed very much darker, as if a storm were brewing.

She was huge, Edna-Mae; threateningly huge, and her body audibly wallowed beneath the shredded remnants of her paper gown. Across her stomach, a long python-like bulge rolled and turned and then swallowed itself back into her abdomen. Her eyes were completely bloodshot, and they quivered in her face the dark crimson patches of chicken embryos quivering in eggwhite.

"Almost time to feed," she said, her mouth sticky with mucus.

She took a heavy step forward, then another. The thick python-like bulge suddenly ran over one of her shoulders, and down her back. She hesitated, coughing, her head turning from side to side as if she couldn't decide what to do next.

"Almost time to—"

Larry held up his gun in front of her face.

"Far enough," he told her.

She stared at him with those blood-clot eyes. "Far enough?" she asked him. "Is that what you said?"

Gradually, creaking with fat, she started to laugh. The laughs made her shapeless breasts heave, and her stomach ripple, and all the time that terrible snakelike shape poured from one side of her body to the other, as if it were frantic to escape from inside her skin.

She tore at the few fragments of paper which were still tied around her neck. Then she dragged one of the sheets off the bed, and clumsily wrapped it around herself, right over her head, around and around her body, so that she took on the appearance of a huge white nightmarish nun.

"You cannot stop me now," she smiled at Larry. "Nothing you can do can stop me now."

As she smiled, the inside of her lower lip brimmed with blood-swirled mucus, and overflowed into a long viscous string, which swung from side to side as she took yet another step forward, and then another.

"That's it, Edna-Mae," said Larry. "One more step and I shoot."

"Well, you poor little cockroach, you know what the consequences of *that* will be."

At that moment, somebody tapped Larry on the left shoulder, and he jumped with shock.

"For Christ's sake—"

"Sorry, lieutenant. Officer Rickenbacker," said a bull-necked man with a shaved head and rimless spectacles. He hefted a huge long-barreled Magnum.

"Just hold off," Larry told him. "We have a special kind of problem here."

Rickenbacker leaned sideways so that he could see past Larry's shoulder into the room. He took one look at Edna-Mae and his mouth slowly opened and stayed open.

"See what I mean?" said Larry.

"That's a special kind of problem, all right," Rickenbacker agreed numbly, his eyes still wide. "What the hell's eating *her?*"

"Just don't shoot unless I say so," Larry told him.

"Wouldn't dream of it, sir."

Edna-Mae shuffled toward them, bandaged in her sheet, her breath rasping. All that Larry could see of her face was the bridge of her nose and those gelatinous eyes. She smelled strongly, too. She smelled of human insides. That sweet stuffy stench that living people exhale when bullets and knives have violently disregarded the sanctity of their all-concealing skin, and torn them open to the outside world. The nauseating richness of raw blood.

As Edna-Mae loomed nearer, the room appeared to grow darker. Maybe it was an illusion. But Larry could almost *feel* it. It was more of an aura than real darkness—more of a concentration of malevolent thought.

There was something extremely cold about it, something extremely cruel.

Edna-Mae reached Larry and Larry placed the flat of his hand against her. Underneath the sheet, he could feel her insides churning and rolling, and it took all of his nerve to keep his hand where it was. His left hand. His moving hand.

"That's it, Edna-Mae. That's as far as you go."

"Christ almighty," he heard one of the officers breathe, close behind him.

There was a split-second when Larry believed that he might actually have managed to stop her. She stayed quite still, and even the maelstrom inside her body seemed to calm down. Her breathing came low and thick, like the breathing of somebody with a heavy cold.

But then he looked up into her eyes and he was hit in the dead-center of his skull by a pain so hard and so cold that he dropped instantly on to his knees. He thought that she had actually smacked an axe into his head. He couldn't see, couldn't hear. He couldn't think about anything except this devastating blow to his brain.

He didn't even feel it when Edna-Mae shuffled past him, and out through the door, driving in front of her a crowd of nervously retreating police officers and medics.

But he did hear Houston Brough shouting, "Rickenbacker! Warn her, then fire!"

Rickenbacker bellowed, "Freeze! Do you hear me! Police officer! Freeze!"

Larry opened his mouth and yelled, "*No!*" but he wasn't sure that any sound came out. He twisted himself around and, with Fay Kuhn's help, lurched back on to his feet, just in time to see Rickenbacker fire the first shot.

There was a deafening bang inside the hospital corridor. The back of Edna-Mae's bedsheet flapped and snapped as the bullet hit it. Larry heard a scream—but it wasn't a scream from Edna-Mae. It was a scream from the stick-like body of the nurse, still lying sprawled on the floor.

"Jesus," said Rickenbacker. "Hit her dead center and she's still walking!"

Larry gasped, tried to say "No," tried to make Rickenbacker understand him. Fay shrilled, "What? What is it?"

But then Rickenbacker lifted his Magnum two-handed and fired again, and again, and again. The back of

Edna-Mae's bedsheet tore and flew into fragments. But inside room 9009, it was the nurse's frail remains that were blasted apart by the full force of Rickenbacker's bullets. Her ribcage exploded, half of her shoulder was blown away, her hairless skull burst like a jug dropped from a third-floor balcony.

Houston screamed, "Stop firing! Stop firing!" But the panic was too great and the noise was too loud. For a few seconds, as Rickenbacker emptied his gun, room 9009 was a staccato blizzard of skin and bone and ripped-apart uniform. The nurse's arm suddenly flapped up as if it were desperately trying to fend the bullets off.

Larry turned back to the corridor in dread. It was his worst nightmare—the nightmare of killing an innocent civilian. The whole floor seemed suddenly silent. No phones, no bells, no loudspeakers. Only gunsmoke, and a high persistent singing in his ears. Only nine or ten police officers and paramedics staring in disbelief as the sheeted form of Edna-Mae retreated slowly out of their sight.

"Want me to get after her, sir?" asked a young Latino officer.

Larry shook his head. "Houston, you take over here. Edna-Mae is mine."

"Six rounds, dead center," said Rickenbacker. still in shock. "Six rounds and she kept on walking."

"You'd better take a look at what you *did* hit," Larry told him, nodding his head toward 9009.

A pale-faced paramedic was already taking a look at what was left of the nurse. "Gunshot wounds," he mouthed, as Rickenbacker came into the room. "Wouldn't have believed it if I hadn't seen it for myself."

One insouciant black paramedic said, "That some kind of new invention, officer? A gun that shoots round corners?"

"The hell it is," breathed Rickenbacker. He dropped on to his knees on the floor.

Larry set off after Edna-Mae. Fay Kuhn came hurrying behind him, her heels tapping sharply on the polished floor.

"What are you going to do?" she panted.

"What do you think I'm going to do? I'm going to follow her."

"How far do you think she's going to get, wrapped up in a sheet?"

"How should I know? She got past me. She got past Officer Rickenbacker. Come on, Fay, that's not Edna-Mae Lickerman inside of that sheet. That's just a whole tangle of human stuff that's being dragged alone like two hundred pounds of variety meats. And where do we think it's all being dragged to?"

"I don't know." gasped Fay. "Where do we think it's all being dragged to?"

"The one who wants to feed on human experience, that's where. Belial or Beli Ya'al or Belly Y'all or whatever he calls himself. There she is, look! She's taken the stairs!"

They turned the corner of the corridor just in time to see the door to the emergency stairwell closing. Larry wrenched the door open again, and he and Fay went through to the ninth-floor landing. Larry paused, and listened. Up the echoing concrete stairwell came the soft swishing of sheet on concrete, and a scuffling padding noise of bare feet.

"Come on," he told Fay, and they quickly and quietly started to follow.

"Isn't there any way of stopping her?" asked Fay.

"If six rounds from a Magnum can't do it, then I don't know what can. Besides—it's more important to find out where she's going."

"You really think she's going to take us to Belial?"

He stopped on the fifth-floor landing. "Fay—will you please stop asking me questions. I don't know any more about this than you do."

She stared at him. "That's the second time you've called me Fay."

She was about to say something else, but Larry lifted his hand and said, "Ssh!"

They could still hear the swishing of Edna-Mae's sheet, and the ratlike scampering of her feet on the concrete stairs. Larry peered over the stair-rail and saw the edge of her sheet flickering past the third landing.

"Come on, let's go! If I can't follow an overweight woman in a bedsheet on Potrero Avenue, Dan Burroughs is going to have my hide for car-seat covers."

They ran swiftly down the remaining flights of stairs. They reached the first floor just as the door to the hospital's side entrance was easing itself shut.

They burst out into the street. Larry looked frantically one way, then the other. "Where the hell is she?" he demanded. "We can't have lost her!"

"There!" said Fay. "Right across the street!"

Edna-Mae was standing on the opposite curb, her torn bedsheet shining in the streelight. Sister Edna-Mae of the Unholy Transformation.

"What's she doing?" frowned Fay. "She's just standing there!"

"Wait, wait, hold back," said Larry. "I don't know

whether she can see us or not. She looked almost blind back up in her room."

They edged back against the hospital wall, so that they were partly obscured from Edna-Mae's view by a parked car. They waited, and still Edna-Mae remained where she was, patiently standing on the curb, her white sheet flapping. Several passers-by turned around to stare at her, but San Francisco is San Francisco, and she didn't attract any exceptional attention.

Houston appeared from around the front of the hospital.

"She's still there!" he said, in surprise.

"What's happening upstairs?" asked Larry.

"I've sealed it off for forensics. There's nothing we can do for that nurse. Rickenbacker's gone to lie down."

They were still talking and waiting when they heard a loud dry squeal of tires. A black Chevy van came speeding along Potreto, and slewed to a halt right beside Edna-Mae, blocking her from view. They heard a door bang, and then the van roared away again, leaving the opposite sidewalk empty.

Houston stared at Larry and Larry stared at Houston.

"She has friends," said Houston, in disbelief.

"The Fog City Satan, of course," snapped Larry, furious with himself for not making sure that he had a car close by.

Houston took out his pocket radio and called for an APB. "Black Chevy van, '81 or '82, no license plates, black-tinted windows. Locate and follow but do not, repeat, do not attempt to stop. Follow them to Eureka if you have to."

"Damn it," said Larry. It was all he could think of to say.

"What next?" asked Fay.

"What's next is I have to hang around here for hours, and you can do what you like."

The street began to warble with sirens as police reinforcements arrived. A van from KCBS television came to a violent stop right beside them, and a tanned bald man in Ray-Bans leaned out of the window and called, "Kuhn! What's happening, my angel?"

"Hold on, Henry!" called Fay. She took hold of Larry's sleeve, and looked at him seriously. "Are you still happy with that story?"

Houston said sharply, "What story?"

"It has to come out sometime," said Larry.

"So I can go ahead? No second thoughts?"

"Hey, what story?" Houston repeated.

"Wait for tomorrow's paper, Sergeant Brough," Fay smiled at him, as she turned to go. "It's about time you learned to read without moving your lips."

Houston watched her go with the expression of a man appreciating a good horse. "Attractive-looking woman," he remarked.

"Sure," Larry replied. "But you and me, we're both old married men."

"All the same, it's not too wise to do things for attractive-looking women unless you're sure you'd be just as happy doing them for ugly-looking old men."

"What's that? Brough's First Law of Faithfulness?"

"Unh-hunh. It's rule 22 in How To Survive In The SFPD."

He didn't get home until well past midnight. Linda had left him a huge turkey sandwich in the icebox, and he sat in the kitchen on his own, with a bottle of Anchor Steam and a large jar of mayonnaise, and loyally chewed his way through it, while he watched *Lobster Men From Mars* on cable.

After he had finished he took a shower, and shaved. When he looked at himself in the shaving-mirror he thought he looked changed. Maybe it did change you, when you started to believe in the supernatural. Maybe it showed in your face; the same way that you can tell when a girl has known hundreds of men.

The boys were still away at Kirby Cove, sleeping under canvas, but all the same he went into their rooms to look at their empty beds. Then he eased himself in beside Linda, who was deeply asleep with her blue velvet airline mask on. He guessed that she had probably taken a sedative. She always found it difficult to sleep when he was working on a dangerous or difficult case.

He switched off the bedside lamp and lay in the dark and wondered what it would be like to go to sleep thinking that you had nothing more important to worry about tomorrow than what to have for lunch; or what book to read; or where to go for a walk. He had forgotten what simplicity was like. He had forgotten what sleep was like.

Although he was gradually piecing together a picture of the Black Brotherhood and their apparent attempt to resurrect Belial, he still found his logical mind rebelling against the things that he had seen. When he thought back over Edna-Mae's grotesque departure from SFG, it seemed more like a television program that he had been watching, rather than reality. Rickenbacker had fired directly at Edna-Mae and yet his bullets had struck the nurse, ten feet behind him and off to his left, and shielded by a six-inch concrete wall. Even the most eccentric of ricochets couldn't have done that.

No—she hadn't been killed by the normal laws of physics.

She had fallen victim to that critically dangerous condition that Wilbert Fraser had warned him about. If any other being steals or borrows your ectoplasm, you daren't attempt to kill it or hurt it—not without killing or hurting yourself. They may have taken your essence somewhere else, but it's still *you*.

And, as Larry had seen before, the spirit world was neither rational nor predictable. It was a world where dead people walked, and flesh flowed like cotton-candy, and lives could be swallowed whole.

He turned on his side and tried to sleep, but sleep slunk away again, and lay sulking in the shadows. He began to wonder whether he had made a mistake in talking to Fay Kuhn. It had seemed like sense at the time. Bold, even rash, but sense all the same. Now, however, in the silence of the night, he wasn't so sure. Dan Burroughs would blow fifteen rows of fuses, he was sure about that. But would the Fog City Satan really care that his real objectives had been brought out into the open? He had shown complete disregard for the police when he had rescued Edna-Mae from the hospital, why should he worry now? He was obviously going to do just what he had set out to do, whether Larry tried to push him or not.

Larry eased himself out of bed and went through to the study. He punched out the *Examiner* number and waited for nearly two minutes for somebody to answer.

"*Examiner.*"

"Is Fay Kuhn still around?"

"No, I'm sorry, sir. She left about a half-hour ago."

"This is Lieutenant Foggia, of the San Francisco police. Do you think you could give me her home number?"

"I'm sorry, sir, I'm not permitted to do that."

"Well, could you call her and have her call me back? It's urgent."

"I'm sorry, sir. I don't think I can do that either."

"How would you like to be busted for obstructing a homicide investigation?"

"All right, sir. No need to get mad. I'll call her now. But I can't guarantee that she'll want to call you back."

"And I can't guarantee that I won't talk to your boss and tell him what an asshole you are."

"Sir, there's no need to be offensive."

Larry took a deep breath. "No," he agreed. "There isn't. So will you please accept my apologies and please put a call through to Ms Kuhn. I'll give you my home number."

Fay rang back almost immediately. "Lieutenant? I was almost asleep."

"Did you write the story?"

"For sure. It's page one, main lead."

Larry dry-washed his face with his right hand. "All right. Tell me what it says."

"Well, the strapline reads Supernatural Only Explanation Says Detective, and the headline reads 'Bizarre Death At SFG.'"

Larry was silent for a very long time. Then he said, "I suppose that's already running now."

"We usually start printing at eleven or thereabouts, yes. We may change the story during the night."

"There's no chance of pulling it, then?"

"Lieutenant!" Fay protested.

"All right, Fay. It was my decision, I guess I'll have to run with it. But in the cold light of rational reflection, it suddenly doesn't seem like such a great idea. You saw how Edna-Mae was picked up, right in front of our noses. This guy doesn't care squat what we do, *or* what we say."

"Lieutenant, I'm sorry, but—"

"All right, all right," Larry told her. "It's not your fault. I think I just made the worst career decision of my entire life, that's all."

"At least you'll force Burroughs' hand."

"What's that supposed to mean?"

"Well… when tomorrow's paper hits the street, he's going to be put into the position of having to come out publicly and say whether he thinks there's anything occult about this investigation or not."

"You *know* what he thinks," said Larry. "It's all fairy-stories, as far as he's concerned."

"Even though he regularly subscribes to *Al Omla La?*"

Larry frowned. "This time you got me. What the hell is *Al Omla La?*"

"*Al Omla La* is a limited subscription magazine produced twice a year by the Night Society, which is a very secretive collective of people interested in things like magic and spells and hallucinatory drugs and out-of-body experiences and the mystic implications of pleasure and pain. It's very specialist, always densely written, beautifully illustrated, if you like illustrations of goats being disemboweled and women's breasts with fish-hooks in them. Not only that, it's a hundred bucks a copy."

"And Dan Burroughs is a regular subscriber?" said Larry, in disbelief.

"Charter subscriber, since the fall of '83."

"So how did you find that out?"

"A good reporter never reveals her sources, lieutenant, you should know that. But it's true, cross my heart and hope to choke on a Chicken MacNugget."

Larry said, "Okay, I'll believe you. Listen, I have to catch some zees. I think I'm going to need all the strength I can get for tomorrow morning."

"Sweet dreams, lieutenant."

Larry went to the kitchen and poured himself a large glass of cold milk. He stood in the darkness swallowing it in palate-numbing gulps. Of course, it didn't necessarily mean anything at all that Dan Burroughs subscribed to some black magic magazine. He probably subscribed to *Guns & Ammo* and *San Francisco* and *Playboy*, too.

But he had been so vehement in his denials that the Fog City Satan case had anything to do with the supernatural that it struck Larry as singularly odd that he should show enough interest in it to part with $200 a year. Maybe he was a sado-masochist. Maybe he was doing his policemanly duty, and keeping a check on what the further-out citizens in the Bay Area were getting up to.

But all the same—There was something here that gave him one of his bad feelings. A piece of jigsaw that obstinately refused to fit, no matter which way around he turned it.

He crept back to bed, and slid between the sheets. Linda was warm and deeply asleep. He tried to remember the last time they had made love. It seemed like about six months ago. In a storm… with rain spattering against the windows. Afterwards they had knelt on the bed and watched the lightning wriggle from Coit Tower and the Trans America pyramid.

He tried to put himself to sleep by reciting as much as he could remember of the *Ode To Coit Tower*. '"O anti-verdurous phallic were't not for your pouring in height like a sick tree—' no, that's wrong '—looming in tears like a sick tree or your ever-gaudy comfort jabbing your city's much-wrinkled sky.'"

God almighty, did I really used to like that poem? Did I really find it a revelation?

But he plowed on all the same. '"—fresh with the labor sweat of cablecar & Genoa papa pushcart.'"

He wasn't aware that he had stopped reciting. He slept, a shallow sleep, no more than lying in six inches of shadowed water. First of all he dreamed of nothing. Then he dreamed that the water was receding and that he was being gradually dragged out with the tide, into the deeper shadows, into the darkness, soundlessly, beneath a Golden Gate bridge that gleamed deathly white instead of orange, out toward the ocean, where nobody could save him.

He was awakened by a rustling sound. A rustling sound so soft, so ghostly, that he wasn't sure at first if it was anything more than his own breathing. He lay with his eyes closed, listening. Then he heard another, sharper rustle, and he opened his eyes wide.

He was so frightened by what he saw that he made a *"wah!"* yelp like a startled dog.

The faintest outline of Roberta Snow, the little girl from Wilbert Fraser's seance, stood beside his bed in her drowned party-dress, with one hand out, staring at him wide-eyed. More than wide-eyed, beseechingly.

Her face was gray as lake-water, and her hair flowed up from her head as if she were still trapped inside that slowly sinking car. Maybe she always would be, forever and ever.

Her mouth moved, and Larry heard a sound like someone blowing down a bamboo pipe.

"What do you want?" he whispered, tautly.

DEAD she breathed.

Larry turned over quickly to see if Linda was awake; but she hadn't moved.

"I don't understand."

DEAD

Larry swallowed. He was so frightened of Roberta Snow that his throat seemed to close up, and none of his muscles seemed to work. Even the heaving apparition of Edna-Mae, swathed in sheets, hadn't paralyzed him as much as this.

"I'm dreaming, right?" he asked her.

She shook her head, and her hair waved from side to side. *DEAD* she repeated, in frustration.

"Dead? You're dead?"

Again, the phantom girl in the party dress desperately shook her head. She flickered intermittently, and sometimes she almost disappeared, as if she didn't have enough energy to sustain her presence in Larry's house for very long.

"You're not dead? You mean, somebody else is dead?"

This time she managed a smile, and nodded.

"Somebody else is dead? Who? Listen to me, Roberta. Who else is dead?"

WIL—

"Will? Will what?"

FRASER

"Are you serious?" Christ almighty I'm soaked in sweat I'm scared shitless and I'm asking a drowning ghost in my bedroom if she's serious. He was so frightened and it was all so ludicrous that he almost laughed.

WILBERT FRASER'S DEAD

"You *are* serious. He's really dead? What happened to him?"

The little girl began to grow dimmer and dimmer. All he could see was the edge of her taffeta dress and the darkness of her eyes.

MAN—she breathed.

"A man killed her? What man? Come on, Roberta, try! What man?"

MAN—

She had almost disappeared now; trembling, intermittent, like the last dull glow of a flashlight before its battery dies; a glow that it is somehow darker than the darkness which it is supposed to illuminate.

She vanished. Larry immediately jumped up in bed and Linda shouted out: "*Larry! For God's sake! Do you have to bounce up and down all fucking night!*"

"I'm sorry, I'm sorry. I just thought of something."

"Do you have to bounce up and down when you think? Most normal men can think without moving."

"Listen, I'm sorry. I'm truly sorry. I'll go sleep on the couch."

She turned over and lifted her eyeshade. "No, come on… you don't have to do that. Why don't you make love to me instead?"

He sat on the edge of the bed exhausted frightened

soaked in sweat. His head was bowed his hair was scruffed up he needed a shave. He hesitated for a very long time and didn't say anything.

Linda knelt up in bed and wrapped her arms around him. "You're so hot! You're not running a fever, are you?"

"No, no. My brain's going around and it won't stop, that's all."

She kissed the back of his neck, and then his cheek and smoothed back his sweaty hair.

"You should've taken your father's advice, and gone into the family business."

He kissed her hand. "I might have done, if I could've found out what the family business was."

"Your father was in import-export, wasn't he?"

"Import-export, that's right. Covers a multitude of nefarious activities."

"Mario's Ghost," she teased him, and kissed him again.

She lay back on the bed. He turned around, and leaned over her and kissed her again, on the lips this time. It was a long, unhurried, romantic kiss, one of those kisses that only lovers who have lived together for a very long time can give each other, because it's not just a kiss but a memory of all of those other kisses; and the reason why all of those other kisses were given.

Larry tugged at the ribbon of her nightgown, and it opened, baring her large rounded breasts, lying to the side of her chest because of their weight. He licked and kissed each nipple in turn, drawing it by suction to the roof of his mouth and drumming it lightly with the tip of his tongue. He could hear Linda breathing quick and low.

His kisses trailed down her stomach, as if he were

dropping a flower on her body with every kiss. His hands caressed her shoulders and massaged her breasts, squeezing them tightly so that they stood up proud and high, their nipples swollen and shiny.

He kissed her navel. He breathed in perfume and perspiration; and the musky aroma of sex.

Slowly, she opened her thighs wider, and let him do what he liked. He opened her lips with his fingers, and let his tongue slide down her slippery, liquid vulva. There was nothing on God's earth that tasted or felt like this. No fruit, no honey, no silk, no flower. The tip of his tongue explored and aroused her clitoris, and the tiny hole from which she peed, and the then the warm embracing depths of her vagina.

He licked her and caressed her until she clutched his hair in her fingers and almost wrenched it from his scalp. He heard her gave a cry that was almost as alien as the cry that he had given when Roberta appeared in the room. He wondered momentarily if humans become something else in moments of intense ecstasy, or intense fear. Perhaps they become less than human: closer to beasts.

He rose up over her, with the taste of her still in his mouth, and slowly slid his penis inside her. She shivered again, and again, with aftershocks, and murmured things that he couldn't understand, but which he knew were descriptions of her sexual fantasies, of people watching while they fucked, of being touched by strangers, of posing for obscene photographs. He made love to her slowly, a long, loping, muscular pace, penetrating deeper with every lope.

He loved her so much at that moment, he was sure that he loved her more than he ever had done, or ever would.

She was his pride, and his redemption. She was his family, his lover, and his friend.

His ejaculation seemed long and slow, warmly pouring rather than spurting. As he closed his eyes in the darkness of his own satisfaction, he heard a voice in the room that whispered *AX*—

He opened his eyes and twisted around, panicky.

Linda said, "What's the matter, Larry? What's wrong? You look—"

"Ssh!" he asked her, "please, ssh!"

"No I won't ssh! You're right in the middle of making love and now you're bouncing around again!"

He climbed out of bed, feeling the wetness between his legs. He went to the bedroom door and opened it. Nobody. Nothing. Not even a quivering shadow. Out in the street he heard the slow tortured grinding of a garbage truck.

"Larry, will you tell me what's wrong?"

He stayed outside the bedroom door for almost half a minute, listening. But it was already beginning to grow light. The windows had changed from glossy black to melancholy gray.

"Larry, come back to bed," she begged him.

He said, "No. You get some more sleep. I'm too wired."

"Larry, I want you to hold me."

Reluctantly, he climbed back into bed, and held her in his arms. She took his hand and held it between her legs. "That's you. That's you and me. Even forensic analysis couldn't tell us apart."

He kissed her ear, kissed her cheek. But his mind kept racing. Had he really seen Roberta Snow, standing in the room? He turned around to stare at the spot where she had been standing, and he couldn't believe it. It must have been a dream. After all, if Wilbert Fraser really was dead, he would have been the first to hear about it.

MAN Roberta had whispered. *MAN* But what man? And why had she come to tell him? *MAN* and then *AX*. Maybe she's got it all ass-about-face, and she was trying to say *AXMAN*.

In spite of himself, he dozed off. But he woke up with a jolt ten minutes later.

"I have to get up," he said, his mouth thick. "Take a shower, get to headquarters."

"Do you want me to make you some breakfast? Maybe some pancakes?"

"Come on, Linda, at ten after five in the morning? You don't want to do that."

"I'm your *wife*, Larry. Wives do things like that."

He kissed her. "Not necessary. Besides, I want to get to the office before anybody else."

She frowned at him. "Are you worried about something?"

"I'm always worried about something. It's my job. If I didn't have anything to worry about it, I'd be worried."

He showered. *AXMAN*, he puzzled. What axman? Ax, man. Man, ax. It didn't make any sense. Yet Roberta had clearly made an enormous effort to appear in his bedroom, and tell him.

Linda had made him some strong coffee and toast while he was showering. She sat in her pale pink robe and watched him eat.

"Something's really bugging you, isn't it?" she said.

"It's this investigation, that's all. It's like nothing I ever worked on before."

"Want to talk about it?"

He shook his head.

"Are you going to be free tonight? I'm picking up the boys at three. Maybe we could all go to 'Cafe Riggio'."

"I don't know. Maybe." Maybe? More than likely, once Dan Burroughs had clapped his eyes on Bizarre Death At SFG. Supernatural Only Explanation Says Detective.

She held his hand, stroked his knuckles. "I'd love it if you could. I'm beginning to miss you."

"I still live in the same house, you know, in the same city. It's not like I've gone off to Darkest Africa for six months."

Linda laughed. "I wish you had. And I wish I was with you. Boy, what I'd do for a magic wand." She held out both hands and said, "Mandrake gestures hypnotically... and Larry and Linda are both together on a slow boat on the Upper Limpopo."

Larry slowly lowered his coffee-cup. Mandrake. Man. Drake. Man. Ax. Mandrax.

MANDRAX. That was what Roberta Snow had been trying to say to him. Mandrax, one of the Black Brotherhood. And possibly the last surviving member of the Black Brotherhood. Wilbert Fraser and George Menzel had burned them in their automobile, but one of them had gotten out alive. Burned, but alive.

The strongest of all of them. Mandrax.

"Larry?" asked Linda. "You look like somebody just dropped a brick on your head from nine miles high."

"I have to go," he told her. He stood up without finishing his coffee and wiped his mouth on a kitchen towel.

"You have to go *now*, this instant? You can't even finish a quarter of a slice of toast?"

"Keep it for me. I'll be back later."

"And what about tonight?"

He shoved his gun into its holster, collected his pale blue cotton coat from the bentwood stand in the hallway, shucked on his right loafer, and hop-skip-jumped to the door while he tugged on his left.

Linda hurried after him and kissed him. "I love you," she said. "Come back safe. The boys'll be home by four."

"Take care yourself," he told her. "And I love you, too. Kissy-wissy-itchy-snookums-huggy-wuggy-bing-bong."

That stopped her dead in her tracks. "Wh-what?" she laughed.

Larry suddenly looked embarrassed; then rueful; then a little sad. "It was something that momma used to say to me, when I was very small. I guess it just came out by itself."

They stood looking at each other under a morning sky that was clear and high. Then Larry said, "I'll call you, okay," and walked down to his car, and climbed in. He drove away without even looking back, and Linda closed the door.

He knocked and rang at Wilbert Fraser's door for nearly five minutes, but there was no reply. He stood in the porch looking out over early-morning San Francisco with its glittering windows and its hazy Bay, wondering what to do. He had no warrant, and no just cause for breaking in.

"Actually, your honor, I was visited in the night by the ghost of a drowned girl who told me that Mr. Fraser was dead. This was a piece of information that I felt it my duty as a police officer to follow up immediately, so I broke down Mr. Fraser's door and scared the hell out of him."

He negotiated the rickety wooden steps down to Wilbert's front yard. He beat his way through thistles and creeper and grostesquely-overgrown hogweed until he found his way round to the side of the house. He frightened a flock of young birds and frightened himself almost as much.

At the side of the house he found the door to the laundry-room. Smearing the dusty window with his hand, he could just make out the shapes of a twin-tub washing machine with a power mangle attached, the kind of washing-machine you would have seen in early series of *I Love Lucy*. He looked around, but the neighborhood was quiet and the street was almost deserted. He picked up a brick from the long grass, and used it to smash the glass.

He found Wilbert almost at once. He was lying pinned to his kitchen table, with a river of red treacle between his outspread legs. His eyes were still open, although blowflies crawled all over his face, in and out of his mouth, and rose in a fierce buzzing storm from the blood that had congealed all over the floor. The glans of his penis had been replaced by a glistening, crawling glans of flies. The whole kitchen was filled with a foul smell, like bad chicken.

Larry carefully picked up the telephone in his handkerchief, dialed 553-1551.

"Houston? You're in early. Listen, I'm over at Wilbert Fraser's house. He's been wasted. Yeah, that's right, and pretty damned viciously too. Unh-hunh. No. Somebody cut off his weenie."

There was a pause, and then Houston said something about Dan Burroughs having already seen this morning's *Examiner*, and that Larry would very likely be sharing the same fate as Wilbert Fraser.

"*He's breathing fire, Larry, I warn you. I mean he's totally breathing fire.*"

"All right, I'll deal with him later. Maybe I should bring some marshmallows and a stick. Will you roust out the coroner, please, and everybody else we're going to need? Let's have Jones and Glass here, too; and maybe the Jolly Green Giant would like to check it out. He knows the m.o. better than anybody."

"*Do you think it's our boy again, or just the revenge of the faggots?*"

"It could be our boy. It's sadistic enough. Any sign of that van yet?"

"*Nothing. A patrol car clocked it in the Mission District, but after that it vanished.*"

"Find out the exact location where they saw it."

"*Okay, lieutenant. And—lieutenant?*"

"What is it, sergeant?"

"*I've got to say this. I don't think it was a particularly hot idea of yours to talk to Fay Kuhn. Not the way things are.*"

"I'm not sure I understand what you mean, 'the way things are'? What way are they?"

Houston hesitated, and then he said, "*I have to think about my career, too, lieutenant. But let's say that Deputy Chief Burroughs didn't assign me to this case for my investigative skills alone. Remember the little birdhouse in your soul.*"

Larry hung up. So Fay was right to be suspicious about Dan Burroughs. But what had Houston meant about "the little birdhouse in your soul". That was a pop song, wasn't it, by They Might Be Giants?

He couldn't even remember the words. Something about blue canaries by the lightswitch, real hippie-type stuff. It had gone down a storm in San Francisco. But then he clearly recalled the hook; the real stand-out chorus in the whole song.

"*I'm your friend… but I'm not actually your friend*" Was that what Houston was trying to tell him?

And then the next line, "*Who watches over you?*"

Larry turned away from the phone and back to the fly-glittering body of Wilbert Fraser. So that was it. Dan Burroughs had appointed Houston Brough to keep an eye on him; and to report back on whatever he was doing. Houston was warning him that for the sake of his own career, he would have to do what Dan Burroughs had told him. But if Houston didn't *know* what Larry was doing, then he couldn't be compromised.

He stood over Wilbert Fraser and crossed himself and said, "*Requiescat in pace*, Wilbert."

His interview with Dan Burroughs lasted less than three minutes. In an office crowded with cigarette smoke and copies of this morning's *Examiner*, Dan asked Larry for his gun and his badge.

"By the time you reach lieutenant, you should have acquired at least a basic grasp of public relations and police protocol," Dan rasped. His eyes looked deader than ever. "I'm disappointed in you, Larry. This mess is going to take days to clear up, weeks. Mayor Agnos is just about biting the fucking carpet. I can't believe you did it. It's like career suicide. 'Supernatural Only Explanation.' For Christ's sake,

Larry! Even if you *are* a wacko, at least have the good sense to keep it to yourself."

Larry said, tightly, "You transferred me to this assignment because you wanted somebody with imagination, somebody who was prepared to investigate any possibility, no matter how weird."

"There's weird and there's weird."

"For sure. And this is *weird* with a capital 'Wuh'. The Fog City Satan is performing a series of ritual murders with the specific intention of raising a demonic being."

"I'm sure you're right," Dan Burroughs protested. "I'm sure that you're absolutely right. But just because the Fog City Satan believes that he's going to raise a demonic being, that doesn't mean that *you* have to believe it, too! Did you hear the TV news this morning? The general opinion is that the San Francisco Police Department have gone totally birdseed. NBC called us the Monster Squad. CBS played the theme from *Ghostbusters.*"

"Dan, there have been certain events in this investigation which have been impossible to explain any other way. Look at what happened to Edna-Mae Lickerman. Look at what happened to that nurse. Go talk to Officer Rickenbacker, and asked him what happened. He fired six times at Edna-Mae and killed a girl in another room."

Dan Burroughs drew an orange manila folder across his desk and opened it up, dropping cigarette ash on it. "According to the doctors at SFG, Edna-Mae Lickerman was suffering a massive endocrinal collapse, a common feature of AIDS. The nurse was a twenty-three-year-old girl named Carole Fremont. She'd been treating AIDS patients at SFG for over eighteen months; and she suffered a similar endocrinal collapse to Edna-Mae Lickerman's. End of story."

"And what about my mother?" asked Larry, in a trembling voice. "I suppose you think that *she* was suffering from AIDS, too."

"Your mother was struck by a Kenworth TransOrient tractor-and-trailer traveling at nearly sixty miles an hour. Pardoning your filial sensitivities, there really wasn't enough left of her for anybody to form an opinion about her medical condition at the time."

"What about the shooting? How do you explain that?"

"Ballistics examined the hospital corridor. Each of the six bullets struck a concrete pillar about twenty-five feet from where Officer Rickenbacker was standing, and ricocheted back into room 9009, hitting Nurse Fremont where she lay. It was a freak accident, no doubt about it. But Officer Rickenbacker has a remarkably steady hand, and that's why the bullets all followed a near-identical ricochet. Here, take a look for yourself."

Dan Burroughs opened another folder and took out three or four black-and-white photographs. They showed the chipped concrete pillar, and the scarred metal hinge at the bottom of the door. Larry didn't even lower his eyes to look at them. Houston Brough and Fay Kuhn had given him enough evidence to know that Dan Burroughs was playing a double game with this investigation, although he didn't understand for a moment what he hoped to achieve.

Nothing in the world could convince Larry now that this wasn't a full-scale psychic disturbance. He had seen three grown women, shrunk down to their bones. He had seen a parrot with his own face. He had seen a drowned girl dance. On his own hand, he had seen the face of a long-dead killer, and heard him talking.

In a tight voice, Larry said, "Dan, I'm going to ask you this once only. I'm going to ask you to back me up, with the mayor, and with the media. The worst we can get is a ribbing. I'm going to ask you to give me *carte blanche* to clear up this case by whatever means it takes. I believe that I'm very close to cracking it. Give me thirty-six hours and I'll bring you back the Fog City Satan, all trussed up and ready for the oven."

Dan Burroughs coughed. "If I back you up, Larry, that's tantamount to my coming out in public and saying that *I* believe in the supernatural, too. You're not just talking about unorthodox methods of investigation here. You're talking about the supernatural! Spooks and vampires and things that go yolla-bolla-wolla in the night! Jesus—the Commissioner would have me playing horseshoes down at the Happy Home for Deranged Detectives before you could say abracadabra. You may want to take a dive down the toilet, Larry, that's your privilege. But I'm not diving in after you."

For a moment, Larry felt all of his Italian fire rise up inside him. Liar! Cheat! Bastard! He could have thumped Dan's desk until everything jumped up in the air. But while he had his father's fire, he had also inherited his mother's self-control. He remembered his father raging from room to room whenever a business deal had gone awry, roaring and slamming doors. He remembered his mother remaining quite serene and still, as if all the shouting and banging in the world would never disturb her. Nobody in the house would dare to speak until the front door had crashed shut, and his father had gone off to the Garibaldi Club to take out his ire on all of his friends, and get drunk on *grappa*.

But knowing what he did about Dan Burroughs, he was able to damp down his temper, and stay relatively calm, even though his heart was racing and his fists were clenched.

Hoarsely, in a voice like Marlon Brando playing Don Corleone, Dan Surroughs said, "I guess that impetuosity has its own price, Larry. You've disappointed me. For Christ's sake, you're not a TV detective. A moral value is a moral value, but there's no point in having moral values if you have no authority to exercise them. That's what you've done to yourself. You've just lost your authority... so your moral values stand for zilch. If only your father were here. There was a man. Mario Foggia. He knew when to stand up for something and he knew when to back off. He had intelligence. Shrewdity. He didn't stand for any crap but he knew when it was time to compromise, too." Dan Burroughs tapped the side of his nose in the age-old gesture of knowingness. "You should learn that. Shrewdity."

"So what do I do now?" asked Larry.

Dan Burroughs crushed out his cigarette. "You hand over your notes and any additional information to Arne. Then you go home and play with your kids. Or maybe go fishing. Take Linda to Big Sur. You're on full pay until this investigation is over, then we'll have a disciplinary hearing. Don't lose any sleep over it. The worst they'll do to you is bust you down to sergeant."

Larry laid down his gun and his badge right on the very edge of Dan's desk. Then he turned to go.

"Larry?" said Dan, as he reached the door.

Larry waited, without turning around.

"I just want you to know that this is nothing personal," Dan told him. "This is police discipline, that's all."

Larry didn't reply. He knew now that it was personal; that Dan Burroughs was engineering something, although he couldn't work out what. Dan would have been better keeping his mouth shut and saying nothing at all. Because Larry knew now that he had entered a different world altogether, the world of lies; the desert of deception; where the truth was never told, and where trust was a word engraved on a tombstone.

8

He drove directly to the "Waxing Moon". He found Tara Gordon at the counter, serving a tall, serious Norwegian sailor who wanted a love potion to make sure that his wife stayed faithful to him while he was at sea.

"You have your three basic ways," Tara Gordon was telling him, while Larry leaned against the counter close by, pretending to inspect a tray of silver amulets. "We have this—" holding up a green glass jar "—this is fat from a buck goat. You smear this on your private parts before you make love to your wife, and she will never *ever* look at another man."

The sailor opened the jar and dipped his large pale nose into it.

"Pff! Smells terrible bad!"

"Well, you don't have to go for that. I have a love potion here which is made of camphor and violets and gardenia. You mix it with two pounds of lard and rub it on your buttocks. Believe me, it makes you pump like a diesel engine."

She turned to Larry and slowly winked. Her hair was brushed up into a large glossy bun and held with a silver hairnet. She wore a sleeveless jerkin of soft black leather, and tight black leather pants. He could smell the musk of her perfume from seven feet away.

"Then there's this," she was telling the sailor. "It's a love-magnet. I call it the Pole-Ariser you hang it around your thing for three days and three nights—then, when you go off to sea, you leave it under the bed. Your wife won't be able to go to any other bed, but any man who tries to get into the bed with her will have to jump out, whether he wants to or not."

The sailor turned the magnet over and over for a long time, mournfully scrutinizing it in every light. Eventually, he said, "I take this one."

"You won't regret it, sir. Polarize your pole and safeguard your hole, that's what I say. That's $68 plus tax, full money-back guarantee."

When he had left the store, Larry said, "Polarize your pole, what kind of sales-talk is that?"

Tara Gordon laughed. "Don't criticize. They *work*. I've sold three hundred in two weeks."

"How do you know they work?"

"Let's put it this way, nobody's brought one back yet. And for reasons of hygiene, we don't exchange."

Larry picked one up, and examined it. "I've discovered something," he said.

"Oh, yes, and what's that?"

"Mandrax is in town. In fact, I think he's the Fog City Satan."

Tara Gordon glanced quickly toward the door, almost as if she expected to see Mandrax standing outside, staring in at her.

"You'd better come back to the office," she said.

She closed the office door behind them. She looked beautiful but pale. Maybe it was the make-up. Maybe it was staying indoors all the time, in this chilly black-velvet emporium.

"Aren't you going to offer me one of your buffalo-chip vodkas?" he asked her.

"Maybe that's a good idea," she said, and poured them each a large glassful. "And it's grass, not chip."

"I'll drink to that."

"How do you know it's Mandrax?" she asked, worriedly.

"Let's say that I had a little visitation from the other side."

"You? You're a police lieutenant. Police lieutenants don't get visits from the other side."

"Well, this one did. And, besides, I'm not a police lieutenant just at the moment. I'm on suspension. I was foolhardy enough to tell Ms Fay Kuhn of the *San Francisco Examiner* that I believed in demons."

"Oh, smart move."

"I'm not so sure that it wasn't. But anyway, sad to tell you, Wilbert Fraser got himself killed last night."

"Oh, no! Oh, I'm sorry! I know he was a bitch and all of that, but—"

Larry nodded. "I know. And he didn't die easily, either. Somebody was out to punish him; and I'm pretty sure that 'somebody' was the Fog City Satan."

"But why should the Fog City Satan punish poor old Wilbert?"

"I don't know for sure. But a reasonable guess is because he opened his big mouth and told me all he knew about the Black Brotherhood and Belial."

Tara Gordon swallowed vodka and shivered. "How could the Fog City Satan have known that he talked to you?"

That question hadn't yet occurred to Larry, although it was a highly logical question for Tara Gordon to ask. If the Fog City Satan had taken his revenge on Wilbert for talking to Larry, then she, too, must be just as much at risk.

Come to think of it, how *could* the Fog City Satan have found out? Only two other people had known that Larry was there: the young uniformed officer who had driven him to Wilbert's house after his mother had been killed. And Houston Brough. And Houston Brough had already tipped him off that "*I'm not actually your friend... who watches over you?*" And to whom had Houston Brough reported back?

"You're looking like you forgot which lady's boudoir you left your shorts in," remarked Tara Gordon, a little impatiently.

Larry slowly shook his head. "On the contrary. I think I just remembered."

"You really believe that Mandrax is back?"

"Yes, I do."

"Because a visitation told you?"

"Do you believe in visitations? I mean, no bullshit, no magnetic Pole-Arisers. Do you really believe?"

"My dearest lieutenant, I was born believing."

"All right, then," said Larry. "The little drowned girl that I saw at Wilbert's seance appeared right by my bed and said 'MAN'. Later, she said 'AX'."

Tara Gordon frowned. "No 'DR'?"

"Ms Gordon, Tara—Mandrax is back, I'm convinced of it. I *feel* it."

She sat on the edge of her desk and thoughtfully swung her legs. "What are you going to do about it?"

"Find the bastard."

"I thought you said you were on suspension."

"Belial and the Fog City Satan killed my mother, not to mention the Berrys, one of the nicest families I ever knew. I don't give a shit about suspension."

"Well—what do you want *me* to do about it?"

"Just let me have Mandrax's last known address… and maybe some of the people who might have known him."

Tara Gordon said, "What if I'm scared?"

"Nobody knows I'm here; not even my sergeant."

She hesitated. Then she put down her vodka glass and went to the steel filing-cabinet. She unlocked it, pulled out the second drawer, and produced a tattered address-book with a picture of a very young Bob Dylan on the front cover.

"Here it is… 3522 Twentieth. That may not have been where he actually hung out, but I went to a couple of parties there once, and I got the impression that he was staying there; or at least crashing for a while."

She licked her thumb and flicked through a few more pages. "My God…"she said, shaking her head. "All these boys I used to know. Look at this! Dwight Kreznick! I can't even remember what he looked like. But I've put three stars beside his name, so he must have been good at something! Look—here's somebody you might talk to—Jack Cole. He used to run a second-hand bookstore on Eighteenth Street. I think it's a bar-b-q joint now, but I'm sure you could find him if you asked around. If you can imagine a six-foot Stan Laurel with jaundice, that's Jack Cole."

Larry left the "Waxing Moon" with a free magnetic Pole-Ariser in his pocket, and lipstick on his right cheek. He drove slowly and thoughtfully to the Mission District. The more he discovered about the Fog City Satan, the unhappier he became. Like the psychic spun-sugar on his moving hand, his investigation was beginning to tangle itself into a recognizable shape. However, he had to make an effort to stop himself from rushing to judgement. So Dan Burroughs subscribed to an occult magazine. So Houston Brough had been keeping a watch on him. Neither of those pieces of information would stand the test of significant proof. Nor would the fact that Houston Brough and Dan Burroughs were arguably the only people who knew that Larry had returned to talk to Wilbert Fraser on the night of his mother's death.

In fact, he was beginning to realize that there was scarcely any point in searching for proof in this investigation. Even if he found it—even if he could get Edna-Mae Lickerman to shuffle up and down the County Court in her bullet-tattered sheets—even if he could produce a parrot with his own eye blinking out of its head—nobody would want to believe that somewhere in the city, there was a dangerous and ancient demon at work—a beast with an insatiable greed for human souls and human flesh.

By accepting the reality of the supernatural, and the anguished spirits on the other side, Larry had lost his case even before he had arrested his perpetrator.

He drew up across the street from 3522 Twentieth. It looked as if he had drawn a blank. Mandrax may have crashed here in 1965, but now it was El Tazumal, the Mexican restaurant. Larry looked around the street to see if there was any sign of the black van that had rescued Edna-Mae, or anybody who remotely resembled Mandrax, but the nearest was a Dominican monk climbing out of a Winnebago and getting his sandal inextricably caught on the footstep. He looked as near as any monk could ever look to saying "shit!"

He drove across to Eighteenth Street, and prowled up and down a few times before locating what looked like the sleaziest local hangout. Bowdre Bar'N'Grill. Coors. Burgers. Try Our BBQ Chicken. Larry parked the car and cleaved his way through a clattering bead curtain into the cold, smoky, fatty interior.

He approached a high polished-steel counter, behind which a man in a paper beanie was aggressively scraping burned circles of hamburger off his hotplate.

"Looking for Jack Cole," he remarked.

The man sniffed, and wiped sweat from his forehead. "Jack Cole? Jack 'King' Cole?"

"I guess."

"You a cop?"

"Unh-hunh."

"Got yourself a business card?"

Larry opened his billfold and laid a ten-spot on the counter. The man made it disappear without even hesitating in his scraping. "Jack Cole's over at Fanny's Bar, cross the street. What's he done now?"

"Nothing serious."

"That makes a change."

Larry crossed the street in the blurry sunshine and found

a narrow red-painted entrance with a broken neon tube outside saying Fannys Bar. Some local wag had added an "e" to the sign in spray-paint. Jack pushed through the single swing door and found himself inside one of those dark, refrigerator-cold bars where the hostesses carry pencil-torches so that they can write your order. There was a smell of yesterday's perfume and cigarettes and disinfected but persistent vomit.

Larry went to the bar and asked for a Coors Lite. The barman was black and non-committal and didn't look like the type you could tell your troubles to. Larry gave him $10 for the beer and asked, "Jack Cole in here?" with the clear implication that he could keep the change if he said yes.

"Skinnah-dood ovah by the play-unt." The $10 vanished.

"The play-unt" turned out to be a dusty vinyl yucca in a potful of cigarette butts. The "skinnah-dood" turned out to be a hangdog-looking man with coathanger shoulders and a drooping felt hat. He was sitting over a draft beer with a bourbon chaser, drumming his long fingers on the table as if he were impatiently waiting for somebody to show. Larry scraped out the chair opposite and said, "Mind if I join you?"

The man gave the barest of shrugs.

"Your name Jack Cole?" asked Larry.

The eyes flickered in the darkness. "What's it to you?"

"Tara Gordon suggested I talk to you."

"Tara? That whore? I haven't seen Tara Gordon since we both got blasted in 2001."

"Listen, my name's Larry Foggi. I'm looking for a guy who used to hang around here in the '60s."

Jack Cole snorted in one nostril. "There's nobody left, man. They all got old, or married, or straight. Usually all three. Some of them even started to vote Republican. What you see now, this is all for the tourists, or for all of those people who think they have too much taste to live in the rest of America. San-Cuteness-on-Sea."

"You're still here."

"Oh, sure. I'm like one of those senile granpas who pinch girls' bottoms and lower their neckties into their minestrone when they're eating and wet the bed every night, but the children can't find a nice cheap nursing-home for you, so here you have to stay. Remember that 'hope I die before I get old' crap? It never works out that way."

Larry took out his billfold and made a play of riffling through his cash. "Jack," he said, "I'm looking for Mandrax."

The silence seemed to go on and on and on. Jack didn't raise his eyes, didn't lift his glass, didn't drum his fingers, didn't reply.

Larry said, "Most people think that the Black Brotherhood were all burned and that Mandrax is dead. But I know that Mandrax isn't dead and I want him."

Jack Cole at last lifted his eyes. "Do you know what you're saying?"

"I think so."

"Do you know that every time you mention that name you might just as well be signing a piece of paper that says, 'I Larry Loggia wish to die as soon as it can conveniently be arranged'?"

"Foggia."

"What?"

"It's 'Foggia'. not 'Loggia'. And, yes, I know all about Mandrax and all about the Black Brotherhood, and believe me, I'd rather not get involved. But it's something I have to do."

"Well... I've heard the rumors," said Jack Cole. "A friend of mine came to me six or seven weeks back and said that he'd seen somebody who looked just like Mandrax driving a van down by the Embarcadero. I didn't pay it any mind, not to start with. But then I heard about some more things, and I guess that convinced me"

"What things? Faces in windows, maybe? Faces on hands? People getting themselves shrunk up? Things that oughtn't to be?"

Jack Cole gave him a long, steady look. "You know all about it. Why're you asking me?"

"Because I want to find him."

"That's like a chicken hunting for a fox."

Larry took out $50. "Come on, Jack. Bend to a little bribery. One address, that's all it takes, and this limited-edition picture of Ulysses S. Grant can be yours."

Jack turned his head and slowly conned the bar. Then he said, "I'd prefer Franklin, if you've got him."

"The rest if the tip turns out good."

"No Franklin, no tip."

Larry reluctantly took out his last $100 bill and laid it on the table. Jack Cole sat looking at it for a very long time, as if he were finding it difficult to make up his mind whether to talk to Larry or not. Eventually, he picked it up, folded it in half, then into quarters, and tucked it into his shirt pocket. "There's an old spice warehouse down by the

China Basin. They were going to knock it down and turn it into something fancy, but in the end they changed their minds. Too expensive, wrong area. It's on the south side of the Basin, just before you get to Pier 48."

"And that's it?"

"You want me to draw you a map?"

"For a hundred you should carry me there on your back."

Jack Cole shrugged, and finished his draft beer. "Information is subject to inflation, old buddy, just like everything else."

"You're sure that Mandrax is there?"

"No, as a matter of fact I'm *not* sure that Mandrax is there. But Mandrax used to say that if ever he needed a place to hide, that would be it. He even took me out to see it once, asked me what I thought. I said it was great. Especially the smell, and the damp. It made Castle Dracula look like a Holiday Inn."

"You must have known him pretty good."

Jack Cole sucked in his cheeks. "Nobody knew any of the Black Brotherhood pretty good. I was *close* to some of them, for sure. But it was the same kind of closeness you get when you stand an inch-and-a-half away from a rattlesnake. Total freezing-cold shit-in-your-pants tension. I guess that was what made them so attractive."

Larry stood up. "Okay, Jack Cole. Thanks for your help. But if it turns out dud, I'm going to be coming back here to Fanny's Bar and I'm going to be asking you politely for my picture back."

Jack Cole managed the ghost of a smile. "Appreciate the warning. I'd better spend it quick, in that case."

*

He called Linda but she wasn't home yet. He ate a solitary lunch at a cozy Cambodian restaurant on Sixteenth Street. He had known the proprietor, an elegant butterfly-lady known to all of her customers as Mrs. Krong, ever since she had first arrived in San Francisco six years ago. Her eldest son had been knifed in a Cambodian gang-fight and Larry had been assigned to find his killers. After six months, he had been obliged to drop the case, still unsolved, and four years later the file was still open.

Every time he ate there, Mrs. Krong asked him politely if he had made any progress. After that formality was over, however, she would feed him on all of her specialties, and laugh and tell him stories about her childhood in Cambodia. Her fish rolls with salad were sensational.

He called Dogmeat at Guido's Bar. To his surprise, Dogmeat was actually there. "Dogmeat, I have an errand to run. Wondered if you'd care to come along."

"*Scusi?* Is this some kind of Joe Cocker?"

"I'm serious. I'll meet you outside Guido's in five."

He went through the usual ritual of offering to pay Mrs. Krong for the food; so that Mrs. Krong could have the pleasure of telling him no, no, he needed his strength to look for the devils who had murdered her son. Mrs. Krong had a sixteen-year-old daughter who always stood shyly outside, in the kitchen. She was so transcendentally beautiful that she often made Larry wish that he were Cambodian, and eighteen.

Dogmeat was waiting outside Guido's at a vertiginous angle, as if he were standing on a hill, or leaning against a high wind. When he climbed into the car, all arms and legs, he smelled as if he had been drinking tequila. Larry knew from experience that Dogmeat and tequila didn't mix. After seven, he would start weeping for the old days, the good old days, when they sang *Sergeant Pepper's Lonely—Sergeant Pepper's Lonely*—as they floated along the streets in the sunshine, and poked chrysanthemums down the muzzles of National Guard rifles, and everybody was permanently over the rainbow.

They all got old, or married, or straight. Some of them even started to vote Republican.

"Where are we headed?" asked Dogmeat, peering from side to side through his flower-power sunglasses.

"China Basin. We're paying a guy a visit and I'd like you along."

"I hope there's some renum—remur—remun—I hope you're going to pay me for this. You're *schneid*ing seriously into my *Trinkenzeit*."

"Shouldn't take long."

They drove along Berry Street and crossed the basin at 3rd Street. Although the morning had been golden, especially on the hilltops, the fog was beginning to billow into the Bay through the Golden Gate, huge white silent banks of it, like prairie schooners carved out of cloud. By the time they reached the approaches to Pier 48, they were already enveloped in a chilly haze, and the surrounding warehouses and offices and quays had all lost their definition.

The spice warehouse wasn't difficult to locate. It was a three-storey building of weathered red brick, with a row of broken windows along the upper floor, and a rusty iron fire-escape slanting down one side. Larry could faintly

read the lettering EAST INDIES & PACIFIC SPICE C°.
He drew the car up against the curb across the debris-strewn
street, and climbed out.

"I would almost pay *you* to discover what we're doing
here, *mon ami*," said Dogmeat, heaving himself out of the
passenger-seat. "*Quel miserable* place."

Larry reached back underneath his seat and took out the
extra .38 he always carried in the car with him. He had
once seen a detective forced to surrender the gun from his
shoulder-holster, and then shot at point-blank range while
he sat like a dummy in the driving-seat of his car. If the
same thing ever happened to him, he probably wouldn't
have time to reach for his second gun, but it was better to
have half a chance than no chance at all.

He tucked the gun into the back of his pants as they
strolled across the foggy street. Dogmeat was walking
loose-limbed with drink and kicking an empty Cesar can.
"Do you want to keep it down a little?" asked Larry. "We're
supposed to be cornering a suspect here."

"A suspect?" asked Dogmeat, suspiciously. "What kind
of suspect?"

"A murder suspect, of course. I'm in homicide, remember,
not in traffic."

"Shit," said Dogmeat, and U-turned, and started walking
back the way he had come.

"Dogmeat, will you get back here?"

"No no no no no. With murderers I do not tangle. *Au
revoir, hasta la vista*, and *bon appetit*, I'm out of here."

"Fifty," called Larry. Dogmeat kept on walking.

"A hundred." Dogmeat U-turned again and rejoined him.
"I must be drunk," he suggested. "I don't usually

accompany Italians on murder busts for less than the union mimi—minimum."

Larry grasped his arm and frogmarched him forward. "I don't care if you're drunk, as long as you can see. I want you to identify this guy before I blow his head off." Dogmeat tried to focus on him. "Did I *écoute* that correctly? You're going to blow his head off?"

"That's right," said Larry, grimly. "You say, 'that's him', and I'll shoot. One, two, just like that. 'That's him!'—*blamm*!"

Dogmeat seemed to like the sound of that. "That's him, blamm! That's him, blamm! Okay, I can live with that. Who is this guy anyway?" He stopped abruptly and stared at Larry in horror. "It must be somebody I know! Otherwise you wouldn't ask me to identify him! I mean, if I *didn't* know him, what would be the point?"

"Come on." Larry urged him, and prodded him up to the corner of the warehouse. He pressed his back to the brick wall, and waited, and listened.

"*Who is it?*" hissed Dogmeat.

"You'll know him when you see him."

"*How can I know him when I see him if I don't know who he is?*"

"You'll know, take my word for it."

They walked softly all the way around the outside of the warehouse, their feet crunching in slag and broken concrete and rusty springs and heaps of shattered glass. The main warehouse was windowless and locked; and from the condition of the bolts and padlocks, it didn't look as if anybody had opened it for twenty years. Larry stopped and listened again, but all he could hear was that strange swallowing roar of traffic crossing the Oakland Bay Bridge, and the distant clanging of the Union Square cablecars. The fog was rolling in thick now, so thick that he could scarcely distinguish the outline of his car across the street.

"I think I'd like to go home now," Dogmeat announced.

"Come on, he may be up here," Larry coaxed him. He pushed Dogmeat toward the fire-escape, and together they cautiously climbed up it, the soles of their shoes crunching on the rusted treads. The whole structure felt highly unsafe, and rust showered down from the upper level as they reached halfway. Below them, they could see China Basin, almost completely fogbound now, and the rooftops of surrounding houses and sheds and warehouses. A damp wind blew from the Bay.

Above them, they could see a flaking brown-painted doorway with cardboard pushed into the broken windows. And Larry saw something else. Down below, parked between two derelict corrugated-iron sheds, half-concealed in weeds and garbage, a black van, of the same type that had rescued Edna-Mae from Potrero Street.

It was possible that it was a coincidence. San Francisco was teeming with black vans. But *here*—at the place where Mandrax was supposed to be hiding himself?

Larry climbed the last few steps of the fire-escape and knocked at the door. "Don't forget," he told Dogmeat. "'That's him!'— *blamm*!"

"Okay, okay, I've got it," Dogmeat assured him.

They waited and waited, listening to the wind waffling through the fire-escape. Larry kept his gun behind his back, but he was tensed up to swing it around, lift it, and fire. No hesitation. No mistakes.

He knew that what he was doing was both illegal and

morally wrong. Even the most sadistic of killers was entitled to a trial. He knew that he would lose his job and probably spend some time in the penitentiary, too. But the Fog City Satan could never be brought successfully to trial. No jury could be expected to convict on supernatural evidence. No judge would even admit it. It was up to him to carry out the sentence, and pray to God and the Holy Virgin to forgive him for taking the law into his own hands.

But he was calm, and he was content. Even if the supernatural side of this investigation were really nothing more than illusions, delusions and hallucinations, he would still be executing a man who had murdered six families with a degree of cruelty that beggared belief. If the supernatural side really *did* exist, he could also be preventing the resurrection of one of the most hideous and voracious evils that America had ever known.

The greatest psychic disturbance in America since the Salem Witch Trials. He waited, tensely, and shivered. There was no reply from inside the warehouse; only the faint sound of something falling, and clanging. He knocked again, and this time he called out, "Anybody home?"

No reply. He knocked again and again, but still no reply. Dogmeat, further down the fire-escape, shrugged in resignation. "*Blamm*! yesterday, *blamm*! tomorrow, but never *blamm*! today," he remarked.

"Yeah... maybe you're right," Larry admitted. His right arm was tensed so tightly behind his back that he had developed a cramp. He stood up straight, and shoved his gun back inside his belt again, and relaxed. "We'll try coming back later, when it's dark."

"Are you out of your arbre?" Dogmeat demanded. "This

isn't the kind of place to go wandering around at night tout seule."

"I won't be *tout seule*. I'll have you with me."

He was just about to start back down the stairs when he saw a large gray bird wheeling around the Basin; and then start fluttering toward the warehouse. He stopped, and shielded his eyes with his hand, squinting against the fog. The bird flew low overhead, and circled around the warehouse.

"Mussolini," Larry breathed. "That's Mussolini! Now I *know* that I'm right!"

Dogmeat swiveled his head around to follow the parrot's progress. "That's a pretty homely-looking seagull," he commented.

"It's a parrot, you cretin," said Larry. "It used to belong to my mother."

Mussolini fluttered past him and perched on the ridge of the warehouse roof. To Larry's surprise, he looked normal again. No lump on the side of his head; no dark-brown human eye. Maybe Larry had dreamed that Mussolini had taken his ectoplasm. Maybe he hadn't dreamed it, and Mussolini had somehow lost it. Or had it been taken away from him.

Larry shivered, watching Mussolini clawing the roof-tiles.

"They're not bad luck, are they, parrots?" asked Dogmeat.

"This one is," said Larry.

"Maybe it's time we were someplace else, then," Dogmeat suggested.

Larry was about to reply when the warehouse door was pushed open, without any warning. It knocked painfully against his arm and almost unbalanced him.

Like an apparition in a stage magic show, a huge man in a black sweatshirt and black leather jeans stepped out on to the fire escape and confronted them.

Dogmeat stared, his mouth wide open.

He didn't say, "That's him!" He didn't say anything at all. He simply retreated step by step down the fire escape, never once taking his eyes away from the man in the doorway, not until he reached the landing. Once he had reached the lower flight, he pelted down the fire-escape as fast as he could, missing three and four steps at a time. Larry could hear him running away across the street, the knobbly hobbling sound of his worn-down cowboy boots.

Larry raised his eyes. He swallowed, but his throat was completely dry. With an extraordinary sense of detachment, he recognized in his own reactions the symptoms of intense fear. Speeding heartbeat, quickened breathing, and that dreadful overwhelming surge of adrenaline. This was it. He had been caught at a critical disadvantage by the bloodiest single killer that San Francisco had ever known.

The man stood at least five inches taller than Larry. He was deep-chested, tense, smelling strongly of sweat and athletic rub and something like hay or herbs.

Larry had expected his face to be terribly burned. What had Dogmeat said? *Worse than Freddie*. But instead he was met by a smooth, Slavic-looking face, with deep-set eyes, and a short straight nose, and a lipless slit of a mouth. Around his neck the man wore a silver chain, with a silver skull on it, with diamonds for eyes. His black-and-silver hair was brushed straight back from his forehead.

But it wasn't his looks that made him so frightening. It was his aura. Tara Gordon had talked to Larry about

349

auras, and Larry hadn't really understood. But he did now. This man had a tangible coldness about him, and a sense of condensed evil. It was almost as if the air actually *fumed* when it touched his skin or his clothes.

Worse than that, Larry saw in his eyes that look he always dreaded. They were the eyes of a man who didn't care whether he lived or died.

In the end, you can never win against anyone who doesn't care whether they live or die.

There was a split-second in which Larry thought that he could possibly raise his gun and fire. But the risks were critical. The man was so close that he could have easily seized Larry's wrist, and pushed him over the railing of the fire-escape. It was forty feet straight down, on to concrete and rusted angle-iron and broken glass.

Apart from that, Dogmeat had fled without saying a word, which had deprived him of his only safeguard against shooting the wrong man. He could argue that this man probably *was* Mandrax, since Dogmeat had looked so horrified. But a look of horror wasn't positive identification, and Dogmeat regularly ran away from a whole selection of people, from black power activists to Chileno crack-runners—anybody on whom he had grassed, which meant at least a third of San Francisco. Occasionally he even ran away from Larry.

Supposing this man *wasn't* Mandrax? After all, his face didn't appear to be burned.

The man stood looking at Larry and Larry looked back at the man. Out of the corner of his eye, Larry could still see Mussolini, awkwardly perched on the roof; but then a foghorn groaned, out in the Bay, and Mussolini lazily lifted himself back up into the fog.

"I've been expecting you," the man said, with unexpected gentleness. His accent was indeterminate, although it had slight Southern vowel-sounds.

Larry awkwardly wedged his gun back down into his belt, and covered it with his coat. "Expecting me?" he said. He wished his voice didn't sound so strangled.

"For sure. Why don't you come along in?"

Larry glanced quickly back down the fire-escape. If he moved now, he could be halfway down before the man had a chance to react. Yet he didn't move. He couldn't. The man opened the door a little wider, and Larry squeezed past him. For a split second, the man's face was only a few inches from his, and they stared into each other's eyes, hunter and hunted, victim and killer. But which was which?

At one time, the top floor must have housed the spice company's offices, because it was divided into dark and separate rooms. There was an overwhelming smell of damp and decaying brick, and that same smell that he had noticed on the man's body... the smell of long-faded spices like cinnamon and chili and cloves.

"Please—go ahead," the man told him, and Larry walked hesitantly along the shadowy corridor until he saw a light flickering at one of the office doors. His feet scrunched on fallen plaster and broken glass, and he could hear rats running throughout the building, as soft and persistent as a heavy rain-shower.

Eventually they reached the last office. It was the largest, with a glass-paneled door on which Larry could distinguish the scratched gilt lettering "...AIRMAN."

The room had been stocked up as a hideout. There were sacks of spices in one corner, which the man obviously used as a bed. In the opposite corner stood stacks of canned food, hot dogs and tomato soup and celery, and stacks of canned beer. Closer to the center of the room, a portable Sony television stood on an upended orange-box, next to pressure-lamp. It was all surprisingly tacky for a killer from hell. But pride of place in the whole room was given to an old hat-stand, on which had been placed a black horned mask, glossy and huge, with dull velvety eyes, like a monstrous insect, or a creature from hell, or Beli Ya'al himself, the first fallen angel, the master of lies.

Larry walked up to the mask and stared at it, and knew that he was looking at the Fog City Satan.

"You're a good detective, you know that?" the man told Larry. "Nobody else has even come close."

"You're Mandrax, aren't you?" asked Larry.

"That's right. Lieutenant Foggia, sir—Mandrax. You have solved your case. The puzzle fits, last piece clicks. It must be a very satisfying feeling, solving a crime. Especially such a horrifying crime. They didn't like this one at all, did they. the people of San Francisco? It made them shiver! Well, hardly surprising. People's legs cut off, people's hands cut off! People nailed to the floor! It must give you quite a sense of *triumph*, solving a crime like that."

Larry turned around and the expression on Mandrax's face made him shiver in suppressed panic. This wasn't just criminal gloating, or the haphazard ramblings of a psychopath. He could tell from Mandrax's face that he was rational, serious, devoted to what he was doing, *and pleased with himself*.

"I didn't come here to arrest you, if that's what you think," said Larry.

"Of course not, lieutenant, I know that. Belial didn't choose me for nothing. But I admire your work, I genuinely do. Let me tell you something, Larry—you don't mind if I call you Larry, do you? All the newspapers do, especially that Fay Kuhn in the *Examiner*. No doubt she'd like to call you some other names, too."

Larry felt: *dread*. He narrowed his eyes. "What do you know about Fay Kuhn?"

"What don't I know about anything, Larry? I'm the original inescapable man of the world." He tapped his forehead. "Or perhaps you could call me the man of *both* worlds, the upper world and the under world. It's all up here, Larry. The good and the evil. The pure and the irrevocably depraved. But who am I to boast? You did a fine job. didn't you, Larry? You were the only detective who was prepared to believe that this case was supernatural, weren't you? I watched every news bulletin; I read every newspaper; and I could tell that you were coming closer. What a professional you are. Larry! You looked at it from *our* side, instead of your own. And you *believed*, didn't you Larry? A true believer, a man of the spirit as well as the body. Just like me."

He shuffled a few paces closer, and Larry found himself involuntarily shuffling an equal number of paces back. God—this man was living death. His coldness and his terrible self-satisfaction made Larry breathless—as if he were starved of oxygen.

"Can I ask you a question?" said Larry.

Mandrax smiled. "You can ask me anything you like. I think you've earned it."

"Okay. Does Belial really exist?"

The smile faded. The eyes darkened. "Are you mocking me, Larry?"

"I'm not mocking you. I just want to know."

The smile returned. "Sure. Sure you do. I forget sometimes that a hundred and thirty extra years can make a whole lot of difference. You get more *knowledgeable*, know what I mean? And you kind of expect it in others. I promise you, Larry—Belial really exists."

He paused, and rubbed his hands together fastidiously, and then he said, "As a matter of fact. I'll do better than *promise* you that Belial really exists. I'll *show* you that Belial exists. You want your teeth to fly out in sheer fear? You want your spine to seize up in total terror? I'll *show* you, lieutenant. I'll *show* you. And if you don't believe after you've seen Belial for yourself, then I'll hold out my hands to you and let you commit me to the madhouse."

Larry cautiously paced around the room. The pressure-lamp threw a huge, distorted shadow of the horned mask on the wall, so that it looked almost as if it were alive. Larry thought of the engraving of Beli Ya'al on which this mask had been modeled, and felt a surge of sudden madness at the thought of meeting a beast which actually looked like this for real.

He stopped pacing, and looked at Mandrax in a chopped-up confusion of fear, and revulsion, and burning curiosity. He still had his gun, of course—and Mandrax could never reach him if he drew it now. One good clean shot should do it. *Blamm!* But Mandrax had said the one thing that made it impossible now for Larry to shoot him.

Mandrax had told him that Belial was real; and he had

said it with such conviction that Larry believed him. Or almost believed him.

If Belial were real, then Larry had to find him, and try to destroy him for good and all; or at least prevent his resurrection. And the quickest and most logical way to find Belial was to let Mandrax take him there; as frightening as that might turn out to be.

Larry said, "When are you going?"

"Soon as it's dark, and the city's settled itself down. It's a good foggy day today, that's the way I like it. You know what they call the fog, in Chile? The devil's breath. What do you think of that?"

"I heard you were burned," said Larry. "You, and the rest of the Brotherhood." He could feel the sweat sliding down from his armpits.

"Lieutenant Foggia," said Mandrax. "I've been burned and hanged and crucified over and over." He sat down on the spice-sacks, and proceeded to lace up his boot. "But you know something... it doesn't matter, when you've got an angel for a friend. All I needed was a little extra ectoplasm, and your mother's parrot was kind enough to bring me that."

"You took my ectoplasm?" asked Larry.

"From hand to coat, from coat to parrot, from parrot to William Mandrax. Nice job, hunh? You can always count on an angel to minister well to the afflicted Fallen or not, they can still work the same high miracles. He's done it for me again and again."

"You're really going to take me to see him?" asked Larry.

"Sure! Sure I am! It's about time you saw what you were supposed to be investigating!"

"And supposing I arrest you? And *him* for that matter?"

Mandrax shook his head dismissively, and grinned, and laughed. "On what count? You know what I've done, you know what I'm *about* to do, but you can't prove anything. Admit it, you're desperate! You must be! You brought Dogmeat Jones along to put the finger on me, didn't you? Holy saints, Larry, you can't arrest me! You can't kill me, either. Because you can't prove anything that's why. You came here to kill me, but it didn't work! One bullet, smack in the head. Judge and jury, that's you! Lieutenant Larry Foggia, knight in shining armor, defender of the faith. A righteous vigilante cop. 'I suspect, therefore I have the right to open fire.'"

"You killed all of those people," said Larry, and for the first time in years he felt genuinely shocked. "You killed all of those families. You *killed* them, for Christ's sake! Don't you understand what you did? Joe Berry was a friend of mine. You raped his wife, you set fire to his children."

Mandrax brushed his hand through his hair. He looked agitated, as if he were trying to think of something else. "They died, yes. I'll have to admit that."

"You tortured them! You cut out their tongues and you cut off their arms and their legs!"

"Yes, yes, quite," said Mandrax, distracted. "But what you don't understand is... the ritual. You know? The ritual."

"What ritual?" asked Larry.

"The means by which Beli Ya'al can be resurrected, my friend. The ritual! Do you think that Beli Ya'al has been lying buried for a hundred and fifty years because he enjoys it?"

Larry took a deep breath and controlled his temper.

"Why don't you show me?" he said. "And why don't you tell me all about it, on the way there."

Mandrax nodded. "That's what I had in mind. We can take your car, yes? Every patrol car in San Francisco is looking for my van. And you don't mind if Edna-Mae comes with us, do you?"

"Edna-Mae?"

"She's here. She's quite well. Beli Ya'al will love her."

He beckoned Larry toward the door. Larry hesitated, and then he followed him. They walked along the corridor a few cautious feet apart; but Mandrax seemed quite confident that Larry wasn't going to attempt to shoot him. Either he realized that Larry needed him to help him find Belial, or else he knew something about Larry that even Larry himself wasn't aware of.

"You've got the hand," he remarked to Larry, almost casually, as they passed one darkened doorway after another.

Larry didn't reply.

"Do you know how that happens?" Mandrax coaxed him. "How people get the hand?"

Still Larry said nothing. He quickly glanced around, to make sure that they weren't being followed. He had the uneasy notion that they were both being watched. He couldn't describe it, but it was one of those strong intuitive feelings that policemen can develop after years and years on the streets.

"It's inherited." said Mandrax. "It's passed down, from father to son."

Larry lifted his left hand. "What are you talking about? This picture? This face?"

"That's right. Once you've committed yourself to Beli

Ya'al, your hand is marked forever, and when you die your eldest son's hands will be marked forever."

"But that's nonsense. My father didn't have the hand," Larry protested.

Mandrax reached the next darkened doorway, and turned around, and smiled. "Your father was Mario Foggia, right? Import-export?"

"That's right. But—"

"But nothing. Sixteen years ago he ran out of money and he ran out of people who were willing to lend him any. He only had one place to turn. His old friend Dan Burroughs, Lieutenant Dan Burroughs of the San Francisco Police Department, as he then was. And he said, save me, Dan; and lo! Dan saved him. But then your father began to wonder if the price of being saved was more than he was prepared to pay; and he went back to Lieutenant Dan Burroughs and said, un-save me. But Lieutenant Dan Burroughs refused. So your father said, either you get me out of this squeeze or else I'm going to tell the Chief of Police that you've been dabbling in things that ranking police officers shouldn't be dabbling in.

"So, do you know what Lieutenant Dan Burroughs did?"

Larry said, tautly, "Am I supposed to believe all this?"

Mandrax gave him a lipless grin. "You can believe what you like. But Lieutenant Dan Burroughs had your father hijacked one night on his way back from the warehouse, and two days later they dropped him into the Bay, weighted down with blocks of salt."

"This is insane!" Larry snapped. "My father died of pneumonia."

"So the coroner said."

"You're trying to suggest that Dan Burroughs murdered my father?"

"I'm not suggesting it, Larry. I'm telling you the truth. Your father wouldn't behave himself. Wouldn't keep quiet. There was no telling what he might have done. And Dan Burroughs was always so keen to resurrect Beli Ya'al before anybody else."

"Now, hold up," Larry told him. "Dan Burroughs wanted to resurrect Belial?"

Mandrax laughed. "Of course. Ever since he found out that Beli Ya'al was someplace in San Francisco—ever since he found out what Beli Ya'al could *do*..."

"You're out of your mind," said Larry.

Mandrax shrugged. "You can think what you like. But your father and Dan Burroughs weren't the only ones. There was a whole syndicate of San Francisco businessmen and lawyers and politicians who wanted in on Beli Ya'al."

"All right," said Dan, "supposing there was. How did they find out about it?"

"Somebody told them. I don't know who. Somebody who needed money and figured that it was worth the risk. Somebody close to the Black Brotherhood, I guess. Somebody who knew what we were into. Maybe it was Edna-Mae. Maybe it wasn't. Whoever it was, when Beli Ya'al rises, they're going to know what it's like to suffer in hell."

"But what would politicians and cops and lawyers want with a fallen angel?"

"Power, of course. Power, straight from heaven. God's power. You don't understand this at all, do you? God is sheer almighty unadulterated power, the kind of power you can't even *look* at. Each of his angels has the power of a hundred nuclear power-stations; except that it isn't the kind of power that lights up freeways and runs factories, it's the power to do anything you want.

"If your father and Dan Burroughs and all the rest of those greedy men had found out where Beli Ya'al was, and how to raise him up, then believe me, Larry, life in San Francisco wouldn't have been worth the living." Larry stared at Mandrax for a long time without saying anything. It seemed ridiculous; this talk of a political conspiracy to raise a fallen angel. If Mandrax were capable of slaughtering and torturing dozens of people without any remorse, he was probably so far distanced from reality that he could invent and believe any explanation for anything—especially his own grisly rampage as the Fog City Satan.

Yet he still seemed so calm and matter-of-fact and rational; and if you could believe that such a thing as fallen angel actually existed. then it wasn't demanding too much to believe that a syndicate of lawyers and politicians and policemen were searching to use its supernatural influence for their own ends.

"The only blessing is that they haven't yet discovered where he is," smiled Mandrax. "They have many clues. Once they came really close. But close isn't close enough. For sure, they can use his influence. They can tap some of his power. He gave them the moving hand so that they could hunt out victims for him. But he never told them where he was because he doesn't know. He's half-asleep, dreaming. That's why you see all those clouds on your hand, all those skeins. Those are dreams drifting by. And do you know what he dreams of?"

Larry looked at his palm again, although there were no pictures on it. "It always looks to me like the same man's face, over and over. Tara Gordon said it was some guy called Sam Roberts, who used to run a wild bunch of vigilantes here in San Francisco back in the 1840s."

"That's right—Sam Roberts," Mandrax smiled. "He was the man who brought Beli Ya'al to San Francisco in the first place."

"Why should he have wanted to do that?"

"Same reason. Power, revenge. Brannan and Leavenworth had chased him out of San Francisco, and he wanted to come back and show them who was boss."

"Where the hell would a man like that find a fallen angel?"

"He'd heard a story from an old Chileno, about a ship that was carrying a strange cargo round Cape Horn, in the 1820s. The cargo was supposed to be the greatest treasure on the whole of God's earth; the greatest power that man had ever known. But the ship went down in a storm, and the cargo was lost. The old Chileno said that any man who found that cargo could be king of the whole world. So after Brannan and Leavenworth chased him out of San Francisco, Sam Roberts went to find it.

Mandrax's eyes took on a strange steely shine, like polished ball-bearings. Larry thought he looked more than psychopathic, he looked inspired, as if he had been visited by a divine revelation. It was eerie, in a man who had butchered so many men and women and children; and the chill half-light of the old spice warehouse made it feel eerier still.

Larry felt that he had reached one of those heart-stopping

moments when the whole world can be catastrophically changed, on the strength of one word.

Mandrax said quietly, "He sailed to Punta Arenas, and then through the Straits of Magellan and all through the islands of Cape Horn. It was the damndest, bleakest, most unforgiving place on the whole surface of the world. But the old Chileno had been right. The ship had run aground on the False Cape Horn, the *Falso Cabo de Hornos*; and the cargo was still lying on the shore beside it, after thirty years, and it was surrounded in every direction by the skeletons and the freshly decaying bodies of thousands of penguins, as far as your eye could see.

Mandrax interlaced his fingers and bent them backwards, noisily cracking his knuckles. "Roberts chartered a ship, and he managed to rustle up a crew who were more attracted by gold than they were frightened by superstition, and he sailed all the way back up the coast of South America; and every day he sat next to his prize and he whispered to it, and every night he slung his hammock over it and dreamed about it, and by the time he reached the Golden Gate he knew what it was all about and how he was going to resurrect it. He was going to let it loose on all of those blowhards and do-gooders and hypocritical house-Betties who were going to take everything that San Francisco had to offer for their own greedy ends, in the name of justice, and the name of God.

"That thing that Sam Roberts brought back from the False Cape Horn wanted its revenge on God, and God's creations. It wanted it so bad you could almost hear its teeth grinding. That thing lives for nothing but devouring lives."

Larry was sweating, shivering, both at the same time. "And *you* want to let it loose?"

Mandrax grinned. "Revenge has a special taste, pal. Sweeter than anything you care to mention."

He checked his watch. "But—wasting time. Let's get Edna-Mae and get ourselves out of here."

Without saying anything else, he led the way into the darkened room. Reluctantly, Larry followed him, and stood in the blackness straining his eyes. He didn't know how Mandrax was able to see anything.

"Mandrax?" he called. "Are you there?"

There was long, aching moment when he thought that Mandrax had completely vanished. The darkness was completely overwhelming, and he could smell that terrible distinctive smell of opened-up bodies. *Jesus*, he thought, *supposing he's left me here alone with Edna-Mae.*

He reached behind him for his gun. His heart tightened; and he held his breath. The room was so silent that he could hear the molecules of air bombarding his eardrums. Outside, in the corridor, fog began to roll in over the windowsills, in a creepily appropriate parody of a Dracula movie.

"Mandrax? Edna-Mae?"

His voice echoed flatly. He kept peering into the darkness but it was too complete for him to be able to make out anything. It was worse than having a black bag over his head.

He was about to step backward out of the room when a huge white shape appeared out of the darkness, shuffling and swaying. For a split-second, he thought that Edna-Mae was unaccompanied; and he was about to break all records for running down a San Francisco fire-escape. But then

Mandrax appeared, too, with a bland smile that wasn't quite straight on his face.

"She's ready, what a beauty."

"Where are we taking her?" asked Larry, backing away.

"You'll see when we get there. You can drive, I'll give you directions."

Edna-Mae swayed and made a terrible dribbling, whistling noise. Under the flap of her bedsheet covering, Larry could make out a flat, cellulite-rippled face, with crimson eyes.

He felt like dropping Mandrax here and now, as he had originally meant to. Blow his head off, finish this grisly charade of superstition and butchery. But if Dan Burroughs had been searching for Belial for nearly twenty years and still hadn't been able to find him, there wasn't much chance that Larry was going to be able to locate him on his own.

Together, an extraordinary and incongruous trio, they descended the fire-escape.

The fog was so thick now that they couldn't see Larry's car across the street. Their feet made a slow scraping sound on the rusty rungs of the fire-escape. The handrail was corroded and cold and wet with the touch of fog. Off to their right, in the Basin, a small boat suddenly let out a high *whip, whip, whooop*, and Larry's heart almost stopped.

They crossed the debris-strewn street, Edna-Mae's bare feet shuffling on the concrete. As he reached his car and unlocked the door, Larry looked around, unsettled. He had that feeling again: that feeling of being watched. Closely observed detectives. He opened the rear door for Edna Mae, and Mandrax helped her in. The car's suspension creaked under the weight.

"All right, let's go," grinned Mandrax, climbing in beside

Larry and slamming the door. "Head for Front Street, and drive due north, until I tell you."

Larry switched on the headlights and turned the car around.

As he drove, he kept flicking his eyes up to his rearview mirror to look at the white shapeless bulk in the back seat. The stench was more subdued now, with the airconditioning turned up to Hi, but there was still a cloying brownish odor in the car.

"Just drive easy and natural and stop at all the reds," said Mandrax. He seemed surprisingly relaxed for a man who appeared to be unarmed, and who had freely admitted to six sickening mass-killings to an armed police officer. Or armed *suspended* police officer. How better could Larry get his suspension revoked than to bring in the Fog City Satan singlehanded?

All he had to do was to ignore the threat of Belial, which was probably all a delusion in any case.

But he kept on driving northwards through the fog because he had seen the other side for himself, and he knew that it was true; and so Belial could be true, too.

"You're wondering why I'm taking you along," said Mandrax, a little more tensely now. "You're thinking to yourself, this man is psychopathic. He's a killer, I'm a cop. I've been hunting him down, and now I've found him, and what's he doing? He's going to show me his greatest secret. He's going to show me everything he's been struggling to do for longer than I can imagine. All I have to do then is arrest him; and arrest Beli Ya'al; and I'm a hero."

Larry cleared his throat. "The thought had crossed my mind."

"Of course it did—and why not? But the point is, you're not going to arrest Beli Ya'al, because Beli Ya'al isn't exactly the kind of being you can arrest. And quite apart from that, you're not going to arrest me, because you, my friend, are Larry Foggia, son of Mario Foggia, and you have the moving hand. Your father said some vows, a long time ago, and made some oaths. In return, a blood vessel burst in your Uncle Sylvester's brain as he was driving to work and your Uncle Sylvester left your father three-quarters-of-a-million dollars which your father sorely needed.

"Your father promised that you would always do Beli Ya'al's bidding; and that your son would always do Beli Ya'al's bidding; and so on, for a thousand generations, when the score would be considered settled."

Larry felt a leaden feeling in his spine, but all the same he said, "I don't have to do anybody's bidding right now. And, what's more, I never will."

"Well, we'll sure see about that," said Mandrax, propping his long scuffed shoes on the dash, and leaning back. "Keep going slow, you're doing fine."

"I could have the hand exorcized," said Larry.

Mandrax looked at him with interest. "Is that so?"

"I know some sensitives. I could get it done."

"Take my advice, Larry—don't. The only people who ever tried to get rid of it were killed."

"I don't know. Wilbert Fraser mentioned a girl. The ectoplasm came out of her hand and then flared up."

Mandrax frowned intently for a moment, thinking—then laughed. "Oh, Shetland Piper. Sure. I remember that. Do you know what happened to her?"

"I'm sure you're going to tell me."

"Shetland Piper's hand never healed. She had a burn that wouldn't close up. In the end she got gangrene, and they cut her arm off up at the elbow. But that wouldn't heal either, because what the doctors didn't understand was that they had cut through an open spirit-channel— straight from her head to her hand. It was like cutting a gas main in halt. They tried cutting off her whole arm and she literally exploded. You've heard about spontaneous combustion? That's what happened to her. Two nurses had their faces burned off and the anthetist was melted to his gas cylinders. The operating table was said to have reached 2,020 degrees Celsius."

"You know a whole lot about a whole lot," Larry remarked.w

"Sure I do," said Mandrax, his eyes shining. "I've been around so long, that's why."

Larry was driving through Walton Park now. Lights gleamed dim and secretive in the fog, and pedestrians moved through the grayness like ghosts. In the back, Edna-Mae let out an awful cackling bubbling noise, and Larry was sure that he could hear the greasy sliding of her skin on the vinyl seats.

Larry said, "What's to stop taking out my gun right now and blowing your head off?"

Mandrax looked almost hurt. "Do you *feel* like taking out your gun right now and blowing my head off?"

"It's another one of those thoughts that's been crossing my mind."

"Well... I couldn't stop you, for sure. But I wouldn't advise it."

"Oh, no?"

"Doesn't anything about me seem familiar?" asked Mandrax.

Larry scrutinized him for a moment. "Not that I can see."

"Didn't Wilbert Fraser tell you anything about me? That I was burned?"

"He did mention it, yes."

"Well, he was right. I *was* burned. Me and all the rest of the Black Brotherhood. I didn't know for years that it was Wilbert who did it, Wilbert and George Menzel. They stopped us from raising up Beli Ya'al when we were only *days* away from doing it. Maybe it was our own fault, we boasted about it too much. We were going to be the power, we were going to take over the whole city. Let me tell you something, pal, the gutters were going to run with blood.

"Anyway, they burned us. Everybody died, except me. Leper was charcoal when that fire died out. Charcoal. The Fire Department tried to lift him out and his arms snapped off. I managed to smash my way out through a window, I don't know how, but I was on fire from head to foot, and if somebody hadn't wrapped me in a blanket I would've died, too. I spent six years convalescing, and even then I still looked like raw meat."

"You look okay now." Larry observed, cautiously.

"Of course I do. I found you. I had to find somebody else with the hand, somebody that I could take ectoplasm out of. And there you were! A gift! I took all that I needed, and then some, and your mother's bird was kind enough to fly it to me. Don't you recognize me? How about my eyes? How about my profile? This is *you* you're looking at, Larry! Your ectoplasm!" He squeezed his cheeks with his fingers. "Your ectoplasm, my face! I'm still burned underneath, but thanks to you, my generous friend, I can walk around looking quite well."

"You mean that damn parrot stole part of me and gave it to you?"

Mandrax grinned. "I have a way with birds, Larry. Comes of spending time with them in jail. I used to know the Birdman of Alcatraz; he taught me a whole lot. How to breed them, how to feed them, how to call them."

"So what happens if I shoot you?" asked Larry, unsteadily.

"Same thing that happened to that nurse, Bizarre Killing At SFG. You fire at me, but you blow your own face off. Want to try it?"

Larry took in a deep breath. Mother of God, what if he'd done what he originally intended to do, and fire at Mandrax as soon as he opened the warehouse door? He rubbed his own cheeks as he drove. It was hard to remember that the supernatural obeyed none of the laws of logic, none of the laws of physics. The ground had opened beneath Larry's feet, and stayed open.

They reached the intersection of Front and Green. Mandrax said, "Turn right into Green. There's an entrance marked GARAGE PARKING about fifty feet along, on the right. Drive straight in, and down the ramp, and keep going."

Edna-Mae gave other sickening, suckling noise. The smell was beginning to grow stronger. Larry waited for the lights, then turned right. He wished that his heart would stop racing so damned fast. He saw the narrow brick entrance with a flaking green-painted sign saying GARAGE PARKING, but a battered pickup was parked halfway across it. Larry hooted his horn, and glanced at Mandrax anxiously. Although the pickup's driver was sitting in it, smoking, he made no attempt to move.

Larry hooted again; but still the pickup stayed where it was.

"Guess I'll have to get out and ask him the polite way," said Larry.

Mandrax's eyes flickered. "Go ahead."

Larry climbed out of the car and walked across to the pickup's open window. The driver was an unshaven bull-necked young man with a red baseball cap, greasy blond curls, and the look of somebody whose everyday attitude to life was an upraised middle finger.

"Er, I'm trying to drive into this entrance here," said Larry.

The young man sniffed. "That's okay by me."

"Trouble is, I have a problem," Larry continued. "You have your vehicle parked across this entrance, making it kind of impossible for me to get in there."

The young man sniffed again. "Looks like you'll have to wait, then, dudn't it?"

Larry thought about that for a moment. Then he said, "You want to make yourself some money?"

The young man's eyes focused on him for the first time. "Pends how much."

"In the palm of my hand is fifty dollars. I shall lay my hand on the side of your vehicle and drop it into your cab. All you have to do then is drive to the nearest payphone and call the police. Ask to speak to a guy called Houston Brough in the homicide squad. Tell him where I'm at. Tell him our boy's here, too. That's all you have to do."

The young man looked bewildered. "Whyn't you do it yourself?"

"Because I am in the company of a criminal who mustn't suspect that I'm calling for backup. You see that guy in the car with me? You've heard of the Fog City Satan?"

"Are you shittin me?"

"Expensive brand of shit if I am," said Larry, and dropped the $50 into the pickup's open window. "Remember... speak to Houston Brough. Tell him our boy's here, that's all."

The young man started the pickup's motor and squealed away, leaving Larry standing in the street. He returned to the car and climbed in.

"The friendly persuader," Mandrax complimented him.

They entered the garage, the car bucking and dipping as they descended the ramp down to the first level. There was dim lighting at each corner of the parking bay, but the garage looked old and damp and disused, with huge encrustations of salt and minerals on the concrete walls, and glistening green algae on the pillars.

"Next level down," said Mandrax. "You'll have to shift the barrier."

Larry climbed out of the car again, and dragged aside a rusted metal fence with a barely legible sign on it that read NO ENTRY: BUILDING UNSAFE.

They drove down the next ramp. Level Two was totally dark, and Larry had to switch on the car's main beams. They illuminated a subterranean world of rusted and abandoned cars; an old '59 Cadillac with no wheels, lying on its belly like a leprous whale. A blue '49 Kaiser, once some family's pride and joy, now dulled with age and damp, its windows fogged over. A bronze Hudson with its hood gaping open. There was other garbage which Larry couldn't identify— things that looked like wet heaps of sacks or trails of slime, and strange wooden constructions, black with damp and orange-spotted with fungus. The car's tires set up a thin wet complaint on the concrete floor.

"Next level down," said Mandrax.

Larry almost missed the down-ramp. It was a tight spiral, its walls streaked with water and saltpeter. He negotiated it as carefully as he could, but his tires kept skittering and shrieking against the curb. The spiral seemed to go around and around for ever, until Larry's arms grew tired of holding the steering-wheel in a sharp left-hand turn. At last, however, they reached the lowest level, with a splash and an echo and a slap of water.

The third and lowest level was entirely flooded, to a depth of two or three inches. Larry drove slowly forward, with the water drumming against the floor of the car, and black glittering furrows trailing behind it. The furrows reached the far wall of the garage. slapped, and then came furrowing back again.

"Okay, this is it," said Mandrax. "You can kill the motor."

Larry switched off the engine and looked around. The parking-bay was cold and echoing. From the darkest recesses, Larry heard a never-ending chorus of loud drips.

"Now what?" he asked, his throat tight.

"Now we get out of the car."

"Is *this* where Belial's been hiding?"

"Larry—now we get out of the car. But watch out for eels."

"Eels?"

They climbed out of the car and stepped into the oily, freezing water. Larry immediately felt it pour into the sides of his shoes. Mandrax helped Edna-Mae out of the back, and Larry heard her gabble something as she stepped into the water. They waded ankle-deep across the parking-bay, and Larry saw at once what Mandrax meant about eels. The shallow water teemed with them—thin, black, whip-like eels, that flicked and flurried at his ankles as he walked.

They followed the path of the car's headlights until they reached the far wall, where a heap of dilapidated furniture lay, rotting and sour and gray with mold. Mandrax heaved aside an old sodden sofa, and behind it Larry saw a low cavity in the brickwork. Mandrax groped around inside until he found what he was looking for—a flashlight.

He forced Edna-Mae's head down, so that she could crouch her way through the cavity. "You next," he told Larry. "And remember what I said about the face."

Larry hunched himself down, and followed Edna-Mae's heaving sheet-swathed back through a narrow tunnel hacked into the brickwork. In some places it was so tight that he scraped his hands and knocked his elbows. The water churned noisily around their feet.

"You remember what I said about Sam Roberts bringing his cargo back from the False Cape Horn?" said Mandrax, as they shuffled forward.

"I remember," said Larry. The smell of mold and stagnant water and Edna-Mae was suffocating him; and all the time, the eels kept coursing over his feet.

"He anchored off Law's Wharf, and there he set out to do what he had to do, in order to resurrect Beli Ya'al. He carried out the seven ritual sacrifices, according to ancient Hebrew legend... the seven ritual sacrifices that would set Beli Ya'al free. He had locked his entire crew below decks, on the pretense that they would be arrested and imprisoned if US Customs officers found them there. Then, on his second night ashore, he let four or five of them out at a time, and ritually sacrificed them.

"Human beings are Beli Ya'al's natural enemies, you see, because they're so beloved of God and he no longer is. Before he can be free from his chains, he has to know that his enemies have every God-given gift stripped away from them. They shan't walk, so his sacrifices have their legs cut off. They shan't speak, so their tongues are cut out. They shan't fight against him, so their arms are cut off. They shan't hear, so their ears are blocked. They shan't see, so they get blinded. They shall be nailed down, as Jesus was nailed down, and their children shall be tortured in front of their eyes, so that they lose their love of God and their love of the life that He gave them, and voluntarily end it. That's an important bit. *Voluntarily*."

Larry's head knocked painfully against the ceiling. He thought about the Berrys, Joe and Nina; Caroline and Joe Berry Jr, and it hurt. "That's six sacrifices," he said, thickly. "What's the seventh?"

"Aha!" said Mandrax. "The seventh is the First Supper, the first feeding on a whole human, not just the spirit or the soul, not just the essence, but the whole human, mind and body. Let me you tell this, my friend, when Beli Ya'al eats you, he eats you in your entirety, and there's no chance of going to heaven. You're gone, Larry. Gone to a void where your whole soul is digested for *centuries*. Like, your whole being is gradually dissolved in the psychic equivalent of stomach acid. No, no heaven for the victims of Beli Ya'al, believe me. If *he* can't get to heaven, then no miserable human being is going to get to heaven, either. What do you think about that? Vengeance for its own sake—nothing more."

After seventy or eighty feet, the narrow tunnel began to open out, until they were able to stand up straight. Mandrax quickly lanced the flashlight beam left and right; and Larry was able to see that they were standing in a large chamber, with curved sides fashioned out of black dripping beams of wood. He peered up at the ceiling, and saw that was raftered with wood, too. And although the floor beneath his feet was two or three inches in water, and alive with eels, he could feel rotted planks through the ooze.

"What's this?" he asked Mandrax. "It looks like some kind of old wooden warehouse."

Mandrax waded proudly across to one of the walls, and slapped at the black encrusted beam. "Wooden, yes. But not a warehouse. You wouldn't know what this place was, unless you'd been in one before; and these days, not too many people have. This is the lower cargo deck of a three-masted sailing ship called the *Cabo Carranza.*

"This spot here, where we're standing, at the intersection of Front and Green Streets, is a block away from the Bay. But when this ship docked here in 1850 it was Law's Wharf. A couple of years later, all of this area was buried in landfill, and all of the old wharves went—Cunningham's, Buckelew's and Cowell's. Law's, too. But in 1850 this was Law's Wharf and the *Cabo Carranza* was tied up here."

Edna-Mae stayed where she was, hunched in her soaking sheet. But Larry paced around, examining the dripping hulk of the ship that Sam Roberts had brought back from the False Cape Horn.

"It's a miracle, isn't it?" said Mandrax, his eyes glittering in the darkness. "They could really make ships in those days."

"What happened?" asked Larry.

Mandrax gave a short, forced laugh. "What happened? What *didn't* happen! Halfway through the rituals... when the decks were smothered in blood and stomachs and chopped-off arms... one of the Chilenos managed to force his way out of a porthole and climb down a rope to the wharf. He didn't go to the Law & Order brigade. He went straight to the Chileno shanty-town, where Lieutenant Sam Roberts was regarded with slightly less benevolence than Satan himself.

"Beli Ya'al was already starting to stir. There was thunder, lightning, earth tremblors! But those Chilenos swarmed on to the dock and on to the ship, and they rescued all of the crew that was left, and then they stove in the ship's bottom so that she sank where she was anchored; and anything that was left above the waterline, they burned. Some witnesses say that they saw Sam Roberts burn, too; but others say they saw him dive in flames into the Bay. In any case, the city demolished the wharves, and filled in the Bay, and what was left of the *Cabo Carranza* was buried under the fill."

Larry looked around. "I wouldn't have believed it if I hadn't seen it with my own eyes."

"It's a miracle," Mandrax repeated.

Larry walked around him, rippling the water, his hands

in his pockets to keep them warm. Mandrax followed him with the beam of his flashlight, around and around. Larry knew what he was going to have to ask next, but if he asked it, it would be an admission that he already believed it.

Did he dare to believe it? It gave him an empty feeling in his stomach; and a huge yawning sense of his own mortality, and the shortness of his own life. He wasn't sure he was ready to face up to that, not yet.

"What?" demanded Mandrax, at last.

Larry stopped walking, and the ripples died away in the darkness.

"*You're* Sam Roberts, aren't you?" he asked.

9

He wasn't sure whether Mandrax didn't answer because he didn't need to; or because the idea was so stunningly ridiculous. He just stared at Larry with those glittering eyes and that tight slit of a mouth, and then turned away, and said, "Come on."

Larry hesitated, then followed. Edna-Mae followed, too, in her winding-sheet. For some reason Larry felt relieved that Mandrax hadn't said "yes." It would probably have frightened him even more than he was already. If Mandrax had said "yes," he probably wouldn't have been able to function. His legs would have simply refused to walk any further.

They splashed the length of the ship's cargo-hold until they reached a further entrance. This had once been a timber doorway, but it had rotted into nothing more than a soggy, mold-encrusted cave. As they approached, Larry saw that there was a dim orange light inside it, swiveling and dipping in the subterranean draft.

"Now you can meet some old friends of yours," said Mandrax. He shone the torch on to an upward slope of gravel and slurry, and with relief Larry climbed awkwardly out of the eel-whipping water on to a damp uneven floor of mixed rubble.

The sight that met his eyes was so unexpected that his first reaction was to turn around to Mandrax and ask if this was all an elaborate hoax—staged by some inventive prankster at the police department to pay him back for his "Supernatural" story in the newspaper.

But at once his sense told him that nobody could have set this up as a hoax. He had at last come face to face with the consequences of believing in the supernatural.

This further room was a wooden-walled chamber; probably a messdeck. Part of the wall had rotted and collapsed, allowing the landfill to slide through and cover the floor. At the far side of the chamber lay a massive metal box, beaten out of lead or some dull grayish alloy. It was twice the size of a normal human coffin, yet there was no doubt at all that it was a coffin. On the lid, it bore the embossed likeness of a man with the head of an antlered beast; and its sides were embossed with cuneiform writing that looked more Sumerian than Hebrew.

Beside the coffin, an oil-lamp stood on an upended orange-box, so that shadows continually danced over its lid, and made the antlered head look as if it were alive. For a moment, Larry was convinced that he saw its chest rise and fall; but it was only the shadows.

At the foot of the coffin, kneeling naked in the rubble, thin and ribby and miserable, bulgy-eyed and short-sighted without his glasses, was Dogmeat. His back was marked with red stripes, as if he had been whipped. His chin was encrusted with blood.

"Dogmeat, for Christ's sake!" said Larry.

Dogmeat said nothing, but coughed blood.

"You can't do this," Larry told Mandrax. "This is where I draw the line. Enough."

Mandrax walked up to Dogmeat and seized hold of his hair, stretching his head back. Dogmeat cried out, but Mandrax ignored him, and looked across at Larry with a wolfish challenge on his face. "This is where you draw the line, is it? A pretty elastic kind of line, Larry—that's what I'd say. This trash has been selling me down the river for years. And tonight he had the nerve to finger me. He always knew the Black Brotherhood would get their revenge. Well, tonight that's going to happen. A thin skinny runt of a feed for Beli Ya'al."

"How the hell did you catch him?" asked Larry. "How the hell did you get him here?"

"Because he isn't alone," said a pricklingly familiar voice, out of the shadows. "Because he has loyal friends, who make sure that anybody who betrays him is brought to justice."

Out of the darkness where he had been concealing himself, in his green rustling raincoat, stepped Arne Knudsen. He stood in the dancing lamplight, smiling at Larry with the same self-satisfied smile as Mandrax.

"Arne?" asked Larry, in astonishment. He felt as if his whole life were collapsing on top of him, like a wave.

"Hallo, Larry!" said Arne. "So, you solved it at last! Quite a roundabout way of detecting you have. Rushing here, rushing there. Talking to mediums, drumming up spirits!" He tapped his forehead. "You should have solved it the way I solved it, by logic and analysis."

"You *solved* it? You found this maniac even before I was assigned to the case?"

Arne nodded. "You shouldn't be so surprised. The Fog City Satan was obviously performing some kind of serial ritual, and all I had to do was to find out which one. If you had taken the trouble to look through *Sacrifical Offerings & Primitive Rituals* at the public library, you would have saved yourself a great deal of legwork. It's all there. Belial, the Master of Lies, the First Fallen Angel. His body was found in Ur when the Babylonians were building their great ziggurats. It was sealed into this coffin and entombed in a hillside cave until Richard Wasey the British archeologist discovered it in 1837.

"It was supposed to have been lost in the Bay of Biscay, while Wasey was shipping it back to England. But, very obviously, it wasn't—although how it came to be shipwrecked eleven years later on the False Cape Horn, nobody knows.

"Anyway, it's real; and everything that Mr. Mandrax has been telling you about it is true. I was down at the warehouse this evening, when you arrived. Poor Dogmeat ran straight into my outspread arms, didn't you, Dogmeat?"

Larry slowly, slowly shook his head. "You *solved* this case? You found Mandrax and you kept it to yourself?"

"I'm afraid so, Larry. I had my first suspicions about it after the McGuire killing. Then the Ramirez massacre convinced me. Somebody was trying to raise Belial. I wrote a new computer model on occult practises in San Francisco, and checked back on every similar kind of killing; and it didn't take long to go through records and find Mr. Mandrax."

"You located him *before* the Berrys got killed?"

Arne looked embarrassed. "I was very sorry that it was the Berrys, believe me."

"You were *sorry*! Jesus, Arne, you could have saved their lives!"

Arne walked around the coffin and looked down at the antlered beast. "I have to say, Larry, that once in a while something comes along that makes other people's lives look very unimportant by comparison. Maybe it's a war, yes? Maybe a revolution. But the whole of mankind doesn't get ahead unless some of us are offered in sacrifice."

"You let this crazy loose on the Berrys?" Larry screamed at him. "He nailed them to the fucking floor, Arne! He set fire to their children! Do you have any idea how much they must have *suffered*?"

"Yes," said Arne, with terrible simplicity.

"And you can still live with yourself?"

"Yes," said Arne. "Because of this. Because of Belial."

"I don't believe what I'm hearing. Those files you gave me... that was only half the story, right? You pulled out anything that would've helped me to track down Mandrax sooner."

"Of course I did. I didn't want you to find Belial too quickly, now did I? We still had life-substance to collect, to build up Belial's strength. Edna-Mae's; your mother's; more than a hundred in all. Most of their bodies are down here."

Larry approached the coffin. It had a terrible aura around it; even colder than the man-made catacombs in which it rested. He felt his skin tingle and his teeth set on edge.

"Can you feel it?" Arne whispered. "That's power for you, Larry. That's a whole new life."

"What's it all for, Arne?" Larry asked him.

Arne smiled, still admiring the metallic beast. "It's to have the kind of life that guys like you and me can only fantasize about, Larry. Real wealth, real influence. Think of the women! Belial wants a thousand thousand lives; that's all. A million miserable lives. Half of San Francisco is already dying of AIDS or crack or God knows what else. What's a million lives?"

Larry looked over at Mandrax. Down by the foot of the coffin, Dogmeat was starting to tremble and shake; and his teeth began to chatter.

"What else has Mr. Belial promised you, besides power and wealth and more women than you can shake a stick at?"

Mandrax said nothing, but smiled tightly.

"A long life, for instance?" he asked Arne, although he didn't take his eyes off Mandrax. "A very, very, *very* long life?"

"Nobody wants to die, Larry," said Arne, obviously trying to sound reasonable.

"How about those million people you intend to toss to the monster? How about Joe and Nina Berry? Do you think they wanted to die? Do you think their kids wanted to die?"

"Come on, Larry. It's a question of attitude."

Larry rubbed the side of his neck. "So you found Mandrax and you found Belial and you quit the case?"

Arne shook his head. "No, no. I didn't quit. I just tried to give Dan Burroughs the impression that I was being agonizingly slow and meticulous. In fact, so agonizingly slow and meticulous that he'd get impatient, and kick me off the case altogether. I'd started to notice that Dan Burroughs seemed to know more about the Fog City Satan than he let on. He kept asking me time and time again if I'd found out anything yet. Before I located Mandrax, I thought that he was just being obnoxious. Now I know that he was absolutely desperate to find Belial before the Fog City Satan could bring him back to life. *Dan* wanted the power. *Dan* wanted the wealth. And all I can say is, I'm going to have his share, so tough shit."

"And what about me?"

"Oh, Dan thinks you're brilliant. He knew you'd crack it, and he knew you'd crack it quick. He knows you haven't given it up, either. He knew you wouldn't, even when he took your badge. But he couldn't afford to come out publicly and say that he believed in the supernatural. Bad for his career. Bad karma all around."

"So why are you telling me this?" asked Larry. "If you think I'm such an upright cop, why are you showing me where Belial is, and admitting your guilt—you and Mandrax, both? Do you know what I'm going to say to you? You're under arrest for homicide in the first degree, for assault with a deadly weapon, for conspiracy, for kidnap, for you name it, you're under arrest for it."

Almost as soon as he had spoken, a deep shudder went through the structure of the building, and the timbers of the *Cabo Carranza* creaked and lurched.

"Tremblor," smiled Mandrax. "They'll get stronger, as the time comes closer."

Arne was smiling, too. "Don't start worrying yourself about arrests, Larry. There was another good reason why Dan Burroughs chose you for this case. You're Mario

Foggia's son. You're one of them, Mario's little Ghost. You've been marked with the moving hand, and that means you're bound to Belial already. Your old man bound you, what can you do? Dan Burroughs knew that he could count on you to find Belial and to understand what it was all about when you did."

Larry looked down at the effigy of the beast on the coffin. There was no question about it—he could feel a hugely powerful influence from beneath that sculptured lid: an influence that felt much more exciting than evil. It was like the rush of skiing too fast on a dangerous slope; the rush of driving too fast on a rainslick road. If you *could* have the power of the angels on your side... You could be anything you wanted. You could have anything you wanted.

There was only one terrible price. Others would have to die. Others had already died. Belial's impending resurrection had been won only at the price of unimaginable suffering and pain.

His father may have sold himself to Belial in return for solvency; but in the end his father had gone to Dan Burroughs and said no. If his father had stood up to Belial and his acolytes, then Larry could stand up to them, too. After all, he loved Linda, he loved the boys, he mostly enjoyed his work... what could an angel give him that he didn't have already?

It was then, however, that something flickered in his mind. An image, bright but only half-realized. A girl in a scarlet dress, dancing. He couldn't see her face: only that whirling, floating scarlet dress, and that night-black, softly curled hair.

Marietta, from high school. Marietta—his first real love.

He could almost *touch* her, almost *feel* her. But then she flickered and faded and all he could see was the beast, embossed on the coffin.

It knows me. he thought, with a bone-marrow chill. *It knows who I am, it knows what I want. It's not offering me money; it's not offering me promotion. It knows that I love my family.*

It's offering me—

As clear and as bright as she had always been, he saw his *momma*. White-haired, elegant, smiling.

"*Why don't you come to see me so often? What are you trying to do, break a mother's heart?*"

Involuntarily, raised his hand. *Momma? But you're dead. I saw the shadow take your whole substance. I saw the truck run over you.*

"*Why don't you come to see me so often, Larry? You were my little frittata, yes?*"

"Momma," he whispered. Even though she wasn't really there. "Momma, I can hear you momma."

"*There's somebody else here, Larry. Somebody else you want to see.*"

Larry steadied himself, pressed his fingers against his forehead, tried to concentrate. But his mother was as bright in his mind's eye as a ballet-dancer in a spotlight, and she wouldn't go away.

And she was right. There was somebody else there. Somebody standing in the darkness on the very fringe of his consciousness. Somebody who loomed huge and influential in Larry's life.

He scarcely dared to imagine that it could be true. He began to shiver—and, as he shivered, he made a quick panting sound. He couldn't stop himself—no matter how cowardly it might seem to Arne and Mandrax. He knew without any doubt at all who that dark somebody was, but he couldn't bring his mind to accept it.

Could Belial, the fallen angel, really offer him *this?* His momma, alive again—just the same as she had been on that foggy day when he had visited her to talk about the World Beyond. And not just his momma but this dark somebody who stood motionless in the shadows, in his vicuna coat and his homburg hat, his face as pale as death, his mustache bedraggled, but his eyes as knowing as ever. His eyes *smiling*, even.

But the ropes that had bound him to three 200-lb blocks of solid salt still hung around his ankles, and the cold water of San Francisco Bay still ceaselessly poured from out of his nostrils, and out of his thick, hand-tailored clothes.

POPPA.

The somebody nodded.

"Poppa?" Larry whispered, his heart breaking.

"*You're a good boy, Larry. I never figured you for good, but you proved me wrong.*"

"Poppa, is that really you?"

"*You don't recognize your old man?*"

"And I could have you back?"

"*Do you want me back, after all of this?*"

"Poppa, I—"

"*Do you want me back, Larry? You could have me back. Me and your mother, all of us back together again, the way things were. I could see the boys, Larry. Take them on outings, tell them stories. We could have ourselves some beer and some* consum *and spend the whole evening making friends."*

"Poppa, this is crazy. Poppa, this isn't even *real.*"

The shadowy figure of his father ebbed and flowed. He turned to look at his mother, but when he turned it wasn't his mother at all, but Arne.

Arne was smiling at him and nodding. "You get the picture?"

"Yes," he said, in the thinnest of voices. He was still shivering; still not totally stable. "I get the picture."

Belial had taken his father and his mother and now he was pretending to offer them back. He must have sensed that Larry wouldn't be vulnerable to cars or women or career opportunities. Larry was a family man: and so Belial had tempted him with nothing more nor less than the family that he had lost. Larry felt such disgust that his stomach tightened and he almost vomited. It was lies, all lies. A trick of the light, a trick of the mind. But at the same time, he still felt a keen and desperate longing to see his father and mother again—to take both of them hand-in-hand, and walk down to the Bay, and tell them he *had* loved them, yes, so very much; because between them they had created the life that was his, and Frankie and Mikey's life, too.

But even if Belial *could* bring his parents back, what was it all worth? Was his own selfish sense of family worth a million lives? Joe Berry, Nina Berry—Edna-Mae Lickerman, and thousands more?

Something else occurred to him, too. Belial was the Master of Lies, the King of Deception. Everything he said was a lie. *Everything.* If he had wanted Larry to believe him, he should have promised him nothing at all: no miracles, no resurrections, no family reunions. Then perhaps Larry might have been able to believe that he was going to get what he really wanted.

The strange part about it, however, was that he could now understand why Mandrax and Arne both believed Belial, although they *knew* what a liar he was. They believed him because they needed to believe him— because, when it came down to what they desperately wanted—their judgement became hopelessly distorted, and they were able to convince themselves that, this time, in their particular case, Belial was telling the truth.

Larry had seen so many defrauded widows; so many abandoned women whose assets had been systematically stripped; so many victims of so many stings. The lies that they had been told were almost always implausible— more often than not, absurd. An insurance executive from Burlingame had given over a million dollars to a man who claimed he had discovered the Lost Dutchman Mine in Santa Cruz—it had been shifted bodily from Arizona— a distance of nearly a thousand miles—by "earth disturbances". A woman in Mill Valley had consented to sex with a strange man because he had told her that he was the last surviving Martian, and her pregnancy would guarantee the survival of the Martian race.

Most of the time, lies were only believable because their victims wanted them to be believable. Larry had found himself right on the brink of believing that Belial would give him his parents back. He had *ached* for it. But he knew that it could never happen. He hoped that it could never happen. He prayed that he was right.

Mandrax stepped up to the coffin. "It's time," he said,

and grasped the lid. Arne took hold of the lid on the other side.

"You're not going to open it?" asked Larry anxiously, taking a step back.

"You'll be pleasantly surprised," said Mandrax. The temperature in the wooden chamber began to drop like a stone. "The beast face is simply a disguise, to hide the reality. The beast face was invented by Aaron, during the Exodus, so that only those who truly worship the fallen gods can see how beautiful they are."

Together, with a heavy grinding noise, he and Arne heaved the lid aside, and lowered it on to the rubble. Instantly, like a flood, the chamber was filled with light—pure, intense light—so bright that Larry had to cover his face with both hands.

He heard a sound like no other sound that he had ever heard before. It was high and thin, and *human*, like a scream, yet it went on and on, unceasingly, in a way that no human voice could ever physically manage. It was like the scream of somebody falling for ever. It had a fear and desperation in it which Larry could hardly tolerate, and he looked from Mandrax to Arne and back again in consternation.

"You'll get used to it," said Mandrax. "He's still dreaming. Still falling. He didn't just jump out of a 747, he was thrown down from heaven, and that's about as far as that—" (he demonstrated an inch, between finger and thumb) "—and as near as the furthest known star. Heaven's inside of your head, and that's how far *he's* falling."

"Come take a look," said Arne, and beckoned Larry nearer.

I'm afraid, thought Larry. *I can't look.*

But he approached the coffin and he looked. And he stood looking for almost a whole minute, electrified, terrified, at the figure which lay shrouded in blinding light.

Belial was almost twice the height of a normal man; but proportionately he was perfect. His long white hair was drawn back tightly by a thin band. His face was exquisitely proportioned; so beautiful for a man that it was disturbing. His nose was finely boned, his lips full, his chin strong. He was dressed in a white cowled robe of strange fabric that seemed to melt to the touch, like snow.

His eyes were closed, and he seemed to be sleeping; although Larry could detect his lips faintly moving.

It suddenly occurred to Larry that he was in the presence of a real angel; one of the mythical messengers of God. It was one of these creatures who had visited Mary; it was one of these creatures that the shepherds had seen in the skies over Bethlehem. The feeling of cold was numbing; the high-pitched screaming was numbing. But this thing was real, and it was beautiful beyond all understanding, and he had found it. He felt like sinking on to his knees, and praying.

But now Mandrax was dragging Edna-Mae forward— the huge, churning Edna-Mae. He guided her over the coffin, and then forced her head down toward the angel's face.

"What the hell are you doing?" Larry demanded, but Arne lifted his hand and said, "Sh, Larry. Let's not interfere with things we don't understand."

"I understand it, for Christ's sake. It's homicide!"

But nothing could stop Edna-Mae from pressing her sheet-shielded face over the angel's cowl. Larry couldn't see anything but shimmering white sheets as the two appeared to kiss.

"What the hell are you doing?" he repeated. His voice sounded choked and strained.

At that instant, however, he heard a gut-wrenching sound. It was thick and turgid, like something being dragged out of a swamp. But then there was a sudden snap, and a muffled scream, *two* muffled screams, two women shrieking together, and Edna-Mae's sheet struggled and boiled and tossed as if somebody were trying to butcher a dog underneath it. It frothed with blood. So much blood that a fine scarlet spray rose in the air, and speckled Belial's robes, and drifted across the rubbled floor. There was a last frantic fight, with blood staining the sheet wider and wider. Then the sheet was flung from the coffin, and Belial was again revealed.

This time Belial's eyes were open, and they were staring at Larry with such intensity that he felt as if he had already done something wrong. They were yellow—strong concentrated yellow, the color of rapeseed flowers, almost too yellow to exist.

Larry slowly knelt down beside the bloody, thrown-away sheet and hesitantly lifted it up. Underneath lay the remains of Edna-Mae Lickerman. She had become no more than a transparent sack of very thin skin, the same color and texture as chicken skin, inside of which were jumbled all of her internal organs, but completely dry. A dry, flat stomach like a leather water-bottle, a dark-red dried-out heart, a hard brown liver. Intestines, coiled like macaroni that had been boiled and then left to lie on the plate for too long. He could see the fragile holes in the skin where her eyes and nostrils and mouth had once been. Men had kissed that mouth. Men had looked into those eyes. People had said to Edna-Mae Lickerman, "I love you," and now what was she?

Mandrax said, "It's time for our prayer. Then the time to feed has come at last."

He stood at the head of the coffin, next to Arne, and closed his eyes. Belial's eyes, however, remained wide open, and yellow, and didn't move once from Larry's face. Dogmeat started to sob and say something about the good old days, the good old days. He looked to Larry as if he had been beaten almost to the point of death.

"O great Beli Ya'al, whose time has now come. O great Beli Ya'al, whose return was written in pages of dust, yet whose name lived on, when every other name was taken by the wind…

"Arise, Beli Ya'al, to feed at last, and to give these your servants their just rewards!"

Instantly, there was a dazzling flash of light; and the wooden chamber began to thunder and shake. Huge chunks of rubble dropped from the ceiling, and burst on the floor below. In the intermittent flashes of light, Larry saw Beli Ya'al begin to rise from his open coffin, his eyes staring, his beautiful face taut with concentration. He rose, and his light spread even more brilliantly all around, and the sound of his falling grew to a shrieking crescendo, until Larry was unable to hear anything but that high-pitched screaming that rubbed his nerves together and made his ears ache.

Soon Beli Ya'al was standing beside his coffin, impossibly tall, in robes that gleamed and stirred in quite different winds from the drafts which blew through his underground prison. He turned his head slowly from side to side, taking in his surroundings.

"*Great Beli Ya'al!*" cried out Mandrax, dropping on to his knees in front of him, and clenching both fists in hysterical delight. "*Great Beli Ya'al!*"

Beli Ya'al said nothing. His eyes were wide and peculiarly wild. When he turned to stare in Larry's direction, Larry was suddenly terribly afraid of him, and took two or three steps back toward the open doorway. He was so frightened, in fact, that he stumbled twice, and grazed his knee.

The ceiling thundered yet again, and a vast vertical beam groaned and dropped two or three feet, dislodging more loose soil and slurry. Beli Ya'al turned his head and the air positively *crackled* all around him.

"Dogmeat!" yelled Larry. "Get the hell out!"

Dogmeat lurched to his feet, and tried to escape across the rubble. But Arne must have beaten his legs so badly that he could scarcely manage more than a hobble.

"Dogmeat!"

But with one flowing step, Beli Ya'al had reached him. Dogmeat turned, twisted his ankle, dragged himself up again. Beli Ya'al was almost smiling. He reached out his hand and laid it on Dogmeat's angular white shoulder. Almost gently, as if he were patting him, like a pet.

For one instant, Larry thought: *Thank God, everything's going to be all right. He's not going to hurt him.*

But then Beli Ya'al grasped both of Dogmeat's upper arms, and held them cruelly tight. Dogmeat stared up at him in awe and fearful anticipation.

"Listen, man. I never did nothing to nobody, never. Don't hurt me, *s'il vous plait*. I'll do anything you want. You do crack? Ice? Snow? I can get you nose candy that'll make this *son et lumière* look like—"

There were two quick, nasty squeaks, followed in quick succession by pistol-sharp cracks, and Beli Ya'al had circled both of Dogmeat's arms around the wrong way, popping them out of their sockets and then bursting them out of their skin. Beli Ya'al swung both arms up into the air, spraying a criss-cross of blood across the rubble, while Dogmeat stood for an instant stupefied, with no arms, and blood pumping out of each shoulder. Then he collapsed.

But Beli Ya'al hadn't finished with him yet. Back stretched those perfect bow-shaped lips, baring white glistening gums, and rows of teeth as ragged and as crowded as a wolf. Beli Ya'al lifted up Dogmeat's thin, bloody body, and without any hesitation forced his head into his mouth, with the relentless orgasmic thrusts of a snake swallowing a sheep. Dogmeat, still alive, woke up from the trauma of losing both of his arms, and found his head inside a wet, stretched mouth, and viciously sharp teeth biting at his neck.

He screamed; but Beli Ya'al crunched, and tore, and it didn't take long before Dogmeat's screaming gargled, and filled up with blood, and stopped altogether. Beli Ya'al; stood silent and concentrated in the middle of the chamber, with static electricity creeping and trickling all around him, forcing huge lumps of bloody flesh and bone and hair down his throat. His yellow eyes betrayed nothing.

Mandrax had been watching Beli Ya'al devour Dogmeat in awe and fascination. Beli Ya'al crunched and swallowed the last of Dogmeat's bony joints, and then Mandrax cautiously approached him. Beli Ya'al turned his head to look at him, his chin bloody, his white robes splattered with blood and quivering strings of tissue.

"What do you want of me?" Beli Ya'al asked. His voice was like the reverberation of a tuning-fork, heard but unheard. Larry could feel it in his bones more than his ears. He recognized it, though. It was the same voice that had spoken from his hand.

Mandrax bowed and said, "Beli Ya'al, you are the greatest of all creation. We welcome you, and we worship you."

Beli Ya'al said nothing, but looked around the wooden chamber with congested eyes.

Mandrax got down on to his knees. "I was the one who rescued you, Beli Ya'al. I was the one who found you."

"Didn't I always promise you that you would have your reward?" said Beli Ya'al. "You shall, when I have devoured the thousand that were promised me."

Larry retreated further to the entrance. He didn't have any idea how he was going to escape; or what he could do to stop Beli Ya'al from slaughtering a thousand innocent people. His chest was too filled up with panic, and he could hardly breathe.

Beli Ya'al appeared to be thinking, or dreaming. Then suddenly, just as Larry made a last scramble down the slope of gravel and clay, his whole body shuddered bright gold, out of focus. There seemed to be three or four Beli Ya'als, standing side by side, in a shimmering chorus. Larry scrabbled for the low, rotting door; but as he did so he heard a sound like a rapid-transit train arriving, a rush of warm wind, and Beli Ya'al was standing right beside him, by the door, bloodied and shining and horribly calm.

"You are the one with my eyes on your hand," said Beli

Ya'al. He was so close that his voice vibrated all the way down Larry's spinal cord, and made his pelvis ache.

"What do you want?" Larry challenged him, gasping for breath. "Haven't you done enough?"

Beli Ya'al's eyelids glutinously closed and then opened again, the sticky eyes of a creature who has slept for innumerable centuries.

"I have watched the world through windows; I have watched the world through mirrors; I have watched the world through water and pictures and the shiny reflection in children's eyes."

The angel slowly licked his lips, and a thin thread of Dogmeat's intestine was dragged across his teeth. "I have watched *your* world, little servant of mine."

Larry swallowed anxiously, and glanced across at Mandrax and Arne. Mandrax was grinning like a trick-or-treat mask, but Arne looked pale and deadly serious.

"I have come here to feed now," said Beli Ya'al. "I have come to dine on the banquet which was spread for me by my greatest foe. But there is nothing so sweet as the banquet that is freely offered."

"I don't understand you," Larry choked. He couldn't stand those yellow basilisk eyes. They unnerved him more than anything. He prayed to God that he could be someplace else, anyplace else; but he realized with a strong taste of bitterness that he had been fated to come here ever since his father had asked Dan Burroughs to bail him out of his bankruptcy. There was no escape. There never had been.

If only his father had known what his house and his champagne and his Lincoln Town Car would eventually cost.

Beli Ya'al said, "I struck down your father's benefactor. Your father promised me everything. *Everything*, including you, and yours. Not that I wish to have you, of course. Not that I wish to taste your family's flesh. What does an aged beast like me want with firm young bodies and sweet young souls—even when they are *freely* given, you understand, offered in sacrifice, offered with adoration? What does a timeworn creature like me want with such morsels?"

Mandrax called, "Larry!"

Larry stared at him, wide-eyed.

"You know what he's asking, Larry!"

"Damn you to hell, Mandrax!"

"Oh, come on, Larry, this is your moment. You give him your family, you can have everything! You're a young man, you can have some more kids! He wants your family, Larry! Freely given, so that he can look up at God and say You may have cast me down but these people adore me. I rule in Your creation, I feed on the people You made in Your own image, and You can't do anything about it, because You gave them freedom of choice, and what they want is power, and wealth, and damn your sanctimonious heaven!"

Beli Ya'al began slowly to grin, baring tooth after tooth. But Larry didn't wait for any more. He pushed his way through the doorway, splashing into the blackened ship's hold, and started to run in cascades of water across the rotting deck.

As he did so, he saw the golden light shimmer again; and the next thing he knew, Beli Ya'al had materialized right in front of him, shining and triumphant. His broken reflection danced in the water beneath his feet, so that he looked like two angels suspended in darkness, one upright, one inverted.

"Your father swore an oath" he said; and his voice sang in Larry's ears like a just-struck church-bell. "Perhaps he regretted that oath, especially when he sank in the Bay. But an oath is an oath. A promise is a promise. Not that I want you to fulfil your father's promise. Not that I want to feed on your family's flesh. I have all of this city to feed on! The very last thing I want is to feed on your family's flesh."

"Larry!" Mandrax panted, catching up with him, his feet sloshing in the eel-infested water. "You know what he wants, Larry! It's the only way! It's the whole reason I brought you here!"

"Fuck you!" yelled Larry.

Beli Ya'al turned to Mandrax and said, "Your ranting is doing no good. Quiet."

"But if he doesn't give you his family—"

"QUIET" said Beli Ya'al, in a pitch that was almost beyond human hearing. He reached out and seized Mandrax by the wrist, then twisted his arm behind him and lifted him halfway out of the water. Mandrax kicked and struggled, one foot splashing. "What's the matter with you? I was the one who saved you! I was the one who performed all the sacrifices for you!"

"Of course you did," Beli Ya'al told him. "You were my most devoted acolyte. You were my *only* acolyte. Why do you think I kept you alive for so many years? Why do you think I cared for you, and promised you so much?"

"Then let me down," gasped Mandrax. "Let me tell you this... my face is made of *his* ectoplasm. If you so much as touch me, his face is ruined, and believe me, you won't get much out of him if you do that."

Beli Ya'al looked back at Larry. "There is nothing so distasteful to me as a whining and conniving servant," he said. "Hold out your hand. You know which hand. Raise it, let me see it."

"What are you going to do?" asked Larry. "You're not going to—"

"HOLD OUT YOUR HAND." It was a command as powerful as a nuclear explosion. In spite of himself, Larry raised his left hand, and held it toward Beli Ya'al.

Mandrax fought and thrashed. "You can't—you can't *do* this! Beli Ya'al! You can't do this!"

"I can do whatever I wish," said Beli Ya'al. And almost at once, a change began to take place on Mandrax's face. It began to distort, and melt, and twist around. His features disappeared in a fog of light; and like a shining scarf, the ectoplasm unwound itself from around his head, and coiled up into the air. The real face of Mandrax was exposed: hideously burned, with a cavity for a nose, and stretched-back eyelids, and a sloping mouth with snarling, exposed teeth.

The ectoplasm poured back into Larry's upraised palm. He felt a warm, abrasive sensation, as if the inside of his arm were being dragged with a nylon pot-scourer. Then the ectoplasm vanished, and he closed the palm of his hand, and he was complete again. He felt heavier, as if he had just finished a huge Italian meal; but his sense of *wholeness* was extraordinary.

Mandrax roared and screamed. "Traitor! Liar! I fought

for years to bring you back! I gave up everything to bring you back!"

He kicked out at Beli Ya'al and the angel dropped him into the water. Mandrax scrambled to his feet, slipped, scrambled up again, and started to run toward the tunnel that would take him to the underground parking-lot.

With a terrible shining smoothness, Beli Ya'al spread his arms and dived into the shallow water. He vanished into it as if it were ten feet deep. Larry saw him shimmering beneath the surface, as fast as a hammerhead shark, swimming right beneath Mandrax's splashing feet. Mandrax saw him, too, and screamed a ghastly distorted scream.

Then Beli Ya'al dimmed and disappeared; and the ship's hold was pitch black, punctuated by the splash of Mandrax's feet, and his terrified panting.

Larry stayed where he was, petrified. He thought he could hear something else, apart from Mandrax's panicky escape. Something like a wave coming, on the shoreline. A deep, huge rushing of water.

Just as Mandrax reached the far wall, Beli Ya'al came crashing out of the water in a fountain of sparkling spray, right in front of him. Mandrax roared in terror, tripped, slid, and tried to wriggle himself away. But Beli Ya'al's mouth stretched open and seized his leg, and blood gushed across the water, alive with bloodied eels.

"Oh, no!" screamed Mandrax. "Oh, no! Oh, Christ! Oh, no!"

There was nothing that Larry could do but stare in horror as Beli Ya'al tore Mandrax's legs into strings and shreds, and ripped into his buttocks and his belly with the ferocity of a buzzsaw. He had never seen any creature with such greed and power. Mandrax was still screaming and begging and splashing his arms in the water as Beli Ya'al buried his muzzle into his chest cavity, crushing his ribs and dragging out his heart. Larry saw his heart pump just once, as Beli Ya'al bit into it, and burst it. Within minutes, the fallen angel arose from the water, his exquisite face a mask of blood, and there was nothing left of Mandrax but a gradually widening stain on the water.

"Now," whispered Beli Ya'al. "You wouldn't have anything to offer me, would you?"

Arne came into the hold, and stood by the doorway. "Mandrax?" he said, uncertainly.

"Mandrax disagreed with something that ate him," said Larry, with undisguised bitterness.

"Oh God," said Arne.

"What will you do now?" asked Beli Ya'al, with a grisly smile. "I don't wish to kill you, but perhaps you leave me no choice."

"Still lying," said Arne. "He'd *love* to kill us."

"Wait," Larry told him. "Let's give ourselves some time to think."

"God, what a liar," said Arne. "God, if only I'd known."

Larry looked at Arne in disgust. "If only you'd known. What kind of an excuse is that?"

Arne held his eye for a moment, then turned away. "You don't know what he promised me, Larry."

"Whatever it was, I hope you think it was worth it. And to think I used to call you Jolly."

"Shit, Larry," Arne raged. "What are we going to do?"

Larry turned to Beli Ya'al and said, as boldly as he could, "You'll have to give me time to talk to my family."

The yellow eyes closed, then opened again. "Why should I do that?" asked Beli Ya'al.

"Because at the very least I want them to know *why* they have to be sacrificed. They deserve that much. Better still, I want them to be happy about it. Wouldn't that make them even sweeter?"

"I have no particular desire for your family," said Beli Ya'al, flatly. "Of course, if they *wish* to be sacrificed…"

The lack of interest in his voice was belied by the greed in his yellow eyes. Larry thought: *I've won some time, thank God. All I have to do now is find out how to send this creature back to the coma he came from. Somebody did it, centuries ago. Somebody trapped him in that coffin. If they could do it in Sumerian times, we must be able to do it now.*

Beli Ya'al swirled the water with his blood-soaked robes. "You have an hour. Then, raise your hand, and summon me, and I shall come."

Can I trust him? thought Larry. *No. If Tara Gordon was right, everything he says is a lie. I'll have to think quick. But some time is better than no time at all.*

Arne said, "What about me?"

"You will wait here, to keep me company," said Beli Ya'al.

"For God's sake, Larry," Arne begged.

Larry shook his head. "You didn't think of my family when you dropped out of this investigation. You didn't think of Joe Berry's family. Whatever you get, Arne, it can't be any more than you deserve."

"Larry!"

Larry ignored him, and waded through the water to the tunnel. The last thing he saw as he crouched down and started back to the underground parking-lot was Arne standing white-faced staring at Beli Ya'al, and Beli Ya'al still swirling his robes in the water. Then he took a deep breath and hunched his way back.

His car was still there; and the lights were still bright, so the battery hadn't run flat. He splashed across to it and climbed in, and for a moment he sat with his eyes closed, trying to pull himself back together.

Who would know if there was any way to beat Beli Ya'al? Dan Burroughs possibly; Dan Burroughs had obviously been dealing with him for years. But he couldn't trust Dan, not now. If he had murdered his father for the power that Beli Ya'al could bestow, then he was just as likely to try to murder him.

No, his only chance was Tara Gordon.

He started the engine, backed the car up, and headed for the tight spiral ramp. As he did so, however, he saw lights coming *down* the ramp, toward him. They flashed and sparkled in the water, and the next thing he knew, a bronze Caprice came splashing down to the lower level, and drew up beside him. The window hummed down. It was Dan Burroughs, with a cigarette hanging between his lips—and surprise, surprise, Fay Kuhn.

"What's happening, Larry?" Dan asked him. "We got your call, came here as quick as we could."

"You know damn well what's happening," said Larry, his voice shaking. "Your precious angel has risen again, that's what."

Dan peered with smoke-slitted eyes toward the cavity

behind the broken furniture. A few thin shafts of golden light shone through it, and played on the scummy surface of the water. "So that's where the bastard was hidden," Dan breathed. "After all these years. *That's* where the bastard was hidden."

"You want to go talk to him, you're welcome," said Larry. "How about you, Fay? Where do you fit into all of this?"

Fay looked at him straight. "Do you think I wanted to be a newspaper reporter all my life?"

"*Et tu, Ms Brute*," said Larry. "Thanks for all of your warnings about Dan playing a double game."

"Oh, don't blame her," put in Dan, coughing. "That was all my idea... thought it would put some salt on your tail, get you moving."

"He's really risen?" asked Fay, her face pale with excitement.

Larry nodded. "I wouldn't open the Dom Perignon just yet, though. He's in kind of a fractious mood. Dogmeat's dead; so's Mandrax. Arne's still with us, the last I saw, but I wouldn't count on him lasting much longer."

"Arne?" said Dan, perplexed.

"That's right, Arne. Go ask him for yourself."

"Arne, what a double-crossing bastard," Dan spat.

"Takes one to know one, Dan," said Larry. He thrust the Le Sabre into 2, and roared off up the ramp, his bumper scraping against the concrete all the way up, in a spectacular shower of sparks.

He reached the second level, skidded sideways on the wet concrete, then jarred-bounced up to the ramp which took him to the street. The Le Sabre cannonballed across the sidewalk and crashed down into the middle of Green Street, barking the side of a Federal Express truck, and setting up a protesting barrage of car horns.

Larry drove southward on Battery at nearly 60, swerving between vans and cars, running red lights with his horn blaring and his popcorn light flashing and his headlights on full. He caught the edge of a Cadillac as he sped over Pine Street, causing it to slew in a circle; but he kept his foot flat on the gas pedal until he approached Market.

He reached the "Waxing Moon" and screeched to a stop, his front wheel mounting the sidewalk.

Tara Gordon was walking across the store as he pushed open the door, spraying the air with musk. She was dressed in a tight black dress, with scores of silver bangles.

"Lieutenant!" she said, in surprise. "You look *awful*! You haven't come to arrest me for using CFCs, have you?"

Larry pressed both his hands flat on the glass-topped counter and took a huge breath. "They've done it," he said. "They've brought him back to life."

Slowly, she put down her aerosol. "You're kidding me," she said. "Come on, lieutenant, no jokes. This isn't something to joke about."

"No jokes, they've done it. He's down in a basement in Green Street."

"My God," Tara Gordon whispered. "I never thought they'd do it. I never thought they could."

"He's there. Ten foot tall, handsome as the devil, and greedy as a goddamned wolf. But they got a lot more than they bargained for. Dogmeat's dead, so's Mandrax." He spoke in short, staccato bursts. He couldn't seem to get his breath back, no matter what he did.

"What's happening now?" asked Tara Gordon. "How did you get away?"

"He's given me grace," Larry gasped. "An hour's grace. He wants my family, my wife and my sons. He's given me an hour. I don't know, maybe less, maybe more. Whatever he says, it's a lie."

Tara Gordon laid her hand on his shoulder. "Relax," she said. "Get your breath back. Give me a minute." She left him, and walked across to her reference library, where she took down two books, and started to leaf noisily through both of them. After a while, breathing more easily, Larry came to join her.

"Anything?" he asked her.

"I don't know. I think so. The trouble is, it's all myth and legend, and you don't know whether it's reliable or not."

"Anything," Larry begged her.

"Well... it says here that no fallen angel can survive on earth without the approval of the people amongst whom he lives. He needs a popular mandate, if you like, in order to defy God's banishment. Look... 'it takes only one voluntary sacrifice for one of the fallen to live out his life as a lord of the temporal sphere. But without that voluntary sacrifice, he must needs creep back to the bowels of the earth and await another summoning.'"

"So he needs my approval," said Larry. "That's one point in my favor, at least."

"I don't know. It says here that those who refuse to give sacrifices to fallen angels are often killed anyway, and suffer eternal agony and unrest."

"Shit," said Larry. "What the hell am I going to do?"

"Hold on," Tara Gordon soothed him. "Whatever you do,

don't panic. This is all about Belial. First of the fallen angels, master of lies… Here, look. 'Beli Ya'al can only be dismissed by causing him to utter a great and indisputable truth. Since the truth is anathema to him, he will be confounded.'"

Larry read the book for himself. Then he looked at the leather-bound cover. "God almighty, Oxford University Press, 1871. How reliable do you think *this* is?"

"Do you have any better ideas?" asked Tara Gordon.

"I don't know. He's like a—well, Christ, he's worse than a shark. He ate Mandrax and Dogmeat in front of my eyes. He just ripped them to pieces, and swallowed them."

"I don't know how else to stop him," said Tara Gordon. She didn't sound very confident.

Larry lowered the book. "How the hell do you make a congenital liar tell the truth?"

"Maybe you do it the same way that I used to do it with my ex-husband. You lie better than they do. He used to say, 'Keep the Porsche, I don't want the Porsche,' just to make me feel guilty because *I* wanted it. In the end I learned how to deal with somebody who comes on like that. I used to say, 'You can have it, you're welcome to it, so long as I know that you really want it.'"

Larry shook his head. "It doesn't seem much to go on, does it?"

"You're drowning, Larry. If nothing else, it's a straw. Do you want me to come with you?"

"I think I'd better go on my own. If this goes as badly as I think it's going to go, I need somebody who knows what happened to survive."

Tara Gordon held his arm. "Lieutenant," she said. "Good luck."

Larry, spontaneously, kissed her. Her lips were soft, cool, remote. Her eyes were very large, like a dream in themselves. "You can do it," she told him. "I can feel it; you're strong. You can do it."

He reached his house on Russian Hill and parked the battered Le Sabre against the curb. The house-lights were shining dimly through the fog; and the flowers in the garden looked as if they were draped in bridal veils. He opened the front door and went in, and immediately he knew that something was wrong.

There was an unfamiliar smell in the house. Like spices, or incense. And nobody came running to greet him.

Oh God, don't tell me they're dead already.

He walked through to the living-room and his eyes were met by a golden glow. *He lied, he's here already.* Beli Ya'al was standing in the far corner of the room, his cowled head almost touching the ceiling, his hands clasped loosely in front of him. His face was bearded with dried blood, and his robes looked like a butcher's apron.

Linda, Frankie and Mikey were huddled close together on the sofa, unharmed, but terrified. Linda looked up desperately as Larry took one cautious step into the room, and tugged the boys back as they tried to jump up. She said nothing; Beli Ya'al had obviously told her to stay quiet; but then she didn't have to.

"You came early," Larry said to Beli Ya'al, trying to sound calm.

"I came at the time we agreed."

Lying again.

"Oh, yes," said Larry. "I forgot."

Beli Ya'al didn't respond to that, but glided forward, his

bloodied robes whispering hideous secrets across the floor. "Of course, I couldn't have allowed my hunger to get the better of me."

"Of course not."

"Larry—" said Linda. "What is this? Who is he? *What* is he?"

"What is he, Daddy?" Frankie asked, his face drawn in terror. "He said he wasn't going to hurt us."

"That's right," said Larry, trying to sound confident. "He's not going to touch you, not at all. That's true, isn't it, o great one?"

Beli Ya'al's yellow eyes narrowed like sunflowers at night. "I wouldn't harm any family so sweet," he replied.

He circled around the back of the sofa. He found it hard to take his eyes off Linda and the boys. He had the same fixed grin as those heroin addicts that Larry had interviewed, with a hypodermic full of methadone on the table in front of them. The same inability to keep his eyes off his fix.

Larry said nothing, but stayed where he was, close to the door, and watched him circle and circle, like a shark in clear water. The tension in the living-room was huge. The floor almost creaked with it. And all the time Larry could hear that keen, high-pitched singing sound; that singing sound that was almost a scream.

"Have you considered?" Beli Ya'al asked Larry, with closely curbed impatience.

Larry nodded. "I've thought about it very carefully, as a matter of fact."

Linda said, "What? What have you thought about?"

But Larry lifted his hand to quieten her. "You said that you didn't want to touch such a young and sweet young family... and I respect your wishes completely. That was a very fine sentiment indeed."

Beli Ya'al frowned at him. "Of course, I *did* say that if such a family were offered voluntarily..."

"You'd want them then?"

"Of course not."

"Then you don't want them?"

"No."

Larry licked his lips. He was aware that this was only word-play; and that if Beli Ya'al grew tired of trying to persuade him willingly to give him Linda and the boys, he would tear them apart anyway; and they would suffer an after-life that was worse than all the ovens of hell.

All the same, he could see how fiercely Beli Ya'al craved a voluntary sacrifice. It would make his saliva run that much sweeter; and win him a life on earth.

"Okay..."he said at last. "You can have them."

Beli Ya'al slowly grinned. He reached back, and dropped his cowl, baring his radiant white hair. He was so beautiful he was terrifying. Beautiful as a statue. Beautiful as a nightmare.

Larry said, "You can have them so long as I know you really want them."

Beli Ya'al, still grinning, opened his mouth to speak. Then he hesitated, and stared at Larry in suspicion. "As long as I really want them?" he said, in that reverberating, unearthly tone.

"Well... just now, you said that you didn't want them. I mean, there's no point in my agreeing to your having them if you *don't* want them, is there?"

"I didn't say that I didn't want them," Beli Ya'al lied.

"Then you *do* want them?"

Perplexed. "I didn't say that, either."

"My friend," said Larry, "you can have them, they're yours. But all I have to know is that you really want them."

Sour gastric juices were coursing down Beli Ya'al's chin and mingling in streaks with the blood of those he had already devoured. His eyes darted quickly from side to side. His greed was overwhelming. The family were here, within his grasp; sweet proffered flesh, sweet proffered souls. And a life on earth, too, where he could feed with mindless gluttony for eternity to come.

"Do you want them?" asked Larry.

Linda was staring at him in bewilderment and horror. She couldn't understand what this creature was; or what Larry was doing. All she knew was that she and the boys were somehow being bartered. Frankie and Mikey hid their faces with their hands.

"*Do you want them?*" Larry demanded. His hard-cop interrogation voice.

"NO," roared Beli Ya'al.

Larry turned his back. He could hear Frankie and Mikey sobbing in fright, and he would have done anything to take them up in his arms and hug them close. But this wasn't the moment. If he failed now, Beli Ya'al would have his teeth in them in seconds.

"All right," said Larry, quietly. "If that's the way you want it. You can't say that I didn't offer."

"Wait," said Beli Ya'al. A different voice, cajoling.

"You've changed your mind?"

"No."

"You do want them, after all?"

"No!"

"You can change your mind. Everybody's entitled to change their mind. Do you want them?"

"No! No! No! A hundred thousand times over, no!"

"Damn it to hell, Beli Ya'al!" screamed Larry. "They're here! They're yours! Just tell me that you want them and you can have them now!"

"*No!*" shrieked Linda.

"YES," roared Beli Ya'al. "YES I WANT THEM."

Larry stood stock still. Yellow eyes stared into brown eyes.

"What did you say?" Larry asked him.

For one long, long moment he was terrified that it wouldn't work; that Tara Gordon's book was all nonsense. Beli Ya'al stood in front of him as tall and as grisly as before, his face contorted with anger and greed.

But the silence went on; and on. And gradually, Beli Ya'al lowered his head.

"You told the truth," said Larry.

Beli Ya'al remained silent.

"You told the truth," Larry repeated.

"No," whispered Beli Ya'al.

"You told the truth! You told the truth!"

"NOOO," bellowed Beli Ya'al. He lifted his head and his eyes were ablaze with dazzling light. He looked as if he were on fire; only brighter than fire; brighter than suns.

His image shuddered and divided, as if they were looking at him through a hall of mirrors. His yellow eyes roared with yellow flame.

NOOOOOO became a wave of noise, rather than a scream, and the whole house began to vibrate. A vase toppled off the table behind the couch and shattered on the floor. Pictures dropped one by one from the walls. With a squeak, splintering noise, the patio window cracked from one corner to the other.

The noise rose and rose until the ground was shaking underneath their feet. Beli Ya'al detonated with fire, white-hot dazzling fire; and Larry staggered across the room and took hold of Linda and Frankie and Mikey and held them close.

"Daddy! He's burning! He's burning!" screamed Mikey.

"I'll tell you another truth!" Larry shouted at Beli Ya'al. "I love my family more than you could ever hunger for anything!"

There was a moment when Larry felt as if the whole world were sliding away.

Beli Ya'al turned to him with a face of fire, and eyes of fire, and a mouth that spouted roaring flames.

"A CURSE ON YOU," he thundered.

Then, with a sound like a monstrous door slamming, he burst apart. The room exploded in a welter of skulls and bones and torn clothes and bloody remains; a huge sickening volcano of undigested flesh and blood. Scarlet muscle was splattered all over the white-painted walls, torsos and hands and thigh-bones emptied out all over the floor.

With a blinding crackle of psychic energy, Beli Ya'al vanished, sucked back to his coffin by the same greed that had resurrected him. Beli Ya'al was back in the limbo to which God had condemned him. Only the grisly half-chewed remains of those he had eaten had remained behind.

Larry led Linda and Frankie and Mikey out of the gore-splattered, smoke-filled room and closed the door. The boys were white and trembling, but silent. Linda had her hand pressed over her mouth.

"What was it?" she said, again and again. "What was it?"

"It's over," said Larry. "It's gone now."

He couldn't think of anything else to say. He hugged his family close and he couldn't even cry.

"Call Houston," he told Linda. "Call Houston and tell him what happened. Then go over to the Marshalls. I'll join you there in just a while."

"What are you going to do?" asked Linda, trembling. "You're not going back in there?"

"I saw something," said Larry. "I have to be sure."

Linda reluctantly took Frankie and Mikey into the kitchen. Larry made sure they were gone, and then he opened the living-room door again, and stepped back in. It was impossible not to tread on blood and stripped-apart skin.

In the tangled heap of human remains he had seen a face; and that face had looked as if it were still alive.

He found Arne's arm. He recognized it by the Rolex wristwatch, blood-smeared but still ticking. He found a white-skinned female torso, bare-breasted, headless, still wearing the pale-blue remnants of Fay Kuhn's tailored suit. He saw a gray bloodstained sock that must have belonged to Dan Burroughs.

And behind the couch, one-legged, one-armed, smothered in blood and mucus and reeking of bile, he found Dan Burroughs himself. His eyes were glazed, but he was still breathing, a shallow bubble of blood swelling out from between his lips.

Larry knelt down beside him, trying to ignore the blood on the floor.

"Dan?" he said, lifting his head in his hands. "Dan, can you hear me?"

Dan coughed, and blood ran out of the side of his mouth.

"I'm dying, Larry. I thought I was dead already."

"Dan, he's gone, Dan. Beli Ya'al's gone."

There was a long wheezing pause, and then Dan said, "Thank God."

"Can you hold on? I'll call the paramedics."

Dan gave a bloody cackle. "Too late for that, Larry. Far too late for that. Just forgive me, that's all. That's all I need, forgiveness."

Larry said nothing, but took hold of Dan's remaining hand and squeezed it.

"He offered so much... money, power... you don't have any idea. He offered so much. I had a shadow—shadow on my lung—and he offered me health—you know that?—and life, and money. Seemed too good to be true."

He coughed up more blood, and then he said, "There's a list, Larry... all of those politicians and businessmen who were in it with me... back at my house... third drawer down... locked."

"Don't worry, Dan, I'll take care of it."

Dan looked at him sideways, despairingly. "He's really gone? Beli Ya'al's really gone?"

"Until the next time, Dan. Until somebody else gets too greedy."

Dan nodded, and died. Larry knelt beside him for a moment, and then stood up, and looked around the carnage of his living-room. Beli Ya'al had gone, for sure. But all he could think about was all the nightmares that he was going to have to endure, before Beli Ya'al would finally leave him be.

Early the next day, Larry guided city engineers down to the lower level of the disused underground parking-lot on Green Street.

They found the cavity in the wall, but the tremors of Beli Ya'al's departure had brought down the walls of the basement beyond it, and blocked it with hundreds of tons of gravel and silt.

Larry stood and watched as city engineers filled the tunnel with concrete. They smoked and whistled while they worked. Two truckloads of concrete wouldn't prevent Beli Ya'al from getting out; nothing could do that. But it would stop anybody else from getting in.

Afterwards, he went to his mother's house, and sat for an hour, looking through his father's old papers and letters. He could find no references to Dan Burroughs; but at the back of the bottom drawer, with its edge caught under the wooden beading, he discovered a faded black-and-white photograph of two men drinking at a bar. They were raising their glasses to each other and smiling in satisfaction, as if they had just struck the best deal of their lives.

The man in the dark suit on the left was Mario Foggia. The man in the gray suit on the right was Dan Burroughs.

Larry stared at the photograph for a long time, tapping it

against his thumbnail. Then he ripped it up and dropped it into the waste-paper basket.

He opened the front door to leave. It was a warm, hazy afternoon: and he suddenly began to feel good again. He was about to close the door, when there was a sudden flurry of wings, and a flustered gray shape flew past him and into the house.

"Well, I'll be—" he said, and walked back into the living-room.

Mussolini was sitting, bedraggled, on his perch. "*Che violino!*" he cackled. "*Che violino!*"

Larry approached the cage and tapped his finger against the bars. "Well, well, and where have you been?"

"*Che violino!*" screeched Mussolini.

Larry opened his coat and took out his .38. He pushed it through the bars of the cage, and without hesitation, fired.

The echoes died away. Smoke drifted lazily across the old, antique-furnished living-room. Gray feathers see-sawed down from the ceiling, one by one.

Larry closed the living-room door behind him, smoothed his hair in the hall mirror, then stepped out into the sun.

That night, as Larry slept exhausted on the couch at the Marshall's house across the street, the skeins began to drift across the palm of his hand.

They drifted lazy and slow, forming themselves into tangles and cobwebs. Then, after a while, a face appeared; a face that moved and smiled like a 16 mm movie from long ago.

"*Time to feed, my friend. Time to feed.*" murmured a flat and familiar voice. Larry stirred, and his fingers twitched, but he didn't wake up.

"...*if you must, dust if you don't*..." the voice went on.

Larry was dreaming that he was wading through ankle-deep water in echoing darkness. He knew that he was approaching something terrible.

He was frightened, in his dream. So frightened that he didn't know whether he could wade forward any further.

But still he didn't wake up.

Still he didn't open his eyes and see that the face on the palm of his hand was his own.

About Graham Masterton

GRAHAM MASTERTON is best known as a writer of horror and thrillers, but his career as an author spans many genres, including historical epics and sex advice books. His first horror novel, *The Manitou*, became a bestseller and was made into a film starring Tony Curtis. In 2019, Graham was given a Lifetime Achievement Award by the Horror Writers Association. He is also the author of the Katie Maguire series of crime thrillers, which have sold more than 1.5 million copies worldwide.